What was I doing?
I am a prince of the realm,
not a beast in the night.

Lynan laughed wryly at his own pride. Some prince of the realm: exiled to the Oceans of Grass, with a future only the greatest optimist would find any hope in, and now plagued by desires that were inhuman. Areava would not be surprised, of course, she always thought of him as almost less than human. He could remember vividly their last conversation on the palace's south gallery only hours before Berayma was murdered; he had seen in her eyes then how she truly thought of him.

With that memory came a very human anger, and the emotion threw out the last vestige of his unnatural hunger. *This is how I control it,* he thought with surprise. *By never forgetting the first cause of my exile and transformation.*

His confidence renewed if not wholly restored, Lynan walked back past the sentry and into the camp. He reached his tent and looked east, back toward civilization, back toward his enemies. He imagined Areava in her throne room, thinking he was dead and celebrating the fact, Berayma's murderers by her side.

If only she knew what had truly become of him.

The *Keys of Power*

INHERITANCE
FIRE AND SWORD
SOVEREIGN*

*coming soon from DAW

FIRE AND SWORD

Book Two of *Keys of Power*

SIMON BROWN

DAW BOOKS, INC.

DONALD A. WOLLHEIM, FOUNDER

375 Hudson Street, New York, NY 10014

ELIZABETH R. WOLLHEIM

SHEILA E. GILBERT

PUBLISHERS

http://www.dawbooks.com

First Printing, March 2004
1 2 3 4 5 6 7 8 9 10

For Guy Miklenda, Janet Delfosse,
and Del Delfosse.
Also family.

ACKNOWLEDGEMENTS

All my thanks to my readers, Alison Tokley and Sean Williams, and to my editors, Julia Stiles, Stephanie Smith and Debra Euler. Thanks to them this is a better book than it would otherwise have been. Many thanks also to my agents, Garth Nix and Russell Galen, for all their wondrous efforts on my behalf.

Hverr of kom Heráss á
hí á land gotna?
Fiskr ór fjanda vim svimandi,
fogl á fjanda lith galandi.

As whom came the god of war
to the land of men?
A fish from the torrent of enemies swimming,
a bird against a troop of enemies screaming.

–from the Eggjum gravestone, Sogn, Norway (based on translation by Peter Foote & David M. Wilson)

IN autumn, when the hot summer winds have passed and the fierce winter storms are yet to come, the Oceans of Grass is the most silent place on the continent of Theare. The occasional breeze will brush the yellow land but make no more sound than a lover's whisper, a dying enemy's curse. Even insects stop their chirruping and burrow deep underground, waiting for spring and fresh rain.

On this day the sun, still with its summer strength, arced high over the plain, making the air above the ground shimmer like silk. The only water hole for leagues around was nothing more than a silted puddle, and the tracks of a hundred animals crisscrossed its muddy ring. A family of karaks drank from the hole, their long ears drooping with thirst. The heat had made them careless and they had not caught scent of the grass wolf carefully studying them from the fringe of growth not more than fifty paces away.

The wolf had been following them for over two hours, always keeping behind, waiting for her chance to charge in and take one of the calves. She sensed the time had come. A sow had moved farther into the water hole and started to roll in it, leaving her calf behind. The wolf measured the distance, carefully noting how far the big boar had wandered from the main group, and tensed her muscles.

And then came a sound so deep it was first felt by the wolf as a vibration in the ground. The karaks sensed something as well. Their ears pricked up, their nostrils flared. The boar grunted and the herd hurried to join him; younger males took up their positions on flank and rear.

The sound swelled in the still air like the thunder of a distant storm. The wolf was puzzled. She had heard something like it many years ago, when she was not much older than a cub, but she could not remember what it meant.

The karaks were getting skittish. The calf the wolf had set on squealed and broke from the group. Again the wolf tensed, ready to take advantage of the herd's confusion.

And then the terrible riders appeared. Their gray mounts kicked up sods of mud, screaming as bits were pulled deep into their mouths. The riders shouted. There was a flurry of javelins and arrows. A young male karak went down, and then another. A sow, trying to protect a calf, took a spear through the neck.

The wolf watched in a daze. The calf she had selected was pierced by two arrows, and squealed for the last time. Her confusion gave way to a great and sudden anger. She leaped from the bushes, charging not toward the karaks, but toward the riders.

The crookback Ager Parmer was flushed with excitement. A crazed laugh escaped from his lips. He wheeled his horse to the right of the group and retrieved his short spear from the flank of a still panting boar. He looked up and saw Lynan corner a karak and pierce it with a javelin. The prince caught Ager's glance and grinned wildly. Ager laughed again, overjoyed to see the pale young man starting to enjoy life once more. Lynan was joined by his Chett friend and guardian Gudon, and the two of them went off in pursuit of more prey. Another rider cut behind them, and Ager turned to see Korigan, the Chett queen. He watched in admiration as she used only her knees to direct her mare, keeping her hands free to shoot with her recurve bow.

Something at the edge of his vision caught Ager's attention; he saw a young sow making a break for the tall grass and spurred his horse after it. The sow saw him and turned away. Ager cursed loudly. Now he would have to put the spear between the karak's shoulder blades, a much more difficult shot, especially with his one eye. He waited until the mare was close enough to trip up the sow and thrust down with his weapon. The spear lodged in the hollow just above the sow's neck. The karak grunted and its forelegs collapsed; it somersaulted into the dirt, jerking Ager's spear out of his hand, and was still.

Ager gave a triumphant cry. *That's my second! Won't Kumul be sorry he didn't come on the hunt!*

He checked to make sure there were no karaks nearby, quickly dismounted, and used his knife to finish off the sow. Then he heard a sound that came from no karak. He spun around and saw something long and gray and half the size of a Chett mare leap from the grass into the clearing. It ran under one of the horses and flashed wide jaws, tearing at the horse's belly. The mare screamed, bucked, and its rider fell heavily to the ground, the horse collapsing on top.

My God! Ager thought. *That's a grass wolf!*

The beast had not waited to finish off its first victim, but raced on to get under another horse. The rider saw the wolf coming and tried to wheel away, but the wolf was too quick; it used its teeth to slash at the horse's throat. There was a whip of blood and the horse went down, her rider still in the saddle. The wolf jumped over the mount and tore at the rider's throat, then leaped away.

Ager could not believe the speed of the creature. Most of the remaining horses clumped together, instinctively trying to get some protection from numbers, but their riders knew this was the worst thing they could do and desperately tried pulling them apart to give them some room to maneuver.

Ager pulled his spear out of the sow and jumped onto the back of his own mare. He tried to get it to charge the wolf, but all she would do was roll her eyes and pull back. He saw the wolf cutting across the clump of horses, trying to find a way in. A javelin whizzed by its ear and then an arrow.

One of the horses broke free of the group and Ager saw its rider was Korigan, her tall golden body leaning low over the horse's neck. The wolf zigzagged away from her, heading for the grass, easily outpacing Korigan's mare. Korigan loosed a short, white hunting arrow. It twanged into the ground only a step in front of the wolf's muzzle and the beast veered back toward the water hole. Without hesitation, Korigan's mare followed it and her Chetts shouted in admiration. And then they shouted in consternation as the wolf double backed, slashing at the horse's fetlocks. The horse stumbled and Korigan flew over the mare's head, landing on her shoulder. The queen pinned her bow to her chest and rolled. The wolf paid her no attention, driving into her horse and disemboweling it with two savage bites.

By now Gudon had broken free from the mass of stamping horses. He threw his javelin wildly, hoping to divert the wolf's attention from his queen. It worked. The wolf leaped, its jaw snapping only a finger's breadth from Gudon's face. The Chett drew his long sword and tried desperately to turn his mount, but again the wolf was quicker almost than the eye could see and was already behind Gudon. His mare panicked, reared back, and Gudon fell heavily to the ground and was still. Korigan sprinted to his side, grabbing for his sword. The wolf howled, the sound almost gleeful, and charged toward the two humans.

And then there was another howl, more terrifying, but it

did not come from the wolf. A third horse split from the main group and Ager saw its rider was Lynan.

"No!" Ager shouted. "Lynan, no!" He dug his spurs so hard into his mare's flanks the horse actually started forward, but even so, he knew he would be too late to stop his prince.

"He shouldn't be out there!" Kumul declared, waving his hand vaguely toward the horizon. Some nearby Chetts instinctively moved back from the giant's reach.

Jenrosa, diminutive next to him, suppressed a smile. "And where exactly should Lynan be?"

"Back here, of course, planning his next move. Instead, he's out gallivanting with Ager and Gudon—both of whom should know better!"

"It was Korigan's idea. She is not someone to be ignored."

Kumul looked around him sourly and lowered his voice. "She may be queen of these Chetts we've landed with, but Lynan outranks her. Instead, he behaves as if *she* was heir to the throne of Grenda Lear."

"He is making friends."

"He has friends."

Jenrosa could not help the smile this time. "Really, Kumul. I know you are an impressive figure, and Ager is a great fighter, but if he's to win back his birthright, he needs more than the three of us on his side."

Kumul harrumphed and returned to staring out over the horizon. "Be that as it may—"

"Besides, Lynan needs to build up his confidence again. He hasn't been on a horse since the battle with Rendle's mercenaries. And he deserves some time free of worry."

"Don't we all?"

"You could have gone on the hunt."

"I've got more important things to do."

"Like standing here complaining about Lynan having more important things to do?"

The giant nodded. "Exactly." He heard Jenrosa laugh, and refused to face her. Just the same, he could not help grinning through his salt-and-pepper beard.

"I must sound like a fool sometimes," he said quietly after a while.

Jenrosa gently touched his arm. "No, never a fool."

Kumul turned to her. He wanted to take her hand and hold it close to him. He wanted to kiss her face. "I suppose you're right."

"I usually am. But about what in particular this time?"

"Lynan. He needs a break from the camp. He's been sick for so long the ride will probably do him good. I hope he's all right."

Jenrosa saw in his eyes the great love he held for the prince. When Lynan was so badly wounded he was at death's door, she had overheard Kumul speaking to him, and for the first time had truly understood that he looked on Lynan as his own son. It was also the first time she suspected she might feel more for Kumul than respect and grudging friendship.

"I worry about him, that's all," Kumul added. "I worry about him all the time, especially since . . ."

"Since the change?"

Kumul nodded. "I know you had no choice. If you hadn't given him the wood vampire's blood, he would have died from his wounds after his encounter with Rendle's mercenaries. You saved his life, Jenrosa. But although we know it's changed his skin and his reaction to light, we don't know what's happened to his mind."

"He'll be fine," Jenrosa said and heard the doubt in her own voice. This time she had to force a smile. "Anyway, what could go wrong when Ager and Gudon are with him?"

*   *   *

The wolf lunged at Korigan. She fended it off with a clumsily aimed blow from Gudon's sword. The beast twisted aside and lunged again. Korigan fell back, tripped over Gudon's body, and fell to the ground. The wolf tensed for a final assault, and Korigan knew she was going to die.

The wolf leaped.

And suddenly was hurled aside. At first Korigan did not know what had happened. There was a spray of dust and a wild melee, the wolf bending over itself to snap at whatever it was that had grappled it. Then she recognized the Kendran prince. His small white figure was attached to the wolf's back. She gasped and stood up, ready to go to his rescue, then realized with shock he needed no rescuing. Somehow he was bearing the wolf down to the ground. She saw one of his arms curl under the wolf's neck and pull up. There was a sickening crack and the beast went limp, its tongue lolling from its great jaws.

A horse skidded to a halt and the crookback Ager was on the ground next to Lynan, pulling him away from the animal, his spear ready to strike.

For a moment no one moved. Ager held his spear, Korigan her sword, and Lynan, not even panting, stood over the dead wolf.

"How did you do that?" Korigan asked in amazement.

Lynan said nothing, but stared at his hands.

"Lynan?" Ager prompted. "That's a grass wolf. It's as strong as Kumul. How did you break its neck?"

Lynan eased off the chin strap of his wide-brimmed Chett hat. His ivory-colored skin shone with sweat. He squinted in the bright light and shook his head. "I don't know." He met Ager's anxious gaze, then Korigan's mystified one. Then he saw Gudon.

"Oh, no," he moaned, and knelt down next to his friend. Korigan and Ager joined him. Ager felt the Chett's thin throat, placed a hand gently on his chest.

"He will be fine," Ager said, and Lynan sighed with relief. "Bring me some water."

Lynan went to Ager's mare and returned with a water bottle. Ager dampened a kerchief and used it to pat Gudon's forehead, then poured some of the water over his lips. Gudon's mouth moved, and Ager let him swallow some of the water.

"Oh, all the gods hate me," Gudon muttered. He blinked and looked straight into Ager's face. "I am in hell."

Ager grunted. "Not yet."

"What happened?" he asked weakly as he tried to sit up. Ager placed an arm under his shoulders. Gudon saw the wolf. "You did that?"

Ager shook his head, nodded to Lynan. "Our young prince did that."

Gudon smiled at Lynan. "Your aim was sure."

"He did it with his hands," Ager said.

Gudon's eyes widened. "Three of our strongest warriors could not have subdued that creature."

Lynan stood up uneasily. He did not know what to do with his hands. "What has happened to me?"

No one could answer him.

ORKID Gravespear, Chancellor of Grenda Lear, found his queen standing on the south gallery of the palace. When he did not find Areava in her sitting room, he had known she would be here. It struck him as ironic that, like her hated brother Lynan had once done, she came to this place when she wanted to be alone. He paused at the wide double doors that led to the gallery, his bearlike frame almost filling the space, and studied her for a moment.

Areava was a tall, blonde-haired woman whose back was as straight as a stone wall. She inherited her beauty from her mother, the late Queen Usharna, but her character was a strange amalgam of her mother's wisdom and her father's selfish willfulness. He had not yet hit upon a method to get his way with her as he had with Usharna.

The thought made him smile ruefully. It had occurred to him after Usharna's death that she had in fact hit upon a method of getting her way with him and making it seem it was the other way around. But Areava was too direct for that and had not yet learned her mother's trick of subtle cajoling.

Areava was staring out over the royal city of Kendra, toward the harbor and Kestrel Bay beyond. She held her tiara in her right hand, and her long hair sifted gently with a cooling southerly breeze.

Orkid coughed politely into a hand and came to her side.

"I need some time alone, Chancellor," she said without looking at him.

"We all need that, your Majesty, but you of all people can least afford it."

He saw her grimace in irritation. "I hear my mother's voice when you speak like that."

"She was the wisest of women."

"Not so wise, perhaps."

"How so?"

"After my father died she married the General and begat Lynan."

Orkid sighed deeply. He had suspected her current mood had more to do with Lynan than with other affairs of state.

"You are being wise at her expense," he said.

She nodded. "Yes. That was unfair of me." She faced him. "Strange, isn't it, how we always refer to Lynan's father as 'the General'? Why not 'the Commoner' or simply 'Elynd Chisal'?"

"Because he was the greatest general Kendra has ever seen."

"Was Usharna the greatest queen Kendra has ever seen?"

"Undoubtedly."

"Then why do we not call her simply 'the Queen'?"

"In time, we may. But you may surpass her, your Majesty. Future generations may quibble about which of you should be called nothing but 'the Queen.'"

"And the other nothing more than 'the mother of the Queen' or 'the daughter of the Queen'? I don't like the sound of that. I don't want to be greater than Usharna."

"You should. If you do not strive to be the very best monarch Kendra has ever had, you will not be doing your duty."

Orkid watched with fascination as the red Rosetheme rage filled her cheeks. "How dare you—!"

"Do I have your attention now?" he interrupted sharply, his thick beard adding to his grim expression.

Areava's mouth snapped shut. Her face was still flushed, but the corner of her lips turned up in a smile she was finding hard to repress. "Is this how you treated my mother?"

"No, your Majesty. She was my teacher in all things."

Areava heard the genuine sadness in Orkid's voice, and felt pity for him. "You are my teacher, then?"

"No, Queen Areava. I am your chancellor. And we have work to do."

She resumed looking out over the city. The trees that filled the gardens and parks of Kendra's richest citizens had turned red and gold, filling the city with splendid color. "I cannot get Lynan out of my head. I had truly believed he was dead and gone forever, and when that mercenary . . ."

"Jes Prado," Orkid said with some distaste.

". . . Prado told me he was still alive, I felt like I had died instead."

"I understand. I felt the same way. But we still have work to do."

"I want to be rid of him, Orkid. I want my kingdom free of his influence, free of his taint."

"He is harmless, your Majesty. He is with the distant Chetts, a petty people living in a wasteland without cities or armies."

"No, you are wrong. While he is alive, Lynan can never be harmless. The *idea* of Lynan is a canker and, like a canker, it will spread if not cut out. He is a mule born of a monarch and a commoner. And he is a kingslayer."

Orkid sighed deeply. "This is something you should discuss with your council. Indeed, there are many pressing matters that you should discuss with your council."

"And what will be their advice, do you think? The same as yours, mayhap?"

"Your Majesty, if I had that kind of influence with the council, I would not be an Amanite. They will support you in all things, but can advise beyond my poor measure to do so."

"Oh, now you tease me," she said disdainfully. "Mother depended on your advice as heavily as I do. And you may be an Amanite, but most on the council look upon your people with a kinder light now."

"Because you are to marry one of us? Maybe."

Areava frowned in concentration. "Perhaps you are right. I will call the council on this."

"They will help you steer the right course, I am sure." He turned to leave, having achieved what he came for. He would tell Harnan Beresard, the queen's private secretary, to issue the summons for the council immediately. Areava needed hard work to drive her out of the despondence brought on by Jes Prado's news.

"Orkid," Areava called after him.

He turned around. "Your Majesty?"

Areava licked her lips, seemed hesitant to speak.

"Is there something else?"

"My brother, Prince Olio. Have you noticed anything . . . peculiar . . . about him lately?"

"Peculiar?" Orkid looked down in thought. "He seems overly tired."

"Nothing else?"

Orkid shook his head. Prince Olio? He had given the young man barely a thought since Prado's arrival at the palace. Had he missed something important? "Is something wrong with his Highness?"

"I don't know. Maybe it is my imagination."

"What exactly concerns you, Queen Areava? I will help if I can."

"He is changing," she said quickly, as if she did not really want to say the words.

"Changing?"

"He is not as, well, sweet as he once was."

Orkid's expression showed his surprise. "Sweet?"

"As gentle. He often seems sullen."

"I am sorry, I have not noticed. I will make some enquiries, if you wish."

Areava nodded. "Yes, but not so he knows."

Orkid bowed and turned again to leave.

"And, Orkid, I may have agreed to call the council, but my mind will not be changed about Lynan. I want him hunted down. I want him killed."

Olio was in a long, dark room filled with a thousand cots, and in each cot was a child. He looked at the first one, saw the rash of milk disease. The child's eyes were half-opened, the pupils so wide there was almost no white; her breath came in short pants, like a stricken dog. Olio placed his right hand on the child's head, and with the left tightly grasped the Key of the Heart. He felt the gentle touch of a magicker on his shoulder and power surged through the Key into his body and then into the body of the child. The rash evaporated, her eyes closed, and her breath deepened as she fell into a healing sleep.

A hole appeared in Olio's chest, narrow as the nib on a pen, but he could see right through it. He heard a moan from the next cot. In it was a boy, tossing and turning, scratching the boils that disfigured his arms and face. Olio placed his right hand on one of the boils; again the power surged through him. The boils dissolved, the child sighed deeply, and smiled up at him. Olio smiled back, then noticed the hole in his chest had widened.

A cry of pain from the next cot. Olio saw another boy, his whole torso scarred by burns, the flesh turned black and red.

Olio healed him. The hole in his chest widened to the size of a spear shaft.

And now the whole room filled with the sounds of suffering children. It battered against him like a storm tide. "I'm coming," he said. "Give me time."

He went from cot to cot, healing each child, and the hole in his chest grew so large he was cut in half by it, its entire circumference no longer visible. He was exhausted, but still the children needed him.

On and on he went, curing the sick, all the while slowly being eaten away until, when he finally reached the last cot, he saw his right hand glimmer, become translucent and then disappear entirely.

He looked into the last cot. It was Lynan, small Lynan, his body white and swollen with the sea, his eyes gnawed away, his lips nothing but torn shreds. "Brother, I will heal you," Olio said, and put out his hand. But there was no hand. Olio was nothing but air and light.

"Oh, no!" he cried. "Not now!"

Lynan's bloated body moved, and Olio saw worms working through the flesh of his half-brother.

"No!" he screamed, and turned away . . .

. . . and fell. Something hard slammed into his head. His eyes opened, and he saw he was on the floor in his own chambers. He groaned, tried to stand up, but could only dry retch instead.

"Oh, God."

He pushed himself up with his hands, slumped against his bed. Something was banging in his head. He held his hands against his temples, then against his jaw. Stubble scratched his palms. His mouth felt as dry as sand, and completely filled with his tongue.

He tried to stand again and got to his feet, but doubled over as the drumming in his head reached a crescendo. He sat on the edge of his bed until the drumming eased, then went to the wash basin. He splashed cold water over his face, and the shock of it seemed to wash away some of the pain.

Someone knocked on his door.

"What is it?" he said thickly, making hardly any sound at all.

"Your Highness, Prelate Fanhow is here to see you." It was the voice of his manservant. "Shall I let him in?"

"Of course you should let him in!" Olio shouted back. How many times did he have to tell the idiot that Edaytor Fanhow should never be barred from him? He looked up at the door, caught his own reflection in the mirror above the wash basin. At first he did not recognize the face.

"No, wait!" he tried to shout but could only make a hoarse cry. It was too late anyway. He could hear the servant's footsteps as he scurried away to fetch the prelate.

He splashed more water in his face and looked at his reflection again. His eyes were red-rimmed, his skin so sallow it was the color of old ivory. Two days' worth of whiskers made him look like a bandit, not a prince of the realm.

There was another knock on the door, and it opened. Prelate Fanhow, genial and round, entered and closed the door behind him. Olio hung his head down between his shoulders.

"Your Highness, are you all right?"

Olio nodded. "Just tired, Edaytor."

"I'm glad to hear it. Should I return later?"

"Yes," Olio said weakly, then quickly: "No. No, stay."

He stood up straight so the prelate could see his face. Edaytor's usually gentle and benign face blanched.

"Your Highness! What's happened to you?"

"I'm not sleeping very well."

"You look like you haven't slept for a month." The prelate found it hard to disguise his shock. Olio's usually childish features had been transformed almost beyond recognition, as if he had aged twenty years in just a few days.

Olio forced a smile. "That b–b–bad, really? I m–m–must stop eating all that rich p–p–palace food."

Edaytor did not return the smile. "You mean all that rich Chandran wine."

Olio's genial expression disappeared, replaced by a mixture of shock and anger. "How dare you—!"

"If I cannot say it to your face, Prince Olio, who can?"

"You p–p–presume too m–m–much—"

"Undoubtedly. Did you drink last night?"

"I don't see how that's any of your b–b–business."

Edaytor said nothing. The prelate was starting to perspire, and was almost overcome by a sick feeling in the pit of his stomach that told him the prince *had* been drinking.

"I don't even like wine," Olio continued after a moment, his tone now feigning anger. "I rarely drink it. I can't . . ." He let his voice trail off.

Edaytor swallowed. "You can't hold it, your Highness?"

"That isn't what I m–m–meant!" Olio spat. "If you can't open your m–m–mouth without m–m–making ridiculous charges about m–m–me, then b–b–best you don't open it at all."

Edaytor opened his arms the way a court suppliant might. "My lord, I mean you no offense—"

"It didn't sound that way."

"I *mean* you no offense. You and I are partners in a great experiment for the good of our kingdom, and I respect and admire you more than any other man I know, but to see you like this tears at my heart." Edaytor swallowed again, this time to keep back his tears. He had been wounded by the prince's manner but was ashamed to show it.

Olio gaped and put a hand on the wash basin to steady himself. His sleeve dunked in the water, and he looked at it absently. "It is I who offended you."

"No, your Highness . . ."

Olio waved him quiet. "No p–p–protestations. We cannot afford p–p–pretense between us." He closed his eyes for a moment, and when he opened them they seemed to Edaytor to be twice as red as before. "I m–m–may have overindulged now and then, m–m–my friend, but I did not lie to you b–b–before. I am not sleeping well. I am having terrible dreams. The drinking helps me sleep. And it helps me forget the dreams I have when I do sleep."

"About your healing?"

Olio's face whitened. "How could you p–p–possibly know?"

"We are dealing with great magic, your Highness. Often those who practice it suffer the consequences. Some of those magickers I've assigned to assist you in the healing complain of exactly the same thing. The dreams always end badly, in grief and failure."

"Yes, yes. That's how it is."

"And the drink would not help," Edaytor added quietly.

Olio ran his fingers through his hair. The throbbing in his head had eased, but was still there. "I swear, Edaytor, it is not the drink."

"Whether it is the drink or the magic, you cannot continue like this."

"B–b–but all the sick! What will they do?"

"Heal themselves, as they often do. When we started the clinic, we were to treat only the dying, and only those dying from misfortune, not infirmity. I know you have been treating every child who comes to us."

"I can't b–b–bear to see them suffer."

"We all suffer, your Highness. Ultimately it is our lot in life. But if you continue to help all who are brought to us, then I fear a time will come when you will not be able to help any, not even those in direst need of your healing power."

Olio sighed. "You are right. I did not recognize m–m–myself this morning. And the dreams are getting worse. They always end with . . ." He could not finish.

"End with what, your Highness?"

Olio shook his head. "It does not m–m–matter." He tried smiling again. "I p–p–promise to look after m–m–myself, Edaytor. I will rest. I will get m–m–more sleep."

"I think more than sleep is needed," Edaytor warned him. "You must not attempt any healing for a while. You need to stop using the Key of the Heart."

"Stop using it? You can't be serious."

"I have never been more serious. It is the source of your nightmares and discomfort."

"B–b–but I can't stop, Edaytor. You know that."

"For a while only. Just long enough for you to recoup your strength."

"How long will that take?"

"You are young. I do not think it will take long. But when you are well enough to resume the healing, it must be as we first agreed: to help only those in mortal peril."

"This is hard of you."

"Only those in mortal peril," Edaytor said more sternly.

Olio nodded wearily. "Very well, m–m–my friend. As you say. You have m–m–my word."

"I do not need your word, your Highness." Edaytor went to the prince and put a hand on his shoulder. "I trust you."

Jes Prado stretched his body, wincing at the pain as muscles locked. "But it is better," he groaned between grinding teeth. He even acknowledged to himself that a lot of the fat he had accumulated as a farmer in the Arran Valley had disappeared from his frame. He was harder and leaner now than he had been since he had fought in the Slaver War many, many years before.

He slumped back into a chair and started clenching and

unclenching his fists. There was almost no pain there at all anymore. He had been practicing with a sword ever since his worst injuries had been treated by the queen's own surgeon, Dr. Trion. *A funny old cutter,* Prado thought, *but he knows his stuff. I wish I'd had someone like that in my mercenary company in the old days.*

He stood up again and dressed slowly. The queen had given him a new set of clothes to replace those torn to pieces during his adventure in the summer. He remembered with a grimace how he had kidnapped Prince Lynan from under the noses of his companions, then was stopped at the last minute from safely delivering him to another mercenary captain called Rendle. And he remembered Rendle's fury at his failure, and how cruelly Rendle had treated him after that with physical punishment and constant threats to his life. And he remembered the long, dangerous, and exhausting escape from Rendle's clutches in the far northern kingdom of Haxus all the way back to Kendra, when he had arrived at Areava's palace more dead than alive.

Rendle, you bitch's son. I will find you one day and gut you while you still breathe.

One day soon, he reminded himself, if the young queen agreed to his plan. But how to convince her to give him an army? The problem had worried at him since his arrival in Kendra, but over the last few days a plan had slowly coalesced in his mind. There was a way, but it had to be explained to the right people and in the right way.

He went to the window. From his small room in one corner of the palace he could look down on the Royal Guards' training arena. Soldiers were practicing their sword skills under the careful eye of their new constable, Dejanus.

I never thought I'd ever see anyone bigger than the old constable, Prado admitted to himself. *Kumul against Dejanus. Now that would be something to see.*

He looked on the training guards with an envious eye. If

he could have fifty of them, he would march straight into Rendle's camp and butcher his whole company. But no, that would be asking for too much.

His plan would work well enough, though. He would still get Rendle in the end.

But first Lynan, he reminded himself. Lynan was the key to the whole thing. The thought struck him as morbidly funny. Imagine that useless whelp playing a role in helping him exact his revenge against Rendle. He realized then it was also right that Lynan should be at the center of the design. After all, everything had started with him all those months ago. He wondered if he should let the prince live long enough to see Rendle die. It would not hurt to have a royal prisoner—no matter how out of favor—should things go awry.

Yes, he thought. *Maybe I'll let the prince live for a while. A little while.*

3

"THE best strategy is clear," Kumul said. He was walking with a slow determined pace around the campfire and the small group gathered around it. In the flickering light his huge size and gray head made him look like something out of ancient legend. Gudon and Ager followed him with their eyes, while Korigan stared straight into the fire. Kumul's hands were behind his back, his head down in thought. "We raise an army here in the east of the Oceans of Grass. We are close to the Algonka Pass, and through there to Haxus and Hume. We can keep an eye on our enemies, and do not have so far to travel when we are ready to move."

Queen Korigan's gaze did not waver from the flames. "No. That is not the best way."

Kumul stopped his striding and looked at her. She was young, not much older than Lynan, but Kumul could tell by the way she carried herself that she was already an experienced warrior. She had a commanding, even haughty presence that sometimes reminded him of Areava. When he had first met her, he had noted the ragged sword scar on her left arm, new enough still to be bright against her golden skin. But, for all that, she did not have his experience in warfare.

"We have both fought in many battles," he said to her.
"Oh, yes, I can tell. But how many wars have you fought?"

"I was fifteen when I slew my first warrior," she said defiantly.

Kumul nodded. "Fighting Haxus or Grenda Lear will not
be the same. I have fought against Haxus, and for Grenda
Lear, almost my whole life. I know them. I am telling you
we need to stay close to their borders; when it is time to
move against one or the other, we must move quickly."

"No," Korigan repeated.

"I cannot believe you are saying this," Kumul said. "You
are a Chett; no one understands the importance of mobility
more than the Chetts."

Korigan nodded. "That is true. But you insist on thinking
about the coming struggle as a military problem. It is more
than that."

"What do you mean?"

"Prince Lynan has my full support in his struggle. My
people have a great respect for the one who holds the Key of
Union, and also a great respect for the son of Elynd Chisal."
She looked up at Kumul then. "And also for the famed captain
of Elynd Chisal's Red Shields. But my support will be
meaningless if the northern Chetts do not, in turn, support
me."

"But you are their queen!" Ager protested. Korigan and
Gudon glanced at each other. Ager did not like the meaning
he read in that. "You *are* their queen, aren't you?"

"Oh, yes," Gudon said, "she is definitely our queen."

"Then what's the problem?" Kumul demanded.

"My cousin is queen in name only." Gudon spread his
wiry arms to encompass the whole camp. "All these Chetts
belong to her clan, the White Wolf clan, and would follow
Korigan even across the Sea Between if she asked them. But
the northern Chetts are made up of many clans, and not all
of those would be as keen to follow her."

"The truth is that some of the leaders of those clans would be queen or king in my place," Korigan added.

"But your father united them."

"My father united them against their will. We had a common cause back then: the defeat of the slavers. Once your General had defeated them, some of the clans believed there was no longer any need for the Chetts to have a monarch."

"But the threat hasn't gone," Kumul said urgently. "Prado and Rendle are back."

"Those clan leaders most opposed to me will not take my word for that. They would suppose I was lying to remain their queen."

"So what do you suggest?"

"That we move to the High Sooq for winter. The clans gather there to trade and arrange marriages. Since my father's time, it is also where the monarch consults with the other clan leaders. Last year there was a move against me, but most of the clans would prefer me—someone they believe is naive and bendable to their will—than one of the current clan heads."

"And truth, that's our problem," Gudon said. "If you want to raise an army of Chetts, you'll need more than our clan. But if Korigan tried to raise the other clans, they will have more reason to depose her."

"The solution's simple—and obvious," Kumul said flatly. "We stay here in the east, watching the Algonka Pass and carrying out raids on our enemies. Word will spread to the clans eventually and they'll join our cause."

"Kumul, how many years do you have?" Korigan asked.

"What do you mean?"

"I mean how long do you have before Grenda Lear will not care whether or not Lynan is alive or dead, forgotten, or reinstated? If they have ten years of peace and prosperity under their new queen, what chance have you of pressing Lynan's claims against those who murdered Berayma? For

it will take ten years to gather an army the way you propose."

"And what do you suggest we do? From what you have
said, the clans would rather depose you than follow you into
war."

"We *all* go to the High Sooq. I try to rally them, but if
they waver, Lynan will be our key. They will believe him."

"Would he be in any danger there?" Kumul asked.

"No one would harm the son of Elynd Chisal," she said.

"Not even if it means getting rid of you?"

Korigan stared at him levelly but said nothing.

"Then I say again, our solution is simple. We stay here.
We carry out raids. We send out messengers to the other
clans, gifts, booty, anything we need to do to make them
rally to our cause."

"You do not understand the Chetts. Gifts and booty are
well and fine, but they do not feed our cattle, they do not
bring rain to the Oceans of Grass, they do not control the
seasons. We need a cause, and Lynan can give them that
cause."

"You mean Lynan can secure your throne for you," Kumul
said sharply. Even as he said the words, he knew he
had overstepped the mark. There was a sudden and cool silence around the fire.

"Kumul, that was unnecessary," Ager said softly.

Kumul nodded. "Ager is right. My apologies, your Highness. You didn't deserve that."

"Better it had been left unsaid," Gudon agreed.

"But Kumul *is* right," Korigan said. "I do need Lynan to
secure my throne." Her gaze never left Kumul. "But do you
not need my support to secure Lynan on the throne of
Grenda Lear?"

Lynan had feigned exhaustion and retreated to his tent
soon after dark. He needed to be alone. He tried to think

about his future, about what needed to be done to return to Kendra, to reinstate Kumul as constable, Ager as captain, Jenrosa as student magicker, and himself as a prince of the realm. Most of all, he tried to think about what needed to be done to revenge Berayma's murder.

Had Areava been a part of the plot? He could not believe it of his half-sister. She had loved Berayma, and anyway would never have done anything to betray Usharna's last command. But how else could the murderers have hoped to pull off regicide? Neither Orkid nor Dejanus, who had performed the deed, could hope to ascend to the throne themselves. They needed one of Usharna's children to succeed to the crown, but they had killed Berayma and tried to kill Lynan, and he did not think for one minute they would try to place Olio on the throne. That left Areava. Did she really believe Orkid and Dejanus' claim that Lynan had murdered his own brother? Or had she been a member of the conspiracy from the very beginning?

Hard as he tried, he could not see his way through it. Something else was occupying his mind. At times just a flash—the exultation he felt when he snapped the neck of the grass wolf—and at other times it was as if he was reliving the whole hunt.

He did not know what happened to him today. He remembered the rage filling his whole being when Gudon's life was in danger, as hot and great as a summer storm. He remembered spurring his horse out of the protective group and leaping off it to grapple with the wolf. But he did not know *how* any of this had happened. And he did not know where his great strength had come from.

He swung his feet off his cot and stood up. The plain gold circle of the Key of Union dangled from its heavy chain around his neck. When he looked outside of his tent, he saw a few fires burning, some with people gathered around. He could also see the shape of the grasslands gently rolling away from the hill on which they were camped. Far away, he could make out clumps of trees. Gudon had called them arrow trees. Lynan could even see individual leaves as sharp and deadly as the weapon they were named after. While he could barely squint in the daylight, at night his vision was as good as a hawk's. He stepped outside. Nearby was a large boulder. He bent over and tried to pick it up. It would not budge. He might as well have tried to move the world. Whatever strength he had during the fight with the wolf was gone now. He was just plain Lynan again.

Moonlight reflected off his the pale skin of his hand. *Not quite plain old Lynan anymore,* he thought. Or ever again. He did not fully understand what he had become, but the callow, frightened, and often self-righteous boy who had fled Kendra was no more.

Suddenly he was alert.

He looked around, but saw nothing out of the ordinary. What had captured his attention?

He pricked his ears, but heard only the sound of snuffling horses, a few snoring Chetts, the indistinct mumble of close conversation, the crackling of the fires. He could smell the fire smoke, too, and the horses' hides. And he could smell something else.

That was it. That smell. He slowly turned on his heels. There, to the northwest. He *knew* that smell, had come across it only recently. Karak. He drew in air through his nose. One karak, he was certain.

And then a new sensation. Akin to hunger, but greater and fiercer.

He strode rapidly toward the source of the scent. He passed a lone sentry, who bowed to him. He broke into a trot. The sentry called after him. He waved at her to keep quiet, and she shut up. In a few moments he was almost out of site of the camp. He hesitated. Part of him wanted to return to his tent, to find rest, but another part, a greater and more urgent part, drove him on.

Korigan's remark left Kumul and Ager speechless.

"You mean you don't intend for him to replace Areava as ruler of Grenda Lear?" she asked, incredulous.

"Of course not," Kumul said, his tone more confused than righteous, staring at the queen. "Areava was next in line to Berayma. And after her is Olio, her brother. No one would accept Lynan being placed on the throne."

"The Chetts would," Korigan said evenly, meeting his gaze.

"Lynan is of royal descent," Gudon added. "He has been wrongfully outlawed. Those who actually murdered his brother now rule behind the throne, and if Areava was not complicit in Berayma's killing, she is certainly taking advantage of it."

"But we don't know that Areava knew of the murderers' plot," Ager argued. "She was crowned because she was next in succession."

"And she gave amnesty to Lynan to argue his case in front of the court?" Gudon said.

"Well, no . . ."

"Then maybe she does not want to hear what Lynan might have to say."

"This is ridiculous—"

"What is ridiculous," Gudon interrupted, "is that neither of you have tried to see to the very end. Whether or not Areava is guilty of conspiracy is meaningless. *She* is Lynan's enemy now, not Berayma's murderers, however just it might be to want to reveal their wrongdoing."

"Lynan will never be safe in Grenda Lear until he is crowned himself," Korigan added. "And as for cause? He has the blood, he has the goodwill of the Chetts and—from what Gudon has told me—the goodwill of the ruler and people of Chandra as well. Lynan has one of the Keys of Power, the Key of Union, the Key that represents all the provinces in the kingdom outside of Kendra itself."

"We're getting ahead of ourselves," Kumul said. Ager thought he looked suddenly gray, and his voice sounded uncertain. "We still have to decide what to do *now*, not years ahead."

"Then shouldn't Lynan be here?" Korigan asked.

"Ager and I have been advising him. When we have all made a decision as to our best course of action, we will present it to him."

Korigan's eyes widened. "Is that how it works in Grenda Lear?"

"Lynan is still young," Kumul explained patiently. "He was never expected to succeed to the throne, so he was never taught how to rule or how to lead. He must learn these things under our tutelage."

"Truly, it is better to learn by doing," Gudon said.

"In the proper time and in the proper way," Kumul said shortly.

As the discussion returned again to whether the clan should move west to spend winter at the High Sooq or stay where it was, Ager found himself no longer listening to the words. He stood up, excused himself and drifted into the night, his crouching walk making him look like a giant spider in the dim light.

Korigan and Gudon's words had shocked him because the idea of Lynan becoming king himself had never occurred to him, but the more he thought about it the more logical the Chetts' conclusion seemed to be. He did not agree with it—his whole upbringing and training as a soldier loyal to Grenda Lear rebelled against it—but he could see the sense behind the argument.

He turned back to the others. The fire flickered dimly in

the darkness, the giant silhouette of Kumul casting an eerie shadow across the camp.

Lynan forced himself to turn back.

What was I doing? I am a prince of the realm, not a beast in the night.

He laughed wryly at his own pride. Some prince of the realm: exiled to the Oceans of Grass, with a future only the greatest optimist would find any hope in, and now plagued by desires that were inhuman. Areava would not be surprised, of course, she always thought of him as almost less than human. He could remember vividly their last conversation on the palace's south gallery only hours before Berayma was murdered; he had seen in her eyes then how she truly thought of him.

With that memory came a very human anger, and the emotion threw out the last vestige of his unnatural hunger. *This is how I control it,* he thought with surprise. *By never forgetting the first cause of my exile and transformation.*

His confidence renewed if not wholly restored, Lynan walked back past the sentry and into the camp. He reached his tent and looked east, back toward civilization, back toward his enemies. He imagined Areava in her throne room, thinking he was dead and celebrating the fact, Berayma's murderers by her side.

If only she knew what had truly become of him.

He was about to enter his tent when he caught sight of Ager standing alone. With his bent body he seemed almost to hover over the ground. Lynan went to him and put a hand on his warped shoulder.

"I thought you would be asleep by now," he said to the crookback. "You were as excited as a child on the hunt today."

Ager grinned self-consciously. "It has been a long time since I've had the pleasure. Since before the Slaver War."

He nodded at his back. "And I have always found it easier to ride than walk."

"Are the others still up? Where's Gudon?"

"With Korigan."

"Ah," Lynan said, misunderstanding. "I'll leave him be, then."

Afterward, Ager was never sure what made him say next: "And Kumul."

"And Kumul?" Lynan blinked. "I see. And you were with them as well."

Ager nodded.

"Why wasn't I told?"

"You had gone to your tent. You said you were exhausted."

"You could have waited until tomorrow."

"Lynan, it's not like that—"

But Lynan was not listening. He turned on his heel and made for Korigan's tent.

"Lynan, wait!"

But Lynan ignored him. As he drew near the tent, he saw the Chett queen with Gudon and Kumul around a fire. When they saw him coming, they stopped talking. He smiled at them but said nothing.

"You could not sleep, lad?" Kumul asked. His lips were pressed close together, and the skin around his salt-and-pepper beard seemed drawn and lined.

"You look like you could use some," Lynan replied.

He waited.

The other three looked at each other uneasily. Then Ager joined them, slightly out of breath.

"Where have you been?" Kumul demanded.

Ager shrugged. "I needed to walk."

"Walk? I could have used your support—"

"Support for what?" Lynan interrupted.

Kumul glanced at Lynan, then at Ager, but Ager was looking determinedly at the ground.

"Truth, little master, it was of no great concern," Gudon said, his tone light.

"The weather?"

The way Lynan held himself, the tension in the skin around his eyes and mouth, told Gudon the prince was in no mood for banter. "No, your Majesty."

"I am not your Majesty, Gudon. Officially, I am 'your Highness.' I believe Areava is still queen of this kingdom."

Gudon joined Ager in staring at the ground.

Lynan caught Kumul's gaze and held it. "My friend. My oldest friend. What were you talking about?"

Kumul's jaw set. "We can discuss this later, Lynan."

"No." He said flatly.

"We were discussing what we should do next," Korigan said suddenly, and got to her feet. She walked to Lynan and stood straight in front of him. Lynan had to look up to see her face. Her skin shone like real gold in the firelight. "In fact, we were *arguing* about what we should do next."

"We? You mean me, don't you?"

"Lynan, there is no need to trouble yourself about this," Kumul said. "Ager and I were going to tell you in the morning everything that transpired here tonight."

Lynan ignored him. "What was the discussion—sorry, argument—about?"

"About whether to stay here in the east of the Oceans of Grass to be near Haxus and Hume, or to go to the High Sooq and recruit the entire Chett nation to your cause."

"Kumul wanted us to stay here," Lynan said, a statement and not a question.

"Yes."

"And you want us to go the High Sooq."

"Yes."

Lynan looked at Gudon. "And you? Which side were you on?"

"There are good reasons on both sides." Gudon shrugged. "But I support my queen."

Lynan turned to Ager. "And you?"

"I lean toward Kumul, your Highness."

"And Jenrosa. Was she a part of this discussion? What side did she take?"

"She has no experience in these sorts of things," Kumul said gruffly.

"Nor have I, apparently, though we both deserve a say, wouldn't you agree?"

"Of course, lad, but we weren't making any decisions—"

"Except what course of action I should take."

"It wasn't like that."

"It's always like that, Kumul. I remember the talks I had with you and Ager before Jes Prado kidnapped me. 'Lynan, we think this is the best course of action. If you don't agree, we'll not support you.'"

"It was never like that!" Kumul said, aghast.

"It was exactly like that," Lynan said without rancor. "But I've changed, Kumul. Being kidnapped, hacked to pieces, and brought back from the door of death does that." He turned and walked away, and without looking over his shoulder said: "We leave for the High Sooq in the morning."

Kumul stayed by the fire after the others had gone. Ager hesitated, but Kumul waved him off and Ager left without saying anything.

"Well, that was a turn," Kumul said softly to himself. He was feeling angry and ashamed, a combination that left him feeling confused. He had always been sure that Lynan would one day come into his own, both as a prince and as a man, but for it to happen so abruptly and in such a manner took Kumul aback.

And then there was the transformation that had changed the prince's appearance so dramatically. Kumul did not know what else the transformation had altered, but could not help being afraid of the possible consequences.

He sighed deeply. He had been wrong to exclude the boy from the discussion, but was sure Lynan's decision had been made in anger. If only Kumul had handled it better, he was sure Lynan would have come around to his way of thinking.

It's not the decision his father would have made, he thought ruefully. *The General would have seen the wisdom of staying close to the enemy.*

But Lynan was not his father, in any fashion. Proven in battle but not yet in war, heir to a blighted inheritance but also heir to the greatest throne on the continent of Theare, outlaw and victim of thwarted justice. Lynan was so much more and less than his father ever was. Where Elynd Chisal was straight up and down, Lynan was a mystery.

And yet, Kumul suspected, Lynan might prove to be the greater. *And he is my son as well.*

Kumul could no longer see into the future with the certainty he once possessed. All the sureties had left his life, and only vague hopes took their place. The thought worried him; he knew that once the challenge of heading into the unknown would have excited him.

And Lynan, for the first time, had spurned him. That weighed on Kumul heavier than all else. He felt he had been rejected, and the feeling made him angry at his own self-pity and childishness.

He threw some more wood into the fire, watching it burn brighter and higher.

So be it, he thought resignedly. *The future is dark to me now, but I will not let Lynan enter it alone.*

4

IT was sunset, and Kendra had become a golden city.

"That sky is the color of my love for you," Sendarus said.

Areava looked sideways at him and saw the smile he tried to hide, but it lit up his face too much. "I have heard crows sing sweeter songs," she said.

"Ah, but no crow ever loved you as I have."

Areava shook her head. "Oh, stop it. You don't have to prove to me you have a sense of humor."

Sendarus got up from their stone seat and knelt in front of her. He took her hands in his own. "But there is so much I want to prove to you," he said seriously.

"We will have time. A whole lifetime."

"It won't be enough."

She kissed him on the forehead and slipped her hands away from his. "It will have to do. Have you heard from your father?"

"Must we always discuss business when we're alone together?"

"Best to get it out of the way."

"You used to have a lighter heart."

"Stop it, Sendarus," she said shortly. "If you want the marriage to go ahead as much as you say you do, you'll help remove the last impediments. The council wants that agreement from Aman—signed by your father—before its members will give our union their full support. This is a particular concern of the Twenty Houses."

"You have no regard for your country's nobility," Sendarus objected. "Why this sudden need to pacify the Twenty Houses?"

"I have a lot of respect for them and their influence in the kingdom."

"And why are you so concerned about the council? It is your creation, after all. You can dissolve it any time you like. I've heard you say so to their faces."

Areava patted his cheek. "A council expects to be threatened by its monarch every now and then. It's good form. But it's not good form to ignore its advice, and its advice is to get from your father a guarantee that my marrying you does not give Aman any rights of succession outside our own issue."

"Such a legalistic expression for the children we will raise. Our 'issue.' That is a term for matters of state."

"And our children, like it or not, will be matters of state."

Sendarus shook his head. "Not to me."

Areava was about to agree when she realized she would be lying. The realization surprised and dismayed her. There was no doubt in her mind that she would love any children she bore, but equally there was no doubt that as queen she would put them to good use for the sake of her kingdom. *As my own mother did with Berayma, and at the end of her life, through the Keys of Power, had tried to do with all of us, even Lynan.*

"Have you heard from your father?" she asked again.

Sendarus sat next to her, his usual cheerful face now as serious as her own. "Not yet. I was expecting a message to arrive last week, but it has not come yet."

"You don't think your father—"

"Will not agree? No. But it is possible he will ask for concessions in other areas. He is a politician at heart."

"As he should be. He is a ruler."

Sendarus looked sideways at Areava. "He will meet his match in you, I think."

"Ironically."

"Why?"

"Because his brother, my chancellor, is one of my teachers."

Sendarus laughed at that, and the sound was so infectious that Areava joined in.

"I'm glad to see you enjoying yourself, your Majesty," said a voice behind them.

They both turned and saw Orkid standing there, looking as severe as usual, an impression always exaggerated by his long dark beard. They both laughed even harder.

"How pleasing to your humble servant to be a source of amusement for your royal personages," he said stiffly and without a trace of sarcasm.

"Oh, Orkid, don't take it to heart," Areava said lightly, and went to him. "You are more than that to me."

Orkid sighed. "Oh, such relief."

"Why, Orkid, I believe you actually tried to be funny."

"Tried?" he asked glumly. "Well, I am employed as your chancellor, not your jester."

"Come and sit with us." She took his hand and drew him to the stone seat. "We were actually discussing matters of state, particularly pertaining to your brother. Why has he not sent his agreement to the council's condition for the marriage?"

Orkid shrugged. "I imagine he is thinking up some way to bargain with it."

"Exactly what Sendarus said. You Amanites all think alike."

"I have come about another matter. One just as pressing."

Areava raised an eyebrow. "What matter could possibly be as important as my marriage?"

"The matter of your brother, your Majesty, the outlaw Prince Lynan."

"Oh." Her jollity disappeared. She slumped down next to Sendarus.

"You asked me to pursue the matter. I believe a solution may have presented itself."

"In what way?"

"You can come now!" Orkid called out. A moment later Jes Prado appeared and stood by Orkid's side. The queen studied him closely. He was looking a hundred times better than the first time she had seen him in her chambers all those weeks ago now, but there was still something hard and cruel about his eyes and the thin set of his mouth, and something threatening about the way he stood, like a cat about to pounce on a mouse. His thickly braided gray hair, scarred face, and crooked nose only added to the sense of menace that accompanied him like a shadow.

"The first time we met you brought me bad news," the queen said evenly. "I hope you have something better for me this time."

"I wish it had not been me who brought you such evil tidings. But I think I can offer your Majesty a remedy to this particular wound."

Areava glanced at Orkid, but his expression gave nothing away. "Go on."

"You know my past?"

"Of course," she said, her distaste obvious.

"Then I suggest you put it to use."

"I will not tolerate the resurrection of slavery in my kingdom," she said quietly.

"Nor should you," Prado replied quickly. "But *mercenar-*

ies still have their use. Even now you employ them on the border with Haxus."

"In small numbers."

"Let me raise my old company, and give me your warrant to raise more. I will set out to hunt down and capture Lynan for you."

"I want him killed, not captured."

"Even easier."

The words sent a chill down Areava's spine. She controlled it, ashamed of her reaction. "What is your opinion?" she asked Orkid. Orkid simply nodded. "Do you have particulars?"

"Not yet," Orkid said. "I wanted you to hear the suggestion yourself before going into any more detail."

"Do so. The council meets in three days' time; give me your report before then and I will present it."

Orkid and Prado bowed and left.

"I do not like that man," Sendarus said.

"You don't have to like a rock to crush a spider with it," she said.

The boy was about four years old. He lay in a tight crumpled heap in his cot, his breathing labored, his face shiny with sweat in the torch light.

"What is it?" Olio asked, running a hand through his unruly brown hair, struggling to fight off the exhaustion that seemed his constant companion these days.

The priest laid a gentle hand on the boy's forehead. "Asthma. He has had it since he was three months old. It has become worse in the last year. He has been like this for several days now. He doesn't eat and throws up most of what he drinks."

"Is he dying?"

"Yes, your Highness, he is dying. He will not live to see the morning."

Olio sighed deeply and looked at Edaytor Fanhow. "I have no choice. I cannot refuse to heal him, despite my assurance to you that I would not use the Key."

Edaytor looked grim. "No. I see that."

Olio nodded to the priest, who stepped back, then laid his right hand on the boy's heaving chest. With his left he pulled out the Key of the Heart—shaped like a triangle with a solid heart placed in its center—from behind his shirt and grasped it firmly. "All right."

Edaytor laid his hands on Olio's slender shoulders. Almost immediately, he felt magickal power surge through the prince. No matter how many times he did this with Olio, the strength of the magic surprised him, but this time he was also surprised at the speed with which it came. The Key was becoming aligned to its owner. He wondered if Olio would soon be able to do without a magicker's assistance at all. The thought worried him.

Olio started to slump, and Edaytor pulled him back from the cot. The prince cried out weakly, then rested against the prelate.

"Your Highness?" the priest asked, concerned. He was newly assigned to the hospice, and had never worked with the prince before.

Olio held his hand up. "I am all right. A little weary, that's all."

"Come, sit down." The priest and Edaytor guided him to a wooden stool. "Do you want me to get you something?"

"No," he answered, then almost immediately. "Yes. Wine."

"Your Highness—" Edaytor started, but Olio's angry glare stopped him.

"Just a cup, Prelate."

The priest returned with the wine. Olio drank it greedily and handed the cup back.

"More, your Highness?" the priest asked.

"No," Edaytor said firmly. The priest glanced from the prelate to the prince and back to the prelate again. "No," Edaytor repeated. "Thank you. I must speak with the prince. Alone."

The priest scurried off.

"I wouldn't have asked for more," Olio said, his voice almost a whine.

"Then I saved you the trouble of telling him yourself."

Olio stood up unsteadily. Edaytor reached out to him, but Olio waved him away. "I thought you trusted me."

Before Edaytor could reply, a little voice said: "I'm hungry." The sick boy was sitting up in his cot. He looked thin and pale, but his breathing was normal. "I'm hungry," he said again.

"I'll get you something," Olio said. "How are you feeling?"

The boy thought about it for a moment. "Hungry."

"Then we'll feed you a mountain." He faced the prelate. "Is this not worth all?"

Edaytor blushed, ashamed he had no reply.

Now that the executive council had met half a dozen times, its members had gravitated to sitting in the same position at the table at every meeting. Areava sat at one end, flanked by Orkid and Olio; down the right-hand side, from Areava's perspective, sat government officials such as Harnan Beresard, Prelate Edaytor Fanhow, and Kendra's mayor Shant Tenor, as well as those members of the Twenty Houses given seats on the council, most prominently Areava's cousin Galen Amptra. On the left-hand side sat the various representatives of the kingdom's guilds and merchant houses, as well as Primate Giros Northam, leader of the Church of the Righteous God, and his secretary and Areava's confessor, Father Powl. At the end of the table sat

Fleet Admiral Zoul Setchmar and Marshal Triam Lief on either side of the new constable, Dejanus.

Sunlight poured into the room from the long glass windows in one wall. The members waited for Areava to start, but she was busy conferring with Orkid. A few were taking notes or catching up on paperwork, one or two looked bored and were stifling yawns. Most simply waited patiently.

"You will have heard my brother is still alive," Areava said suddenly. One or two members jumped in their seats.

"We have heard rumors, your Majesty," Father Powl said, "but not the whole story."

"Lynan did not drown. He has escaped to the Oceans of Grass."

There was a soft murmur, but—Areava was glad to hear—no urgency or panic in the voices.

"He is still in the company of former Constable Kumul and former Captain Ager Parmer, and the female magicker . . ." She searched for a paper on the table in front of her.

"Jenrosa Alucar," Edaytor Fanhow said quickly and softly, as if ashamed she had been a magicker.

". . . yes, from the Theurgia of Stars."

"*Was,* your Majesty," Edaytor corrected.

"Was. Yes. They are with the Chetts."

"Then they are harmless," Marshal Lief said. "They cannot harm the kingdom from the Oceans of Grass."

There was general agreement from the council.

"While he is alive, Prince Lynan is dangerous," Areava said softly. Somehow the words carried through the hubbub, and everyone instantly fell silent. Olio looked at her with something like dismay. Sitting there, pale and golden-haired, she reminded him of one of the old gods—as unmerciful as they were beautiful.

"Your Majesty?" the Marshal asked.

"What does he hold?" she asked.

"Nothing except grass now," Shant Tenor said jovially.

"And the Key of Union," Areava said.

"Is it worth anything by itself?" the mayor said, holding his hands up and looking from councilor to councilor as if he were directing the question to all of them.

"It is worth something to me," Areava said sternly. "I want the Key of Union for another purpose."

"Sister, you already have two," Olio said gently.

"My husband-to-be has none."

Olio seemed surprised. "Ah, of course," he said eventually.

"Your Majesty, this is a delicate matter you have raised," Xella Povis, the head of the Merchant Guild, said. "We still have not heard from the king of Aman about his guarantee on the issue of succession."

"Correction," Areava said, and put out a hand. Orkid handed her a rolled parchment which she opened and flattened on the table in front of her. "His courier arrived yesterday afternoon." She paused, glancing up at all the expectant faces. "And he agrees."

The council exhaled as if it were a single, large animal.

"With two conditions," Areava finished.

The animal held its breath again until Galen Amptra said: "Which are?"

"He wants another dock built for Amanite merchant ships in the harbor."

"That would give them the same number as Lurisia, and two more than Chandra or Hume," Xella Povis said.

"Which is undoubtedly why he wants it."

"And the second condition, your Majesty?"

"That the Tithe of Gelt be reintroduced."

There was an uproar. Everyone started talking at the same time.

Areava's disappointment was clear in the look she gave

Orkid and Olio. She waited until the noise subdued. "Is there a problem with this?"

The uproar started all over again, this time directed against her. Areava's face paled. "Enough!" she shouted. And just like a summer storm the tempest passed as quickly as it had come. "Is this how you address your queen?"

"Your Majesty, I am sorry," Xella Povis said, "but one of the reasons Kendra went to war against Aman all those centuries ago is because they imposed the Tithe of Gelt on any shipping passing by and through the mouth of that river, a tithe they imposed with force. Is Aman suggesting we submit to this piracy voluntarily?"

Areava felt Orkid stiffen beside her, but he kept his control and said nothing. *If only all my councilors were as disciplined,* she thought.

"It is nothing so fierce," Areava told the merchant. "They are asking that every merchant ship that passes by or through the Gelt River pay a tithe worth one part in a hundred of its cargo. As I understand it, the old tithe was one-third the worth."

"That is true," Xella Povis admitted, somewhat mollified, "but the principle involved . . ."

"The principle involved is that in exchange for these two conditions, Aman not only will sign the guarantee of succession, but undertake to construct and permanently man a beacon fire on Triangle Rock at the mouth of the Gelt. Is it not the case, Xella Povis, that even today we lose half a dozen ships a year on that rock?"

The merchant nodded.

"And, compared to that loss, how much is a tithe of one part in a hundred?"

"It is a good bargain," Xella Povis admitted, bowing to the queen in apology and in surrender.

Areava smiled lightly. "Am I to take it, then, that there

are no more objections to my marriage with Prince Sendarus going ahead?"

There was no disagreement. Galen Amptra and one or two others seemed unhappy about it, but there was no longer anything they could do.

"And to come back to our original point of discussion, is it fair and just that my husband and consort should be without one of the Keys of Power when the outlaw Lynan still possesses the Key of Union? And who better to wear that Key than Prince Sendarus, an Amanite who will join in union with your monarch?"

"All well and good, your Majesty," Marshall Lief said gruffly, "but how do you propose we go and get the Key?"

"Are you suggesting the army of Grenda Lear is incapable of marching into allied territory to find a single group of outlaws?" Areava asked. "And especially a group so conspicuous? One prince, hardly more than a boy and holding a Key of Power, one giant ex-constable, one crookback ex-soldier, and one female magicker."

"The Chetts won't like it. And sending soldiers into the Oceans of Grass could raise tensions with Haxus even higher than they already are. King Salokan would have to wonder if we are preparing for a move against him."

"We can make it up to the Chetts—they had no objection to our armies marching through their territory when we were clearing up the slavers for them. And I don't care in the least if the move disturbs King Salokan; I only wish everything I did disturbed King Salokan."

"I'll lead a force," Dejanus said quickly. "I'm afraid of no Chett."

"That was not my concern—" the Marshal began testily, but Areava held up her hand.

"Constable, how well do you know the Oceans of Grass?" she asked.

Dejanus balked, suddenly frightened. Did she know of

his previous life as a slaver? Did Orkid tell her? He thought desperately for a moment.

"Constable?" Areava prompted.

All eyes turned to him. His normally red face blushed even deeper. His cheeks glowed with color.

No, she could not know. Otherwise I'd be in a cell right now.

"Not at all well, your Majesty. But there are maps—"

"Unnecessary, Dejanus, though I applaud your enthusiasm," she said, throwing a glance at the Marshal who blushed and looked away.

"Then what does your Majesty suggest?" asked Dejanus.

"We send those who know the Oceans of Grass and the Chetts better than any of us here. We hire a mercenary captain, one of those who fought in the last war."

"A slaver?" the Marshal said indignantly. "This Jes Prado, for instance? The one who is said to have brought you the news about Lynan?"

"No longer a slaver. And yes, I am thinking of Jes Prado."

"What would *he* do?" Olio asked.

"Hire a force of mercenaries to pursue Lynan."

"And capture him," Olio finished for her.

"No. Kill him."

Everyone in the room became still.

"Sister, our b–b–brother is not tried yet for his alleged crimes."

"Was his flight not enough?" Areava demanded, her voice rising. "Is the overwhelming evidence against him not enough?"

"B–b–but he could still b–b–be captured," Olio insisted.

Orkid spoke to the council for the first time. "We cannot risk it, your Highness. If he is captured and escapes, how much stronger will his position be?"

"With whom, Chancellor? He has no supporters among

us, surely, and none among the other provinces that I have heard. He is almost forgotten by the p–p–people."

"And if he is killed, alone and deserted on the Ocean of Grass, he will be forgotten entirely," Areava said to Olio, and then to the council: "He is a traitor, he is an outlaw, and he has committed regicide. He deserves to die."

"And it will not cost the kingdom much to raise a force of mercenaries large enough to hunt him down," Shant Tenor said.

"Prado's commission would be wider than that," Areava told the council. "He has told me of a mercenary recently hired by us to help patrol the border with Haxus—a certain Rendle—who took our gold and then fled to Haxus to serve her king. I am convinced he must be found and punished as well, or all our mercenary units may come to believe they can do the same with impunity."

"Then why trust this Prado?" Dejanus asked. His face wore the quizzical smile he so often gave when he thought he had an advantage, as if he was puzzled by good fortune. "He is nothing but another mercenary. Your Majesty, give me leave to take a regiment of our own horse to the Oceans of Grass. Prado can be our guide, if you like, and our loyalty is unquestioned."

Orkid shook his head. "We cannot so easily dispatch such a regiment. Our forces are thin on the ground after so many years of peace, and although we are mobilizing against the possible threat of Haxus, if King Salokan should invade soon, we will need all the loyal units we have."

"And in the short term, hiring mercenaries is cheaper," Areava added. That put a smile on some of the councilors' faces, she noted. They liked the idea of not spending more money than necessary, a fact she was counting on.

"But how reliable is this Prado?" the Marshal insisted.

"He will be reliable," Orkid said. "I will make sure of it. I give the Council my word on it."

There were no more disagreements, and only Orkid noticed the sour look cast him by Dejanus.

Areava and Sendarus spent the night together for the first time in several weeks.

"We should have done this more often," Sendarus said to her in the morning.

"That would have been difficult before the council gave its final approval to the marriage. It would have seemed as if we were flouting all my advisers and many of the common people, too."

Sendarus leaned over Areava, used his hand to trace her jaw and neck, then her breasts and the flat of her stomach. "Instead, you flouted me," he said, pouting.

"Keep that up and I'll flog you," she said, and pushed him away. He roared in mock fury and tried to fling himself over her, but Areava got out of the way and leaped on him instead.

"You're too slow, Amanite."

"Slow to come," he said, "better in bed."

Areava laughed. "Oh, you are cheap."

Sendarus twisted around underneath her. "You are less careworn today."

"I feel it. Learning that Lynan was still alive shook my confidence, I admit. But I am back on top now."

Sendarus grunted. "In more ways than one."

Areava slammed a pillow into the side of his head. "This is the natural state of things. I am queen already, you are a mere prince."

"Yes, your Majesty."

She lay down against his length and held his head in her hands. "I love you, and always will, prince or no." She kissed him quickly and moved to get out of bed.

"Already?" Sendarus complained. "I was hoping for a second engagement."

"Tonight, perhaps. I have much to do."

"Will we be taking a honeymoon after our marriage?"

"Of course. The morning after our marriage, I will stay in bed an extra hour. That should be enough time."

"Too fast for me," he said.

"But not for me," she countered, already half-dressed. She went to the east window and opened it. Down below, the guard was changing, their spear tips and helms gleaming in the dawn light. She saw another figure, small, lonely and sad-looking, coming through the main gate. With a shock she realized it was Olio. In her depression about Lynan over the last few weeks she had not spared him much time, and he seemed to be getting worse from day to day. What was happening to him? Why was he changing so much? She did not want to gain a husband but lose her dearest brother.

Sendarus noticed her face fall. "What is it?" he asked, concerned.

She shook her head, said nothing.

Prado was filled with nervous impatience. "When can I go?" he demanded.

Orkid studied him carefully. Prado had been a wretched creature when he first came to the palace—malnourished, bruised, and cut—but now he looked every bit a warrior, lean and strong despite his middle age. On hearing of the council's decision, the mercenary had immediately gone out and bought a new set of breeches, jerkin, boots, and gloves, and a fine Chandran sword and knife, all on credit. If anyone could find and slay Lynan, he could, Orkid thought.

"Soon. The queen should sign your warrant today, and I already have your promissory note from the treasury. You have enough to hire a small army for a period of several months. I hope it is enough, for you shall get no more."

"It will be enough," Prado said with arrogant confidence.

"I will bring you two heads in repayment: Prince Lynan's and Rendle's."

"One head will be enough. Rendle's remains you can leave where you slay him."

"Oh, no. I have plans for that trophy."

Orkid grimaced. "Your mission is to kill Lynan. Achieve that at all costs."

"I will."

"And do not fail me."

"You?" Prado barked. "I thought I was serving your queen."

"*Our* queen," Orkid hissed. He stood right next to the mercenary. "And on this commission you answer to me. I will not brook failure."

Prado's eyes hardened. "I will not fail, Chancellor, but I do not like being threatened."

"I promise you, Jes Prado, if you *do* fail me, I will have you hunted down like a crazed karak."

There was such menace in Orkid's voice and large, dominating figure that Prado retreated a step. He avoided the chancellor's gaze. "I've already told you: I will not fail."

Orkid nodded and moved to his desk and retrieved an official-looking parchment. He held it out to Prado. "Your promissory note."

"Good," Prado said, taking the parchment.

"Come back this evening for the warrant. By the way, it will have an extra clause the council does not know about, and which they must not know about."

"Extra clause?"

"You will be given the rank of general in the Grenda Lear army. It will give you the authority to commandeer regular troops on the border if you need them."

Prado gasped. "Me! A general in your army? This is a turnaround."

"Where will you go first?"

"To the Arran Valley. Many from my old company live there, and will form the core of my force. From there north, picking up groups where I can find them."

"Where will you base yourself?"

"On the border with Haxus, not far from the Algonka Pass. That way I can move in either direction, depending on which target presents itself first."

"When do you leave?"

"If I get the warrant tonight, first thing in the morning." He grinned up at the chancellor. "And the palace will be rid of me at last!"

"I will let the queen know," Orkid replied. "She will be so pleased."

5

AS far as Kumul was concerned, one part of the Oceans of Grass looked much the same as the next. He had marched through parts of it during the Slaver War with the General's army and had never understood how their Chett guides knew where they were going. He knew north from south and east from west, sure enough, but where exactly in the north or south or east or west had always eluded him. Everywhere he looked tall grass, yellowing with autumn, covered the undulating landscape. Although there were creeks, there were no rivers or valleys and nothing taller than the occasional clump of spear trees. He knew the impression of absolute flatness was misleading, that you could reach the crest of one rise to find an army waiting for you on the other side, hidden by the gentlest of elevations, but he felt himself longing for some real geography—a wide river, a forest, a mountain or two—anything to break the monotony.

Ager rode up beside him. "This place takes some getting used to," the crookback said.

"I'll never get used to it," Kumul answered grumpily. "How do we know there is an end to it? We might ride until we are old men and not get to the other side of it."

"There are worse fates. The Oceans of Grass has a special beauty."

Kumul looked at his friend with alarm. "All your wounds are softening your head. There is no beauty here. It is . . . I don't know . . ."

"Unrelenting," Ager suggested.

"Yes, that's it."

"Lynan seems at home here."

"He is quarter Chett. Besides, he feels safe here."

"And you don't?"

Kumul grunted. "I won't feel safe until Lynan is reinstated in Kendra and I wear the constable's uniform again."

"Reinstated as what?" Ager asked after a moment.

"You've been thinking about the words we had with Korigan and Gudon last night?"

Ager nodded. "They made sense."

"Lynan is not the rightful heir to the throne of Grenda Lear, Ager. There is a moral and legal distinction between us helping him right the wrong of his outlawry and helping him usurp Queen Areava."

"Areava is his sworn enemy. He is the son of the hated commoner who replaced her beloved father as Usharna's husband and consort. She has never liked him. Reinstating Lynan in the palace will not make him secure."

"What do you mean?"

"He will still be seen as a threat by the Twenty Houses; probably even by Areava herself."

"We can deal with that."

"And don't forget, Areava may always have been in league with Orkid and Dejanus."

"I'll never believe it."

Ager leaned over to take Kumul's reins and pulled up. "And even if Areava wasn't part of the original conspiracy, she must be relying on Orkid and Dejanus now. She cannot have Lynan back."

Kumul tugged his reins free. "You don't know what you are saying, what it will mean for all of us."

"It might mean our salvation."

"We could be hanged as traitors."

"If we're caught, they're going to hang us as traitors anyway."

Kumul spurred his horse on so he did not have to listen.

"Or probably just cut our heads off as soon as we're captured!" the crookback shouted after him.

Damn! Ager thought angrily. *That was about the worst way to go about convincing Kumul of anything.*

Jenrosa came abreast of him. "What was all that about?"

"Policy discussion," Ager said offhandedly.

Jenrosa snorted. "You two have never disagreed before." She glared at him pugnaciously. Even the freckles on her face seemed to glare at him. All the sun she was getting riding on the plains was making her look more Chett than Kendran, except for her sandy hair which was starting to look as if it had been bleached.

Ager shrugged, smiled easily. "He doesn't like the Oceans of Grass. It's making him crabby."

For a moment they rode together in silence, then Jenrosa said, "It's more than that, isn't it?"

"Some," Ager admitted, unwilling to say more. Jenrosa was silent, but her presence demanded an answer. She was very good at getting what she wanted. "Don't worry about it. Eventually one of us will come around to the other's thinking. Well, I'll come around to his; that's how it usually works."

"It was about Lynan, wasn't it?" she persisted.

"When are our discussions about anything else? Where is he, by the way? I haven't seen him all morning."

"With Gudon, behind the riders."

"And with Korigan, too, I bet."

"No. She leads. You don't like her, do you?"

Ager thought about the question. "I don't dislike her, necessarily. I don't think Kumul likes her much."

"Kumul is like a father watching his only son being wooed by a woman he doesn't approve of."

Ager nodded. "I hadn't seen it like that, but you're right."

"Kumul told me about his confrontation with Lynan. He doesn't know whether to be angry or sad about Lynan standing against him."

"Last night was difficult for other reasons."

"He told me he and Korigan had argued."

"Did he tell you about what . . ." Ager's voice faded.

"What's wrong?"

Ager pointed toward the van of the column. Jenrosa looked and saw that the lead riders were galloping forward toward the nearest crest. She watched them reach the crest and then disappear over the other side. Other Chetts started joining them. The horizon was slightly hazy with dust.

"Rendle?" she asked.

Ager did not answer but dug his heels into his mount. Jenrosa did her best to keep up, but he was a better rider and pulled ahead. She watched him reach the crest and then suddenly pull up, his horse's hooves digging into the soil. A few seconds later she was by his side and looking down. Her breath caught in her throat.

Some five leagues away was the biggest herd of cattle she had ever seen. She had no idea how many beasts there were, but they seemed like a dark tide on the yellow and pale green plain.

Lynan and Gudon appeared by her side. Lynan's eyes widened despite the bright sun.

"It is bigger than I remember," Gudon said in a kind of hush. "Little master, this is the wealth of the White Wolf clan. *My* clan."

As well as the cattle, Jenrosa now could also make out what looked like two long trains of small brightly colored insects, one on either side of the main mass of the herd. Soon she could see they were large tents carried on wide carts, each cart drawn by four or more horses. Single horses carried Chetts around and in and between the cattle, keeping them moving and together. There seemed to be almost as many Chetts as cattle.

"How large is your clan?" Jenrosa asked Gudon.

"One of the largest," he said proudly. "We have been riding with the Left Horn, Korigan's personal guard of one thousand warriors. There is also the Right Horn and the main group of five thousand warriors, the Head. Unless we are at war, the Head always stays with the herd, while the two horns take turns scouting ahead and to our flanks, usually many leagues distant from the main body."

"I don't understand, Gudon," Lynan said, his expression still showing his surprise. "I thought the Chetts lived in groups of a hundred or so. You told me so yourself on the journey to the Algonka Pass."

"We lived like that for centuries until the Slaver War. Korigan's father realized we had to unite to fight the incursions of raiders like Rendle and Prado. But before he could unite the clans, each clan itself had to unite. There were as many squabbles and rivalries between each clan's families as there were between the clans themselves. Now each clan moves and fights as a unit. It means they have to move a lot more, else the combined herd would destroy all the pasture, but it is worth it for the increased safety."

Ager was carefully observing the clan below. "It seems random at first, the way the clan moves," he said. "But I can see now how the outriders don't keep to the same station. They are always moving, but always to another station." He looked over to Gudon. "This is very impressive. I don't think anyone in Grenda Lear realizes how organized the Chetts have become."

"They think us simple herders," Gudon agreed. "We prefer it that way."

"They're stopping," Lynan said.

The Chett outriders had closed in on the herd and slowly, like honey on a knife, it oozed to a halt. The carts carrying the tents then formed a corral enclosing all but a dozen of the largest beasts that were led away and pegged nearby.

"The bulls," Gudon explained.

"Why so many?"

"Trade. Our herd is a large and healthy one. Other clans will give a great deal to have one of our bulls, thinking they are the secret of our clan's success."

"And what is the secret of your clan's success?" Ager asked.

"Our queen," Gudon said simply.

"Look, there's Kumul," Jenrosa said. She had spotted him halfway down the slope. Like the rest, he was transfixed by the sight of the clan and its herd. None of the easterners had expected to see anything of this scale on the Oceans of Grass.

"And here is Korigan," Gudon said, pointing to a single rider coming their way. Tall and lithe, so confident on a horse, she was easy to pick out. When she reached them, she stopped in front of Lynan.

"Welcome to the heart of the White Wolf clan, your Majesty." Her beautiful golden face beamed with pride. "You will always be welcome among us."

Lynan nodded, still in awe. "Thank you, Korigan. I am honored."

"My people are waiting to meet you all," she said to everyone, and led the way down the slope to the corral, Kumul joining them as they passed.

As they drew nearer, small children jumped out of the tents and gathered around them. Like most Chetts, they were dressed in simple breeches and shirt, made from either linen or hide, with a cloth poncho over their shoulders. Their hair was cut short, again like most of the adults. Gudon had once told Lynan that among his people hair was a precious resources, used for binding and stitching.

Most of the children's attention was given to Kumul and Ager, the first so huge he must have seemed like a mountain on legs to them, the second so bent over they were surprised he could ride at all. At first they ignored Lynan; in his poncho and wide-brimmed hat, he could almost have been one of them.

The children were soon joined by a few of the outriders, and the procession finally wound its way to the biggest tent, sitting astride the largest wagon Lynan and his companions had ever seen. The tent was made from several panels of boiled leather, stitched together with thick strands of twined sinew. Each panel was painted a different color, the one above the door also carrying a pictogram of a white wolf.

Before the riders halted there was the sound of a fast-approaching horse. They looked behind them and saw an outrider, his hat hanging from his neck by its cord, his heels dug into his mare's flanks.

"Gods!" cried Gudon, his face breaking into a wide grin. "It's Makon!"

The one called Makon waited until he was only a few paces from the group, neatly reined in his horse and leaped from the saddle. To the surprise of the newcomers, he landed on the back of Gudon's horse. Thin, wiry arms wrapped themselves around Gudon's waist.

"Gudon! My brother! You have come back to us at last!"

Gudon half-twisted in the saddle and hugged back, giving his brother huge slaps on his back. "I told you I would, karak!"

They fell off the mare and landed in a heap on the ground. The Chetts around them laughed, including Korigan. Lynan and his friends looked on bemused, not sure what to make of it all.

Gudon and Makon stood up, still holding on to each other, their faces split by the widest smiles Lynan had ever seen worn by a Chett.

"This is my younger brother!" Gudon declared loudly.

"We would never have guessed," Kumul said dryly.

"My queen, what have you been feeding him? He is too tall to be from my family."

And indeed, now that they were standing, Lynan could see that Makon had at least a hand's span on Gudon.

"Your life in the east has shrunk you," Makon said. He waved at the strangers. "And who are these friends you have brought home with you?"

Gudon went to Jenrosa and placed his hand on her shoulder. "This is Jenrosa Alucar, famed magicker from the Theurgia of Stars in Kendra!"

The crowd cheered before Jenrosa could tell them she was only a student and not famous at all.

Gudon went to Ager next. "Ager Parmer, one of the most renowned warriors in Grenda Lear! His injuries come from the Slaver War, where he fought nobly under Elynd Chisal!"

More cheering, and Ager actually blushed. The children that had been staring at him curiously huddled closer, some reaching out to touch him.

Gudon moved to Kumul. "And this is a warrior whose renown is known even to us. The right-hand man of the General who ended the slavers' attacks on the Chetts. Kumul Alarn, Captain of the Red Shields!"

Lynan thought his ears would burst with the calls and ululations that followed Gudon's announcement. Even the outriders now dismounted to gather around. All eyes were on Kumul, and Lynan could hear the awe in their voices. "It is him! It is the General's giant! It is Kumul!"

Lynan was watching Kumul's reaction. His pale skin

flushed deep red; even the gray roots of his close-cropped hair seemed to gain color. Dazed by the adulation, he could say or do nothing. Gudon waited until the cries started to die before moving to Lynan. As he moved to place his hand on Lynan's shoulder, he stopped and stepped back. Lynan looked around and saw Korigan come to stand next to him. The crowd fell silent then, and waited for their queen to speak. She reached across and removed Lynan's hat. He squinted hard in the sudden rush of light. When he managed to open them wide enough to see what was going on, he was met by the staring eyes of every Chett around them. One small girl dared to touch Lynan's pale white hand, but quickly withdrew. Lynan smiled down at her, but she was obviously too frightened to smile back.

"This is Lynan Rosetheme, son of Queen Usharna and General Elynd Chisal. He is a prince of the realm of Grenda Lear. He is a holder of one of the Keys of Power.

"He is the white wolf, and he is come back to us!"

For a moment nothing happened, and then, without a word between them, the crowd as one bowed low as if they were a stand of wheat struck by a single scythe. Even Korigan was bowing. Lynan blinked, his eyes watering from the harsh sun.

After a moment Korigan stood erect, and the other Chetts followed her example. She replaced his hat and held him gently by the arm. "For as long as you wish it, this clan is your family and your home."

"The white wolf?" Lynan asked Gudon. They were sitting together on a crest overlooking the Chett camp, their mares cropping grass behind them. Above them stars sprinkled a perfectly clear sky, and beneath them dozens of small fires outlined the corral. They could hear faintly the lowing of the clan's herd, and occasionally the rumbling call of the bulls.

"Long ago, little master, when my clan was nothing more than a small tribe of two or three families, legend says we were protected from the predations of other tribes by a lone white grass wolf. He could only be seen at night, from far away. He became our totem, and eventually one of our gods.

"And here you are. You came to the Chetts near death, and then were resurrected with skin as white as a mare's milk, and on your first hunt, single-handed, you slew a grass wolf that threatened our clan's queen."

"I was trying to save you," Lynan said bluntly.

"Truth, little master. But you can see why Korigan would call you the white wolf."

Lynan hugged his knees. "I don't want the clan to expect too much of me, Gudon. I don't want to disappoint them."

"That will not happen."

For a while neither of them said anything, until a shooting star flashed above them. Gudon pointed at it. "A good sign. We are protected, you see."

"I have a feeling you are not nearly so superstitious as you make out," Lynan said. Gudon looked at him questioningly. "You are a pragmatic Chett. Like your queen."

"That would not be unexpected. We are cousins."

"And destinies can be made."

"Now what can the little master mean by that?"

"When we first met on the river, you told me that destiny serves no one."

"Truth."

"Not truth, Gudon. You saved me from Jes Prado, for which I will always thank you, but you knew who I was."

Gudon nodded.

"And you knew I would be valuable to your queen."

Gudon sighed deeply, then said: "You wanted to go to the Oceans of Grass."

"And you wanted me to go to the Oceans of Grass, but

not fall into the hands of another clan, especially one whose chief was in opposition to Korigan. Truth?"

"Yes, little master," the Chett said, his voice low.

"I will help your queen, but the price will be high."

"Korigan understands this," Gudon said without hesitation.

"How long before we reach the High Sooq?"

"Many days, especially with the herd. It will be winter when we get there."

As autumn deepened, the cold started to take hold of the plains. The first sign of oncoming winter was a frost in the morning, at first so gentle it disappeared soon after the sun rose, but after a few days thick enough to survive until midmorning. When the herd was started, the brittle grass could be heard crunching under their hooves. At this time Korigan ordered the slaughter of the steers, and the clan spent two days at one camp so the meat could be salted and the hides cured. The meat was kept in special tents, painted a bright white to reflect the sun's light and keep cool the meat still waiting to be cured. While the steers were being culled, as much grass as possible was gathered, some of it bundled as feed for the cattle in deepest winter, and the rest winnowed for the seeds necessary to make bread. Whenever the clan came across trees and bushes, their fruit was collected and stored.

Compared to their progress before catching up with the herd, Lynan thought they were crawling along at a snail's pace, but he enjoyed not being in a rush to get somewhere or in a rush to get away from someone. He spent most of the day with Gudon riding on the edge of the clan, learning about the Oceans of Grass, its creatures and plants and clans, and about the seasons, about the Chett gods and beliefs and customs. Lynan drank in anything Gudon could teach him, and when Gudon's memory was faulty or incomplete, Makon would join them to fill in the gaps. Lynan never stopped asking questions.

For most of the time, Kumul, Ager, and Jenrosa rode with the main group, sticking together for company and to keep out of the way of the Chetts trying to keep the herd moving. They were never alone for long, since children and outriders on rest often accompanied them, plying them with questions about the east and about Lynan. Ager and Jenrosa enjoyed the journey. Like Lynan, they appreciated being secure for the first time since leaving Kendra all those months ago, but Kumul felt the frustration of inaction. He regretted every day wasted by not working on getting Lynan back to Kendra and every day that took them farther and farther away from civilization and deeper into the unknown Oceans of Grass.

After a few days, Ager began spending more time away from Kumul and Jenrosa and started mixing with the Chetts themselves. On one day he drove the queen's wagon under the supervision of its master, an old and nearly toothless Chett named Kisojny. It took him a while to get used to pulling such a huge load and controlling eight horses, but Kisojny was a patient teacher. Once Ager got the hang of it, they spent the rest of the day telling each other jokes. Ager was surprised to learn that the Chetts—not merchant seamen—possessed the crudest sense of humor in the world, and he decided that living with a huge herd of cattle and a dozen bulls all their lives probably explained it.

Ager's drift from his companions was driven partly by his curiosity and his need to do something other than let his mare guide him across the Oceans of Grass, but mostly it was to give Kumul and Jenrosa time together. They did not mean to exclude him from their conversations, but increasingly the two talked to each other, leaving Ager on the boundary. He was glad Kumul had Jenrosa to distract him from his own growing depression, but wondered if it was for the best. Jenrosa was with them because she had been with

Lynan on the night King Berayma was murdered, and had to flee the palace with the prince. Ager did not know what Jenrosa had been doing with Lynan that night, but he was sure they had not been discussing the history of Grenda Lear. How did Lynan feel about Jenrosa now?

It was certainly clear to Ager who Jenrosa preferred to spend time with.

Lynan rode from the corral into the cold night air. For the second time he felt he was being flooded by a dark hunger, and the smell of the cattle was driving him insane. A wind was blowing from the south, numbing his cheeks and hands; on the horizon, lit by moonlight, he could see masses of anvil-shaped clouds heading toward him.

When the corral was out of sight, he stopped and twisted his hands into the reins; his eyes were knitted shut and his jaws clamped together. He wanted to feed and drink, wanted to feel the taste of warm blood on his lips. The mare underneath him was tense and wanted to run, but Lynan kept the reins hard into the pit of his stomach.

Slowly, the wind blew away all scent of the herd, and his head started to clear. He breathed deeply and slumped in the saddle. The mare relaxed underneath him and started cropping at the grass.

It had been easier this time to deal with it, and he wondered if it was because he was farther away from Silona and her supernatural influence. Somehow, he was sure, more than the vampire's blood now flowed through his veins. He looked east and remembered all the things—good and bad— that he had left behind. The homesickness he had felt for the first few weeks of his escape from Kendra was now little more than memory. His gaze turned west then, out over the great plains that seemed to have no boundary. He was nothing but a speck out here, and the feeling of insignificance appealed to him. The wind picked up and his poncho winged around him. He tightened the hat toggle under his chin. The horse started to whinny; it wanted to be back with her sisters.

A rider was coming toward him. A Chett. Too tall for Gudon. Maybe Makon. No, he told himself, recognizing the rider's obvious self-possession. It was Korigan. She pulled up beside him. "I wondered what you were doing out here by yourself, especially on a night like this."

"I like nights like this," he said.

She looked around, and Lynan could see the pleasure in her face as she gazed out over the Oceans of Grass, the same pleasure he felt.

"I like them, too," she admitted. "They are wild, and somehow free of all humankind. It's as if our race did not exist at all. Have you ever felt that?"

Her words sent a shiver down his back; he remembered his dreams of Silona, and imagined she must have existed long before humanity ever did.

"Only out here," Lynan answered quickly. "In the east you cannot ignore the existence of civilization."

"This *is* your home, isn't it?"

Lynan nodded. "I feel it is so."

Korigan bowed her head in thought for a moment, and then said: "I am sorry I came between you and Kumul."

"We did not need you to come between us. He still thinks I am nothing but an overweened, somewhat irresponsible child."

"You are not that."

"Not anymore."

"He loves you."

"I know, and I love him. He has been my father for as long as I can remember."

"Have you told him that?"

Lynan blinked. "No. It is not something he needs to hear."

Korigan shrugged. "But I need to hear something from you. Did you choose to go to the High Sooq because you thought it was the best course, or because it would cross Kumul?"

"Both, probably. I find it hard to remember what I was thinking that night; I just remember the anger."

"He was angry that night as well."

Lynan snorted. "He thought I would always follow him."

"Well, now that you are coming into your own, I think you will find he will always follow you."

There was a gust of wind. Snowflakes fell onto Lynan's hand and instantly melted.

"The Sleeping Storms," Lynan muttered. Korigan's expression showed her surprise. "Gudon told me that these cold autumn southerlies almost always brought snow, and that it marked the time when many animals start their hibernation."

"You have been spending a great deal of time with Gudon learning about the Oceans of Grass and we who live on it. That is good. But it is not the hibernating animals that give the storms their name."

"No?"

"I remember a late autumn when I was campaigning with my father against a rebel Chett clan. We got caught by one these storms. The next day we found two of our outriders had frozen to death. They fell asleep and never woke up. That is why we call them the Sleeping Storms." More snow flurried around them. "We should go back."

"I will not fall asleep," Lynan said.

"But your horse may."

"There is a storm coming," Ager said.

"It's just a breeze," Kumul replied. He was using a whetstone on his sword and was barely conscious of the wind starting to howl around the tent they were in.

"I can feel it in my bones. Ever since my back was sliced open by an ax, I've been sensitive to storms. They make my muscles ache."

"Rubbish," Kumul grunted.

"I have heard similar stories from others with serious wounds," Jenrosa said reasonably, restraining the urge to snap at Kumul; she was getting tired of his abrupt manner. She knew he worried constantly about Lynan and the changes that had been wrought in him—partly through her own intervention when she saved his life—but she and Ager were also concerned. Lynan was their friend as well, after all.

Kumul wiped the blade clean with a corner of his poncho, then licked his thumb and ran it along the flat near the sharp edge. The edge started to pull on his skin and he knew it was sharp enough. He now quickly sliced the whetstone along the edge at contrary angles, slightly serrating it, then repeated the test with his thumb. He nicked it twice.

The tent's flap snapped open and waved furiously in a sudden gust.

"God's death!" Kumul cursed and reached across to retie the flap. A whirl of snow blew in before he could finish.

"I told you there was a storm coming," Ager said smugly.

Kumul gave him a sour look. "Snow. That's all we need. It'll halve the clan's pace."

"After all our rushing around in summer I thought you'd appreciate a more sedate pace."

"There are things to be done, and we can't do them here."

"Lynan made a decision for himself," Ager said gently. "It's what we've always wanted him to do."

"It wasn't just for himself," Jenrosa pointed out. "He made a decision for all of us."

"He's our prince," Ager countered. "And now he's our leader as well."

"He'll be a damn sight more than a prince if this Chett queen has her way," Kumul said.

"What do you mean?" Jenrosa asked.

Ager and Kumul exchanged quick glances. Ager nodded.

"Korigan believes Lynan should seek the throne," Kumul said stiffly.

"I don't understand. Why would Korigan want Lynan to become king of the Chetts?"

"Not her throne," Ager answered. "Korigan thinks Lynan should usurp Areava."

Jenrosa's gray eyes widened in surprise. "Oh."

"And Kumul disagrees," Ager finished.

"And you?"

Ager shrugged. "I don't know anymore."

"You agreed with me the other night," Kumul said.

"I agreed with you about not going to the High Sooq. I said nothing one way or the other about Lynan taking the throne of Grenda Lear."

Kumul stared down at the ground. He seemed to draw in on himself. Jenrosa sat next to him. "Kumul, is there another way?"

"What do you mean?" Kumul growled.

"Can Lynan return to Kendra and take up where he left off? Is that possible?"

"I don't see why not. If we reveal Orkid and Dejanus as the murderers of Berayma, nothing can stop Lynan from resuming his position in the palace."

"And you will be constable again, and Ager a captain in the Royal Guard."

"And you back to your studies with the Theurgia of Stars. Yes. Isn't that what we all want?"

"Is that what you want, still?"

"Yes."

"And what of Areava and the Twenty Houses?"

"Areava's not stupid. She will make up with Lynan. The Twenty Houses will do what they're told."

"What if Lynan decides to go for the throne? Will you stop him?"

Kumul looked up at Jenrosa, startled. "No. No, he wouldn't do that."

"Lynan has changed. Ager said he has become a leader. Can he go to war against Areava and in the end not take the throne from her'?"

Kumul stood up quickly. "No. Lynan wouldn't do that. I know him."

"You knew Lynan the boy," Jenrosa said. "How sure can any of us be that we know Lynan the white wolf?"

"White wolf?" Kumul barked. "Pah!"

Jenrosa stood up, too. Kumul tried to avoid her gaze, but she reached out and held his jaw. "Have you been listening to the Chetts?" she said, her voice suddenly fierce. "They almost worship him, and he's only been with them a short time. If he decides to go for the throne, and Korigan supports him, do you think the Chetts will hold back?"

"He'll need more than the Chetts to win the whole of Grenda Lear."

"Are you so sure?" Ager asked. "This is just one clan. Seven thousand warriors. How many clans did Gudon say there were? Seventeen major ones, at least."

"They are all horse archers," Kumul said dismissively. "In the hills and fields and rivers in the east they would be trapped and slaughtered."

"Unless they're trained to fight differently."

"Why should we train them? So Lynan can go after Areava's crown?"

"We were going to raise an army to force the issue anyway," Ager argued.

Kumul did not reply.

"Weren't we?" Ager insisted.

"Yes." Kumul had to squeeze out the word. His blue eyes glared at Ager.

"And what were you going to do with the army?" Jenrosa asked him. She stood in front of him, feet firmly planted, arms akimbo, as if she was confronting a particularly stubborn mule.

"Force Areava to submit," he said numbly. "Force her to bring Orkid and Dejanus to trial." His voice suddenly rose. "Force her to right the wrong of Berayma's murder and Lynan's exile!"

"And having done all these things under duress, how long would Areava let Lynan be left free in the palace? How long would any of us remain free?"

Again, Kumul did not reply.

"I am tired," Ager said. "We can argue about this later."

Jenrosa followed Ager to the entrance; when the flap was untied, he held it open for her to go through, but she shook her head. He gave her a quizzical smile, then shrugged and left, soon disappearing in the flurries of wind-swept snow. Jenrosa tied up the flap behind him and turned to face Kumul.

"He did not mean to corner you like that," Jenrosa said.

"I know. But I do not . . . I cannot . . . agree with him, or Korigan or Gudon."

Jenrosa stood in front of Kumul. "I know," she said.

"What they want to do isn't right."

"I know."

"You must be tired, too."

Jenrosa pursed her lips. "Do you want me to go?"

Kumul became very still. "No." He reached out and gently stroked her hair.

Jenrosa leaned forward, stretched up to tiptoes, and kissed him on the lips.

⬡ 6 ⬡

WHILE Orkid talked at him, Prado adjusted his horse's saddle straps. The chancellor was spouting something about the heavy responsibility the queen had entrusted to him, but it went in one ear and out the other. All Prado could think of was what lay ahead. It would take him a few days to get to the Arran Valley, and at least a month to recruit and supply his own mercenaries, then another month or so to get to the border with Haxus, picking up more troops on the way. Then a month, less if he was lucky, to get reliable information about Rendle's movements and the location of the Chett tribe protecting Lynan. He was impatient to go. But Orkid was still mouthing.

"And don't overuse your office. Remember, the queen can turn you into an outlaw as easily as a general. Don't drain our forces on the border with Haxus for your little expeditions."

Little? The idiot knows nothing about military operations.

"Queen Charion of Hume has been informed of your eventual arrival, and instructed to give whatever assistance is necessary. But step warily with her; Charion is a clever woman."

"I've heard worse about her than that," Prado said offhandedly. "Some say she's a deceitful bitch who hates Chandra more than Haxus."

"Be that as it may, she is Queen Areava's subject. Treat her with the appropriate courtesy."

"If you say so."

"And who are these gentlemen?" Orkid asked, looking around at the six large and rudely dressed riders waiting for Prado.

"My first recruits."

"Where did you find them?"

"Taverns, mostly. They are all ex-soldiers or mercenaries, a little down on their luck but interested in useful employment." He half smiled at Orkid. "Useful employment in the queen's service, of course."

"I hope the caliber of your other recruits is slightly higher," Orkid said distastefully.

"They'll do for the job at hand," Prado said shortly. "I'm not creating a parade unit, Chancellor. I want experienced warriors, and warriors used to not asking awkward questions." He mounted and sat comfortably in his saddle. "Anything else before I go? Any messages for Prince Lynan?"

"Just do your job, Prado. That's all I ask."

"Then ask no more," he said, and spurred his horse.

He left the palace knowing he would soon have a large force of mercenaries at his command. Never during the long years of his retirement in the Arran Valley had he thought this would ever come about. Perhaps, just perhaps, he considered, the good old days would come back again. The world had turned around, and once again it had need of men like Prado and the services only they could provide.

Orkid watched as Prado left the palace courtyard, his six followers close behind. The chancellor shook his head, angry at the obvious contempt in Prado's voice.

Well, let him keep his arrogance, he thought. *If he survives, he can be cut down a few pegs.*

From her chambers Areava, too, watched the departure of Prado and his men. Like Prado, she sensed that the world had turned, but for something new not something old. The age to come would be unlike any that had come before, and she was unsure if it was for good or ill. Her gaze lifted to take in the whole of Kendra. It was still one of the most beautiful sights she had ever seen, refreshing her spirit whenever she looked out upon it, yet some of the sheen had gone. More and more it seemed less an idea given form, an idea about statehood and the rule of natural law, than simply a place where power resided, and she was learning that power was like mercury, ready to flow whichever way fortune led it.

Her private secretary, Harnan Beresard, coughed politely from behind his small writing desk. He was a thin, reedy man who looked barely strong enough to support his own weight when he stood. Sandy hair, sparse on top, made him look younger than he really was. Areava looked at him blankly for a moment. "What were we up to?"

"Your correspondence to King Tomar and Queen Charion regarding their trade dispute."

"Oh, yes." She brought her mind back to the matter at hand, and started dictating. "While I see it as my duty to ensure both your states have appropriate access to Kendra, there is little I can do to fix tariffs within your own domains. My mother saw fit to leave local affairs to local rulers, and I am reluctant to change that policy."

Still gazing out from her window, she saw Orkid striding across the courtyard to his own offices when a postrider suddenly galloped through the main gate. Instead of stopping for an attendant to take her horse, the rider went straight up to Orkid and handed him a message. Areava watched him read it, saw his figure tense. He said something to the messenger and she immediately rode off again.

"Your Majesty?"

"Where was I up to?" she asked absently.

Orkid looked up toward her chambers and saw her. He changed direction and headed toward her section of the palace.

"You are reluctant to change your mother's policy about noninterference in local matters," Harnan summarized.

"However, I am deeply concerned at this ongoing dispute between two such loyal subjects, and wish to see it resolved as soon as possible."

She heard Orkid's heavy footsteps coming up the stone stairs outside, then along the corridor to her chambers.

"To this end," she continued, "I am therefore resolved to establish a party of learned councilors who will advise me on this issue and other issues regarding trade and tariffs."

There was a knock on the door and a guard opened it. Orkid stood there for a moment, looking grim and displeased. Areava absently wished he would soften his appearance by shaving off his beard.

"And I would, of course, expect each of you to send a representative to sit on this council. In kindest regards, so on and so forth. For my signature this afternoon."

"Your Majesty," Harnan said.

"Orkid? You look like a startled bear."

"May I see your Majesty privately for a moment?"

Areava nodded. "Thank you, Harnan. I will call you when I am ready."

Harnan stood up promptly, gathered together his writing materials and small desk, bowed to the queen, and shuffled out. Orkid shut the door behind him.

"I saw a messenger arrive for you," Areava began.

"She came from the docks. I have a post down there."

"I know. I pay for it, remember?"

Orkid looked uncomfortable.

"Oh, come now, Chancellor. You can't expect to keep all your secrets for yourself."

"My operations are an open book for you, your Majesty, you should know that. Something else troubles me."

Areava nodded.

"The message was from one of my agents on a Lurisian ship that came in today. The ship recently completed a long voyage along Theare's east coast, north to Chandra and Hume . . . and Haxus."

"So, Salokan is still letting trade get through? That's a promising sign."

"The last, I'm afraid," Orkid said somberly.

Areava felt her chest tighten. "What word have you?" she demanded.

"The agent managed to journey with a caravan from the Oino delta to Kolbee itself. He reports the city came under curfew while he was there. Over several nights he heard large numbers of troops moving south through the streets. He assumed they came from the royal barracks. On his last morning he visited a market place near the barracks, and no one would open for business since there was no longer any business to be had. The Kolbee garrison had gone—all of it."

"Salokan is mobilizing." She tapped her fingers together. "And it ties together the fragments of intelligence we are getting from other traders and our spies, that Salokan is storing more grain and cattle than usual for winter, and that he is limiting the trade in iron ore in his own country." She looked up at Orkid, unable to hide completely the fear in her eyes. "The king of Haxus is preparing to go to war."

Orkid sighed heavily. "Yes, your Majesty, I believe so." He cast his gaze down and his fingers fidgeted.

"There is more?"

"The agent reports there are rumors among many in Kolbee that Lynan has been seen in Haxus."

"That isn't possible. He escaped Rendle. Prado told us so himself."

"That doesn't mean Rendle—or some other captain—did not capture him subsequently, or that Lynan did not go to Salokan of his own accord."

Areava felt unsteady. She grasped the back of a chair then sat down. "No. I won't believe it. Not even of Lynan."

"He killed Berayma, your Majesty. Fleeing to Haxus is a small treason beside that."

Areava did not reply. Her skin had paled to the color of ash and her hands rested in her lap like dead weights.

"There is more," Orkid said, his voice straining.

"Go on," Areava said shortly.

"Some of the rumors insist that Lynan has been made commander-in-chief of the Haxus army to march south into Grenda Lear."

Again, Areava did not reply.

"If true, there can be no greater proof of his guilt," Orkid continued. "And there is nothing Lynan could do that would more alienate the people of Grenda Lear."

"He would lead an army against his own people?" Areava asked, but Orkid knew the question was not directed toward him. "He would take arms against his own country?" Her skin now darkened with anger. She stood up suddenly, her hands bunched into fists. Her ice-blue eyes seemed to glimmer.

"How long ago was your agent in Kolbee?"

"About three weeks, your Majesty."

"Three weeks!"

"He returned as soon as he could, but he had to be careful getting back to the ship in the Oino delta."

"And how long would it take the Kolbee garrison to reach the border with Hume?"

"About the same amount of time, as long as it was not stopping to recruit new members or pick up extra units on the way."

Areava started striding up and down the chambers, her fists still bunched and kept behind her back. "It is too late for them to attack. It will be winter in a month."

"I agree, your Majesty, but King Salokan—or Prince Lynan—is well in place to launch an attack as soon as the spring thaw starts."

"Then we must mobilize now and send regiments north."

"The first snows will have come by the time they are ready to leave the south."

"I don't care. They have to march north. Our defenses must be ready by the time winter is over."

"You'll need to increase taxes, your Majesty. Our treasury is healthy, but will not withstand the expenses of war for very long."

"Call my council immediately. They will support me."

"As will all Grenda Lear," Orkid said.

She looked at him grimly. "I hope you are right, Chancellor, for all our sakes."

Somehow, despite his fogged mind, Olio had found the old library tower. He made his way to the top, carefully ascending each step with exaggerated caution. He stood in the middle of the chamber and turned in a circle, looking at all the old books unread by anyone for hundreds of years because no one could understand the writing.

All this knowledge waiting for someone to unlock the secret, he thought. *What magic do they hold?*

The question wearied him, and he slumped to the floor, careful not to smash the flagon of expensive red wine he was holding. He took a good swallow from it and grinned to himself.

I bet Edaytor and the theurgia would hate the idea that

there's power here they know nothing about and cannot use. What a joke.

Morning light crept in from the tower's single window. He looked up and saw that the shutters were slightly ajar.

Lynan liked it here, he remembered. He was probably the last person to look out that window.

Olio stood up unsteadily and opened the shutters wide. He could see only part of the city, but in the distance he recognized the coastline of Lurisia and the distant mountaintops in Aman. And westward were the Oceans of Grass. Somewhere out there was his brother. *God, Lynan, are you still alive?*

He collapsed to the floor again, overcome by sudden grief.

I wish you were here, Lynan. I wish you were home.

The tears came unexpectedly, and he scolded himself for blubbering. He tried to hold back, but he could not stop crying.

After a while, exhausted, he lay down on the cold stone floor, hugging the flagon close to his chest. Sleep came quickly, and he dreamed that his younger brother was sitting with him in the chamber, watching over him.

The council received Orkid's news with silence. No one knew what to say. Areava let them think a while on what it meant for the kingdom, and then asked Marshal Lief about the state of readiness of Grenda Lear's armies.

"On your command last summer I mobilized a few regiments, mainly cavalry, to bolster our border units in Hume. They are there now."

"Will they be enough to thwart a full invasion from Haxus?"

"No, your Majesty. Nowhere near enough. They can deal with any minor border incursions, but if they encounter anything stronger than a couple of enemy divisions, they'll be scattered. I never really believed Haxus would actually go to war without some border raids to test our strength."

"Nor did I," Areava said bitterly. "Chancellor Orkid, what are our estimates of Haxus' strength?"

"Twenty thousand infantry, at least five thousand cavalry. That's their regulars. We don't know how many militia they can call up."

Marshal Lief said, "Your Majesty, in the last war they had a similar-sized army, but not the logistical support to send them too deep into our territory."

"That was fifteen years ago," Orkid said dismissively. "We don't know how good their logistics are now. Besides, if they move quickly enough and capture Daavis, they would have the supply base they need to move on to Chandra, and from there onto Kendra itself."

"How long would it take to mobilize our entire army, Marshal?" Areava asked.

"Three months at least. We don't have the equipment and weapons in our armories to field an army much larger than twenty thousand ourselves, although over time, as our weapon smiths, cloth makers and granaries went to a war footing, we could double or even triple that. But contingents would have to come from Lurisia and Storia and Aman, and that will take time as well. And if the bulk of our troops are in Hume to stop an invasion, we'll need the fleet's help to keep the army fed and clothed; we'll also need the navy to move much of our southern forces north."

"Which raises another problem," Admiral Setchmar added. "Most of our fleet is laid up. It's too expensive to maintain all our transports and warships during peacetime. It will take us at least two months to get them ready and crew them all. Even if they were ready sooner, it would be foolish to risk sailing a fleet against winter's storms; we could lose everything."

"How many troops can you have on the border with Haxus by the end of winter?"

"Twenty thousand," the marshal said despondently. "Maybe. Including the regiments that are already there."

"You're not including the heavy cavalry, Marshal?" Galen Amptra asked in an arrogant voice.

Lief blushed. "I would not presume . . ."

Galen waved him silent and turned to Areava. "Your Majesty, the cavalry from the Twenty Houses can be riding north in a week. That's three thousand of the best soldiers on the continent."

Yes, and risk the Twenty Houses taking control of my army in the north, Areava thought. She hesitated.

"Your Majesty, that is the perfect solution," Shant Tenor said. The news of Haxus' mobilization had almost made him spasm with fear, but then the thought of his city's industries gearing up for war and the profits that would bring Kendra had calmed him remarkably quickly. And the thought of selling the food and extra supplies the heavy cavalry from the Twenty Houses would need almost had him salivating.

"We are going about this the wrong way," said a new voice, calm and measured. All eyes turned to Father Powl. In the four meetings since he had been one of the council members, he had hardly spoken at all. Even Primate Northam looked in surprise at the priest. He was a small, thin man who often wore a smile but whose hard gray eyes never seemed amused at all.

Areava considered him. "Father?"

"I think sending our army north piecemeal is inviting disaster."

"But the kingdom is under threat!" Shant Tenor exclaimed. "We can't wait until our enemies reach the walls of Kendra itself!"

"Which is what will happen if King Salokan is allowed to destroy one regiment here and two regiments there. Even the renowned cavalry of the Twenty Houses could do little by themselves against an army more than ten times its size."

"He speaks the truth," Marshal Lief said despondently. "We have been caught by surprise, and our forces are too scattered or not up to full strength."

"Not completely by surprise," Father Powl said, "thanks to the offices of Chancellor Orkid Gravespear." Priest and chancellor exchanged courtesy glances. "And there is a way through this problem."

Shant Tenor could see all the city's short-term profits evaporating before his eyes. "With all due respect to Father Powl, I think military planning is best left to the marshal."

"Go on, Father," Areava said, throwing the mayor a warning look.

"I suggest we reduce the border garrison to a line of look-outs. The remainder should be sent to garrison Daavis. In the meantime, a proper army is gathered here and sent north as soon as spring comes."

"But we would be surrendering almost all of Hume!" Galen said.

"Only for a few weeks at most," Marshal Lief said. "The priest is right. If the forces already in Hume garrisoned Daavis, the city should be able to defend itself against the army of Haxus long enough for our army to relieve it."

"There is another factor to consider," Powl said. "Prado and his force of mercenaries. He will be in Hume before winter bites too hard. He could reinforce Daavis, or support those forces we leave on the border."

"Or change sides as soon as Salokan crosses the border," Dejanus growled, still stinging over losing the command of that expedition.

"He will not," Orkid said firmly. "He hates Rendle, and Rendle is with Haxus."

"I would not see Prado deterred from his mission," Areava objected.

"If Prince Lynan is indeed with Salokan, Prado's mission and our need dovetail, your Majesty," Powl said.

"Thank you, Father," Areava said. "Your words have made the situation at once less dire and its solution much clearer."

Powl nodded graciously. "There is one more issue."

"Yes?"

"Who will lead the army north?"

"I will, of course," Areava said quickly.

"Forgive me, your Majesty, but that is inadvisable," Orkid said. "No one can deny your skill with weapons—after all, your mother gave you command of the kingdom's armed forces—but your place is here, in the palace. What if some other emergency should arise in your absence? And your absence would be a long one. The same applies to the marshal. He needs to be in Kendra to organize the army's mobilization, and then its continued supply."

"Then who do you suggest?" she asked the chancellor.

"Why not someone from the Twenty Houses?" Galen asked.

"Or Prince Olio," Father Powl suggested. "It would be fitting for Grenda Lear's army to be led by a prince of the realm, especially if the enemy army is being led by another."

There were nods around the table, and then everyone noticed that Olio was not present. He was usually so quiet that his absence had not really been noticed until now. The queen looked puzzled.

"Harnan? Was Prince Olio notified of the meeting?"

"My clerks could not find him," her private secretary said. "I could send them out again."

Areava shook her head. "No. There is much for me to consider. I will consult with my brother in private over this matter." She stood up and everyone else immediately stood as well. "You have served me well today."

*   *   *

When Olio finally awoke, the muscles in his back were knotted into painful bundles. The side of his face that had been resting on the tower's stone floor was numb with cold. He groaned and lifted himself into a sitting position. His head beat with a sound like a hammer striking an anvil. His hand was in something wet. He looked down and saw a great red puddle of wine. He stood up uneasily. He moved toward the steps and his foot knocked aside an empty flagon. It rang on the stone floor, and he had to close his eyes in pain.

"God's death," he muttered, holding his hands to his head.

After the pain eased, he made his way slowly down the tower stairway and then along the corridors to his chambers. When he opened the door, he was met by a room filled with light. He squeezed his eyes shut and tottered into the bedchamber, closing the door behind him.

"Leave it open. I won't stay long."

"Sister?" He squinted, and could just make out Areava's tall form sitting in a chair near his bed.

"You missed a council meeting."

"I'm sorry. I was otherwise . . . disposed." He made it to his bed and sat on the end. "Was it important?"

"Haxus has mobilized its army. We cannot meet it with our full strength. Hume may fall by the middle of spring. Otherwise, no, nothing important."

Olio shook his head to clear it. It did not work. "I didn't quite get all of that."

"You smell of wine. Are you drunk?"

"N–n–no, n–n–not drunk. M–m–my head hurts."

"I needed you. You weren't there."

"I said I was sorry, Areava. Tell m–m–me again. What happened in the council?"

"In four months, maybe less, we will be at war with Haxus."

Olio's eyes sprung open. "War?" Areava nodded. "With Haxus?" Areava nodded again. "B–b–but the m–m–marshal and admiral were there, surely? And Orkid?"

"Your name came up."

Olio sighed. His eyes were adjusting to the brightness.

"What is happening to you?" Areava asked.

He shrugged. "N–n–nothing is happening to m–m–me. I had a b–b–bad night, that's all." Distractedly, he ran his fingers through his brown hair.

"I see you wandering in and out of the palace at all hours. We don't talk anymore. My servants have heard your servants complaining that your clothes always reek with wine." She shook her head in frustration and asked again, "What is happening to you?"

"N–n–nothing is happening to me!" Olio spat.

Areava gasped in surprise.

Olio moaned and put his hand out to hold hers, but she jerked away from him. "I'm sorry, sister, I didn't m–m–mean . . ." She made no move to take his hand, and he eventually dropped it.

"Clean up," she said imperiously, standing up. "Get changed. Get shaved. Get rid of that terrible smell. I want to see you in my chambers in an hour. Be there or I'll send one of the guards to bring you."

Olio forced a laugh. "Areava, you can't be serious."

"Be there," she repeated, her voice hard, and left.

Orkid knocked on the door of the primate's office and entered without waiting to be called in. Father Powl was sitting behind a huge desk reading through a sheaf of papers; when he saw Orkid, he stood up hurriedly.

"Chancellor! It's rare to have you visit this wing of the palace. You've missed the primate, I'm afraid. He's gone into the city."

"Good. It was you I came to see."

Father Powl looked surprised. He waved his guest into a chair and sat down himself. "How can I help you?"

"I wanted to commend you on your contribution to the council meeting this morning."

"I was glad to be of service to her Majesty."

"You are still her confessor, I understand?"

"Less of late, I'm afraid. Father Rown now relieves me of most of that duty. I'm kept busy with the pressure of office as Primate Northam's secretary."

"Your advice at the council came as something of a surprise to most of us. After all, one hardly expects a cleric to demonstrate such a clear understanding of military strategy."

Father Powl spread his hands. "I have been a student of knowledge since entering the priesthood. Our library here deals not just with religious subjects; there are histories and biographies, accounts of journeys and myths, records of previous military campaigns. The appropriate course of action seemed obvious to me, and it would have been remiss to remain silent. I am quite sure the marshal would have offered the same advice eventually."

Orkid smiled easily. "Lief is an old soldier who came into command during the great years of peace following the Slaver War. Before that, he was a fine field commander. Grand strategy was never his strong point."

"He may learn," Father Powl countered.

"He will have to," Orkid said dryly. "However, his burden will be eased by good advice. Advice from the queen. Advice from me. And, I suspect, advice from you."

Father Powl looked shocked. "Chancellor, I would never bypass the council."

"I was not suggesting you would. But there are times when the council may not be the appropriate forum."

"Forgive me for being abrupt, Chancellor, but I'm at a loss to see where you are going with this."

"I would appreciate being the beneficiary of your learning."

"You are suggesting I go to you with any contribution instead of the council?"

"Indeed not. The queen relies on her councilors to speak directly. But if, for example, you had some insight that might bear on urgent events, there is no need for you to wait for the council to be convened. If you were to come to me, I could convey your advice directly to the queen herself."

Father Powl rested back in his seat and made a steeple out of his fingers. "I would have to clear this with the primate."

Orkid shook his head. "No, I don't think so. Let this stay a matter between you, myself, and Queen Areava. Better that way. Fewer channels to slow things down."

"Let me state your position clearly, so there is no misunderstanding between us. I am to have direct access to you?"

"Yes."

Father Powl smiled over the steeple. "I feel honored."

"Do you agree?"

The priest nodded. "I agree. I think this is a relationship that will benefit both our offices."

And those that occupy them, Orkid thought.

Areava tried to sit as regally as possible, but it was not possible in front of her brother. Olio stood before her, scrubbed and ashamed. He almost looked like an innocent young man again. She wanted to wet her hand and dampen down his unruly mop of hair.

"If my words seemed harsh—" she started, but Olio interrupted.

"M–m–my apologies, sister, for m–m–my b–b–behavior," he blurted. "I cannot explain why you saw m–m–me in that condition—not yet—b–b–ut it will not happen again. I p–p–promise."

Areava sighed and took his hands in her own. "I was

worried. I have never seen you like that before. So much is happening now, and I need you strong by my side."

"I will always b–b–be at your side, Areava. You know that."

She nodded and smiled up at him. "You are to be a general."

Olio blinked. "A general?"

"We are creating an army to counter Haxus. We believe they will march south into Hume as soon as winter eases. Their army is already massing on the border. There are rumors that their captain is Lynan."

"My God." Olio shook his head. "I don't believe it. Not of Lynan."

"And I, for one, would never have suspected Lynan capable of murdering Berayma!" Areava snapped. Olio opened his mouth to object, but Areava spoke over him. "We are ordering what forces we have in Hume to hold the province's capital against a siege. Our army should be ready to march north in the spring; it will have contingents from all the southern provinces, and the heavy cavalry from the Twenty Houses. It needs a leader who will be higher in rank than all its captains, a leader all will obey. I must stay here in Kendra. That leaves you. It will be a close-run thing, Olio."

"I understand. I will do it, of course, b–b–but I have no experience in soldiering."

"So few have, brother. We have been at peace for a long time. But the same applies to the army of Haxus. In that at least, we are equal."

"What m–m–must I do?"

"Be near me. Give me your advice. Liaise with the marshal and Orkid. They will advise you."

"When will this b–b–be announced to the p–p–people?"

"I'm arranging for couriers to be sent to all our provinces; they will leave this afternoon. By then everyone in Kendra will know. Councilors like Shant Tenor and Xella Povis are hardly likely to keep quiet about it."

"Are you going to declare war on Haxus?"

Areava shook her head. "Let them make the first move. Let all of Theare know who is the aggressor in this matter. It will not be Grenda Lear."

Olio smiled. "You are m–m–more and m–m–more like our m–m–mother."

"I hope I have her luck in war."

"You will have no need of luck."

Areava could already hear the sounds of battle in her mind. She could smell smoke and blood and fear. She could see heaps of dying and wounded, and battered pennants waving from broken spears. "Perhaps," she said quietly. "But I will take any I can get."

7

THE riders halted at the crest of a small hill. Some distance away was a glade of arrow trees circling a permanent lake, something rare in the Oceans of Grass. The glade was surrounded in turn by a deep green carpet of vegetation that spread out for leagues in every direction. Regularly spaced around the glade were collections of brightly colored tents, each collection marked by different pennants, and around the tents milled thousands of cattle.

"The High Sooq," Korigan said, stretching in her saddle, looking even more lithe than usual. For a moment Lynan felt a twinge of desire; the urge surprised him.

"This is the richest grazing land on the continent," she told him. "From here, you can see the entire wealth of the Northern Chetts."

Lynan could not believe how many cattle there were. "Surely they will eat it out?" he said.

"Most of the grazing will be gone by midwinter. Then we give them the feed we've stored. By the end of winter that will be gone, and the clans will scatter to find spring grass. By the time we all meet here again next year, the land here will have regenerated."

"Do we wait for all your people to arrive before moving

down?" Kumul asked. The riders had left the White Wolf clan the day before.

"No," Korigan answered. "We go down now. There will be a meeting tonight of the clan heads, and I want to see how hard my opponents will push me before they're aware that Prince Lynan is among us." She glanced quickly at Kumul. "Or you."

Kumul did not feign modesty. It had been a long time since his reputation as captain of Elynd Chisal's Red Shields had given him any pleasure or fed his pride. It was just a fact of his life and had served him better than worse in the years since the end of the Slaver War—it was his reputation that had secured him the position of constable under Queen Usharna. "So you are concerned for Lynan's safety?" he asked sourly.

"Of course," she admitted. "But it is time for his Majesty to take these risks."

Kumul shook his head. "I wish you wouldn't call him that."

"Will you stop talking about me as if I wasn't here?" Lynan said, but without anger. "What is your plan, Korigan?"

"Tonight's meeting will be a test for me. If it ends in my favor, we announce your presence. If it does not, we keep you a secret; I will not risk your safety unnecessarily."

"It won't be a secret once the rest of your clan arrives," Kumul said. "They will all be eager to tell their news."

"News is the currency of such gatherings," Gudon agreed.

"If the meeting goes badly for our cause, your Majesty," Korigan said, "then I will give you an escort of a thousand warriors to take you back to the east of the Oceans of Grass. There you can follow Kumul's plan, if you so wish, and I will join you when I may, or you can travel to some other part of the kingdom to find support among the people of Chandra or Hume."

Lynan said nothing, but his heart felt truly heavy for the first time since recovering from his wounds at the end of summer. He knew if the Chetts did not support him, no one else would, even if they sympathized with his cause: Areava was the rightful queen of Grenda Lear, and none of the rulers among the eastern provinces would willingly stand for Lynan against her.

A hand rested on his arm, and he turned to see Ager looking at him. "*Whatever* happens, Lynan, your friends will stay with you."

Lynan smiled then, and the weight in his heart eased. "We should go down," he said lightly. "Let us see how the clans treat a queen." He bowed a little to Korigan.

Korigan returned the gesture and matched his smile. "Or, indeed, a king," she said.

On the way to the sooq they rode past three encampments. Lynan, Ager, and Kumul all stayed in the middle of the group, their hats pulled low over their faces. Jenrosa, who was not so differently shaped from the Chetts, and after spending most of the autumn on the plains not much lighter in color, happily rode on the edge, although she had to hide her long sandy hair under a wide-brimmed hat. She was fascinated by the patterns the clans used to decorate their tents and ponchos. There seemed to be no rule to the colors anyone used, but the designs themselves were unique to each clan.

Gudon was riding by her side. "This the Sun clan," he told her. Their design was a bright yellow circle surrounded by white crooked rays, like lightning flashes. The motif was repeated everywhere within the clan, but with subtle differences: one tent had the motif on a blue field, another in the middle of a series of concentric circles.

"The Sun has long been an ally of the White Wolf," Gudon continued, "since one enjoys the day and the other the night and they do not get in each other's way. This next clan is a different matter."

"Let me guess," Jenrosa said, laughing. "The Owl clan." There was no mistaking their motif.

"Yes, and like the White Wolf, a predator of the night. Its chief is Piktar, and he was an enemy of Korigan's father. That animosity has been passed to my queen."

Animosity or not, the Chetts inhabiting the camp seemed as interested in their passing as those of the Sun clan. "They don't seem hostile," she said.

"We are not at war," Gudon explained. "And this is the High Sooq. There will be no fighting here. Indeed, it is not unheard of for young White Wolf warriors to take a husband or wife from the Owl clan." As he said the words, he found time to smile and wave at a particularly lithe Chett riding by in the opposite direction, the owl design clearly blazoned on her poncho. She smiled and waved back.

"A Chett can marry anyone she wants?"

"Truth. A warrior can also choose which clan to ally herself with after marriage. Sometimes, to avoid disharmony, two warriors from different clans may marry and join a third, neutral clan."

"I thought your clans were family based."

"They still are, largely, but the clan tradition and history is more important than any bloodline."

The last encampment they rode by had a design of three wavy lines. "The River clan?" Jenrosa suggested.

Gudon shook his head. "The Ocean clan."

"The Oceans of Grass?"

"No."

"That's odd, isn't it? Your people belong to the plains, not the sea."

"Now, but our oldest stories are about the sea. We came from across the ocean may centuries ago."

"Which ocean?"

"The Sea Between."

"You come from the Far Kingdom?"

Gudon shrugged. "Who can tell what is truth or myth in the old stories? None of us is that wise."

"Are they your clan's enemy or ally?"

"Ally most recently. They were the first clan defeated by Korigan's father in the war to unite all the clans under his leadership. They have been loyal ever since."

Something in Gudon's voice made Jenrosa wonder if he really believed the Ocean clan had ever been an ally, but before she could ask more questions they were riding between tall arrow trees, and their mares, who now could smell the water above the smell of the cattle filling the land around, picked up their pace. As they continued, the trees grew closer together, tall bushes filling any empty space. The trail became crisscrossed with the shadows of branches and leaves.

Their first glimpse of the sooq was a hint of azure glistening behind the vegetation. As they got closer, the arrow trees started thinning out, replaced by palms and ferns. Brightly colored birds scattered into the sky. Permanent, mud-brick homes started to appear, built like those Jenrosa had seen at the Strangers' Sooq.

"Which clan owns the sooq?" she asked Gudon.

"No clan. Those who live here permanently are not like other Chetts. They do not keep their own cattle."

"Then how do they make a living?"

"They receive a tithe from the clans who visit in winter and make some profit from trade. There is plenty of grass for their bread, and the trees here produce the most succulent fruit, and the lake is filled with fish. It is an easy life compared to that led by most Chetts."

They reached the lake shore and dismounted. Suddenly they were surrounded by smiling children who took their reins and led the horses down to drink. Adults clustered around Korigan, most with clay platters laden with food. Jenrosa watched Korigan carefully take something small from each plate and eat it. As her hand touched a platter, its owner would briefly place her or his hand on top.

"They are greeting her in their way," Gudon told Jenrosa. "By sharing their food, she is bound to protect them."

"They do this with all the clan leaders?"

Gudon nodded. "This way no one is their enemy, and the clans know that no other clan can take the sooq and hold it against them in winter."

When Korigan had finished, the locals started singing, a slow ululation that rose and descended in pitch like waves.

"They seem very happy about it," Jenrosa said.

"Truth, for one year came when Korigan's father did not take the food." Gudon's voice had become grim.

"He took the sooq from these people?"

"Not as such, but by refusing to protect it, he was throwing a challenge to all those clans not allied to him, a challenge they could not ignore. In that winter was the greatest and most terrible battle in our civil war. Many warriors fell."

"What happened?"

"Korigan's father became king," Gudon said simply.

"So anyone opposed to Korigan could do the same thing?"

"Only if they had the support of enough clans."

The singing stopped, and one among the locals, a woman slightly bent with age and with hair as gray as smoke, came forward, her hands extended in greeting. Korigan took them in her own. The two spoke a few words to each other, which Jenrosa was too far away to hear, and then went arm-in-arm to one of the houses and disappeared inside. The locals started to disperse. Korigan's own followers split up into small groups, most of which sat on the ground or went to the lake's edge to look out over the water. Jenrosa and Gudon were joined by Lynan, Kumul, Ager, and Makon.

"That went well," Makon said.

"Who was the old woman? The local chief?" Jenrosa asked.

"Herita. She is their oldest, and so speaks for them. They have no chief as such."

"What did Korigan and Herita say to each other?" Gudon asked his brother.

"Korigan asked about the other chiefs. Herita said they all took food, but a few of them seemed grim."

"That's not good news," Kumul said.

"There are many reasons to be grim in this life," Gudon pointed out. "But, yes, we could have hoped for a better sign."

"Who can come to this meeting tonight?" Kumul asked.

"All of us, but only in the second circle."

"The second circle?"

"The first circle—the inner circle—is for the chiefs. Their followers, the fifty they may bring with them, form the second circle around them."

"Do the followers bring their weapons?"

"Have you ever seen a Chett without one?"

Kumul shook his head. "Does this meeting ever end in bloodshed?"

"Sometimes, but never between the chiefs, only their followers. There has been no such violence since Korigan's father became king."

"You never give him a name," Lynan said.

"Who, little master?"

"Korigan's father."

Gudon looked steadily at the prince. "His name means many things for us Chetts, even those of his own clan. It means unity and purpose. It also means bloodshed and strife. We use it only when we have to."

"May I know the name?"

Gudon nodded. "It was Lynan."

It was almost dark. Korigan and her party made their way to the meeting of the two circles. Jenrosa and Kumul walked at the back of the group and briefly—too briefly for either of them—held hands.

"I wish we had more time alone together," Jenrosa said.

Kumul laughed. "It was hard enough when we were with just the White Wolf clan. Now that we are with the whole Chett nation . . ." He shook his head in frustration.

"Maybe we can volunteer for scouting duty," she suggested. "Just the two of us and a tent."

Kumul considered the suggestion. "Do you think we'd get much scouting done?"

"That would depend on what we were looking for."

"Yes, I can see that. Would we need a map, or maybe a Chett guide?"

"I already know the way," she said.

"Well, that's useful."

As the party passed the camps of different clans, its reception swung from easy greetings to sullen silence.

"Do you think Korigan will be in danger tonight?"

"Almost certainly. I am more concerned for Lynan's safety. He does not understand what he is getting himself into."

"Do any of us?"

Kumul shrugged. "Maybe none of us has since fleeing Kendra." He loosened his sword in its sheath.

Jenrosa risked holding his hand again. "Please be careful. I want nothing to happen to you."

*   *   *

The meeting was held away from the sooq at the end of the long shallow valley now inhabited by all seventeen major Chett clans and dozens of the minor ones. Nearly thirty chiefs had elected to come, most with fifty followers. The first circle sat around a blazing fire. The second circle, filled with well over a thousand warriors, was packed tightly, its members standing to make more room. Lynan and his companions were near the inner rim of the circle, but the dark helped disguise them; only Kumul's height stood out in the crowd, but everyone's attention was focused on the chiefs.

Herita, without clan or supporters, spoke first, welcoming all to the High Sooq; she then asked if anyone wished to speak. Lynan expected Korigan to claim the right to speak first, but she stayed seated and said nothing. Even Herita looked at her expectantly, but after a short while asked again if anyone wanted to speak.

"What is Korigan doing?" Lynan asked Gudon.

"Waiting to see who dares to take her privilege," Gudon said. "If her opponents are well organized, there will be one clan chief leading them, and she or he will take this opportunity. Korigan wants to know who it is."

But no chief answered Herita's call.

Herita returned to stand before Korigan. "My queen, will you not speak to your people?" Some of the other chiefs echoed the call.

Korigan stood up slowly. "I accept the honor of speaking first."

There were cheers from the second circle, and not just from her own followers.

"There is news from the east," she said, her voice carrying across the whole meeting, strong and determined. "The mercenaries have returned."

For the briefest of moments there was a sudden silence, and then the whole meeting erupted in furious tumult. Several of the chiefs shot to their feet and shouted, some in alarm, some in angry denial.

"Ah, now we see who oppose her," Gudon said.

Korigan waited until the some of the noise had subsided. "My people have fought with them. Thirty mercenaries were killed."

"Whose mercenaries?" a man's voice demanded. All eyes turned to a chief on the other side of the fire from Korigan. He was big for a Chett, wide and strong-armed. His face was pitted and crevassed, his nose squashed flat, his lips wide and thin.

"Rendle's," Korigan answered.

"How do you know this? Was Rendle with them?"

"No, but you know, Eynon, that I have sources of information outside of the Oceans of Grass."

"Your spies," Eynon spat.

Gudon whispered into Kumul's ear: "He is chief of the Horse clan. His father was the most determined and the strongest enemy of Korigan's father, and the one defeated here at the High Sooq in the last, great battle. It is no surprise that he is opposed to Korigan."

"My spies?" Korigan said, her voice cold. "*Our* spies."

"We had no need of them before . . ." Eynon let the sentence hang, but everyone knew he meant before Korigan's father had united the Chetts.

"Before the Slaver War?" Korigan said. "Maybe that was why we suffered so cruelly at the hands of Rendle and his ilk."

"Oh, nicely done," Ager said admiringly. "She turned that around."

"Rendle is a mercenary first and foremost," another voice said. Another chief stood up, a woman. She looked as old as Herita, but stood straighter. "His presence on the Oceans of Grass does not mean he has returned to take slaves."

"Akota," Gudon told Lynan. "Chief of the Moon clan."

"Another old enemy?"

"No, but the clan has always fiercely independent. Its warriors always doubt what they themselves have not seen."

"Whatever else Rendle may or may not be, slavery was his trade in the past; how do we know he has not returned to it?" Korigan demanded, asking the question of the entire first circle.

"But the great queen in Kendra would not allow the slavers to ride again," another chief countered, standing to get everyone's attention. "She promised us they would never return!"

There was a loud sound of agreement from many of the chiefs and their followers.

"The great queen is dead!" Korigan announced.

The chief who had spoke froze. Akota slumped to the ground. Even Eynon looked bewildered.

"Dead?" he asked. "When?"

"The beginning of summer," Korigan said.

"But her son would not tolerate slavery any more than she—"

"Berayma was murdered before he could be crowned. Areava, his sister, now rules Grenda Lear."

Now even Eynon sat down.

"Every time you speak you deliver a blow to us," Herita said hoarsely. "Your spies have told you all this?"

"I did not need spies for this news. You know my clan's territory abutts the Stranger's Sooq. The news of Usharna's death, and that of her son, was common knowledge."

Akota stood up once more. "But Areava—or any of Usharna's children—would never allow the slavers to work again."

"Areava is not Usharna," Korigan said evenly. "I know that Rendle and others were commissioned under her authority."

"For what purpose?" Akota asked. "And what others?"

"To guard their border with Haxus, or so Areava says. And others? Jes Prado for one."

Again the chiefs and their followers let loose with loud cries, some in alarm, some denying Korigan's words. All the chiefs were standing now, speaking all at once.

"Haxus is not at war with Grenda Lear!" shouted one of the chiefs. "Why would Areava use mercenaries instead of her own troops?"

"Someone is lying!" Eynon declared, and all other voices were stilled. "Either Areava or Korigan! And I know which queen I believe!"

Before Korigan could say anything, Akota said: "What kind of loyalty is this you show for our queen?"

Eynon laughed harshly. "Our queen? Which one?"

"You know whom I speak of, Eynon. Again I ask, what kind of loyalty is this?"

Eynon pointed at Korigan. "Rather you should ask: what kind of queen is this?" He turned to face the second circle, and as he spoke, he turned slowly, his arms wide and encompassing them all. "This girl has inherited her title! She has not earned it! She knows she is not welcome among some of the clans, and she knows the only way she can unite us all behind her is to make us think the slavers have returned! There are no slavers! There are no mercenaries! There is only Korigan, a shadow of everything her father ever was!"

"And what would you have?" Korigan demanded, her voice rising above his. "A new ruler in my place? Someone like yourself?"

Eynon faced her squarely and shook his head. "I would have no king or queen in the Oceans of Grass. One queen in distant Kendra is enough. We need no more."

"The world has changed since our fathers' day," Korigan replied. "We cannot count on help coming from Kendra. We cannot even count on Kendra looking on us with any favor now that Usharna has gone. We *must* be united!"

"Against whom?" Eynon said. He turned to one of the chiefs, a young man who looked barely old enough to shave. "Terin! Your clan territory is closest to Haxus! Have any mercenaries raided your people?"

Terin shook his head uncertainly. He looked at Korigan with an expression of helplessness. He was obviously no friend to Eynon, Lynan saw, which was undoubtedly why Eynon had chosen him: if even Korigan's own allies could not support her story, why should anyone else believe it? Lynan started to move forward, but a heavy hand grasped his arm. He looked over his shoulder and saw Kumul.

"It is too dangerous, lad," Kumul whispered fiercely.

Gudon gripped his other arm. "He is right, your Majesty."

Eynon again faced the second circle. "Has anyone seen these mercenaries?" No one would answer him. "Will no one stand for Korigan?" The derision in his voice was unmistakable.

"Her clan stands for her!" Gudon shouted and, releasing his grip on Lynan, he stepped forward from the second circle.

"Who speaks?" demanded Herita.

"I am Gudon, son of Kathera Truespeaker, cousin to Queen Korigan."

"Gudon?" Eynon asked suspiciously. "You have not been seen or heard from for many years. How do we know it *is* you? Come into the light!"

Gudon strode to the fire and took off his hat. Herita, Eynon, and Akota came up close to study his face.

"I am not sure," Herita said.

"Maybe it is not him," Eynon suggested.

"It is he," Akota said with certainty. "I knew the Truespeaker, and this is her son."

A murmur passed around the two circles like a breeze across the plains.

"He seems well known," Ager muttered.

"Where have you been all this time?" Akota asked.

"In the east." Gudon smiled humorlessly at Eynon. "I was one of Queen Korigan's spies. It is I who brought back word about Rendle and Prado. They ride again."

"This is ridiculous!" Eynon said angrily. "Because he is the son of the Truespeaker does not mean he is one himself! He is Korigan's worm!"

Gudon's hand went to his sword hilt. "I am no one's worm," he said coldly.

"There is no need for insult and threats here," Akota spat, and she and Herita stood between Eynon and Gudon. Eynon stepped back a pace, his hands clearly well away from his own weapon, and Gudon let his own hand drop.

"My words were hasty," Eynon admitted, but then turned once more to the second circle. "But if we do not believe Korigan, why should we believe her cousin? I ask again, has anyone seen these mercenaries? And I do not ask this of the White Wolf clan, for we know where their interests lie."

Lynan moved so quickly he broke from Kumul's grip before the giant could tighten it.

"God's sake, lad!" Kumul hissed, but Lynan ignored him. He stepped well into the light of the fire. His hat cast a dark shadow across his face and hid his features. Eynon and the other chiefs turned to face him. Gudon groaned. Korigan came up to him and said under her breath: "Lynan, you do not have to do this!"

Lynan looked squarely at her and said: "I made a choice to come to the High Sooq. Now I have to make that choice work."

"And despite my words, yet another from Korigan's clan comes forward," Eynon cried loudly. "Her followers are loyal to a fault, but not so good of hearing." Many in both circles laughed at the small figure who had appeared in front of them.

"I am not born of the White Wolf clan," Lynan said loudly enough for all in the first circle to hear. "And I have seen the mercenaries."

"Then whose clan were you born into?" Eynon asked, his voice still jesting.

"A clan you know well, Eynon. The clan of the kestrel."

"I have never heard of this kestrel," Eynon said. "And certainly know of no such clan."

"You would know it by its other name."

"First, my little Chett, by what name should we know *you?*"

"My name is Lynan."

Eynon's face turned sour. "That is not funny. No Chett may be called Lynan after the last of that name passed away." There were murmurs of agreement from all the chiefs. "His name is not one we cherish."

"I am not a Chett."

Eynon was too startled to speak, but Herita said: "If you are not a Chett, what right do you have to speak to the two circles?" She turned to Korigan. "Will you break with our tradition so easily?"

"I have the right," Lynan said before Korigan could reply, taking off his hat and drawing out the Key of Union from beneath his poncho. The firelight gleamed off his white skin and the Key. He heard gasps all around him.

"Do you recognize this?" he asked of all the chiefs.

"I have never seen it," Akota said under her breath, "but I know it. All Chetts know it. It was the symbol of Usharna's sovereignty over us."

"The Key of Union," Eynon said numbly. "How come you to have it . . . ?" His voice drifted off as he realized the truth.

"I am Lynan Rosetheme, and the sea hawk is my family's

emblem. As son of Queen Usharna, I have the right to be heard before the two circles. And as son of Elynd Chisal, who was born of a Chett woman, I have the right to be heard before the two circles. And as the White Wolf returned, I have the right to be heard before the two circles."

In the uproar that followed, Ager turned to Kumul and said, "He's getting quite good at this, isn't he?"

Kumul grunted, but could not deny the sudden joy in the cries of the Chetts around him.

"I wouldn't be surprised if there's a prophecy or something foretelling Lynan would appear like this," Ager continued.

"If not," Kumul said, "we can always make up one."

They watched Lynan stand in the firelight, holding up the Key of Union for all in the two circles to see. Korigan stood beside him, her relief obvious in her expression. Gudon moved to stand beside the pair, a grin as wide as the Gelt River across his face. But both Ager and Kumul were watching Eynon; it was his reaction that would determine what happened next.

Eynon surveyed the second circle, listening to the cheering and excited cries. He approached Lynan and an apprehensive silence fell across the meeting.

Lynan stood his ground, looking haughtily at the chief. When Eynon was no more than two paces, the chief bowed his head. For a moment nothing else happened, then Akota and Herita stood before Lynan and bowed as well. Then each of the chiefs in the first circle paid obeisance. When the last chief had bowed, every Chett in the second circle bowed as well.

"Impressive," Ager muttered under his breath.

"It is," Kumul admitted, and could not help but feel great pride in what Lynan had achieved. "It is not the way I would have done it, but it is the way it should have been done."

Jenrosa put an arm around Kumul's waist. "You are used

to the ways of the east, of the royal court. Lynan seems to know instinctively how to behave with the Chetts."

"Well, that might explain his lack of success back in Kendra," Ager said. "Lynan is a barbarian at heart."

Ager's words sent a shiver down Kumul's spine. "For the kingdom's sake, I hope you are wrong."

8

FREYMA was scattering the last bale of feed in the paddock when he saw the group of horsemen approaching along the south road. He thought quickly, and realized he would not be able to reach his house to get his sword before they arrived. There was a pitchfork in the barn, though, and that might be handier than a sword against a mounted foe. He called to his five cows and they lazily lumbered across the paddock to pick at the feed. Pretending to be as casual as his beasts, he sauntered to the barn, opened just one of the old, creaky wooden doors, made sure his pitchfork was within reaching distance, and waited for his guests.

One rider galloped ahead of the rest. He saw Freyma but ignored him at first, instead riding around the yard, looking through windows and around corners. He was dressed in good leather gear, the chest piece hard and shiny from boiling; a long cavalry sword was in a scabbard attached to the saddle. When at last he halted in front of the barn, he looked down on Freyma with something like curiosity.

"Hello, friend," Freyma said.

The rider nodded but did not reply.

"I hope you've just come for water or to buy some eggs."

The rider shook his head, and pointed to the rest of his group, six riders, now passing the farm gate.

Can't do much against seven, Freyma thought. *But if I take this one out now, I'll make at least some account of myself.*

His leaned against the barn door and grasped the pitchfork in his right hand. "One of your horses is lame," he said. The stranger looked over his shoulder, and as he did so, Freyma quickly moved forward, bringing the pitchfork up and around.

"Hold it, Freyma!" cried a harsh voice, and the farmer hesitated. The rider Freyma was about to impale whipped around, his sword already in his hand. Before Freyma could do anything the pitchfork was spinning out of his grasp.

"God's death, you're fast," Freyma said, and waited for the sword to bite into his neck. But the rider just grinned down at him.

By now, the other riders had reached the barn. One of them dismounted and slowly took off a pair of black gloves. "Age has slowed you, my friend," the man said.

Freyma stared at him in surprise. He recognized the voice, the well-muscled frame and horribly scarred face with its crooked nose. "I don't believe it. Jes fucking Prado."

Prado put his hands on his hips and roared in laughter. "You should see the color of your face. You'd think I was a ghost."

"I thought *I* was going to be a ghost," Freyma said. He waved at the other riders. "Who are your friends?"

"My escort."

"Escort? Since when does a farmer in the Arran Valley need an escort?"

Prado shook his head. "News still travels here slower than a corpse. I've been gone from the valley for over half a year."

"Gone? Where? Who's looking after your farm?"

Prado snorted. "I never thought I'd hear you sound so concerned over a few square leagues of dirt."

"It's how we feed ourselves, remember?" Freyma said resentfully. He looked at Prado's companions again. "Or did. You've obviously moved on."

"How much do you make here, Freyma?"

"None of your business."

"After you've paid your taxes, and for transporting your milk and grain and eggs. How much? A dozen gold pieces a year?"

"Still none of your business."

"And how much did you make when you rode with me? Some campaigns you made a dozen gold pieces a day."

"Those days are gone, Jes. I'm just a farmer now."

Prado grinned and put his arm around Freyma's skinny shoulders. "I'm here to tell you that those days are back again."

Freyma did not have enough food for all seven guests, so Prado paid him three gold pieces straight off for one of the cows. For that amount Freyma said they could have the vealer, and three hours later they were eating rare fire-roasted beef and downing a few flagons of his best cider and mead.

"So you're actually working for the Rosethemes now?" Freyma shook his head disbelievingly. "I never thought that'd happen. Not in a thousand years."

"That's right. I've even got her commission."

"They made you a captain?"

"A general," Prado said. "I want you to be my captain."

Freyma's eyes narrowed. "I told you, Jes, I've got my farm."

"I'll pay you three times what you get from your farm. And there'll be booty."

"Slaves?"

Prado shook his head. "No. Areava's munificence won't extend that far. But there's plenty of rich takings in Haxus, and the Strangers' Sooq."

"That's true," Freyma admitted. He rubbed a pockmarked cheek with a long finger. "How long does this commission last?"

"Six months, a year. Until we do the job."

"You goin' to stretch it out?"

Prado's eyes hardened. "I want Rendle dead. I want Lynan dead. The only thing I want to stretch are their necks."

Freyma's brow creased in thought.

"I know what you're thinking, you dog. You can be my captain, get rich, and be back here before next summer." Prado chuckled. "Well, that's fine by me, if that's how you want to play it. But I have a feeling there'll be more work for us after this job is done."

"I haven't got many good years left in me, Jes. I don't want to die with a sword in my hand."

"None of us is young anymore. I reckon if I recruit most of the old company, and take on their sons and daughters who can ride and use a sword, we'll be back to almost full strength."

"You'll need more than that to take on Rendle, especially if Salokan's backing him."

Prado nodded. "I hear Black Petra settled his company near Sparro."

"That's right. I ran into some of them at the Sparro fair this autumn past. But Black Petra's dead, Prado."

"Gored by one of his bulls, no doubt. He liked farming, too, I seem to remember."

"Knifed. Got in a brawl with a local."

Prado sucked his teeth. "No way for a soldier to die."

"No way for a farmer to die either. You thinking of recruiting his people as well?"

"As many as I can get."

"Sal Solway put her company down near Black Petra's. That's another hundred or so. She'll join up, at any rate. I hear her inn was burned down."

"We'll make the biggest company Theare has ever seen," Prado said, his eyes gleaming.

"We? I haven't said I'd join up, Prado."

"You didn't say, that's true."

"You'll pay me six times what I make from my farm, and I leave in summer with all the booty I can carry."

"Anybody would think you were a mercenary."

Freyma laughed, and the two men shook hands.

Prado set up in the second largest inn in the valley's largest town. His men wondered why he did not stay in the largest, but Prado would not tell them the largest inn was where he had kidnapped Lynan, slaying the owner of the tavern in the process.

Once word got around he was recruiting, over eighty of his old company came to see him and sign up, many of them bringing their children to sign up as well. By the end of the first week, he had over two hundred on his roll.

He sent Freyma to spread the word among any other mercenaries he could find closer to the Chandran capital, Sparro, and by the end of the second week his numbers had swelled to four hundred, many of them veterans, and even including a few locals with no military tradition but eager for adventure and easy money. Freyma had been right about Sal Solway, and Prado now had his second captain. She was a short, solidly built woman of middle years with short black hair. He let Freyma and Sal choose their own lieutenants and sergeants, and within a month of arriving in the Arran Valley had a force of five hundred mercenaries, all mounted, and divided into two companies of roughly equal strength. Freyma wanted to start training right away, but Prado told him to wait until they were on the border with Haxus.

"I want to get north and find billeting before spring."

"They can't train in winter," Sal complained.

"They can and will," Prado said harshly. "They'll do whatever they have to do if they want to stay in my company."

"How long before we leave the valley?" Freyma asked.

"Another day or two, then we head for Sparro, picking up any of Sal's and Black Petra's old companies that still want to join, then north, recruiting where we can until we get to the border with Hume. I hope to have at least two thousand under me before I start calling on Queen Charion for some of her regiments."

Sal was impressed by Prado's ambition. "Two thousand! We can do a lot with two thousand mercenaries."

"We only have to do two things," Prado reminded her. "Kill Rendle and kill Lynan. If I can avoid using Charion's regulars, I will."

"You said it was Areava who first commissioned Rendle . . ." Freyma began.

"What of it?"

". . . did she employ other companies at the same time? Could we get them to join us?"

"They've already taken Areava's gold. She wouldn't look too kindly on us paying them again."

"Not whole companies, maybe," Freyma mused, "but a troop here and there?"

Prado grinned. "Well, maybe a troop here or there. I'll leave that to you."

"I'm surprised you don't have at least two others with you now," Sal said to Prado.

"Who do you mean?"

"Bazik and Aesor. They were your sergeants once, weren't they? Stuck closer to you than ticks on a dog."

"I was wondering when they'd turn up," Freyma added.

"They won't be here," Prado said darkly, and something in his tone told Sal and Freyma to leave well enough alone.

On their last day in the valley, as their company gathered with their mounts along the main street, Prado still kept open a table for any last-minute recruits. He was glad he did. So far, five more locals, each armed with their own bow and arrows, had signed up, and there was a short queue still waiting to be processed. He wanted as many of the Arran Valley archers as he could get his hands on: there were none better in Theare.

"Have you been in combat before?" Freyma was asking the next in line, a boy barely old enough to shave, but he had weapons and a horse.

"No, sir."

"Then your pay is one gold piece a day, and one share of any booty after each battle."

"Good enough."

"Can you write?"

"No, sir."

Freyma pushed over the page he had been writing on as he asked his questions. "Make your mark here," he said, handing him the stylus. The boy did so, and Freyma then gave the stylus to Prado to countersign. "Right, report to Lieutenant Owel at the end of the line; she's the one with a roan mare and a scar shaped like an arrow point on her forehead."

The boy nodded, bowed a little to Prado who patted him genially on the back, and made way for the next in line, a man who had seen better years and came with the yellow sash of the grieve's office and a dress sword that would be good for little except sticking fruit.

Well, we can't expect them all to be warriors, Prado thought to himself, then brightened when he saw a small group of riders approaching from north of the town. They were well mounted and well armed. Now these were the kind of recruits he wanted.

"Name?" Freyma asked the man in the yellow sash.

"Goodman Ethin."

"Occupation?"

"Clothier by trade."

"Any military experience?"

"None. But I am currently grieve hereabouts."

Freyma nodded. "That will do." He pointed to Goodman Ethin's sword. "We can't afford to arm you with anything better. You fight with what you bring."

"I'm not here to sign on to Jes Prado's company," the man said.

"Then why in God's name are you wasting my time?" Freyma spat.

"To arrest your general." The man turned to Jes Prado. "Sir, I am placing you under arrest to answer charges of murder and kidnapping."

Prado stared at the grieve in astonishment. "What are you on about, man?"

"I am charging you with the murder of a local innkeeper, Yran, and the kidnapping of a youth, on a night during the summer past."

Freyma laughed at the grieve. "You must be joking?"

Some of the locals in the queue started drifting away.

Prado's face went red with anger and surprise. "Do you have any witnesses to either the murder or the kidnapping?"

"You deny the charges?" the grieve returned.

"Do you have any evidence at all?" Prado insisted.

"I have the testimony of patrons that you were among the last customers in the inn on the night of these events. At any rate, I am arresting you until the charges can be proven or cleared."

"You can't do that!" Freyma shouted indignantly. "He's a *general* in Queen Areava's service!"

Goodman Ethin regarded him coolly. "Even the queen is not above the law."

"The youth in question was an outlaw," Prado said.

"So you do admit it!" the grieve declared.

Freyma stared at Prado. "Jes, what are you talking about?"

"I admit nothing," Prado said. "I took the youth into custody. He was to be delivered to the queen for trial."

"To the queen, you say! And why would she be interested in him?"

"Because he was Prince Lynan, murderer of King Berayma and traitor to the crown."

The grieve's face went white. "No."

"Oh, yes. You might remember his companions?"

"Of course . . ."

"Kumul Alarn, ex-constable of the Royal Guard, Ager Parmer, ex-captain of the Royal Guard, and Jenrosa Alucar, student magicker. *All* outlaws."

"The big one was Kumul Alarn? Kumul of the Red Shields?" The grieve's eyes were almost popping out of his head. He shook his head. "But what of Yran? Do you deny murdering him?"

"Killing him? No. Murdering him? Yes. He tried to defend Prince Lynan."

The grieve shook his head. "This is incredible." He regarded Prado carefully. "Nevertheless, the charges still stand. If you are right in what you say, then you will be found innocent and can continue with your business—"

"I don't have time for this. I am on an important—a vital!—commission for the queen. Nothing must stop me."

"For certain," the grieve said, his voice starting to quaver, "the law will stop you, sir."

Prado could see more of his potential recruits moving away, and then he saw the group of riders he had noticed earlier gathering around. He did not want to lose them as well.

"Freyma. Take care of this interfering fool."

Freyma smiled thinly. "With pleasure." He stood up and drew his sword. The grieve backed two paces and drew his own slight weapon.

"Hardly a fair fight," said one of the new arrivals. All eyes turned to the speaker, a tall, thin man with long, graying hair and eyes as dark as a hawk's. He was mounted on a black stallion, and was dressed in a short coat of well-made mail dented and scraped from many blows. A long sword in a plain scabbard was strapped to his back.

"Maybe you would like to lend him your sword?" Freyma suggested sarcastically.

"No one but myself may ever touch Deadheart."

"You give your sword a *name?*" Freyma sneered, and many of the mercenaries laughed. "And *Deadheart* at that?"

"I did not name it," the stranger said equably. "My father's father called it Deadheart. I saw no reason to change it." He rested his hands across the pommel and leaned against them, looking for all the world as if he did not particularly care which way the conversation went.

"This is none of your affair," Prado cut in. "This man is interfering in the queen's business."

"And he is King Tomar's grieve, and since King Tomar is Queen Areava's subject, he is also on the queen's business."

Prado placed his hands on his hips and said in his most authoritative voice: "I have the queen's commission. My duty is urgent and cannot be interfered with."

"I know," the stranger said evenly.

Prado and Freyma exchanged quick glances. "Who, exactly, are you?" Prado demanded.

"My name is Barys Malayka."

Prado's eyes narrowed. "I know that name."

"So you should, Jes Prado. I am King Tomar's champion. I led the Chandran cavalry against your company at the Battle of Sparro."

A low murmuring started among the older mercenaries.

"Yes, I remember. You caused me grief."

"And you and your company caused Chandra great grief during the Slaver War. I tried to reach your banner. I wanted your head to give to King Tomar."

Everyone looked at Prado, expecting him to explode in anger, but instead he smiled easily. "That was then. Now we are on the same side."

Barys considered the statement. "Regrettably."

"Are you here to sign on?" Freyma asked. Prado chuckled.

Barys shook his head. "I'm here on official duty."

"What duty would that be?"

"King Tomar heard from the queen that you would be recruiting here. He sent me to make sure your methods had changed since the last time you recruited in Chandra."

"Why didn't the king come himself if he was so concerned?" Freyma asked chidingly, earning another chuckle from Prado.

"I did," said a new voice, and one of the riders behind Barys moved his horse out from the group.

Prado's eyes boggled. There was no mistaking the large, bearded man who emerged from his bodyguard. His hair was grayer than when last Prado had seen King Tomar, but his brown eyes were still the saddest he had ever seen; they seemed filled with the pain of the whole world.

The locals immediately went to one knee, including the grieve. Goodman Ethin was by now sweating profusely, feeling like a rat caught between two very hungry snakes. He wished he had stayed a clothier.

The mercenaries remained standing, but except for Prado all averted their eyes from the king's gaze. Prado bowed his head the merest fraction. The king ignored him and addressed Goodman Ethin.

"You are carrying out your duty as grieve with commendable bravery," Tomar said. "Unfortunately, what Jes Prado told you is true. Queen Areava has full knowledge of his actions in this valley last summer, and has given him a special commission which cannot be delayed. All charges against him are dropped."

The grieve, not daring to look directly at his king, nodded vigorously. "I understand, your Majesty."

"Stand up," the king instructed, and the grieve did. Tomar drew his own sword out of its saddle scabbard and handed it hilt-first to the grieve. The grieve took it, his hands shaking like autumn leaves on a tree. "As a sign of my trust in this man, and my determination to see that such devotion is rewarded, he will now carry my sword when acting as grieve in the Arran Valley. If he is in any way harmed or interfered with, I will ensure the perpetrators are hunted down and punished."

Tomar stared directly at Prado. "Is that understood by all?"

Prado nodded stiffly. No one else said a word.

"How long do you intend to stay in Chandra?" Tomar asked him.

"We leave the valley today. We will pass within a day's ride of Sparro, then north into Hume."

"It should take you no more than four weeks."

"Four or five, depending on how the recruiting goes."

"Four," Tomar insisted.

Prado sighed. "Very well."

Tomar turned to Barys. "Stay with the mercenaries until they leave Chandra."

"Your Majesty."

"I hope we never meet again, Jes Prado," Tomar said to the mercenary, and turned his horse. His guard followed, except for Barys, who dismounted and stood next to Goodman Ethin.

Prado grunted once, and ordered Freyma to continue with the recruiting.

"But there are no more recruits," Freyma said, and it was true. All the locals who had queued up to sign were gone.

"Time to leave the valley, I think, General Prado," Barys said lightly.

9

OLIO was leaning against the wall of a house. The timber was old and frayed and he could feel a splinter digging into his back through his shirt. It made him open his eyes. He tried to swallow, then stand erect. He slumped back against the wall. In his right hand he held an empty leather bottle. He held it upside down and a few drops trickled down his hand.

"None left?" he said out loud.

He dimly remembered scrounging the bottle from one of the palace kitchens after his evening meal. If he was going to be a general, he might as well have one last drink. No one saw him take it, and no one stopped him leaving the palace after that. He had walked the streets for what seemed like hours, visiting at least two taverns on the way to resupply.

Olio looked around. It was dark, and he could not see much of the street he was standing on. Judging by the manner in which the buildings leaned in over the street, he assumed he was in the old quarter of the city. There was no one else around. Ten paces from his feet there was a dead dog, small and pale, its eyes milky, with something inside it rummaging around in what had been its stomach and making the dog's hide ripple.

He tried to stand again, but could only manage it if he kept his free hand against the wall. He took a step, then another, and had to stop. The ground seemed to whirl under his feet and he fell down. Again he tried to swallow, but it felt as if his tongue had been glued to the top of his mouth.

He heard footsteps behind him and he turned. A young woman, her head buried in a shawl, was trying to get past without him noticing. She was dragging along a small boy with a snotty nose and bare feet.

"Mumma—"

"Don't look. We have to get home."

"He's sick, mumma."

"I'm not sick," Olio said loudly. "I'm a general. Get me my horse." Again he tried to stand, but without success. "Better yet, get my carriage."

"Mumma?"

But mumma just walked faster, actually lifting the boy off his feet to get him past the drunk man.

Olio watched them go, feeling a little affronted. "I'm a prince, too!" he called out after them, but they just kept on going.

"I should have worn my crown," Olio told himself. He was right next to the dead dog. A rat's head poked out of a hole in the dog's belly, sniffed the air, disappeared again.

Even though he was now sitting, the ground still seemed to spin. He put his hands out to steady himself, but they never seemed to connect with anything. He collapsed sideways and lay crookedly, his hand finally letting go of the leather bottle. A moment later two hooded men stood over him. One bent down and gently shook his shoulder.

"He is ill," said the one still standing.

"He's pissed," said the one bending over Olio. He could feel rich cloth under his hand. "A nobleman, perhaps." He grabbed Olio's jaw and turned the man's face so that he could see it. "It can't be."

"Who is it?"

"It can't be." He stood up. "Get Father Powl. I will stay here with him."

"Father Powl?"

"Quickly! As fast as your legs will carry you!"

Primate Giros Northam was woken by a lay brother.

"Your Grace, I have an urgent message for you from Father Powl."

Northam shook his head of the last dregs of sleep and sat up. The lay brother handed him a wooden cup filled with warmed wine. He swallowed it thirstily, the loose flesh around his neck wobbling like a turkey's wattle.

"He brings the message?"

"Another lay brother left it with Father Tere, who is on vigil tonight."

"Give it to me."

The lay brother took the empty cup and handed him the note. Northam read it quickly, and the words made him groan out loud.

"Is it bad, your Grace?"

"Is the lay brother who brought this still here?"

"Yes."

"He is go to Father Powl and tell him I am coming immediately. Father Powl is to wait for me."

"Yes, your Grace."

The lay brother left and Northam dressed quickly.

"I knew it would come to this," he said under his breath. "I knew it would end badly. I *knew*."

Later, as he left the palace, the guards could hear him still muttering under his breath.

Father Powl sat in the room where his two student priests had laid out Prince Olio. He had dismissed the students and was now alone with the prince. He cupped his chin in one hand and wondered if God had delivered to him a great opportunity or a great burden.

Powl had heard stories about Olio, of course, but thought them nothing but gossip about a man who seemed to have no obvious vices. But here Olio was, reeking of wine and, Powl was even more disconcerted to discover, urine. To think that the prince would get so drunk he would lose control of his bladder was both a shock and a revelation to the priest.

This could be the lever Powl needed to open up the primate, who had, since Usharna's death, become quite distant. Powl had been hurt by the colder relationship with his superior, one that before had always been so warm, but had shrugged it off and got on with his duties. This might create a new intimacy between them, the sharing of secret—indeed, almost sacred—knowledge.

The burden, of course, would be the weight on his mind and in his heart of Olio's downfall. Powl stopped himself. He was not the Righteous God and would not judge his fellow man, let alone a crown prince. Nevertheless, it shook Powl's conviction in the basic rightness of society's structure. He had wanted to believe that the members of the royal family were more than human, that they contained in them some spark of the divine. Naturally that could not be expected of the outlaw Lynan, whose royal blood at best ran diluted in his veins and at worst perverted. But here was Prince Olio himself, the gentlest of the all the Rosethemes, brought low by the most common of all vices: excess.

He heard the primate enter the chapel, have a few hurried words with the local priest, and then make his way to the room. Father Powl stood up to greet him. The door opened, and the primate entered. He did not even look at Powl but went straight to the prince. He leaned over and smelled Olio's breath and then, something Powl thought quite strange, pulled out the Key of the Heart from under Olio's shirt and gently held it for a moment before putting it back.

Powl cleared his throat. "Your Grace?"

Northam glanced at him, looking distracted. "Hmm?"

"Two of my students returning from duties on the docks found him in a street nearby. They summoned me immediately."

"Has anyone else seen the prince?"

"Only the chaplain here."

Northam shook his head. "Too bad. That's too bad."

"We can trust the chaplain's discretion, surely, your Grace? And I will speak for my two students."

Northam studied the priest more carefully then. "You are sure the students will keep quiet?"

"I carefully explained to them the gravity of the situation; they will not repeat what they have seen tonight to another living soul."

Northam turned back to Olio. "This isn't the first time."

"I have heard . . . stories."

"Yes, everyone in Kendra is hearing the stories now, but none of them know the true story."

"Your Grace?"

Northam brushed his bald pate with a large hand as if there was still hair there to part. "It doesn't matter. You don't need to know."

"I am your secretary, Primate. Surely, if you carry some terrible burden, I can help you carry it."

"That is a generous offer, but I must refuse you." He faced Powl again and grasped the smaller man by the shoulders. "The queen must never hear of this, do you understand."

"I am her confessor, your Grace; she is not mine."

The primate released him. "Yes, of course. I know." He closed his eyes in exhaustion. "You must do me a favor."

"Anything."

"Find the magicker prelate and ask him to come here straight away."

"Edaytor Fanhow? What has he to do with this?"

"No more questions. I can say nothing else to you on this. Just get me the prelate."

"Of course, your Grace," Powl said and left.

Northam took the priest's seat and held Olio's hand. *I don't trust that man,* he thought, and immediately felt guilty for having such thoughts about his own secretary, someone who had once been his friend.

And if I let him, could be again. But that would be too dangerous.

Olio dreamed of children again. He searched every cot for his brother. He could hear Lynan's voice, calling out to him, but he could not find him. There were children ravaged by disease, sores, and injuries, but he ignored them. The room seemed to extend forever, the cots lined up in three neat rows, each one holding a child who needed his healing. But no Lynan.

Then he noticed that the faces of all the children were starting to look the same. They all became boys. Their hair became brown. Their heads became round. They were all Lynan when he was about seven or eight years old. Olio remembered looking after his brother when he was that age.

But the faces kept on changing. Skin became the color of ivory, and the whites of the eyes became a golden yellow.

"Olio!" all the children called. "Heal me!"

He ran from cot to cot, placing his hand on every forehead, feeling his own life draining away from him as he healed each Lynan.

Exhausted, he stopped, sinking to his knees. The children got out of their cots and surrounded him, their pale hands reaching for the Key of the Heart.

"No, Lynan, stop!" he cried out. The Key burned against his chest like a branding iron.

"No . . . !"

He woke with a silent scream, every muscle in his body knotted in pain, sweat drenching his clothes. He shot up in the bed, scrabbling for the Key, trying to pull it away from his skin. He found the chain, yanked on it. The Key popped out from underneath his shirt. He touched it, then let go with a gasp and blew on his fingers. He opened his shirt and looked at his chest, saw the burn mark over his heart in the shape of the Key. He tugged the chain over his head and hurled the Key away from him. It clattered onto the floor.

Gasping, Olio swung his legs out of the bed and buried his head in his hands. He started sobbing, his chest heaving. He was afraid and ashamed and confused all at the same time. He did not know what was happening to him. When at last the crying eased, he looked up and realized he did not know where he was. A small room; a single bed. Panic started to well up in him, then he heard two voices, distant, like the echoes of a memory.

Olio stood up unsteadily and went to the door. It was slightly ajar, and he listened through the crack.

"On the street, Prelate! Do you know what could have happened to him?"

He knew that voice. Old, with fading authority.

"He promised me he would stop the drinking."

He knew that voice, too. Contrite, desperate.

They were his friends, he was sure of it. He should go to them.

"We have to stop him, for his own sake." The old voice again. "He could even die. Or be murdered. Or fall into the harbor. God knows."

"How? He won't give up the healing, but it exhausts him and gives him nightmares. That's *why* he is drinking."

"Then make sure he gets more rest."

"It isn't just physical exhaustion. It's as if the Key is taking more from him than just his energy."

That was Edaytor Fanhow. He was a good man.

"What do you mean?"

And that was Giros Northam. He was a good man, too. And they were talking about him. They were worried about him. He had done something wrong.

"His nature is changing. Did you ever imagine he would become like this?"

"No, of course not. I would never have cooperated with you and the prince if I knew this was going to happen."

"I don't know what to do."

"We will stop him, that's what we'll do."

"But he *won't* stop, I'm telling you. He's driven to heal those who need his help."

"He will stop," the primate said determinedly. "We will tell Areava."

"God, no!"

"What else can we do? We can't let it go on like this."

Olio realized they were talking about him. What had he done? He shook his head to clear it. Something stank. He backed away from the door, but the smell came with him. He looked down at himself, saw the burn again, then noticed the stains on his shirt and breeches. He had pissed in his breeches. There was something else, too. He could smell wine. Cheap, resinous wine.

He heard Edaytor say something, but could not make out the words. He went back to the door.

"Close the hospice!" The primate was speaking now. "I can't do that. Too many of the poor know of its existence, know that the dying come but leave completely healed."

"Then move it so that Olio cannot find it."

"How do we stop him? He is the prince."

"Then someone must be with him all the time, someone we trust."

"Who?"

"A guard, a priest, a magicker. I don't know."

"He won't allow it."

"He will," Edaytor said, his voice suddenly firm. "He will, or we *will* go to Areava. He would agree to anything to stop us doing that. He is terrified she would put a stop to his healing, maybe even force him to surrender the Key."

For a moment neither man said anything or, if they did, Olio could not hear them. Footsteps, coming his way. He hastily retreated from the door, ran into the bed, and stumbled. He sat on the floor with a jarring thump and put his hands out to stop himself from falling backward. His right hand landed on the Key. Startled he glanced around, and at the same time the door opened wide. He looked back and saw the grim faces of the primate and the prelate staring down at him. They seemed curiously matched, Olio thought: Northam long and large, with huge hands and feet, and Edaytor shorter but almost as heavy, with the face and gentle nature that seemed priestlike to the prince.

"He overheard," Northam said.

"But how much?"

"M–m–most of it, I think," Olio admitted, his voice not much more than a hoarse whisper.

"What happened tonight?" Northam demanded.

"I . . . I don't know. I m–m–must have been drinking."

"You broke your trust," Edaytor said sadly. "I did not think you would ever do that."

"I didn't want to," he said weakly. He turned his face from them.

"We are going to stop the healing," Northam said.

"I know."

He picked up the Key and looped the chain over his neck. It was cold against his skin now.

"It has burned you," Northam said, pointing to the

prince's chest. "Do you know why it has done this?" he asked the prelate.

Edaytor shook his head. "No one really knows or understands the full extent of the Keys' powers. Obviously they were never meant to be used as often as this one has been since his Highness has had possession of it."

Tears came to Olio's eyes again. "B–b–but all the children. I could not let them die."

"They will die as children have always died in this city," Northam told him. "As they have always died in every city in Grenda Lear."

"Let the hospice continue," Olio pleaded. "I will stay away from it, but I can still support it. That will save some of them."

Northam bowed his head in thought. "Very well," he said at last. "But the moment I hear you have been using the Key, or that you have been drinking again, I *will* close it . . . forever."

Olio seemed to shrink in on himself. To Northam and Edaytor he looked at that moment like a lost child himself, abandoned and afraid.

10

A THIN layer of snow had settled across the grasslands around the High Sooq. Cattle licked the snow for water and then ate the yellowed grass underneath. Their breaths filled the shallow valley with clouds of steam. Above all the sun shone, distant and weak, but a welcoming sight in the cold, empty blue sky. Lynan sat in the saddle, trying not to grin as he looked out over the strength and wealth of the combined clans.

I belong to them, he thought.

It had been some time now since he had last felt the inhuman rage and yearning that had visited him in the autumn or experienced any terrible nightmares about Silona and her forest, and he could enjoy the day now that the temperature had dropped. For the first time since fleeing the Strangers' Sooq he felt whole and entirely his own.

With a twinge of guilt he remembered the way he had treated Kumul, but it reminded him he was entirely his own in another way, too. He now made the decisions that affected his future. He had grown up, he realized, and was proud of it.

And with that came new responsibilities. Kumul and Ager had taught him that his decisions affected more than himself; as a prince, his thoughts and actions determined what happened to his followers. In a strange way, the realization reinforced his confidence; he had been right to come to the High Sooq, but he understood that did not mean Kumul had been completely wrong. Ultimately, his future—and the future of his followers—would be determined in the east. That is where he had to look.

Two things I need. An army and the will to use it.

He thought he had the second, and now it was time to go about achieving the first.

Two riders approached, intruding on his isolation. He wished them away, but they came on anyway. He soon recognized Korigan, but it was not until they were much closer that he identified the second. It was the young Terin, chief of the Rain clan and close ally of Korigan. He remembered then he had mentioned to Korigan he wanted to meet with Terin, but had not meant this very morning.

"Korigan said you wanted to see me, your Majesty," Terin said, a little breathlessly. Lynan, forgetting his own youth, could not help thinking Terin was far too young to be a clan chief.

Lynan opened his mouth to ask him not to call him "your Majesty" but changed his mind. He had asked Korigan and Gudon the same thing, several times, but it made no difference. "Thank you for coming," he said instead.

Terin looked surprised, as if Lynan requesting his presence was an order he must carry out without hesitation and required no thanks. The idea unsettled Lynan.

"Last night Eynon asked you if your clan had any contact with the mercenaries."

"That's right, your Majesty. To the best of my knowledge, no one in my clan has had any such contact."

"Have you noticed any strange happenings across the border? Any movements of troops or other military activity."

Terin frowned in thought. "No . . ." He stopped. "Although in autumn we lost two outriders who were patrolling that part of our territory."

"What happened to them?" Lynan asked.

Terin shrugged. "Every clan loses some outriders to wolves or a startled boar karak. I sent troops out to find them, but they came back with nothing, not even their mounts."

"Is it rare to lose the horses as well as the riders?"

"It happens, but not often. The mares know how to find their way back to the clan."

"They may have seen something," Korigan suggested.

"Possibly."

"What do you want me to do?" Terin asked.

"How soon before your clan can safely leave the High Sooq?"

"Not for another two months, your Majesty, but if you order us to go, we will leave tomorrow . . ."

"No. I will not place your clan in danger."

Terin simply nodded, but the look of relief on his face was obvious. "I *can* send out small troops, though. They can take extra horses with supplies."

"What do you have in mind?" Korigan asked Lynan.

"I need to know what's happening on the border. I need to know whether or not the mercenaries are planning to raid into the Oceans of Grass. If they are, and they are going to make their move in spring, there will be some sign of it."

"My riders can do that," Terin said. "They know that region better than anyone, and if they know what to look out for, they will not be caught by surprise."

"They are not to start a fight," Lynan said quickly. "I need information."

"What if an opportunity arises to capture a prisoner?" Korigan asked.

"Good, if they can do so without alarming the enemy."

"They can, your Majesty," Terin said with confidence.

"Can they leave tomorrow?"

Terin grinned, making himself look almost childlike. "I will send two troops out today. They will be on the border in a week."

Lynan could not help grinning back. The young chief's enthusiasm was infectious. "Thank you, Terin."

Terin bowed his head, wheeled his horse, and galloped back to his camp.

Korigan kneed her horse closer to Lynan's. "What are you planning?"

"Planning? Nothing at the moment. I have no idea what the mercenaries are intending, if indeed they are intending anything at all. But I think the sooner we give the Chetts something to worry about, the sooner they will unite behind your banner."

"They will unite behind you whatever may come," Korigan said confidently.

Lynan shook his head. "No. The surprise we pulled at last night's meeting will wear off soon, and some of the those chiefs who are opposed to you will realize there is no danger in opposing me. I have brought no army with me and the affairs of the east are not important to them."

Korigan thought about Lynan's words, and nodded. "You may be right. But Terin's troops may not return with information for several weeks, if they return with anything."

"Then we must keep the clans busy."

"How? They are already busy with winter."

"Then they must be kept even busier," Lynan said. "We must train them. We must make an army."

It was rare for the two circles to be called twice in one winter, but none of the chiefs refused Lynan's request. It was held soon after dawn, and the first circle gathered eagerly around the central fire to warm themselves.

When Herita called Lynan to speak, he immediately declared his intention.

"The mercenaries pose a real threat to the Chetts. Many of you will remember what they did to your clans before the Slaver War. We must stop those times from coming back. The only way to do this is to ride against the mercenaries before they ride against us."

No voices were raised in disagreement, and there were even a few cheers.

"For a Chett army to operate effectively, it will have to be trained to fight as one."

His words were met with a stupefied silence.

"Trained?" Akota asked after a while. "*Us?* Trained to fight?"

"Yes," Lynan said evenly.

"But we are the Chetts," she said, obviously confused by the notion. "We are trained as warriors as soon as we are old enough to ride, and that is before we are old enough to walk."

"Nevertheless, to fight against the mercenaries, to fight in the east, you will need training, and to fight against Areava, if she is directing mercenaries against you, you will need training."

Akota looked as if she was about to continue, but shook her head. Instead, another chief stood up.

"My name is Katan, and I am chief of the Ocean clan."

Herita glanced at Lynan, and he nodded for Katan to continue.

"What exactly can anyone from the east teach us about fighting?"

There was a general murmur of agreement from the gathered Chetts.

Lynan smiled slightly. "No one doubts the worth of the Chetts when it comes to courage, and to skill with bow and saber. I do not think anyone on the continent of Theare could teach the Chetts anything in that regard."

"Then what training are you talking about?"

"Great fighters do not necessarily make great soldiers."

"They are just words," Katan said derisively.

"They are more than words," Kumul said, stepping forward to stand beside Lynan. "I have seen what happens when a trained army fights an untrained rabble. It is always a massacre. No fighter, no matter now brave or skilled in the individual use of weapons, can match a trained soldier."

Katan puffed out his chest. "I can prove otherwise."

Lynan regarded him for a moment, then said: "Very well. What do you suggest?"

"My fighting skill against the best soldier from the east. I challenge Kumul Alarn."

The members of both circles gave an approving roar.

"I accept," Kumul said. There was another roar of approval. Kumul held his head high and pulled back his shoulders, his hand on his sword. Lynan felt suddenly small next to the giant. Even Katan wilted a little, but he did not recall the challenge.

Lynan waited until the noise subsided and said: "No."

Kumul gaped at him. "Lad, who else—?"

"Ager."

Ager shuffled forward to stand by Lynan's other side. He was grinning like an amiable dolt.

"This is foolishness!" Katan blustered. "Defeating your crookback would prove nothing!"

"On the other hand, if my crookback was to defeat you, it would prove everything." He put his arm around Ager's shoulder. "Captain Parmer was trained as a soldier, not simply as a fighter. He fought during the Slaver War as a commander in the Kendra Spears. In a battle, I would trust him with my life."

"Do you revoke your challenge, Katan?" Herita said loudly enough for both circles to hear.

"No," the chief grumbled.

Herita turned to Ager. "You are challenged, Ager Parmer. What weapon?"

"Katan can fight with any weapon he chooses," Ager said offhandedly. He patted the saber by his side. "I will fight with this."

"As will I," Katan agreed.

The first circle widened to make space for the combatants.

"And the rules?" Herita asked the two combatants.

"I would not have this to the death," Lynan said. Both Katan and Ager agreed.

"The first to lose his weapon?" Herita suggested.

"The first to draw blood," Katan said.

Herita looked at Ager, and he nodded. "Very well. The first to draw blood. If either is killed accidentally, the other will pay full five cattle to the dead man's family, including a bull not older than four years."

"I will pay for Ager," Korigan said from the second ring.

Ager grinned his thanks to the queen, and drew his saber. Katan, still obviously unhappy at being involved in such an unfair fight, drew his own. The two men stood ten paces apart.

"Start," Herita said.

Katan immediately charged forward, whirling his saber in the air above his head. Instead of retreating from the attack, Ager ducked and lunged forward. The blades snickered and Katan's saber was suddenly flying through the air. It landed in the ground point first, vibrating like a reed.

"Just as well we're going to first blood," Ager said lightly.

Katan cursed loudly, retrieved the saber and again advanced on the crookback, but more cautiously than before.

For every step Katan took forward, Ager took one back. Lynan watched with amused understanding, having himself dueled with the captain.

Katan lunged with exasperation. Ager easily deflected the blade, then took one step closer, half-lunged, and scraped the edge of his sabre along Katan's arm, opening a long cut. Katan roared and retreated, clutching his sword arm with his free hand; blood seeped between his fingers.

"And that's that," Ager said with mild satisfaction, sheathing his weapon.

"The duel is over," Herita announced. "Captain Ager Parmer was victorious. Katan of the Ocean clan is defeated."

Lynan spoke to both circles. "No one doubts Katan's courage or skill. But all of you must now see how Ager's training—despite his crookback and one eye—gave him the advantage."

"You would all train us to fight like the crookback?" came a voice from the second circle. "Like a beetle scuttling under the grass?"

There was some laughter, but most of the Chetts remained silent; they knew Ager had more than proved himself in a fair fight.

"In hand-to-hand combat on foot, none of us could do worse than fight like Ager," Lynan replied without anger. "But Kumul will also train some of you to fight like cavalry."

"No disrespect to Kumul Alarn," Akota said, "but we are already horse warriors."

"And that will be a great advantage to the army," Lynan said equably. "But Kumul will train those selected as shock cavalry."

"We will lose our mobility," another Chett from the second circle said.

"Well trained cavalry never loses its mobility," Kumul countered.

Eynon stood up, and Herita nodded to him to speak. "How large will this army be?"

"At first, each clan will give ten of its warriors," Lynan said. "Those ten will help to train ten others, and so on until each clan has given the equivalent of one of its horns to the army. That will leave more than enough for each clan to protect its families and cattle."

"And who will command it?" Eynon demanded. "Korigan?"

"I will not command it," Korigan said. "Lynan Rosetheme will."

"But you will ride with it."

"I will, Eynon, but so may you if that is your wish."

"In what role?" Eynon asked. "I will not be reduced to an outrider." There was a rumble of agreement from the other members of the first circle.

Lynan went to Eynon and stared up into his scarred face. "No good commander would waste such an experienced leader as yourself."

Eynon turned his eyes away. The prince's hard, snow-white skin sent a shiver down his spine. "As it should be," he said quickly.

Herita waited for any other chiefs who wished to speak, but none stood to claim the right.

"It seems you will have your army," Herita said to Lynan.

Jenrosa could not believe the heat put out by the small stone furnaces. The High Sooq was covered in several fingers of snow, but in this part of the village the snow melted even before it reached the ground. She watched Chetts stripped to the waist raking carbon beds, pumping small, horn-shaped bellows, taking out red-hot cups filled with molten steel, and pouring them into molds. Ever since the two circles had agreed with Lynan to create an army, the clans had been busy casting new weapons—sabers, spear heads, and arrow points, including a new spear head and sword according to designs specified by Kumul and Ager.

She had been to the large foundry in Kendra, controlled by the Theurgia of Fire, and though their construction was impressive, the heat it produced was nowhere near as intense as that produced by these primitive Chett furnaces.

She noticed a Chett who crouched near the furnace mouth but seemed to take no part in the activity around her. Her face and throat and small breasts glimmered with sweat, and her eyes were shut tight in concentration. Jenrosa watched more closely, and saw the Chett's lips moving.

She is a magicker, Jenrosa thought with surprise. She knew the Chetts had shamans, practitioners of magic looked down upon by the masters of the Theurgia, but this woman was more than a mere shaman, Jenrosa was sure.

Just then Jenrosa was politely hustled out of the way by two men pulling a hand-drawn cart. They quickly unloaded empty molds by the furnace, then loaded up again with filled ones. They left, panting with the effort of pulling so much weight. Jenrosa returned to her position to watch the Chett magicker, but there was a man there now, his lips moving in a silent chant. Jenrosa looked up, saw the first magicker standing to one side and stretching her muscles. The woman glanced around and saw Jenrosa staring at her.

"It is hot work," she said, smiling.

"You were performing magic," Jenrosa said.

"Oh, yes," the woman said, and walked over to where there was some snow. She picked up handfuls of it and rubbed them over her face and chest.

Jenrosa approached her diffidently. "I did not know any of the Chett could do that."

The woman looked at her strangely. "Why should we not be able to?"

"You have no Theurgia."

The woman nodded genially. "Truth. Does that matter?"

Jenrosa did not know what to say. She had always believed that magic occurred because the Theurgia existed to organize and practice it; magic could not exist without the combined weight of knowledge accrued—painstakingly slowly—over centuries. Anything else was illusion or simple shamanism, that minor magic that could be gathered from the natural world.

The woman looked around for her shirt and poncho and quickly dressed, and then, before Jenrosa could react, reached out for Jenrosa's hands and studied each carefully. "Ah, I see you have some ability."

"I was only a student."

The woman looked surprised. "I sense a great deal more than that." She looked carefully at Jenrosa's face, her large brown eyes gentle, unblinking. "Truth, I sense something very great in you."

Without knowing why, Jenrosa admitted: "I can work magic across disciplines."

"Disciplines?"

"I was able to perform magic from several theurgia: fire, air, water . . ."

"This was special?"

"Yes. In Kendra."

The woman laughed and shook her head. "Not on the Oceans of Grass. Imagine learning to crawl, but not to walk or run or climb. This is a mystery to me."

"Are you a teacher?"

The woman shrugged. "Lasthear is many things," she said. "I am rider, warrior, mother, magicker and sometimes, only sometimes, a teacher."

"Are there many like you?" Jenrosa asked, surprised.

"Every clan has at least one magicker; some have two or

more. I am a good one, many will tell you, but no Truespeaker."

"A Truespeaker? Like Gudon's mother?"

"Gudon of Korigan's clan?" Jenrosa nodded. "Yes, she was the Chetts' last Truespeaker. Alas, a Truespeaker is rare, maybe one every two or three generations among all the Chett. They are honored by every clan. Gudon's mother taught me when I was young. Since she died, none have come to claim her place."

"Lasthear, could you teach me?"

It was Lasthear's turn to be surprised. "I would like to teach you, but you are with Korigan."

"Why is that a problem?"

"I am Ocean clan. It would not be proper for me to teach you. You should find a magicker in the White Wolf clan."

"But the Truespeaker taught you, and she was of the White Wolf clan."

"The Truespeaker belongs to no clan, no matter which one she is born into."

"Oh."

"I know there are good magickers riding with Korigan," Lasthear said.

"I have two, in fact," said a voice behind them. Jenrosa turned to see Korigan herself. For a moment she could not help feeling envious of the queen's noble and athletic frame, not to mention her beautiful Chett face.

"The weapon-making goes well," Lasthear said.

"I can see," the queen said, but did not seem interested in what was happening at the furnace. She joined them, smiling easily at Jenrosa. "Could we talk?"

"Of course."

"You must excuse me," Lasthear said diplomatically. "I am tired and must rest before it is my turn again to sing to the fire."

Korigan nodded and Lasthear withdrew. Jenrosa looked

after her with some regret. She wished they could have continued their discussion.

Korigan put an arm through Jenrosa's and started walking toward the lake. The still blue waters seemed like the sky turned upside down, and the reflections of clouds scudded across its surface.

"What is it you wish to talk about?" Jenrosa asked.

Korigan hesitated, then said: "About Lynan."

"Lynan?"

"I think he has demonstrated a great deal of maturity for one so young."

"You mean by agreeing with you on matters of strategy?"

"Perhaps," Korigan said uneasily. "I was thinking more of the way he handled his responsibilities as a leader."

"Essential qualities for a future king."

Korigan stopped suddenly. "Are you making fun of me?"

"I don't even understand you; how can I make fun of you?"

"My motives are clear enough."

"Are they? I know you want Lynan to be king of Grenda Lear. But why should you risk the whole of the Chett nation on such an unlikely horse? The Oceans of Grass are practically inviolate."

"They weren't once. You are too young to remember the Slaver War."

"You've banded together since then. The mercenaries aren't a threat to your people."

"You underestimate the ability of the mercenary captains to learn and adapt just as we have."

Jenrosa nodded, conceding the point. "But this is about more than Rendle and his ilk, isn't it?"

"What do you mean?"

"This is about you and your crown."

"I cannot pretended that Lynan has not made my position among my people more secure."

"But it isn't enough, is it?"

"Not for the Chetts. Ever since we came under the sway of the throne of Grenda Lear over a hundred years ago, we have paid obeisance to distant monarchs. It has cost us nothing. Now it may cost us a great deal."

"Because you support Lynan?"

"Of course, but there are other factors. If Grenda Lear is unstable, then Haxus may try and bring us under its influence, and its king sits much closer to our territory. Or what if Hume secedes from the kingdom? Where can they expand? Not south into Chandra—Kendra would never allow that. North into Haxus? No, they are too small, and would fall to Haxus instead. They can only expand west, into the Oceans of Grass."

"But why push Lynan to be king?"

"Because I know that Hume is pushing the throne for increased trade benefits. Now that Areava needs all the support she can get, she is likely to give way to those demands."

"What has that to do with Lynan?"

"Hume can only increase its trade two ways. The first is at the expense of those trading rights given to its greatest rival, Chandra. Areava won't do that because she also needs King Tomar's support."

"What's the second way?"

"Areava can give Hume control over the Algonka Pass, the only link between the east and west of this continent for most of its length. As far as anyone in the east is concerned, ownership of the pass would give Hume symbolic control over the Oceans of Grass."

And suddenly Jenrosa understood. "But King Lynan would support you against Hume."

Korigan nodded. "We don't want possession of the pass. We want it to remain a free caravan route, belonging to no king or queen. That way trade continues to flourish between east and west."

"For someone isolated in the Oceans of Grass, you have a very good grasp of kingdom politics."

"Don't make Kumul's mistake of thinking we are nothing but nomad barbarians." Jenrosa opened her mouth to object, but Korigan held up her hand to stop her. "You know it is true. I can see it in everything Kumul says, in the way he looks at me and other Chetts. Most in the east look down on us as being little more than herders and horse warriors and potential slaves; Kumul may be more generous than that, but we are still barbarians to him.

"We may not have great cities or palaces, Jenrosa, but that does not mean we are stupid and ignorant."

"No. No it does not."

"I see you have some influence with Kumul."

Jenrosa looked up sharply. "Meaning?"

"You and Kumul are more than friends."

"Have you been spying on me?" Jenrosa demanded.

Korigan smiled ruefully. "You are in *my* kingdom now, Jenrosa Alucar. Nothing happens here without my knowing about it. But I did not spy on you. Your relationship with Kumul of the Red Shields is common knowledge among my people. Although I cannot say if Lynan is aware of it, I think not."

"It is none of your business."

"In and of itself, no. But I am concerned what effect it might have on Lynan if he learns that you and Kumul are in love with each other."

Jenrosa blushed, making her sandy hair stand out even more than it usually did among the Chetts. "Who said anything about love?"

"I will speak of it if you won't. I don't think Lynan is in love with you, but am I right in suggesting he once thought he was in love with you?"

"That's something you should ask him."

"But I'm asking you."

"Perhaps he once thought that."

"The fact that he may no longer think that will not stop him being jealous of Kumul. Losing love is one thing, but losing it to another is a hard blow."

"I can't change the way Kumul and I have . . . grown . . . to feel about each other."

"Will you tell Lynan, then?"

Jenrosa moved away from Korigan. "I told you, this is no one else's business."

"I wish it were so," Korigan called after her, but Jenrosa did not answer.

Away from the lake village, real winter had hold. Cattle huddled together, their heads bowed against the cold southerlies. A band of ten mounted Chetts huddled in the lee of a shallow hill wishing they were back in their huts or around one of the hundreds of campfires. They were from different clans and did not talk to each other. Kumul stayed apart from them, seemingly impervious to the weather.

"You have no armor to speak of," he was saying to them. "What you call spears are nothing more than javelins. Your horses are well trained but don't ride well close together. You're not cavalry."

Some of the Chetts looked defiantly at him.

"I repeat, you are *not* cavalry." Kumul bit the words out. "You see that single arrow tree three hundred paces north?"

The Chetts looked over their shoulders. One or two nodded.

"Take your mounts there and back here."

"Is that all?" one of the Chetts asked.

"Keep them to a walk."

Six minutes later the group were back, still cold. Their mounts looked even less happy.

"Now do it again, at a fast walk."

A little less than six minutes later they were back again.

While the Chetts looked as miserable as ever, and even more confused, the horses seemed more aware of the world around them.

"Now do the distance at a trot. When you get back, do it at a canter, then a gallop."

By the time they had finished the three runs, both mounts and riders were warmer; the exercise had also piqued their interest.

"Again," Kumul told them. "At a fast walk. Line abreast, and no more than three paces between each of you."

This time, Kumul watched them carefully. He had never seen anyone sit on a horse more naturally than a Chett, and the bond between a Chett and his mare seemed almost telepathic to him, but Chetts rode together with less discipline and grace.

"You had trouble keeping the distance close," he told them when they got back.

"It got crowded," one of the Chetts said.

"Get used to it. This time keep the same distance, but move at a trot."

The result was even more disorganized. Kumul made them do it at a fast walk again, and this time the mares and riders managed to reach the arrow tree in something like a dressed line. He then told them to do it at the canter. A mess.

"Now again, but slow to a trot."

Better, and by now the Chetts were getting the idea behind the changing pace and constant distance. Their mounts were getting used to working close to other horses.

"Let's try it at a gallop!" one of the Chetts said excitedly.

"Not yet," Kumul said firmly. "That's enough for the day."

"But we're just getting started!" the same Chett complained.

Kumul could not help grinning at them. He liked their enthusiasm. He knew they would need it in the days and weeks to come.

"I said that was enough for the day. Back here tomorrow, same time."

The Chetts nodded and drifted away.

"Now the saber is an interesting weapon," Ager said, "and useful from the back of a horse. But when you're on foot, there are better weapons."

The group of Chetts gathered before him watched and listened with keen interest. As with Kumul's group, they were from more than one clan. News of the crookback's victory over Katan had spread like a grass fire, and they wanted to learn how he did it. They were also curious about what was inside the sack he was carrying.

"But Chetts do not fight on foot," one of them said.

"Not yet," Ager said under his breath, then out loud: "The lessons you learn from me will be useful if you fight standing, riding, crouching, or crawling." He pointed to the Chett who had spoken. "What's your name?"

"Orlma."

"Come here, Orlma."

The Chett looked nervously at his fellows but did as asked. Ager dropped his sack and pulled out two wooden swords, one shaped like a saber and the other shorter and broader in comparison.

"The short sword," Ager said, and the Chetts heard something like reverence in his voice.

"This is heavier than any saber I've ever used," Orlma said, hefting the dummy weapon.

"And by the time I've finished training all of you, your own sabers will feel as light as a feather. Attack me."

The Chett grinned. "I will not make the same mistake that Katan made, Captain Crookback."

"Glad to hear it. Now attack me."

Orlma moved forward cautiously, his saber held slightly above waist level, its tip raised slightly. He expected his opponent to retreat before his longer reach, but instead Ager waited with what seemed like boredom.

"Get on with it, will you?"

The Chett scowled and raised the saber above his head to slash down, but before he could do anything more he felt the hard tip of Ager's weapon punch him in the chest and he fell back on his rump. He could not believe the one-eyed crookback, who usually moved with evident difficulty and lack of grace, could move so fast.

"Again!" Ager ordered. The Chett scrambled to his feet, held out his saber again, and waited to see if Ager would advance. He did. Seeing his chance, Orlma turned his wrist and swept the saber inward, aiming for the crookback's stomach. Ager retreated half a step, letting the saber whistle past, then lunged, catching his opponent on the chest again.

"I will figure out how you do that," Orlma said, picking himself off the ground for a second time.

"No need," Ager told him. "I'll tell you. Stand as you were before."

The Chett did so. Ager stood within striking distance of him. "Could either of us miss at this distance?" he asked the other Chetts. They all shook their head. "Slowly, start your attack," he told his opponent. Orlma swung his arm back, and Ager simply jabbed forward so the point of the short sword rested over the Chett's heart.

"My enemy has to make two moves with his saber to strike me," Ager told his audience. "I only have to make one. This is the advantage of a stabbing weapon over a slashing weapon."

"But when you beat Katan, you were using a saber," one of the Chetts pointed out.

"That's because I know how to fight on foot, and Katan doesn't. If you only have a saber or cutlass, keep your movements as small as possible. It's not necessary to cut off your enemy's head to kill him. Severing an artery will do the job as well, and almost as quickly. More importantly, it isn't necessary to kill your enemies to win a battle; you can put them out of action and kill them later. Draw your sabers." Ager inspected three of the swords. "Just as I thought. You whet them on the same plane."

"It is the only way to make them properly sharp," Orlma said.

Ager drew his own saber and invited Orlma to feel its edge.

"It is rough."

Ager pulled a short branch from his sack and laid it over two rocks. "Cut it with your saber," he told Orlma.

The Chett swung as high as possible and slashed down. His blade sank deep into the branch. He tugged and pulled at the weapon to free it, then held up the branch to show the others how deep he had cut. "If that was an enemy's body, it would have sliced through his kidneys!" he boasted.

Ager grinned. "How true. Put it back."

Ager now slashed down with his own saber. The blade did not cut nearly as deep, but it came out of the wood without effort and the cut it left behind was wide and jagged. He held up the branch. "If this had been an enemy's body, it would have destroyed more than his kidneys. A wound like this cannot be repaired, and my saber comes out easily."

There was an astonished murmur from his audience.

"I want you to go now and make a wooden saber and a wooden short sword for yourselves. Have them done by tomorrow, and we'll start your training."

After the evening meal Lynan stepped back from the campfire and his circle of friends. He found himself more at peace when alone, something which confused him. He had grown up alone, Kumul's careful guardianship a light and sometimes forbiddingly remote presence, but during their flight from Kendra to the Oceans of Grass he had learned to rely on the steady companionship and protection of Kumul and Ager, Jenrosa and Gudon. He still cared for them all dearly, but increasingly felt the need to set himself apart, to keep some distance between his new life and his old.

The firelight reflected off his hard, pale skin, and he traced a blue vein on one arm with a finger. He felt a pulse and ridiculously felt relief. He knew he was no vampire, but he also knew instinctively that he was no longer entirely human. He wondered how much of his new-found confidence—his changed nature—was due to Silona's blood. He wanted to be a creature of his own making, based on his own experiences and learning, but could not shake the thought that something of Silona's single-mindedness and grim need for isolation had been transferred to him.

He watched his companions, crouching for warmth around the fire. Gudon was smiling, head bowed next to Ager's. The two had become firm friends, and Lynan could see some similarity in their spirits, a combination of cynicism about and acceptance of the way the world was ordered. Next to Ager was Korigan, someone Lynan felt was as torn as he between two natures. Not much older than he, she was already wise in the ways of a monarch. In her was a fierce determination that frightened him a little, but was also something he now recognized in himself. Then there was Jenrosa, who still seemed beautiful to him despite her familiarity. She never snapped at him anymore, nor made fun of him in front of the others. When she looked at him, he saw sadness in her eyes, and guilt at what her actions in saving his life had made him become. He did not know how to tell her that she had done right, and it occurred to him that he did not yet know himself whether in fact she had done right. And beside Jenrosa was Kumul, father-not-father, guardian and bully, adviser and old war horse. There was a tension between them now, and it saddened Lynan.

As Lynan watched, he saw Kumul and Jenrosa hold hands. The contact was brief, but sudden awareness hit him like a blow to the stomach. He stopped breathing.

No. It isn't possible.

The two quickly glanced at each other, a joining as brief and intimate as their holding hands.

Lynan turned from the fire and walked into the night.

"We have some of the new swords you asked to be made," Gudon told Ager. "Only a handful so far."

"Already?" Ager was surprised. The forges had only been working for three days.

"We would have had them yesterday, but the first mold cracked."

"Can I see them?"

"Of course. We must go to the village."

The two made their excuses and left. Ager gathered his poncho around him as the warmth of the fire receded. He looked with envy at Gudon, striding along as if it was a balmy summer afternoon. He did not think the cold was something he would ever get used to. His breath frosted in the night air and he had to hurry to keep up with the Chett. Their feet crunching on brittle grass was the only sound except for the distant lowing of the cattle.

They passed between arrow trees, catching glimpses of other campfires. Ager could not see anyone else, but could somehow feel the weight of the thousands of Chetts that surrounded them.

There must be as many people here as there are in the cities of Sparro or Daavis, he thought, *but they may as well be ghosts.*

As he drew closer to the village, he could hear the sound of the furnace and hammer, of fiery steel hissing as it was poured into molds. Mechanical sounds, and out of place here on the Oceans of Grass. Up ahead he saw the yellow glimmer of molten metal and the angry red of hot coals.

Gudon directed him to a hut before they reached the furnaces. New weapons were stacked neatly against wooden frames. He saw his short swords and eagerly picked up one by its tang.

"When will they be finished?"

"Soon. We are using bone for the hilt, and leather and sinew to finish the grip. What do you think?"

"Hard to tell before the grip's finished, but the weight feels right." Ager took it out of the hut and held it up so he could study it under moonlight. The blade was unpolished, and seemed flat and dull. "They need some work, but I think they'll be fine."

"If we'd had more time, we would have forged them, but to get the numbers you want we had to use molds."

Ager grunted. Still holding the tang, he placed the sword point on a large rock and stepped on the blade. The point skidded across the rock, sending sparks into the air. "It's strong." He whacked the edge of the blade against the rock and heard a satisfying *thwang*. "The blade is not brittle at all. This is good work." He replaced the unfinished sword in the hut.

"Let's get back to the fire. I'm freezing."

Gudon grinned at him. "You will have time to get used to it."

"Is that supposed to make me feel better?"

"I hope not."

They were halfway back when Gudon stopped. He frowned and cocked his head as if listening for something.

"What's wrong?" Ager asked.

"Something is not right."

"What exactly?"

"I don't—"

Before he could finish, three dark shapes rose from the darkness around them. Ager saw moonlight glimmer off steel. Without shout or cry, their attackers were upon them. Ager had time to draw his saber, but it was knocked out of his hand before he could raise it. He threw himself forward against the legs of his closest assailant and they went down together. Ager clawed for his enemy's face, found something soft, and gouged as hard as he could. A woman screamed. He rolled off the body and felt on the ground for his sword. He heard a blade whistling through the air and rolled again, heard it bite into the ground where his head had just been. He lashed out with his foot and kicked the sword away, then scrambled to his feet. A fist whacked into his ear. He shouted in pain, ducked, and charged forward, but his attacker had moved and he stumbled back to the ground. He turned onto his back in time to see a dark silhouette looming above him, a sword raised high. Then the figure jerked and fell, and Ager saw Gudon whirl away to meet the surviving attackers.

Cursing, Ager got to his feet for the second time, retrieved the fallen enemy's sword, and joined Gudon. The pair split apart, forcing the attackers in different directions. The moon swung behind Ager and he gasped in surprised.

"Katan!" he hissed. The Chett tried to retreat, but Ager was furious and redoubled his efforts. Their blades struck sparks into the night. Ager lunged, lunged again, trying to use the point, but Katan was too quick and had learned something from their first bout in front of the two circles. Ager parried a swipe at his neck, crossed his right leg over his left and swung a full circle. He hard Katan's sword swish past his ear. The edge of his saber sank into the Chett's flank and shuddered when it hit the rib cage. Katan moaned, his eyes looked up in surprise, and he fell in a heap.

Ager spun around and saw Gudon wiping his blade on the poncho of the dead woman at his feet.

"It was Katan," Ager said, pointing at the chief's corpse.

"Katan's wife," Gudon said. Together they went to the first enemy Gudon had slain.

"Katan's son?" Ager asked.

Gudon nodded. "Neither father nor son were that good with the saber. The woman was very good. Better than me."

"How did you beat her?"

Gudon grunted. "She was bleeding from one eye."

"Ah." Ager threw down his borrowed saber and found his own. "Who do you think they were after? You for supporting Korigan, or me for humiliating Katan in front of the two circles?"

"Or was Katan working to whittle away some of Korigan and Lynan's support?"

"On his own initiative?"

Gudon shrugged. "No way to tell. Were you hurt?"

"My ear's numb and I hear bells inside my head."

"At least you're not hearing air whistle through a cut throat."

Other Chetts appeared, carrying torches. In a short time they were surrounded by a small crowd.

"We should move on in case others from the Ocean clan make an appearance and decide to take their revenge," Gudon said in a low voice.

They soon left the crowd behind. "If Katan was after us to weaken Lynan's position," Ager said, "and Katan was only one among however many disgruntled chiefs, then they could try and kill Lynan himself."

"Truth."

"He needs a bodyguard."

"Truth."

"And a bodyguard needs a captain. Someone who knows how Chetts think. Someone who will choose only the most loyal warriors."

Gudon considered the suggestion. "Do you have an ideas?"

"I'm sure something will come to you," Ager said, and then: "I don't think you'll have to look far."

11

AREAVA was cold in her bedchamber. There was a fire blazing in the hearth and the morning sun shone through the east window, but still she was cold. Her handmaids busied themselves with her hair and then dressed her. She could not look at them. When her gown was finished, the handmaids put on her rings and her simple gold tiara, and then a wreath of white star flowers, the only ones that bloomed in winter. Finally, they carefully draped the Key of the Scepter—star-shaped with a vertically placed scepter in its center—and the Key of the Sword—square-shaped with two crossed swords pierced by a spear—around her neck, their heavy gold chains a symbol of their burden as well as their power.

Someone knocked on the door and it opened slowly. Harnan Beresard's old face appeared. "Your Majesty?"

"You can come in, Harnan. I am finished dressing."

He took a few steps, then stopped and gawked at her. "Your Majesty! You are . . ." His mouth worked, but he could not make the word come out.

Areava turned to face her secretary. Her gown, layers of white wool with individual threads of gold through it, swished on the wooden floor. Its tight-fitting bodice revealed her slender form to best effect, and the full skirt seemed to flow from her waist. Harnan shook his head in wonder. He thought if winter could be personified, it would look like his queen. Tall and pale, severe, achingly beautiful. All but the eyes, which seemed lost.

"What is wrong?" he asked.

Areava nodded to her handmaids and they quickly scurried from the room. "Am I doing the right thing?" she asked.

Harnan blinked. He had never expected to hear the queen voice that question. "Your Majesty?"

"Marrying Sendarus. Is it the right thing to do?"

Harnan spread his hands helplessly. "All Grenda Lear rejoices. They are happy for you. Overjoyed."

Areava looked disappointed, but nodded. Harnan blushed, knowing he had said the wrong thing but not knowing what would have been the right thing.

"What did you want?"

"To let you know that King Marin has arrived."

"Oh. Good."

"He wanted to know if you wanted to see him right away."

She shook her head. "Let him greet his son first. They have not seen each other for several months. I will have many opportunities after the wedding to talk with the king . . . with my father-in-law." She swallowed.

"As you wish." Harnan bowed and moved to leave, but hesitated. He could not help feeling she should not be left alone.

"Is there something else?" Areava asked tonelessly.

"No, your Majesty." He bowed again and went to the door. It opened before he got there and Olio entered. Harnan breathed a silent sigh of relief.

"Good m–m–morning, sister," Olio said brightly.

"Am I doing the right thing?" she asked him immediately.

Olio threw a glance at Harnan; the secretary raised his eyebrows but said nothing, then left.

"About what?"

"Don't be obtuse," she snapped, then closed her eyes. "I'm sorry."

"Do you love Sendarus?" Olio asked carefully.

"With all my heart."

"Then you are concerned for the kingdom."

Areava nodded. "I am its queen."

"You are also a woman. No kingdom demands its ruler stay celibate." He smiled immediately at his own choice of words, knowing that celibacy was not the problem. "Or indeed, unwed."

"But outside of the Twenty Houses."

"Our m–m–mother wed outside of the Twe—" Olio's mouth snapped shut, and he cursed himself.

"And produced Lynan."

"You are not m–m–marrying a commoner," Olio said. "You are m–m–marrying a p–p–prince."

"And I am marrying an alliance."

"You cannot m–m–make an alliance with a subject p–p–province."

"By marrying Sendarus I raise Aman from its knees. It need no longer genuflect before Kendra."

"M–m–maybe not a bad thing."

Areava looked at him with something like desperation. "Do you mean that?"

"Yes, if Grenda Lear is to b–b–be m–m–more than Kendra."

"I want to believe that, but wonder if I am making excuses for my love for Sendarus."

"The p–p–power of the Twenty Houses m–must be diminished. Introducing new royal b–b–blood will help to do that." Areava did not seem convinced. He went to her and took her hands in his own; they were surprisingly cold to the

touch. "Although I do not think you have your equal anywhere in Theare, I suspect Sendarus comes closest. Your
union will strengthen the kingdom, of that I am sure."

Areava leaned over and kissed her brother's cheek.

He grinned bashfully and stood back, spreading her
arms so he could look at her properly. "You are m–m–
magnificent."

"I feel like ice," she said dimly.

Olio glanced at her with concern, but she would not meet
his gaze. "You will warm up when Sendarus is by your
side," he said, and hoped it was true.

The palace clerk Harnan assigned to guide Marin to his
son waited patiently for the Amanite king at the entrance
to the guests' wing. Marin was still looking over the city
from the vantage point of the palace, his aides and several
of his guards by his side. The clerk could tell from the expression on the king's face that he was amazed at what he
saw. He was not far from the truth, but what was going
through the king's mind at that point was a more complex
rush of emotions.

*Look at the size of this place. I knew it was huge, but had
no idea what that meant.* His own capital, Pila, was counted
among the largest cities on the continent, but Kendra was on
a different scale altogether. *And my son will be wed to its
mistress.*

He shook his head and smiled ruefully to himself. Kendra
had so impressed him that he easily mistook Kendra for the
whole kingdom, and for the first time understood how
Kendra's citizens could fall into arrogance. *Their pride is
not misplaced.*

He heard the clerk clear his throat. He turned from the
view and followed the clerk into the wing, then stopped
again. Stone walls rose on either side of him like the sides
of mountains. The ceiling seemed so far away it could al-

most have been sky. He noticed his companions were
equally awestruck. *We must seem like nothing more than
country bumpkins to this scribbler,* Marin thought. "Well,
maybe we are."

"Your Majesty?" the clerk asked. *He looks like his
brother the chancellor,* he thought, *only shorter and grayer.*
He was not sure he relished the idea of two such large and
stern-looking Amanites being in the palace at the same time.
If only they could shave their beards . . .

Marin shook his head. "Where is my son?"

"The prince's quarters are not far from here; if you would
follow me . . ."

They passed rooms with tapestries that covered whole
walls, and murals and frescos as colorful as a summer
meadow. Clerks and courtiers and the occasional noble
passed them, their heads nodding a silent greeting. They
came across a section of wall made up of nothing but glass,
and for a breathtaking moment the visitors could see Kestrel
Bay and the lands beyond, and great Kendra sweeping out
from the foreground, framed like a living painting.

Eventually the clerk stopped at a hall bisecting the corridor at right angles, turned left, and stopped again before two
large double doors. He knocked and opened them, then
stood aside for Marin and his party to enter.

Sendarus was surrounded by servants helping him dress;
he looked like a fruit tree being attacked by a flock of birds.
The prince's back was to the door. Orkid stood at the other
end of the room, gazing fixedly out a window

"Who is it?" Sendarus asked.

None of the servants recognized Marin, but quickly
guessed who he must have been. They stood away from the
prince so he could turn and see for himself. His face broke
into a wide smile when he saw his father, but Marin put a
finger to his lips, and Sendarus, puzzled, said nothing.
Marin walked over to stand behind Orkid and looked over

his shoulder. In the far distance he could see the highest mountains in Aman, dim and dark against the horizon.

"You miss your home?" Marin said.

Orkid nodded. "More and more." Orkid frowned. The voice had sounded like Sendarus', but was deeper, richer. He looked over his shoulder and saw Marin. His jaw dropped.

"Hello, brother," Marin said and held out his arms.

Orkid gave a cry of joy and embraced his brother, pounding him on the back. "Lord of the Mountain!" he cried. "Lord of the Mountain! I knew you would make it!"

Marin hugged back as fiercely. They separated, but still stood holding each other's arms. "Our ship docked less than an hour ago. A storm slowed us four days out of Kendra."

"I thought we were going to drown," said a voice from Marin's party.

"Amemun!" Sendarus and Orkid cried together.

The old Amanite bowed to them, sweeping back his mane of silver-white hair as he straightened. "In the flesh, no thanks to the gods of the sea."

"Amemun exaggerates," Marin said. "The storm was over in a day."

"Two days," Amemun retorted. "And I was not exaggerating."

The two brothers still held on to each other, almost as if they were afraid if they let go they would not see each other again for another twenty years. Sendarus joined them and put a hand on his father's shoulder.

"Well, you are safely here now."

"Not even the gods of the sea would keep me away from your wedding," Marin told him. Orkid let him go so he could embrace his son. "So what is she like?"

"Areava?"

"Who else, boy! Amemun has been giving me these

glowing reports about her. I don't believe any of them, of course."

"She is glorious, father. She is the most beautiful woman in Theare. She is—"

"Enough!" Marin cried, holding up a hand. "Now you are sounding like Amemun, and one of those is quite enough, thank you."

"This is the respect I get after decades of toiling in your father's service," Amemun said to the prince.

"Amemun and Sendarus speak the truth about Areava," Orkid said. "She is exceptional."

Marin nodded. "You, I believe," he said. "You are so somber and level about everything that if you say this Kendran queen is exceptional, then indeed she must be someone unique."

"You will see for yourself at the wedding this afternoon," Sendarus said.

Marin nodded. "It will be a great culmination."

Sendarus looked at him quizzically. "Culmination?"

"Of the love between you and Areava," Orkid said quickly.

Marin coughed behind his hand. "Yes."

"Where are we lodged?" Amemun asked to change the subject.

"Right here!" Sendarus said brightly. "I'll not need these chambers after the wedding, after all. What do you think of the palace?"

"It is very spacious," Marin said carefully.

"It is overwhelming," Sendarus said. "I am still not used to living here."

"Do you miss the mountains?" Marin asked.

"Yes. And the forests." He fell quiet for a moment and then added: "The Lord of the Mountain seems very far away."

"He is still in Aman, and still hears your prayers," Amemun said kindly.

"He has certainly smiled on me," Sendarus agreed, his eyes looking far away. Marin smiled with sudden pride for his son. He was slender for an Amanite, especially an Amanite from the royal Gravespear family, but he was young and keen and handsome and bright.

The prince shook his head impatiently. "You must want to refresh yourself after your long journey." He turned to one of his servants and asked for hot water and perfume. The servant beetled off. "I have a large tub in the room next to this one. Where are your bags?"

"Not far behind us," Amemun said.

"I will see they are sent in."

Marin laughed. He turned to Orkid. "Are we being dismissed?"

"The groom has much to do before the wedding," Orkid replied diplomatically.

Sendarus kissed his father on the cheek. "I can never dismiss you, father. You are always in my thoughts."

Marin patted Sendarus' cheek. "Not tonight, I think. But thank you." He turned to his entourage. "Well, come on. We must stink like great bears before a rutting."

Another servant led the visitors to the next room, leaving Sendarus and Orkid behind. The two men beamed at each other for a moment.

"I did not realize how much I missed him," Orkid said.

"I know he missed you as well," Sendarus said kindly. "You were never far from his thoughts."

Nor the plan, Orkid thought. *And now at last we both have done what we can for Aman. All else is fate.*

Areava, still cold, sat on her throne wishing she was somewhere else. She felt Olio's hand rest on her shoulder, and she turned her head to look up into his eyes. She saw they were filled with love for her and her heart lightened. She glanced to her right, where Orkid stood, and was surprised to see his face less than stern. *A first for him,* she thought. Did she detect a hint of a smile on the chancellor's lips? If so, she would never tell him; he would be horrified to learn he could be as human as the rest of the court.

Before her the throne room was filled with people, most of them commoners, and as she looked at them, she could not help feeling proud to be their queen. *These are my people. I serve them as they serve me. They understand.* Then she glanced at the representatives of the Twenty Houses, between the throne and the throng, and could see through their forced smiles. Oh, how they wished the people did not understand. *They cannot break our bond, no matter what they do.*

The great doors at the end of the room reverberated with a deep boom; the sound echoed through the high space. Some of the people jumped. There was another boom, a pause, and then a third. Two guards opened the doors, and there stood Dejanus, Constable of the Royal Guard, a great oak spear in one hand. Behind him stood another ten of the Royal Guard and then the groom's party; ten more Royal Guards brought up the rear. With a slow and measured step, Dejanus led the procession into the throne room. All eyes watched Sendarus as he came in; even his enemies admired the figure he cut in his wedding finery of dyed linen pants and a coat made from the tanned hide of a great bear. Except for a fine gold coronet inlaid with small rubies, the prince was bare-headed. As the line approached the throne itself, the guards peeled away to form a line on either side of the causeway. Dejanus stood before the queen, with Sendarus and his followers still behind.

There was a moment of silence then as even more commoners crowded into the room, all craning forward to get their own glimpse of the majesty they demanded from such state occasions. All the players were perfectly still, waiting for the next act.

Areava gently touched Olio's hand and he stepped forward.

"Who comes b–b–before Areava Rosetheme, daughter of Usharna Rosetheme, queen of Kendra and so through it queen of Grenda Lear and all its realms?"

"It is Prince Sendarus, son of Marin, king of Aman," Dejanus replied formally.

"What does P–p–prince Sendarus son of M–m–marin want of Queen Areava?"

"To submit to her will."

Olio turned to his sister. "And in this m–m–matter, what is Queen Areava's will?"

Areava stood, and the audience, seeing her full gown for the first time, let out a collective sigh. She let her gaze sweep over all the people in the room, settling finally on Prince Sendarus. She swallowed but dared not hesitate. "To take him to me, body and soul. For he is the most loyal and loving of all my subjects."

The commoners erupted in an approving roar, cheering and clapping. Sendarus' face broke into a smile of happiness and relief. At that moment Areava felt as if her own personal sun had appeared over her head, and her cold and dread evaporated as if they had never been.

I have done the right thing, she knew with certainty. *I have done my duty according to my conscience and my heart.*

As was the tradition in Kendra, the wedding ceremony itself was a small and private affair, attended only by Areava with Olio for her guardian, Sendarus with Marin for his, Primate Giros Northam and two witnesses—Harnan and Amemun.

Northam beamed at the couple, and looking a little like a

large, overprotective vulture, delivered the marriage rites with stately precision and then joined their hands together. The prince kissed the queen's palm, and with that became her husband, her consort, and her first subject above all others in the kingdom. For a long while the couple stared into each other's eyes, the others holding back with a mixture of pride and embarrassment, as if they were overstaying their welcome.

Primate Northam coughed politely into his hands. "Your Majesty, your Highness, your people are waiting. They want a celebration."

Areava nodded, still locked in Sendarus' gaze. "Yes, of course. Lead the way."

Northam went to the door, followed by Harnan and Amemun, then Olio and Marin. Areava and Sendarus stayed where they were. Olio returned to the couple, gently touched his sister's arm, and whispered to them: "If we return to the throne room without you two, your p–p–people will lynch us."

Dejanus stepped into the throne room, aware that all eyes were on him, if only for that moment. His huge chest swelled with arrogant pride.

"Her Majesty, Areava, queen of Grenda Lear, and his Highness, Sendarus, the royal consort," he announced.

Applause filled the chamber as he moved aside to let the wedding party return. There were cheers for Northam, the two guardians, two witnesses, then wild cries of joy as the newly married couple made their first public appearance as queen and consort. Dejanus sensed everyone's gaze settling on Areava, who looked like a goddess in her gown and with her crown of white flowers, and could not help feeling a little jealous. His chest deflated a little.

The constable watched their procession along the causeway with ironic amusement, knowing the last person in his office to perform as herald had been Kumul, and the occasion the wedding between Usharna and her beloved General, Elynd Chisal. At that time Dejanus had been fighting as a mercenary for the slavers, something unknown to any but Orkid Gravespear. And now here he was, respectable and honored. And powerful.

He looked around the crowd with a great deal of smugness. He noted the city mayor, Shant Tenor, and knew as constable he wielded more power. He saw Xella Povis, head of the merchant guild, and knew he was more powerful than she. He saw the heads of other guilds and dismissed them in his mind. He saw the clerics and magickers, and knew he held more power in his hands than any of them. He saw the chancellor and hurried on. Orkid was easily his match, but he was only one of a very few in the court. The queen, of course. Olio, perhaps, although he was hearing things about him that promised a way around him—or through him if need be. And Sendarus? He was a likable fellow, but weak, Dejanus suspected. The new consort would be no threat. And then the nobles of the Twenty Houses, the traditional source of power in the kingdom. He despised them as much as Areava and Orkid did; if anything, it was this that welded him and Orkid to each other, together with the terrible secret of their crime against Berayma.

As constable of the Royal Guard, he might be able to do something about those inbred pigs. They were parasites, and not worth the clothes they wore so ostentatiously. Dejanus smiled to himself. He needed a new challenge. And once the Twenty Houses had been tamed, there was no need for him to maintain an alliance with Orkid.

Duke Holo Amptra felt like a hollow man. He had learned to tolerate Usharna when she was queen. At first they had ensured she married within the Twenty Houses, but his fool brother—her second husband—had thrown away any control the nobles had over Usharna by siding with her enemies during the Slaver War. Usharna had married the General—the slavers' greatest enemy—and those who thought like Holo believed it was the beginning of the end. But then a glimmer of hope. Berayma, her first-born and successor, had come to them voluntarily, had sought alliance and friendship among his father's family and clan, and the Twenty Houses believed that Usharna would prove to be the exception, the only black mark, in the long line of rulers controlled by the nobility.

And then tragedy again. Usharna died, and soon after Berayma was murdered by the worm in the court, the half-commoner Prince Lynan, offspring of slaves. Now the kingdom was ruled by Holo's niece, a woman who hated the Twenty Houses even more than her mother had. And on this day she might once and for all have broken the power of the Kendran nobility by marrying outside of Kendra itself.

He was an old man, and knew the misery of this world would not torment him for much longer, but he had wanted so much to leave the kingdom strong and united for his son Galen. He snorted. Galen himself did not seem to appreciate how much the kingdom had changed since the old days. It was hard to blame him for that, though, since he was born under Usharna, and would likely spend the rest of his life under the reign of another woman, his cousin Areava.

Holo watched Galen talking among the nobles of his own generation. They were all young, warrior-trained, and haughty. They only had thoughts of the coming war with Haxus, anxiously awaiting spring when they might prove themselves on the battlefield. *Don't be too hard on them,* he told himself. *You were no different at their age.*

Galen saw his father and joined him.

"You are so somber, father."

"This is a somber day."

"Not so somber, perhaps, as you feared. At least Areava has married another noble."

"An Amanite."

"A *noble* Amanite. A good man, too."

"I have no doubt," Holo said gruffly. "But I should not complain. This is your time now, not mine. In spring you will win your battle honors and return to Kendra in glory. I do not blame you for thinking of the future instead of the present."

"We will return from battle with more than honor. We will have gained more power as well."

"Eh?"

"I told you before that the time would come when Areava would learn to rely on us once more. The coming campaign gives us the perfect opportunity to find favor with our ruler. Who knows, we may even be able to win over her chancellor."

Holo grimaced. "Nothing will ever convince Orkid Gravespear to view the Twenty Houses with anything but spite."

"We may work on him through Sendarus. Win over the prince consort, and we may in time win over both the queen and the chancellor. But first we must prove our loyalty."

Holo looked offended. "No one has ever doubted our loyalty to Kendra!"

"True, but many have doubted our loyalty to Usharna and her family. We must rectify that. What is a kingdom without a throne? And what is a throne without a monarch?" He smiled easily at his father. "And what is a monarch without nobles?"

Father Powl had left his position of honor among the invited guests soon after Areava and Sendarus' entrance. He strolled among the common people who had made it to the throne room, listening to their excited babbling. They were so proud of their queen, and more than one was already making comparison between Areava and her mother.

The priest could not help feeling a sense of pride at the queen's popularity. He had been her confessor for a long time and liked to think he had helped her mature into adulthood. Their relationship had been a formal one, but for all that he had learned intimate details about her life, and had a good idea about how her mind worked. He knew she was good at heart, strict with herself and others, disciplined, short-tempered, with few vices. True, her capacity for hatred had been unknown to him until Lynan had killed Berayma, and he was surprised how much her prejudice against her brother had fed that hatred. But he was certain that in her core she was a good woman of noble purpose.

He watched farmers and tanners, cooks and cleaners, carpenters and clothmakers all bustling among one another to get a glimpse of their beautiful monarch and her handsome consort. They liked the idea of her marrying outside of the Twenty Houses, just as they had been overjoyed when Usharna had married a commoner like them. It gave them the feeling that they, too, shared in some of the queen's power, had some stake in the kingdom.

Father Powl was not so naive to think Areava did not realize the political advantage of courting the commoners, but he knew she also had a deep affection for and pride in them. Theirs was a happy union that not only predated her marriage to Sendarus but one that may ultimately prove more important for her reign.

He stopped his wandering, lost for a moment in his reflections. Power could came from the most unlikely source, but only those with the wisdom and perspicacity to seize it would profit by it. He studied his hands and wished he had endured a harder youth. There was something wrong in such soft palms, such uncallused fingers, holding the influence he knew he now possessed. He should have been raised in a logging camp or in a fishing village or on a farm; perhaps he would have been if his unknown parents had not left him as a swaddling babe at the door of a chapel of the Righteous God. But all his life he had been cloistered from such labor, protected from the toil and danger the common people endured to support the state. He was not feeling guilt, it was deeper than that. He felt undeserving.

Favored by circumstance, once patroned by the Primate himself, made Areava's confessor, and now with the ear of the chancellor and holder of secrets that placed him near the middle of an intricate political web, he felt utterly undeserving.

Olio refused the wine a servant offered him.

That's twice this afternoon. I must be doing all right. His hands shook a little, and he would have done almost anything for a drink, but seeing his sister's happiness made it easier for him.

Don't make the effort for yourself. Make it for her.

People said things to him, and he said things in return, but only moments afterward he could not remember what words had been spoken. He hoped he had not promised half the kingdom to some supplicant from Lurisia or Hume. It seemed to him he was drifting through the throne room, walking on air. He wondered if the light-headedness was caused by his deprivation of alcohol or some side effect of the Key of Healing. He fingered the amulet. It rested cold against his skin. Cold and heavy.

At one point the burly King Marin put his arm around him and gave him a bear hug. "If your sister is now my daughter-in-law, does that make you my son-in-law?"

"As m–m–much as the idea appeals to me," Olio replied gently, "I don't think it works quite like that."

"Ah, I think you're right. Pity. You could have called me 'father.' " Marin laughed suddenly, and Olio pretended to join him. Marin went off, looking for someone else to grin at.

I wonder if he's had too much to drink? Olio wondered. He suspected Marin never got drunk, and he felt a twinge of envy.

He saw Areava and Sendarus walking from group to group, thanking them for their wishes. They leaned against each other the whole time, holding hands, giving each other a kiss now and then, their eyes as bright as lamps. A feeling of relief washed through him.

Areava has him now to draw on for strength. My failures are diminished.

The thought made him feel edgy, as if he was giving in too easily to his own demons. Without thinking, he glanced around for the rest of his family; the realization that he and Areava were all that were left sent a ripple of nausea through his stomach.

No, there is still Lynan. Somewhere.

The nausea did not go away.

Afterward, Marin invited Orkid to his rooms. There, with the servants sent away, the two brothers and Amemun sat in deep comfortable chairs with some bottles of fine Storian wine on a small table between them. As soon as they had sat, Orkid and Amemun started talking about the new political situation now that Sendarus was married to the ruler of Grenda Lear. Marin sat silent, pretending to listen, content to gaze quietly at the face of his only brother, a man he had not seen for many, many years. When Orkid asked the king a question without receiving a reply, Amemun told Marin to stop being so maudlin.

"You haven't lost Sendarus, your Majesty. And soon, if the union is blessed, you will have grandchildren to worry about."

"I am not feeling maudlin, old friend," Marin said seriously. He looked around the room. "I do not like this place."

Orkid glanced up in surprise. "I must be used to it," he said.

"It is not the palace, brother. It is who lives in and around it. All day I have been feeling the stares of a hundred Kendrans bore into my back. I have an itch I cannot reach right between my shoulder blades." He leaned forward suddenly and grasped one of Orkid's hands. "My son will be safe here?"

Orkid sighed deeply. "As safe as anywhere except Pila itself. I will protect him, Marin, although I suspect Areava herself will make sure my protection is unnecessary."

Marin rested back in his seat and nodded glumly. "She is a fine-looking woman, and strong," he admitted. "But I don't like the nobles, and some of the officials—like that mayor whatsisname—"

"Shant Tenor."

"—Mayor Shant Tenor and his ilk make me want to take to them with my ax."

"Would it help if I told you that Areava feels the same way?"

Marin waved his hand. "I know all that. I read your reports myself, Orkid, whatever you may think."

"I never doubted it."

"This place is askew," Marin said urgently, his body stiffening. "There is something wrong about it, something deep."

"It is an ancient place of intrigues and plots," Orkid said. Berayma's dead face flickered in his memory and he could not help wincing. "Nothing here is ever quite what it seems."

"They must come to Pila," Marin said.

"Who?"

"Sendarus and his bride, of course."

"Need I remind you that *this* is the capital of the kingdom, not Pila."

"I mean for a visit. And soon. I want to see how Areava behaves outside of her own den, and I would like to see my son away from this court, if only for a short while."

"I'm sure that can be arranged," Orkid said. "Maybe next summer? I could suggest it as part of a tour of all the kingdoms. It would be good for morale if the war with Haxus starts in the spring."

"That's an idea."

"Now relax," Orkid told him. "The event we have been planning for so many years has at last come to pass. Aman will no longer be considered a small backward province of Grenda Lear. The next ruler in Kendra will share our blood."

"It is you who did all the work. For that I am grateful beyond words."

Orkid bowed his head.

"What next?"

"We get the Key of Union off Lynan and make sure it is given to Sendarus," Orkid said.

"Better he get the Key of the Sword," Marin replied.

Orkid looked up in surprise. "What?"

"We convince Areava to hand Sendarus the Key of the Sword. If the marriage sees him accepted by the majority of Kendrans, then being bearer of that Key will make him acceptable to all. Even the Twenty Houses would not move openly against him."

"And how do we manage that?"

"By getting him command of the army to move north in spring."

"I thought Prince Olio had that command," Amemun said.

Marin regarded his old tutor for a moment. Amemun had tutored two generations of Gravespears, including himself, teaching them almost everything they knew about Aman and the larger world outside. He felt a surge of affection for the man and his mane of white hair.

"Can Olio be persuaded to surrender it?" Marin asked Orkid.

"It is Areava we have to persuade," Orkid said.

"Well, I'm sure you can handle that," Marin said smugly.

"Be careful, brother. She is her own woman, just as her mother Usharna was."

"I'll keep it in mind. Nonetheless, I have seen how she looks to you, and now that your nephew is her husband, I think she will be even more amenable."

"You may be right. Time will show us one way or the other."

"And time," Marin said, "is something we have plenty of."

Wedding parties were going on throughout the city. From her window, Areava could see bonfires in almost every square. Lanterns were hauled up the masts of every ship in the harbor. Snatches of song drifted up to the palace in the evening breeze.

"We have made them happy," Areava said.

Sendarus stood behind her, his arms around her waist and his chin resting on her shoulder. "I am glad some of our own joy has spilled out." He kissed her neck, and raised one hand to trace a finger along her jaw.

"In one year I must learn to be queen and wife. It is more than I ever expected."

He kissed her ear and then her temple. He felt her tense. "Is something wrong?"

She giggled nervously. "I am afraid."

"Of tonight?"

She nodded, felt like a little girl. "It's silly, isn't it? It's not as if we haven't . . ." Her voice trailed off.

"We have never made love as husband and wife before.

That is different. We are more than lovers now." He stood back and turned her around, then kissed her on the lips. "We are one life; we have one future."

She knew the truth of the words as she heard them, and kissed him back, and even as she felt her breath quicken and her skin flush with blood, the Keys over her heart seemed to come alive with a warmth all their own.

12

SNOW was falling lightly, but the ground was warm enough to melt it right away. The road had become a long trail of slush. Riders picked their way carefully, but still horses and pack mules slithered and sometimes fell. Jes Prado sighed heavily as another of his mounts had to be put down because of a broken leg and its rider sent to the back of the column with whatever gear he could carry.

Freyma shook his head. "That's the third today."

Prado said nothing.

"It's a bad time to be traveling. Even waiting for the weather to turn colder would be better."

"We don't have the time," Prado said curtly. "We have to be in north Hume before the end of winter."

Freyma used the point of his dagger to pick some of his lunch out from between his teeth. He knew they would lose more horses, and maybe even a few riders to broken necks if Prado did not change his mind. Not that the losses meant much in a company this size. He shook his head in wonder at what Prado had managed to do. No single mercenary captain—*general*, Freyma reminded himself—had ever commanded such a large force. He had over two thousand riders on his rolls, and nearly another five hundred foot, mostly

Arran archers: the best in Theare. The column stretched five leagues from scout to rear, and took a good three hours to pass a single point, and that was on a good road. In this muck it would take five hours or more.

No, it was not the effect on numbers he was worried about, but the effect on morale. Freyma knew from experience in the Slaver War how poor morale could lose a battle even before it had begun.

But Prado was determined, and no one questioned Prado, not Freyma, not even Sal Solway, who had once been a mercenary commander in her own right.

He glanced at Prado, wondering what was going through his mind and what was driving him so hard. There was some demon in there. A shout brought his attention back to the column. A mule was slipping off the road, and its handlers could do nothing to stop it.

"Get the bloody packs off!" Freyma yelled at them, then swore under his breath. He spurred his horse in the vain hope he could get there before it was too late, leaving Prado alone with his own thoughts.

But Prado did not notice. He did not see the struggling riders pass in front of him, even those that offered greetings, and he did not see the mule fall sideways, pinning one of its handlers underneath. He was thinking about Rendle, and wondering what the bastard was doing right now tucked away in his Haxus refuge. His lips were curved in a kind of smile as he thought how surprised Rendle would be when he saw Prado and his mercenaries riding down on his own pitiful company. It was a thought that kept Prado warm even on the coldest nights.

Prado would have been disappointed to learn that Rendle had not paid him a single thought in months, not since the night Prado had escaped his clutches. He had been far too busy with his own plans, and they had nothing to do with revenge.

"Well, my mercenary friend, what do you think?"

Rendle looked up from the map he was cradling in his lap. The man in front of him looked old before his time and overtired, but Rendle noticed the way the man held himself and the look of ruthlessness in his eye and was not fooled. "Your Majesty?"

King Salokan of the kingdom of Haxus—thin, ascetic, and proud—looked vaguely irritated. "What do you think?" He swept his arm out to encompass the military camp that lay before them.

Rendle grunted. "Good. There are four thousand, as you promised?"

"Of course, all mounted."

"And I have their command?"

Salokan pursed his lips. "Well . . ."

"That was one of the conditions."

"I know! I know!" the king snapped, his irritation with the steely little man before him genuine now. "But these are proud men, Captain Rendle. They are not used to serving under a . . . under a . . ."

"Soldier for hire," Rendle finished for him, his voice unsympathetic.

Salokan shrugged. "There you have it! It was hard to convince my officers—"

"Who is the brigade commander?" Rendle interrupted.

"What?"

"Who is their brigade commander? I assume he voiced the greatest opposition to my taking over his troopers."

"General Thewor. A loyal soldier. Many, many years of service—"

"Did he fight in the Slaver War?"

Salokan frowned in thought. "Yes, yes I think so."

"Then he probably served under one of your mercenary commanders back then. Maybe even me."

"Possibly."

"Then, your Majesty, I suggest you remind him of that," he said in a tone that let Salokan know he was not prepared to suffer Thewor gladly. "If he served under me once, he may have the honor of serving under me a second time."

"I don't know that Thewor will accept the logic."

Rendle breathed heavily and threw the map away. The king jumped a little, and his personal guard stared threateningly, but Rendle sized up the former and ignored the latter. Salokan was a butcher. He had a cunning mind, an acute sense of survival, and—surprisingly to the mercenary— huge reserves of patriotism; the last was something Rendle could never understand.

Salokan had never forgiven Grenda Lear for defeating his father in the Slaver War all those years ago and was determined somehow, someway, to pay them back for that humiliation. Rendle knew he was one of Salokan's keys for that revenge.

"I will not lead a force that is not completely behind me into enemy territory."

"You will do what you are ordered to do," Salokan said coldly.

"No, your Majesty. If you want Lynan, only I can get him."

"I will kill you," the king said, his tone suddenly mild. "One of your under-officers will lead your company into the Oceans of Grass under the command of my general."

"If you really believed that, your Majesty, you would have killed me months ago."

Salokan tried to feign offense, but could only snigger instead. "We read each other too well. That's dangerous."

"For whom?"

"For you, of course. I'm king."

Salokan said the words without arrogance, and Rendle knew it was true.

"I'll be gone in a few short weeks. You won't have to worry about me then."

"But you'll be back. At least, I hope you'll be back, with Prince Lynan as your prisoner. That is what all this is about, after all."

Rendle shook his head. "No, your Majesty. This is all about your invasion of Grenda Lear. You will invade whether or not you have Lynan. The kingdom is confused and in more turmoil than it has seen for over a quarter century. Lynan's presence in your army gives the invasion greater legitimacy, but that is only a political thing. You win or lose on your army."

"And a portion of that is riding with you into the Oceans of Grass; which brings us back to our original point of contention."

"Indeed. You want my mission to be a success. I can't have some civilized dignitary in charge of it. I know the Oceans of Grass, I know the Chetts. Your General Thewor wouldn't know which way was up once he was on the plains, and wouldn't recognize a Chett if one came up and bit off his prick."

"I won't argue the point."

"But you will argue with your general?"

"I suppose I must." Salokan looked away. It was a small defeat, and stung his pride mostly, but he resented it more than he should have; he knew that, and kept his temper. His army was strong and ready but lacked experienced commanders; he could not do without Rendle. Not yet, at least. After he had beaten Grenda Lear and won back Hume—and who knows? maybe even conquered Chandra?—Rendle could be dealt with. Or promoted. Salokan had found that a good way to bind men to him, and some women. As long as they weren't promoted too far; no point in giving them ideas above their station, and certainly not above Salokan's station.

The king stood to leave. Rendle copied him. "Would you like to come with me to visit the general?"

Rendle smiled tightly. "Oh, I'm sure you can handle it."

Salokan nodded. "Undoubtedly. Still, I thought you would have liked to see Thewor's face when I tell him the news."

Rendle shook his head. "I bear him no spite."

Yet, Salokan thought. "As you say. We will meet again tomorrow."

Rendle wanted to ask why, but thought he had pushed his luck with the king enough for one day. "I look forward to it."

"There is the border post," Prado said, pointing to the thin red pole by the side of the road. "We are marching into Hume. Another three weeks and we will be on the border, and the company can rest until the thaw starts."

Freyma and Sal nodded, less cheered by the fact that they had reached Hume at last than they were depressed by the thought of another three weeks of marching in these conditions. The last two days had seen heavy snowfalls, and the temperature had been low enough to keep the snow on the ground. With over two thousand men and horses tramping over it, the road was still slush, but the margins were more stable. Still, the cold at night was terrible, and it was hard getting the company moving again in the morning.

After this, campaigning will be easy for them, Freyma thought, but at the moment it gave him little consolation.

He looked up into the sky and grimaced at the darkening clouds. It would snow tonight. If it fell after the tents were put up, it would keep them a little warmer, but not by much. Speaking of which, they would have to make camp soon. Winter days were so short, and a good portion of each day was spent getting the company in order for the march.

He looked down the trail, saw that another hour would see the last of the mercenaries pass out of Chandra. Prado would probably call the camp then. His gaze stopped suddenly on the tall thin man sitting on a black stallion on the side of the road not one hundred paces from the border post.

Barys Malayka. I'll be glad to see the last of that bastard. He's been following us too close for my comfort, he and his sword. Freyma smiled to himself then. *His sword Deadheart. I'd like to give him a dead heart.*

For his part, Malayka was as happy to see Prado and his mercenaries leave Chandra. He could ride back to Sparro now and let King Tomar know the plague had left his lands. He was disappointed to see so many of Arran's archers following Prado, but guessed most were out for adventure and were too young to remember what Prado and his ilk had done to the countryside during the Slaver War; then again, the Arran Valley had been virtually untouched. Prado and other mercenary captains had settled there after the war and brought it some prosperity. Thanks to Usharna's amnesty, King Tomar could not go after them as he had wished.

But maybe now that war was coming again, an opportunity would present itself. Malayka liked the thought of that. He still wanted to give Tomar the head of Prado; the king would put it on a pike and stick the pike in the middle of a midden. Or maybe preserve it and keep it as a warning to all other mercenaries.

He waited until the last of the company had passed over the border, then turned his horse back to the road and started the long journey back to the Chandran capital. It would be several days' ride thanks to Prado's buffoons mucking up the way, and in the spring Tomar would have to pay to have it pounded and flattened again. Worth it, though, to remove any trace of Prado.

Malayka glanced over his shoulder, but could see nothing

in the growing dark. The company had disappeared as if it had never been, and in that moment felt in his bones that none who marched with Prado would ever return to Chandra alive. He repressed a shudder. Times were grim enough without entertaining flimsy premonitions, and why should he care anyway? Good riddance. Good riddance to all of them.

13

THE camps around the High Sooq almost seemed deserted. Some of the fires had old men and women and the youngest children around them, but everyone else was training or forging or herding. Lynan hunched down to the ground and cleared away the snow with his hands. Underneath, the grass was brittle and yellow, the ground hard with frozen water. According to Gudon, once the earth became cold, winter was at its peak. From now on it would get warmer.

He stood up and shrugged off his new poncho—a long, fur-lined garment given him by Korigan—because it was starting to make him sweat. He hardly felt the cold at all anymore, something he put down to that part of him that was Chett rather than to his new nature. He had been so busy since reaching the High Sooq he had not had much time to consider the changes wrought in him by Silona's blood, and was relieved for it. Silona was not someone he wanted to consider in any way or form.

The air was filled with the smell of burning cow dung, an unexpectedly sweet aroma. In the middle distance cattle clumped together for warmth. He could hear, but not see, the training: the clash of wooden swords, the trot, canter, and gallop of the cavalry, the barked orders.

Lynan recognized Kumul's voice and kept down the anger and jealousy that rose in him like bile. He hated himself for feeling this way. He had no claim on Jenrosa, had even stopped thinking about her in that way, but the thought of Kumul together with her made him feel spurned. He thought he could have handled it had it been Ager or Gudon or Korigan . . . in fact, anyone who hadn't been so important in Lynan's life as Kumul.

What did she see in the old fool, anyway?

He cursed himself loudly. Kumul deserved better from him. In fact, Kumul had *always* deserved better from him.

He closed his mind to it, delved deeper to try and make sense of everything that was happening. There were some days when he wished everything would just get on, that winter would finish, that he could ride east and force the issue with Areava and have it decided one way or the other. Then there were other days when he wanted nothing more than to slow everything to a crawl so he had time to understand fully what was happening, especially now that he was making decisions not just for himself but for thousands—tens of thousands!—of other people. He could not even conceive what it must have been like for his mother, who had ruled over millions. Was it something she became inured to?

Lynan could see as far as the end of winter. He would have an army then. But what to do with it? East into Hume? He nodded to himself. He had to secure the Algonka Pass, the only easy way for an army to cross from Grenda Lear's eastern provinces into the Oceans of Grass. South was desert, occupied by the wilder and even more warlike Southern Chetts, a people about whom he knew nothing, and about whom even the Northern Chetts knew little. If an army trying that route did not die from thirst, they would be butchered in its sleep. That left the north. The plains were protected from Haxus by a spur of the Ufero mountain range that divided the Chetts from the east, and was pierced by a few narrow and dangerous passes that no army could successfully navigate; at least, that's what Gudon assured him. Assuming that to be true, the Algonka Pass was the key to everything.

And once the pass was in his hands? What next? He shook his head in frustration. He did not know. It would be hard to make a decision about that without more intelligence on what Areava was doing. And there was only one way he could be sure to get that intelligence.

It took him twenty minutes to walk to Ager's training area, filled with a hundred warriors practicing hard with wooden short swords. Many of them were just beginning and insisted on using the weapon in great slashing arcs; they were paying for it with bruised ribs as their more experienced opponents jabbed at their chests and bellies. Ager was with a small group of Chetts that included Gudon. He was surprised to see that the right hand of a number of the training Chetts were dyed a bright red. Ager was holding the wrists of one of the warriors so her movements had to copy his own as he fenced with Gudon.

"You see that?" Ager told the warrior. "Keep your movements short, concise. Never move just for something to do. Don't lose your balance on the attack. The only time you lengthen your pace is when you thrust!" With the last word he lunged forward suddenly, his whole body angling over his right knee, his right arm extended; the warrior almost toppled over, but managed to stay on her feet, her body stretched to its limits. Gudon backed up, barely deflecting the blow. Ager stood and freed the warrior. "You see? You don't lunge as far as you might with a long sword, but you can still get the reach of someone flashing a saber around."

She limped away, smiling gratefully. She looked up and saw Lynan, bowed deeply, then hurried on.

"What was that about?" Lynan asked Ager.

"Fencing lesson—"

"Not that. The bowing."

Ager glanced at Gudon, who seemed pleased with himself. "You *are* a prince of the realm," Ager said offhandedly.

"I was one of those yesterday, too, and no one bowed to me like that then."

"Ah, but yesterday no one belonged to the Red Hands," Gudon said.

"The red what?"

"Like the Red Shields," Ager explained. "Except with them it's their hands. Shields would have been difficult since the Chetts don't use them as a rule."

"Red Shields? Red Hands? What are you getting at, Ager?"

"Your bodyguard, your Majesty," Gudon said.

"My bodyguard?" Lynan was astounded. "I don't need a bodyguard. I need an *army*."

"You'll get both," Ager told him. "The Red Hands are sworn to protect you, no matter what comes. They will die for you. You should be proud."

Lynan closed his eyes. *I don't want anyone else to die for me.* He sighed. *Then throw away the army,* he told himself. *Leave the Chetts; flee the continent altogether.*

He knew he would do none of those things.

He opened his eyes and nodded wearily. "How long have you two been planning this?"

"Since three nights ago," Ager said cheerily.

"Why?"

Ager and Gudon exchanged one of those glances again.

"Something happened three nights ago, didn't it?" Lynan asked.

"Yes, your Majesty, but not directly against you."

"Ah, I see. It was directed against you, or Gudon."

"Truth, little master," Gudon said, "perhaps both of us at

the same time, or maybe against you through us. We don't know."

"Was anyone hurt?"

"Yes," Ager said bluntly.

"When do my bodyguards start . . . well . . . bodyguarding."

Gudon looked over his shoulder and nodded to someone. Lynan heard two sets of footsteps behind him. He turned and saw two large Chetts, one female, one male, each with bright red right hands. They bowed deeply to him, then waited. Their faces were impassive. He saw from the designs on their ponchos that the man belonged to the White Wolf clan, and the woman to the Owl clan.

"They start now, your Majesty."

"And who is their captain?"

Gudon bowed low this time. "If the little master will accept me."

Lynan felt a surge of affection for his two friends, and pride. "But their captain cannot stay with them."

Gudon looked at him questioningly.

"I have a mission for you." He turned to Ager. "Go back to your training, old crookback. I need to discuss matters with my new captain of the royal bodyguard."

"The Red Hands, your Majesty," Ager corrected him.

Lynan smiled slightly. "Indeed. My Red Hands."

Ager finished the training soon after Lynan and Gudon left; he had more training scheduled for the afternoon and needed to rest. A group of four Chetts were waiting for him behind his tent. He recognized the symbol of the Ocean clan on their ponchos. Three of them were middle-aged, the fourth a young woman. All were armed.

Wonderful. Where's Gudon when I need him?

He looked around for other support, but there was no one else in sight. He glanced down at his wooden sword; his own saber was in his tent. With his crooked back he could never run away from them. He breathed deeply and walked straight up to them.

"I'm tired," he told them gruffly. "Get out of my way, please."

The young woman stepped forward; a long scar ran down her cheek. "This won't take long, Ager Crookback."

Ager nodded. "Who's first, then? Or is it all of you at the same time?" He hefted the wooden sword in his hand. Its weight gave him some comfort. If he connected with a head or two before he was skewered, he might survive the confrontation.

The woman looked at him strangely. "We don't understand."

"You're going to kill me. Let's not twaddle around."

"Kill you? Why?"

"For slaying your chief, his wife, and his son. Pretty good reasons in clan politics, I daresay."

The woman's expression changed as she understood. She laughed suddenly, the sound warm and lively. She was pretty, and the scar added something mysterious to her beauty rather than detracting from it. Ager did not want to kill her. "We have come to pay you allegiance."

"It is to Korigan you should be paying your allegiance."

"You do not understand. She is our queen. You are our chief."

Ager blinked at them. "I am not a Chett."

"You defeated our chief in combat. His wife and child were killed with him. There is no one left of his immediate family. Katan killed his own brother when he was only fourteen to make sure he had no rivals within the clan. You are our chief now."

"I see," he said, not really seeing at all. The Chetts stared at him impassively. "Is there some kind of ceremony?" he asked and, uninvited, the thought of ritual scarring or circumcision popped into his head.

The woman shook her head. "You became our chief the moment you killed Katan. No one has risen to challenge you."

"What if I don't want to be a chief?"

"There is nothing you can do about it," the woman said flatly.

"I see," he repeated. For a moment longer the five of them stood in front of his tent. Ager shuffled his weight to another foot. "I have to rest now," he said.

"Of course," the woman said, and the group started walking away.

Ager suddenly realized he had no idea what was expected of him in his new position. "Wait," Ager said. The group stopped and looked back at him. "What's your name?" he asked the young woman.

"Morfast," she said.

"I will come and see you tonight," he said to the group.

Morfast nodded, and the group left.

For a while longer Ager stood there, bewildered, then shook his head and entered his tent.

Jenrosa's head was resting against Kumul's chest. She could hear his heartbeat, and in some way being that close to him was more intimate than their lovemaking. His right hand coiled and uncoiled her hair, his left hand stroked her arm. It seemed strange to her they could share this moment of peace and solitude in the middle of the High Sooq, their tent surrounded by the tents of thousands of others.

"I think the training went well today," Kumul said after a while. "I have never seen a people so accustomed to being on horseback, but I thought discipline would be a problem. I was wrong."

Jenrosa said nothing. She did not want to talk about the preparations for war.

"Have you found someone to take on your magic training?" he asked.

"No. There is no Truespeaker among the clans right now."

"But the White Wolf clan has magickers."

"I haven't talked to Korigan about it." She did not mention that after their last encounter she did not want to talk to Korigan at all.

For a moment they fell silent again, then Kumul asked: "Have you talked with Lynan recently?"

"No. You?"

"No. But I should. He must know that we . . . that you and I . . ."

"Are lovers," she finished for him. Why did he hesitate? "Do you think that's wise?"

"What do you mean?"

"How will he take it?"

"He is our prince. He has a right to know."

"He has no such right," Jenrosa said firmly. "I don't remember lovers reporting to the queen in Kendra. Why should we do as much for Lynan?"

"It isn't the same."

"Because he was interested in me?"

"No." Kumul sat up.

Jenrosa disentangled herself from his arms and sighed deeply. Their peace and solitude was gone. Lynan might as well have been standing in front of them.

"Because *I* owe it to him," Kumul went on. "I did not understand how much he had grown up since his exile, and it caused a breach between us. I tried to keep information from him. That was wrong." He rubbed his temples with the fingers of one hand. He went on in a quieter voice. "He has changed too much. Is still changing. He needs our support more than ever, or who knows what may become of him."

"Our love for each other is not a matter of state. It is our business."

"He is not just our prince," Kumul said gently, and put his arm around her.

"No. He is your son." *And I am partly responsible for turning him into what he now is. Lynan the White Wolf. Silona's Lynan.* She could not stop a shudder from passing through her. She half expected Kumul to edge away, but instead he pulled her even closer.

"Yes. Ever since his father died, he has been my son."

A cold finger seemed to trace its way along her spine. The words had sounded more like a premonition than a confession, and she could not help the feeling of dread that settled in the back of her mind. She closed her eyes and tried to pretend that nothing was different.

Korigan could not sleep. The future loomed before her like a dark wall; she stood on the brink of great victory or great disaster, and she could not tell which. The fact that it was a future of her own making made her situation ironic but did not change it. Ever since her father had died she had struggled to secure her throne, and when Gudon's message had reached her from the Strangers' Sooq all those months ago she had known immediately she had a way to do it. Gudon saving Lynan's life and bringing him west with him had been a gift from the gods, and she had used the gift to best effect. But the cost . . .

She shook her head. There were no choices anymore. She had put her people behind Lynan, and now they must go where Lynan led them. It was a further irony that she secured her own throne by so demonstrably placing it under the will of an outlaw prince. If Lynan lost, Korigan knew her people might suffer terrible retribution at the hands of

Areava, and yet if Lynan won the crown of Grenda Lear, his control over the Chetts risked making her own authority obsolete.

Unless she could make events follow a third path, and therein lay the greatest risk of all. It was not a matter of choice anymore; it was a matter of riding over the brink and hoping you were not falling into an abyss.

She felt incredibly older than her twenty-two years.

A lonely guard huddled against the cold directed Ager to Morfast's tent. He called to her, and the flap was quickly unlaced. He ducked and entered.

"Thank you for seeing me," he said. "I need to talk to you about . . ."

As his eyes adjusted to the dark, he realized Morfast was standing in front of him completely naked. He could not help staring at her.

". . . about this . . . chief business . . ."

Morfast said nothing. She tried to look relaxed, but Ager could see she was as tense as the string on a drawn bow. Ager looked away.

"Aren't you cold?" he asked.

"Of course," she said testily.

Ager rubbed his nose. "Then why aren't you dressed?"

"Ah," she said, "you want to undress me yourself."

"What?" he said, and looked up. And then he understood. "Oh, fuck." He quickly looked away again. "I've made a terrible mistake. I'm sorry . . ."

"You don't want me?" She made it sound like an accusation.

"No!" He shook his head.

"I'm not beautiful enough for you? I could get someone younger."

"No!"

"Do you want a man?"

"A man? No, I don't want a man. I don't want a woman. And before you ask, I don't want a horse. What I want is for you to get dressed."

He waited until he heard her put clothes on before looking at her again. She had slipped on a poncho. She looked almost as confused as he felt.

"Look, I'm sorry, Morfast. I wanted to see you tonight to ask you about this chief thing. I've never been a chief before. Are you sure you want me?"

"For chief or—"

"Yes, for chief!" he said hurriedly.

"If not you, then the Ocean clan must submit to the will of the two circles. They may choose a chief for us from another clan, or make us join with another clan."

"Who would they choose?"

"Someone who could kill you in single combat, since you killed Katan."

"I see. And if you join with another clan?"

"Then everything we are will be lost. Our young ones may adjust, but those of us who remember our own traditions and customs will be like children without a mother or father."

"But I don't know your customs and traditions," he pleaded.

"We will teach you," she said simply.

"God," he said, and put his head between his hands.

"Do we shame you?"

"No. Never that. But I am with the prince. I cannot desert him."

"You would not desert him."

"But he must go east. He must go to Kendra or perish in the attempt. And so must I."

"Then we will go to Kendra with you, and perish if we must. The gods decide our fate."

He sat down heavily on her sleeping blanket. She sat down next to him, and he edged away.

"You do not find me beautiful," she said sadly.

He caught her gaze and shook his head. "That is not true. You are very beautiful. But I cannot take you simply because I am your chief."

"Then you accept that you are our chief?"

Ager nodded resignedly "It seems I have no choice. I won't throw you to the two circles." He remembered how close Korigan had come to being dethroned. "I have seen for myself how fickle they can be."

She smiled at him. "All in the clan will be happy. We have a chief again, and our ways will not disappear."

He stood up. "How many of you are there?"

"Of us," she corrected him, "there are nearly four thousand, and two thousand of them are warriors. We have over a thousand head of cattle. We are not the biggest clan, nor the richest, but we are one of the oldest, and have much respect in the Oceans of Grass."

"And who are you, exactly?"

"I was the niece of Katan's wife, her only living relative. That is why they chose me to come to you today."

"And who were the others who came with you?"

"Those most respected in the clan for their courage and their wit. I can call them if you wish to see them now."

"That won't be necessary."

"What do you wish us to do?"

"To do?"

"You are our chief. You must guide us."

"Whatever it is you do while camped at the High Sooq. Afterward . . ." He paused, still trying to get used to the idea of being chief of a Chett clan. ". . . afterward, we'll see."

He reached for the tent flap, but Morfast's hand rested on his. "You do not have to go. I am glad you would not force me to sleep with you, but I see now that was not your intention. I would be pleased to share my blanket with you."

Ager smiled at her. He could see her shape under the poncho and felt the first faint pricking of desire, something he had been without for more years than he could remember. But he could not take her now, and not like this. He gently removed her hand from his and left.

14

THERE were two children, a girl about five with a high fever but resting peacefully, the other a boy about three with a cough.

"And you're sure neither is in any danger?" Olio asked.

The priest shook his head. "No, your Highness. The girl's fever has come down in the last hour, and the boy's cough is improving. They will both be well by week's end."

Olio nodded, but his hand still held on to the heart-shaped Healing Key, as if it might be needed at a second's notice. It felt warm to his touch, even on this cold night. *It wants to be used,* he thought. *But I gave my word. And tonight, at least, there is no temptation to use it.*

"And there are no others?"

Again, the priest shook his head.

"Isn't that rare for winter?"

The priest met his gaze. "Not really. We are coming out of the coldest months of the year. The two times when the greatest sickness comes to the poor are when there is ice on the streets and when the nights are so hot the poor leave their doors and window shutters open to cool their homes. We get a lot of the shaking sickness in summer. Winter is for the chest sickness, mainly."

"I see." He turned to the magicker who had accompanied him from the palace. He could not remember his name. "Where is Prelate Fanhow tonight?"

"He had an important meeting with the theurgia, your Highness. Something to do with the army we are sending north in the spring."

Olio remembered then that Edaytor had said something to him about the meeting. For a moment his thoughts went to the planning of the campaign; he had been involved peripherally so far, but from now he would have to attend war councils; after all, he was going to be the army's general. The idea used to amuse him, but as the time came nearer for the army to march, the prospect of leading experienced men into battle was weighing him down. He thought of himself as a healer, not as a warrior. He believed his role in life was to bring people back from the brink of death and not lead them to it. But his sister—the queen—had given him the commission and he could not surrender it.

"We have some refreshment ready for you, your Highness," the priest said, and led him to the kitchen. There were bowls of fish stew already laid out on the rough wooden table, with thick seed bread and dough cakes on plates. And a flagon of red wine sat in the middle.

"Excellent," Olio said carefully, then pointed to the flagon. "But take that away. Some new cider would better clear my throat."

"Of course." The priest disappeared with the flagon. Olio waited for the twinge of regret, but it did not come.

Some things get better, he told himself.

The priest reappeared with a small cider cask, and the prince sat down with him and the magicker. At first his two companions talked too deferentially, but as the night wore on they became more comfortable, and Olio, to his surprise, actually found himself enjoying the meal.

* * *

Areava placed her hands over her belly. *Yes,* she thought. *A girl.* She was filled with a sense of wonder, and laughed with joy. Sendarus, asleep next to her, mumbled something and turned, flopping an arm across her chest. She laughed even harder.

How long had she been pregnant? God only knew. She and Sendarus had slept together so often since falling in love, at night, in the morning, once in the straw in the royal stables, once in his chambers while his father was waiting to see them.

She felt the baby would come in early to midsummer. Maybe her daughter would share her own birth day. The kingdom would have another Usharna. And what sisters and brothers would Usharna have? Another Areava, perhaps, and a Berayma, even an Olio. And why not a Marin? Or even an Orkid? That would put a smile on the chancellor's face, and—just as pleasing—a grimace on the faces of every noble in the Twenty Houses.

And by the end of autumn Haxus should be subdued and Lynan killed. Nine months and the kingdom would find again the peace it had enjoyed under the first Usharna, and have a new heir as well.

"Maybe we won't stop at defeating Haxus' armies," she told her daughter. "Maybe we'll take Haxus itself, and then all but the desert of the Southern Chetts will belong to Grenda Lear. I will make you ruler of Haxus, and that can be your training for my throne when my time has come." The idea appealed to Areava; one fault of her mother had been to keep the reins of control too tightly in her own hands. Berayma's apprenticeship had been too late and too little, she appreciated that now.

Areava let herself drift to sleep, her husband's arm still across her, and dreamed of the future.

*   *   *

Dejanus sat at an ill-lit corner table of the Lost Sailor Tavern, his cloak wrapped around his huge frame. No one who saw him enter could doubt who he was, but newcomers would not notice him. He sipped slowly on a good Storian wine, which as constable of the Royal Guard he could now afford, and waited for the woman he had been told worked here most nights.

She came in close to midnight, looking hurried, and disappeared into the kitchen. A little while later she reappeared dressed in a stained white apron and carrying a wooden platter with change on it. Dejanus watched her as she moved from table to table, taking orders, smiling easily, pocketing tips. She was buxom and pretty in a voluptuous way. *It figures,* he thought to himself. *She's his type.* When she at last realized the dark corner table was occupied, she came over.

"I'm sorry, gentle sir, I did not see you here out of the light. Can I get you something?"

"Another wine." He handed her his empty cup and she left. When she returned, he paid for the wine and then held up a silver crown. Her face broke into a wide smile and she reached for the coin, but Dejanus pulled his hand back.

"Sit down."

The woman's smile disappeared. "I see," she said unhappily, but sat down anyway.

"I need your help," he said.

"I can imagine."

Dejanus laughed humorlessly. "Not that kind of help, Ikanus."

The woman stiffened. "How do you know my name?"

"We once had a friend in common."

"I have a lot of friends."

"This one was called Kumul Alarn."

The woman gasped and made to stand up, but Dejanus' hand shot out and held her down. "Who are you?"

With his free hand Dejanus showed her the coin again. "A new friend. To replace the old."

He let her go and she did not try to leave. "You didn't answer my question."

"I will answer it, Ikanus, but it will be the last question you ever ask of me. I am Dejanus."

Her eyes widened in surprise and fear. Dejanus could see she was fighting the urge to run away from him, but her gaze was fixed on the silver crown.

"There is no need to be afraid. I hold nothing against you for knowing Kumul. Even I was his friend before he turned traitor." He handed her the coin, and she slipped it down her blouse, between her ample breasts.

"Information," he continued. "I need to know the same things Kumul did. I want you to tell me whenever something happens you think I should know about. Anything illegal, anything against the interests of the kingdom. Anything against *my* interests. *Anything* unusual or unexpected."

Ikanus nodded. He could see she was still frightened, and that was good. It was important she understood he was someone who would hurt her as soon as reward her if she crossed him.

"You've taken my coin. You work for me now. I will come here now and then, and you will tell me everything you see and everything you hear that I should also see and hear. If you do well, there will be more crowns. Fail me and I will kill you."

She nodded again and stood to leave.

"I haven't finished," he said quietly, and she dropped back to her seat. "We can start now. I want to know who else Kumul paid for information."

A minute later she was gone, and Dejanus sat back, relaxed and happy with the way things had gone. Within a few days he would completely revive Kumul's old network of down-and-outs and drunks and whores, the same network which had kept him informed of goings-on in the old quarter of the city; it had played no small part in Kumul's success as constable. It was a network that would rival Orkid's own; indeed, it would allow Dejanus to keep an eye on Orkid's own activities in Kendra, his main reason for tracking down Ikanus and her ilk. He finished his wine and left, pleased with himself and the power of a single silver coin.

Orkid and Marin stood on the small terrace outside of Marin's guest room. The glittering city gave way to the dark, placid waters of Kestrel Bay. They looked west, to their homeland, and Marin sighed deeply.

"You miss the mountains," Orkid said.

"And my court. I know it is a petty one next to Areava's, but I feel more comfortable there than here. Too many play for power in Kendra; back home I know my back is safe."

"Especially now you have united our land so closely with the kingdom."

"Yes, it was well done," the king said without arrogance. He patted his brother's shoulder. "By all of us. But now we must use it to advantage."

"So soon? Shouldn't we wait for things to settle before advancing our cause once more? It will be some time before the Twenty Houses—not to mention the rulers of Grenda Lear's other provinces—repair their pride."

"I know that was our plan, but circumstances have given us the opportunity to further advance our cause by rendering even greater service to Grenda Lear."

"What circumstances?"

"Salokan's planned move against the kingdom in spring, and Prince Lynan finding refuge in the Oceans of Grass—or with Salokan, if rumors are to be believed."

"How do these favor us?"

"You have been in Kendra too long, and your brain is used to following the most circuitous route. Let's deal with the problem of Lynan first. Think, Orkid. If he is in the Oceans of Grass and under the protection of the Chetts, what would unsettle the Chetts more than anything else?"

"The reintroduction of slavery."

"Other than that. I don't think Areava would sanction it, for one thing, and slavery has always been distasteful to our people. We are related to the Chetts, remember?"

"Then I'm at a loss—"

"I have given you the clue." Marin smiled mysteriously at Orkid and stroked his graying beard.

The chancellor frowned in thought, but shook his head in resignation.

"Aman was created by Chetts. We still have some connection with them, especially those in the south who border our own lands. We could use whatever influence we have, together with sizable bribes, to stir them against the Northern Chetts. That should distract them at least, making Jes Prado's task easier."

Orkid nodded. "That must help. It would weaken any support Lynan may have gained. And what of Salokan?"

"Remember our discussion about getting Sendarus the command of Areava's army? I can sweeten the offer. I'll send a thousand of our best light infantry to supplement Areava's army, and that's on top of what she'll conscript from Aman anyway. She'll be pleased to receive professional soldiers."

"It might do the trick," Orkid mused. "I don't think it would be hard to persuade Olio it would be best. With him on our side, it will be easier to sway Areava, and once she's on our side, the council will follow."

"And once Sendarus has command," Marin said slowly, "Areava will give him the Key of the Sword."

"Lord of the Mountain! You don't want things by half, do you?"

Marin shrugged. "We have a chance here to make permanent our influence in Kendra. If all goes aright, Aman will be seen to have saved the kingdom. From there, anything's possible."

Orkid said nothing for a moment, almost overwhelmed by his brother's vision.

"I must leave soon," Marin continued eventually. "Two days from now, I think. It will take me five days to reach Pila, and as soon as I do, I will send the infantry. They can sail up the Gelt River to Chandra to save Areava paying the cost for their transport herself. I will also make contact with those southern Chett tribes we trade with. The rest will be up to you."

"I will do what I can." Orkid shook his head. "I had hoped our days of planning and scheming on such a scale, and at such risk, would be over once Sendarus married Areava."

"We are born for this planning and scheming, you and I," Marin told him. "I do not think either of us will ever stop."

15

THE two men led their horses out of the defile and stopped. Before them spread the Oceans of Grass, and with a great sense of relief they realized they had completed their mission. The younger of the two wanted to go farther.

"Rendle will be twice as pleased if we find a river or sooq nearby. The company will use most of its water getting through the mountains."

"If there's a river or sooq nearby, so are the Chetts," his older companion said shortly, wiping snow off his fur-lined jerkin and helmet. "We've done our job. Let's clean the horses' shoes and head back. We won't reach our camp for another week as it is."

"It's still winter, Sergeant," scoffed the other. "All the Chetts are away at the High Sooq."

The sergeant lifted one of his mount's legs and used a knife to dig out stones from the worn shoe. "Suit yourself, but I'm not hanging around. You'll have to catch up."

The young man cursed the sergeant under his breath. He did not fancy riding out into the Oceans of Grass by himself despite their apparent emptiness and his bravado, but did not want to seem a coward or fool.

"I won't go far," he said, and spurred his horse.

The sergeant said nothing, but shook his head. When he had finished with the horse, he found a rock bare of snow and sat on it, letting the stone warm his backside, and chewed on a long strip of beef jerky. The last four nights he had dreamed of nothing but hot stew and fresh brewed beer. His horse nibbled on yellow grass nearby. He looked up into the sky. The pale sun was still an hour from noon. He would wait until then . . .

A terrifying wail pierced the air, and the sergeant's heart froze. He scrambled to stand on the rock and anxiously searched the grass before him, but saw nothing. Then he heard another sound, the long victory howl of a grass wolf. A moment later his companion's horse galloped into sight, empty stirrups slapping against the stallion's flank.

"That's it," the sergeant hissed, as he jumped onto his own horse. He whipped the reins and dug his spurs in, sending the startled horse back up the defile, ignoring the danger of loose stones and a steep climb. His mount was reluctant to keep going until the riderless horse skittered past, then needed no urging from his rider.

The terrified mercenary could hardly breathe. The wild-looking Chett had one knee on his chest and a short knife pricking his throat. The Chett seemed to be listening for something, and after a while grinned and stood up.

"Don't k–k–kill me!" the mercenary begged.

The Chett looked down at him with disdain. "No. Not yet anyway." Then he grinned again. "Not yet." He lifted his head back and howled a second time.

The mercenary pissed himself, but he was too afraid to be ashamed.

Four hundred leagues away Gudon was working on the docks at Daavis. He knew from his time as a pilot on the Barda River how busy the capital of Hume could be in winter, but it was nothing like this. Huge baskets of grain, barrels of wine, and crates of dried meat were being shipped in from Sparro in Chandra. As well, there were more soldiers than usual, all looking grim. He learned from other workers about the rumors of a coming war with Haxus, rumors that were substantively the same from whatever source; on the other hand, the rumors about what exactly Queen Areava was doing about the situation were as varied and wild and almost certainly unreliable.

Another barge slid up to the dock, and with a handful of other workers he hurried up to help unload it before the dock foreman gave him a tongue lashing. Then with a jolt he recognized the man with the scarred face and crooked nose standing impatiently at the bow and quickly ducked his head. He hid behind a particularly large stevedore with a rope brace around his shoulders; Gudon helped him lift a bale of horse feed over his head and into the brace, then slid behind crates of cabbages and corn to work from the stern of the barge. He glanced up quickly and saw Jes Prado bark orders to the foreman and then disappear among the harbor throng.

He breathed a deep sigh of relief, and the shock he felt at seeing Prado gradually melted away.

"You! Chalat! Get a move on there! I don't pay you to stare at your feet!" Gudon bowed quickly to the foreman and joined the queue of workers at the stern waiting to unload goods. In a few minutes the barge was empty. It was pushed away from the dock, and another barge quickly took its place. This one was filled with mercenaries, tired and worn, and about six mounts that looked as ill as their owners. A wider plank was hitched over its gunwales and the mercenaries and their mounts started to disembark.

From this part of the dock Gudon could see all the way downriver, and all he saw was a line of barges loaded with troops and horses.

"What is happening?" he asked the worker behind him.

The worker shrugged. "More reinforcements for the coming war. Queen Charion will be angry. She wants regulars, not these hired mongrels." The worker spat. "At least it means less cargo for us to take off."

There may have been less cargo, but the number of barges more than made up for it. Gudon could not remember working so hard in his life. His thighs and shoulders ached with exhaustion, and the palms of his hands were beginning to blister.

Toward evening the barges stopped coming in, but instead of slacking off, the activity in the harbor actually increased. Empty barges were tied together from the end of the dock, two across, until they connected with a ferry quay on the other side of the river. Then huge planks were laid down on the barges and tethered in place with rope almost as thick as hawsers. When finished, the pontoon was twenty paces wide and two hundred long; the current tugged at the whole structure, bowing its middle. Gudon and the other workers helped construct the pontoon, then busied themselves tying ropes to iron loops in stone anchors and throwing two off the side of each barge. As soon as they were finished, the workers were hurried off, and a column of men leading horses appeared at the ferry quay on the opposite bank.

Although the workers were dismissed around midnight, several of them, including Gudon, stayed behind to watch the procession make its way across the Barda and into the city. Gudon scratched a mark in a crate for every ten men. After a hundred marks he whistled in wonder; there was still no end to the column. He had never seen so many mercenaries under one command before.

Are they for the war? he kept wondering. *Or is Prado going after Lynan again?*

Gudon saw the foreman by the pontoon bridge where it

met the dock and went to him. "How long are we keeping the pontoon?" he asked. "We don't get no barges in while it's up."

The foreman grunted noncommittally. "Don't know. Don't care. As long as we're paid for the time off, you shouldn't care either."

"Guess they're coming for the war."

"Guess so, although why we need more cavalry on the border is beyond me. It's infantry we need, infantry to garrison Daavis. Cavalry isn't worth spit in a siege."

"Yah," Gudon agreed sympathetically. "But the rumors been goin' for weeks now, so how come Kendra ain't sending infantry?"

The foreman gave Gudon a look of mild disgust. "Weeks? Don't know who you've been talkin' to, but the first I heard about it was less than five days ago."

Gudon slipped away. A cold sweat broke out on his brow. Prado could not have put together a company this size in less than a month. The mercenaries were not here for the war.

He walked quickly to the small room he rented in a run-down riverside inn. He went in the back way and quickly gathered together his few belongings, including the sword he had hidden under a loose floorboard. From there, he made his way to a stable, woke the irate owner and paid the difference he owed for the keep of his two horses, then rode north out of Daavis at a fast trot. By dawn, he was well clear of the city and the river. He switched horses and kept up a good pace, but he could not help wishing he had wings on his feet. Even at the best speed he would not reach the High Sooq before the start of spring, and by then it might be too late.

Normally Prado lost his temper when he was forced to kick his heels, but he made a special effort on this occasion; so far into his plan, he was not going to allow anything to stop his progress. Officials in Queen Charion's court bustled by him, paying him scant attention; at first he had pestered each of them to find out when the queen would see him, but they would shrug helplessly and maneuver out of his way, so eventually he gave up.

He had heard from the court sergeant-at-arms the news that Areava was mobilizing for a war against Haxus, and he was afraid she had sent orders for his company to be conscripted into the defense of Daavis. The news certainly did away with any intention he had of asking Charion for a troop or two of her regular cavalry to help him in his mission.

It doesn't matter, he told himself. *I can do it with the twenty-five hundred I have, as long as no one gets in my way.*

About mid-morning he was joined by Freyma and Sal.

"Have you heard—" Freyma started excitedly.

"About the war?" Prado spat. "Of course I've heard."

"And the other rumor?" Sal asked.

Prado's eyes narrowed. "What other rumor?"

"That Lynan is leading the armies of Haxus."

Prado could not hide his surprise. If true, it would almost certainly mean Areava had ordered Charion to join his forces with her own. He thought furiously, pacing up and down the ornate tiled atrium and glancing nervously at the bronze doors that led to the queen's throne room. He was not so sure he wanted that audience with her now.

If the rumor was true, then Rendle had returned to the Oceans of Grass and captured Lynan. But how? Prado had been with Rendle when his first attempt to capture the prince had failed—presumably foiled by the Chetts; if that was the case, the Chetts would have made sure Lynan was safe, which in turn meant Rendle was riding deep into the plains in late autumn—or worse, in winter—to capture Lynan.

He shook his head. No, it was not possible. It must be nothing but a rumor.

"Lynan's still with the Chetts," he said aloud, but to no one in particular.

"How can you be so sure?" Sal asked.

He looked at her sternly. "I just *know.*"

Over the last two months, Sal had learned what that expression meant. She did not argue the point.

The bronze doors opened and a harried-looking official scurried to Prado. "The queen will see you now." The official glanced disapprovingly at the mercenaries' dress. "Be brief."

He led the three into the throne room. The space seemed small after Areava's throne room in Kendra, but it was richly decorated. Courtiers, soldiers, and secretaries were everywhere, yapping with each other, poring over documents on makeshift tables, looking strained. Charion herself was on the throne surrounded by an anxious throng of attendants, and among them all she seemed like an oasis of tranquillity.

She was short and finely built, like a figurine. Her face was round and pale, and black hair tumbled loose over her shoulders. Brown eyes coolly regarded the mercenaries as they approached her.

"Your Highness—" Prado began, bowing low.

"I have received messages from Queen Areava concerning your mission," Charion interrupted. Her voice seemed unnaturally low for such a small woman. "It is an annoyance."

"I am sorry, ma'am, that we have come at such an inconven—"

"The messages also stressed I was not to interfere," she continued. "By which I gather she means I cannot second your company."

"It is mainly cavalry, your Highness. No good in a siege."

"A siege? Who said anything about a siege?" Her voice was as hard as steel.

"Everyone is talking about it, ma'am," Prado said hurriedly. "And the supplies we have seen—"

"Farben?" she said.

The official who had showed in the mercenaries scampered by them and kneeled before Charion. "Your Highness?"

"I thought I ordered the supplies to be stored as soon as they arrived? I don't want Salokan's spies knowing what we're about."

Farben shrugged apologetically. "We're storing them as quickly as we can, but work was disrupted last night by . . ." he glanced at Prado, ". . . by the arrival of the general and his company."

Charion looked sourly at Prado. "Another reason to be unhappy with you."

"We had no idea, your Highness," Prado pleaded. "If we did—"

"You would still have made your grand entrance. I know your type, General. And I know Areava."

Prado did not know what to say, and anyway she would only interrupt him, so he bowed again. Freyma and Sal stood well back, studiously staring at their feet.

"Why are you here?" she demanded.

"To gather supplies," Prado told her.

"Not possible," she said. "You can see we need all the supplies for ourselves. Salokan will march on us when the thaw starts." She looked at Farben again. "When do my magickers say that will be?"

"Four, maybe five, weeks, your Highness," Farben answered.

"So you see, General, supplies are out of the question."

Prado licked his lips. "Your Highness, I understand your predicament, but my mission is vital."

Charion leaned forward. "What exactly *is* your mission?"

Prado blinked. He had not expected this. "Your Highness?"

"Oh, God's teeth, General, don't play the fool. The question was straightforward enough."

"I assumed Queen Areava would have informed you of it."

Charion sat back again, and her pale face flushed with anger. "Obviously an oversight on her part. These are busy times for us all, and something as simple as that might be overlooked. So, what is your mission?"

"Far be it from me to withhold information, your Highness, but I am under instruction from the queen not to discuss it." He hoped he was lying convincingly. If Areava had not told Charion, she had her reasons. Or rather, Orkid had his reasons. Was the chancellor afraid Charion would interfere? Or take on the mission herself? Yes, that was it. In her struggle with Chandra, she would do anything to curry favor with Areava.

"I see," Charion said icily. "Then you had better get on with it."

"I need supplies, ma'am."

"I've already told you I cannot spare any."

"But my mission—"

"If I knew what your mission was, General, then maybe I could see my way to giving you what you need."

"Or we could send a carrier bird to Kendra to clarify the position," Prado said quickly, and bowed his head a third time, but this time to hide the swallow that bobbed in his throat. He held his breath, expecting a scream of outrage.

There was a terrible silence. It spread from the throne outward through the room like a ripple in a pond. Prado dared look up. Charion's face had become almost as white as Areava's.

But she is no Rosetheme, he reminded himself. *She is*

angry because she has lost. He resisted the urge to sigh in relief.

"Farben." She spoke the name with a voice like ice. "Accompany this man to the main storerooms. He will be given what supplies he needs. He must sign for them."

Farben bowed and scraped and backed away, plucking at Prado's sleeve for him to follow. As Prado retreated, Charion said: "I do not ever want to see your face again, General. If I do, I will have your head cut off, and I will send that to Areava instead of a carrier bird."

Prado turned his back on her and followed Farben out of the throne room.

Rendle listened patiently to the sergeant; the man had served with him for nearly twenty years, and he knew him to be as brave as any mercenary had a need to be, and responsible as well, something Rendle found rarer than courage. When the sergeant had finished, Rendle patted him kindly on the shoulder.

"You did the right thing. If the young fool had done as you advised, he would still be alive."

The sergeant nodded helplessly. "Aye, Captain, I know."

"And most of all, you've found the route is navigable."

"But steep and slow and cold, Captain. Even if you started now, you'd not get our whole force across it by spring."

"All right. Get some rest."

The sergeant left, his head still bowed.

Rendle went inside the tent and checked the map which had been laid out for several weeks. On it were marked several trails leading to the Oceans of Grass, which his riders had scouted for him. With blue ink he carefully traced a line from his camp to the Oceans of Grass, going across the pass the sergeant and his late companion had followed. He now had three blue lines leading through the mountains; mainly old trails, naturally formed. All the other lines were marked in red: all dead ends or impassable by horse during winter. Most importantly, the three passable trails were no more than forty leagues from each other, two days' comfortable ride on the Oceans of Grass. He could get his whole force across into the Oceans of Grass and hit the Chetts as they returned, tired and hungry, to the summer pastures. He did not expect to be lucky enough to find Lynan among the first clans he attacked, but one of them would have information about which clan was protecting the prince. With luck, he would be able to attack that clan, get the prince, and retreat back to Haxus before the Chetts could muster any effective resistance. It was a big gamble, but that was a part of any mercenary's life: choose the wrong side in a war and even if you escaped with your life, you made no profit from it. If it had not been for the profit he had made in trading slaves, the last war would have left him high and dry and without a company.

Someone behind him coughed politely.

"What is it?" he growled. "Can't you see I'm busy?"

"These are busy times," replied a soft voice.

Rendle groaned inside. "King Salokan," he said, turning. "What a pleasant surprise."

Salokan smiled thinly. "You don't mean that." He regarded the shorter man for a moment, mildly jealous of the mercenary's knotty build. He went to the map. "I see you have your third way across."

"Yes. I can get the troops through the mountains in two weeks."

"You will be divided."

"Briefly." He pointed to the middle trail. "We'll rejoin here. Two days after reaching the Oceans of Grass we'll be the largest military force on the plains."

"Until the Chetts organize. How long do you think you'll have?"

"Five weeks, maybe more. At any rate, I intend to be back within a month. How goes your own deadline?"

"Everything is on schedule. We'll cross the border in two weeks."

"You still intend to invade Hume before the thaw?"

Salokan nodded. "You'll be crossing the mountains; compared to that, we'll have an easy time of it. Besides, by now Areava will know we're on her border. If she's been able to put together an army in the meantime, it will march in spring. That would only give us a few weeks. By moving early I can sweep aside her border patrols and be at Daavis before her army takes its first step. Once I have Daavis, she must retreat to protect Sparro and her line of supply."

"And by then you'll have Lynan, and with him you can work on Chandra to change sides. King Tomar has always had a soft spot for the General and his whelp."

Salokan carefully studied Rendle. "If your plan works."

"And if your plan works," Rendle countered. Damn if he was going to take responsibility for the success of the whole invasion.

"We are in each others' hands," Salokan said easily. "We will both do our part."

"And we will win."

"*I* will win," Salokan corrected him. "*You* will help me."

Rendle bowed slightly. "Your Majesty."

"Indeed." Salokan sighed heavily. "I'm leaving for the border today. Pity. I've enjoyed our little chats. When do you start?"

"Now that I have my mountain passes, two weeks."

"By the way, have you discussed your plans with General Thewor?"

"Yes."

"I trust he gave you no trouble? I had a good word with him about this command thing."

"No trouble. He was as meek as a lame horse. How did you convince him?"

"I told him I was thinking of starting a new elite bodyguard to protect my person, and that if he gave you any trouble he would find himself in command of it."

"Why would that deter him?"

"It would be a bodyguard made up entirely of eunuchs."

16

AGER woke with the sun, having only slept a few hours. He dressed quickly and limped out of his tent, scratching his belly with one hand and his head with the other. He realized almost immediately he had an audience of about two hundred Chetts, all regarding him with greater respect than he felt he deserved at that moment. He stopped his scratching and lowered his hands.

"Hello," he said, a little awestruck. His breath frosted in the air.

Morfast stepped forward from the crowd and went to his side. "I assembled the Ocean clan's family heads as soon as possible. They must swear their loyalty to you—"

"All of them?" Ager interrupted, startled. "This morning?"

"—or else they must leave the clan."

"Oh." Ager glanced around to see if anyone else was watching. A few passersby stopped to look on. "All right."

It was over remarkably quickly. One by one the family heads came to Ager and placed his hand on their bowed heads, then left to make way for the next one. Although Ager did not even have time to get really cold before it was done, it lasted long enough for a crowd to gather around the ceremony.

"Have you any more surprises for me?" Ager asked Morfast.

"I was going to suggest we go to Korigan to let her know you are now chief of the Ocean clan."

"Can it wait until after breakfast?"

"No need," she said. "She and the White Wolf were watching the whole thing."

"And a fine ceremony it was, too," Korigan said, and came before Ager, Lynan standing a little behind her. The prince was smiling broadly at the crookback, from pride and amusement.

Morfast elbowed Ager in the side.

"What?" he asked. "I'm *new* to this, tell me what I have to do."

"As your family heads gave themselves to your service, now you must give yourself to me," Korigan answered for Morfast.

Ager blushed, glanced at Lynan. "Ah. And what of my loyalty to my prince?"

"Since I regard Lynan as my liege, he will still be yours."

Ager looked uncomfortable.

"What is wrong?" Korigan asked.

"What if . . . I mean, if it comes about . . ." Words failed him. He felt he had been ambushed.

"I think I understand," Korigan said kindly. "What if Lynan and I part ways?"

Ager nodded. "Exactly."

Korigan smiled. "Would it make it easier for you if I said here and now—in front of members of your clan—that I will never ask you to do anything that would work against his Majesty?"

Ager sighed, and nodded again.

"Then I proclaim that Ager Parmer, soldier of Grenda

Lear and chief of the Ocean Clan, will never have call to take arms against Lynan, who is the White Wolf returned." Korigan held out her hand for Ager to take.

He smiled his thanks at the queen, took her hand, and rested it upon his head.

Lynan came beside him and said: "That was well done. For a lost and lonely crookback I first met at a tavern in Kendra, you have come a long way."

Ager stood as erect as he could. "Haven't we all," he said heartily, starting to think that maybe inheriting Katan's clan had been one of the more fortunate accidents to befall him. Lynan made a noncommittal sound and glanced at his pale hands.

"Some of us more than others, perhaps," Ager added quickly, trying to tell the prince he understood.

For a moment they met each other's gaze, and Ager caught a glimpse of the pain and uncertainty deep in Lynan's mind. The crookback swallowed and looked away quickly.

"Riders," Morfast said, pointing, "and coming toward us."

"It is Terin and another," Korigan said, and Ager noticed her and Lynan stiffen. He tried to remember who Terin was, then recalled he was a fellow-chief, one who supported the queen.

A fellow-chief, Ager thought. *I like the sound of that.*

The riders pulled up in front of Lynan and Korigan, their horses kicking snow into the air. Lynan took Terin's reins. "What news?" he asked urgently.

Terin was very young, Ager saw, even younger than Lynan. Terin nodded to his fellow. "It's best if it comes from Igelko." All eyes switched to the second rider, who was obviously exhausted, and his mare close to being blown.

Igelko tried to speak but could only gasp.

"Catch your breath," Lynan commanded. "Someone take his horse and care for it."

Someone from Ager's clan rushed forward and helped Igelko out of the saddle, then led his mare away.

"Your Majesty," Igelko breathed heavily. "We caught one."

Lynan and Korigan exchanged quick glances.

"Caught one what?" Ager asked.

Igelko glanced at him. "Mercenary. By the north spur of the Ufero Mountains."

"The north spur?" Morfast said, surprised. "How did they get that far into the Oceans of Grass?"

"They came over the mountains," Igelko said.

Morfast's face went white. "From the north? Are you sure?"

Ager put a hand on her shoulder. "This is not your interrogation," he said softly.

"Your M–majesty," Morfast stuttered. "I'm sorry. But the news—"

"Is grim, I know," Lynan said for her. He went to Igelko and helped him stand straight. "How are you feeling?"

"Better, thank you, my lord."

"Where is your prisoner?"

"A day behind me. My brother has him."

"How much has the prisoner said?"

"Only that he works for Captain Rendle."

"Rendle!" Korigan spat. She looked fiercely at Lynan. "Now we have our proof. Even Eynon will be convinced."

"Terin, send a troop to escort this man's brother and the prisoner. I want nothing to go wrong."

"Already done," Terin said, proud that he had thought of it.

"Well done," Lynan commended him, then slapped Igelko's back. "And to you and your brother. I will buy five cattle for each of you."

Igelko bowed deeply. "Thank you, your Majesty."

"Make sure this man gets some rest," Lynan told Terin. "As soon as the prisoner arrives, I want to question him."

Terin nodded and left, walking his horse and talking earnestly with Igelko. The young chief was smiling broadly.

"Terin will add a bull each to your five cattle," Korigan told Lynan. "He knows how much esteem Igelko and his brother have won for the South Wind clan."

"Can you do me a favor?" Lynan asked.

"Of course."

"Lend me ten cattle?"

As she did most days, Jenrosa was down by the furnaces watching and listening to the Chett magickers weave their spells to make the fires run hotter. She tried to read their lips, but nothing she thought she could decipher made any sense to her theurgia-trained mind. She found it deeply frustrating, and more and more she realized she would have to go to Korigan and ask to be assigned to one of the White Wolf magickers for training. The thought of asking Korigan for anything made her hackles rise, but the alternative, to be the only one of Lynan's original companions without a purpose or place during their exile, was unthinkable.

Someone called to her, and she recognized Lasthear, the Ocean clan magicker. "I see you here every day."

"I want to learn," Jenrosa said simply.

"You will not ask the queen for help."

Jenrosa sighed. "I will have to, but it is not something I want to do."

Lasthear studied her carefully. "I will not ask why, it is not my place. You are aware of the changes in my clan's fortunes?"

"I'm aware Ager is now your chief."

"If he asked me, I would feel compelled to take on your training myself."

"I thought—"

"Ager could ask Korigan for dispensation to let me teach you. I do not think she would say no."

"I will ask Ager right away," Jenrosa said excitedly.

"There is no hurry. I cannot take you on while I am working so hard here at the furnaces. But later, when we leave the High Sooq, we will have time."

"Thank you." It was all Jenrosa could think of saying.

"It will be an interesting exercise, Jenrosa Alucar."

Jenrosa blinked. "How do you know my name?"

"All Chetts know of Prince Lynan's companions. You have become heroes to us."

"I'm not sure why," Jenrosa said bluntly. "Kumul and Ager I can understand, but I am no warrior."

"You saved the life of the White Wolf."

"That was no magic," she said grimly.

"But it took great courage. And if you truly wish to learn the way of our magic, you will need great courage."

No one asked him his name. He would have given that as willingly as he had all the other things he told them. The crazy-looking Chett sitting in front of him, slowly testing the edge of his sword, never took his eyes off him.

"I don't want to die," he said for the tenth time.

"You're going to die," said the tall female Chett who walked around him. "It's only a matter of how quickly."

The mercenary had long run out of tears, and all he could manage was a jerky breath.

"How many Haxus regulars will Rendle be taking with him?"

"I don't know, not exactly. A brigade I was told."

"You must have seen them."

"Not all of them. We left to scout the pass before they'd all arrived."

"Two thousand? Three?"

"I don't know."

"How many were there when you left?"

"A lot. Maybe two thousand."

"Maybe more?"

"Maybe."

There was a pause, and the Chett on the ground eagerly looked up at the female. She shook her head, and the Chett looked disappointed.

"So Rendle has a thousand riders himself now?"

"I already told you."

"And at least another two thousand regulars?"

"I think so. Maybe more."

"When are they moving into the Oceans of Grass?"

"I told you before, I don't know. They don't tell me those sorts of things."

"You must have heard rumors."

The mercenary closed his eyes. He had given away so much already, if only he could hold on to some of his secrets, the Chetts might yet pay for what they were going to do to him.

"No."

"All right," the female said. At first the mercenary slumped in relief, but then realized she had been talking to the Chett with the sword who was advancing on him. Just then the tent flap parted and another Chett walked in.

At least, the mercenary thought, he dressed like a Chett. But he was shorter than any Chett he had ever seen. The man's hat was low over his face and he could not see what he looked like.

"Have you got what we need?" the newcomer asked.

"All except when," Korigan said.

"Leave me with him."

The two other Chetts left. The mercenary sat up straighter, struggled uselessly against his bonds. The short Chett just looked at him.

"I told the woman everything I know."

Still the man said nothing.

The mercenary licked his chafed lips, but his mouth did not have enough spit left to do any good. "Just kill me. Get it over with."

The man removed his hat, and the mercenary got his first glimpse of his face. He used his heels to push himself away.

The man crouched down and his right hand shot out to grasp the mercenary by his cheeks. The mercenary yelped but could do nothing against the strength of that grip. He was forced to look again at the scarred, ivory-white face.

"What are you?"

"You do not know me?"

"You're hurting me."

"I'm going to kill you," the man said. The mercenary closed his eyes, waiting for the worst. "Unless you tell me what I want to know. Let's start with your name."

"Arein," the mercenary said. He opened his eyes again, feeling a slender thread of hope for the first time since his capture.

"Arein, I need to know when Rendle is coming over the mountains."

"I don't know."

"Do you know who I am?"

Arein tried to shake his head. "No," he said pitifully.

"I am the White Wolf."

"Oh God, oh God . . ."

"I am going to eat you alive."

". . . oh God, oh God . . ."

"Tell me what I need to know, and I promise you will live."

"Why should I trust you?"

"Because the White Wolf never lies."

"I don't know any white wolf."

"You know me, Arein. You know Prince Lynan

Rosetheme." The man took an amulet from beneath his poncho.

"The Key of Unity!" Arein looked up surprised. "No, you can't be the prince."

The man grinned mirthlessly. "I have changed. But I am Prince Lynan. I told you the White Wolf never lies. I have no need to. Now, tell me when Rendle is coming over the mountains."

"Before . . ." Arein stopped himself. No. He *was* going to die. This mad thing was going to kill him, he was sure. The grip on his cheeks tightened and he cried in pain. "Before winter is over!" he blurted, and the pain went away.

The man straightened. "Before winter is over. Are you sure?"

"Rendle wants Prince Lynan to help Salokan invade Grenda Lear." Arein looked up at the man's face and again saw the Key of Unity. "He wants *you*."

The prince turned on his heel and opened the tent flap. "We have what we want," he said to someone, and the woman returned, this time accompanied by a man who was as huge as the prince was small.

"Good," the giant said. "We can kill him now."

"No," Lynan said.

Kumul looked as if he was about to argue, but remembered they were in front of the prisoner. He glanced at Korigan, who seemed as mystified as he was. "Your Highness, can we talk outside for a moment?"

As soon as they were outside, Kumul asked Lynan if he had other questions he wanted to ask.

"I've no more questions," Lynan admitted.

"We can't just let him go—" Kumul started.

"I didn't say we would let him go. At least not yet."

"We can't keep him with us," Korigan said. "The clan has no one to look after a prisoner."

"He will stay here, at the High Sooq, after we have gone.

There will be no need to set a guard on him because he cannot go anywhere. When it is time to release him, we will send a message to Herita."

Kumul scratched his head. "I don't understand your reasoning, Lynan. Why not just kill him?"

"First, because I told him if he told the truth I would spare his life. Second, because I want our enemies to know that if they surrender to us, they will not be butchered out of hand."

"The Red Shields never took prisoners," Kumul said gruffly.

"Nor have the Chetts," Korigan added.

Lynan thought it ironic they were on the same side at last, but in opposition to him. "I will be fighting my own people," he said. "I cannot help it. Sooner or later, I go up against the armies of Grenda Lear. You will be with me, Kumul. Both of us will almost certainly be facing people we once knew."

"War can be like that," Kumul said.

"We don't kill those who surrender to us. I will not have my own people butchered by my own soldiers."

Kumul jerked a thumb at the tent. "He is a mercenary. Will you spare all of them as well? What of Rendle? Would you let him live if he surrendered? And Jes Prado?"

"It will be hard for the Chetts to take any mercenaries prisoner during a battle," Korigan said. "There is too much hatred for what they did to us in the Slaver War."

Lynan looked uncomfortable. "I do not include the mercenaries in any amnesty. But this one lives because I gave him my word."

Korigan nodded. "So be it," she said.

Lynan stared down Kumul until the giant reluctantly nodded his head. "I will do as you order," he admitted. Then he looked up again, his eyes bright. "And now that we know what Rendle and Salokan plan, what will you do?"

"When will the clans leave the High Sooq?" Lynan asked Korigan.

"The time is near. I would say within ten days."

"If we wait that long," Kumul said, "we will not make the Ufero Mountains in time."

"In time for what?" Lynan asked lightly.

"To trap Rendle against them, of course," Kumul declared, as if it was obvious. Lynan said nothing. Kumul shook his head. "You're not going to do that, are you?"

"I don't know yet," Lynan said. "I want more information."

"God's death, Lynan, we have a good idea of how many ride with Rendle, and when and where they are coming over. What more could you want?"

"It is still not enough. I want to know what is happening in the east before committing our forces."

"Surely they will be busy with Salokan," Korigan said. "From what our guest revealed, Hume will be hard-pressed to survive the onslaught from Haxus."

"We have no word from Gudon. Until then, I will commit to no strategy."

"You will stay here like a paralyzed bug?" Kumul demanded.

"No. We leave with the White Wolf clan. We will head east, taking our time."

"The spring grass will not be able to feed our whole army for long, your Majesty," Korigan said.

"I don't intend for the army to be on the Oceans of Grass for long."

"But the army is here *now*," Kumul said, his voice rising. "You have the instrument in your hands to destroy Rendle and his force as soon as he enters the Oceans of Grass."

"His force will be destroyed," Lynan said. "But not then." He faced Korigan. "Tell Terin to take his clan out as soon as he can. I want him to patrol those passes Rendle will

be using to get his army across the mountains. Terin is not
to attempt to attack or harass them. When Rendle himself
appears, Terin is to let us know. Once the mercenary force
has left the mountains behind, Terin is to destroy any guard
left behind and secure the passes so Rendle cannot retreat
that way."

"I will see Terin right away," Korigan said, and left them.

Lynan nodded to a guard. "Bring out the prisoner." The
guard nodded and disappeared into the tent, reappearing a
moment later with Arein. The mercenary was shaking, obviously thinking he was now going to be cut down.

"You will stay here until I send word you are to be freed,"
Lynan told him. The mercenary slumped in relief. "But if
you try to escape, the Chetts will kill you outright. And if
you have lied to me about Rendle and his movements, I will
come back here and eat your heart."

Arein nodded numbly.

"Let him go," Lynan ordered, and the guard released his
grip. Arein stood there uncertainly. "If you go to the heart of
the sooq, you will find an elder named Herita. Tell her who
you are, and what I have said. She will give you work to do,
as well as shelter. The guard will show you the way."

The guard started off, with Arein following behind.

Kumul shook his head. "I think this is a foolish thing you
do," he said quietly.

"What particularly? Letting the prisoner go, or not attacking Rendle outright?"

"Both."

"Neither is something my father would have done, I assume."

"No."

"Then I am already one up on my enemies," Lynan said,
and left Kumul to gape after him.

ORKID found Olio in the palace forecourt watching the Royal Guard at training. The chancellor had seen the prince at training himself as he grew up, and although competent with a sword, he did not have the inclination to be a warrior. The question was, did Olio think so, too?

"If only your army was as well equipped and trained as these fine troops," Orkid said.

Olio turned and smiled thinly at Orkid. "I did not hear you arrive, Chancellor. Forgive m–m–me for ignoring you."

Orkid waved a hand. "I was not offended. Have you seen any of your own soldiers yet?"

"The Twenty Houses have almost finished m–m–mustering. I expect them to b–b–be ready within a few days. The first detachments from our other provinces arrive this afternoon; from Storia, I b–b–believe."

"I would have thought Kendra itself could have supplied you with some sword and spear companies."

"Three, in fact. They are already in b–b–barracks near the harbor, and will ship out as soon as Admiral Setchmar determines the worst of the winter seas are finished."

"And yourself? When do you leave to be their general?"

"With the m–m–main b–b–body of troops. Twenty days at least. We m–m–march north from here to Sparro."

"Then on to Daavis and glory," Orkid added.

Olio looked at the ground, his uncertainty obvious. "Indeed," he muttered.

Orkid stood by his side. "Will you be taking the consort with you?"

Olio looked up in surprise. "Sendarus? Why, no, of course not. He is just wed. I doubt he is so keen to leave Areava's side. At any rate, m–m–my sister would not allow it."

"Sendarus might wish to go," Orkid mused. "He is, after all, an Amanite warrior. It will be hard for him to see others marching to war while he stays behind to . . ." He let his voice fade.

"Coddle the queen, Chancellor?" Olio asked, his voice betraying his anger. "You at least should not think so p–p–poorly of your nephew."

"I would never doubt Sendarus' motives. He is a good and honorable man. He would wish to go for the queen's good, not his own."

If only it was Sendarus who was general instead of me, Olio thought miserably. *Then he could go and I could stay behind where I will do the least harm.*

"At any rate, since you are general, he cannot go," Orkid added offhandedly.

"What do you mean?"

"Well, it would make him subordinate to you."

"Only in the army. B–B–Besides, I do not think p–p–pride is one of Sendarus' vices. Indeed, I am not sure he has any vices at all."

"I was not suggesting the problem stemmed from human vanity. It is only that he possesses, next to the queen, perhaps the greatest authority in the kingdom. There would be political and legal problems if that authority was submitted to your own."

Olio thought the point a fine one, too fine for him to consider seriously, but it did give him the germ of another idea. The Guards had finished their training and were marching back to their barracks. He started walking back to the palace. He motioned for Orkid to accompany him.

"Do you think Sendarus is concerned that he is not going north with the army?"

"Undoubtedly. But he understands the reasons. He is not angry with you, if that is your worry."

Olio shook his head. "No." He frowned in thought for a moment, then said: "Do you think that if he had b–b–been consort at the council m–m–meeting that nominated m–m–my generalship, they would have given him the office?"

Orkid pretended to consider the question. "I am not sure. Perhaps." He pretended to think on it some more. "It is likely," he said in a considered voice. "Now that you mention it, I think that it is likely. It would have been another way for Sendarus to prove his loyalty to Grenda Lear, and would have ensured the safety of the two surviving loyal Rosethemes." The chancellor shrugged. "But such was not the case."

"No," Olio said, more to himself than Orkid.

"Do you need me for anything in particular, your Highness?" Orkid asked.

Olio stopped and looked absently at the chancellor. "No. Thank you, but no." He turned and continued, his head bowed in thought.

Orkid watched him go, a smile crossing his stern face. *That was easier than I had any right to expect.*

Primate Giros Northam was sitting behind his desk, his hands in his lap firmly clasping one another. He heard a knock at his door and swallowed quickly. "Come in," he said, trying to keep the quaver out of his voice.

Father Powl entered, closed the door behind him. "A brother said you wanted to see me, your Grace."

Northam nodded and indicated the priest should sit down. Powl took a chair and looked evenly at the primate, his features calm and interested.

"There is something we must discuss," Northam started "Something important to you and to the Church of the Righteous God."

Northam saw Powl stiffen slightly. The priest had an inkling, then, of what he was leading to. "We have been friends for a very long time," he went on. "Once, we were very close."

Powl evaded Northam's gaze this time and nodded a little curtly; his face reddened slightly.

"You do not agree?" Northam asked uneasily.

Powl shook his head. "Of course I agree, your Grace. But that closeness . . ."

"Has gone, I know."

"And through your actions, not mine," Powl added hurriedly, his eyes almost pleading.

"I know that, too." Northam sighed heavily, making his wattled neck shake slightly. "I wish it could have been done another way."

"You wish *what* could have been done another way?"

"I am not sure how to explain this to you. It is a conversation we should probably have had months ago. You deserve the truth."

Powl's face became calm suddenly, as if intuition warned him of what was coming. "This is about your successor, isn't it?"

Northam nodded. "You are not to know the true name of God. You cannot be its protector."

Powl nodded, too, echoing the primate's movement, as if

to say: "I understand. Of course." But his eyes became hard and bright and he found he could not look at the primate's face, so he stared at his superior's bald head instead. "This is not right," he said tightly.

"It *is* right," Northam stressed. "But it is not easy. Not for you. Not for me."

Powl's head was now shaking. "No, your Grace. It is not right. How can it be? For decades you have trained me for this."

"I have never said so," Northam said defensively.

"Your intent was unmistakable," Powl said. "You were not grooming me simply to be your secretary."

"You were a good novitiate, Father. You gained the attention of all your superiors. But you exceed your learning in believing you knew my thinking."

Powl fixed Northam in the eye. "Look at me, your Grace, and tell me you did not intend for me to be primate in your place when you passed on to God's kingdom."

Northam could not. He averted his gaze, but saved some of his pride by not trying to lie about it again. "It was the queen," he said hurriedly, then closed his eyes in shame. It was no longer any of Powl's business how the decision had come about, and he should not have mentioned her in this business.

"Areava?" Powl said disbelievingly. Not his Areava, surely . . .

"Usharna," Northam said. "She told me you could not be primate. She would not tolerate it."

"Usharna?" Powl looked mystified. "Why? And why are you obeying her now, when she is dead? What does her daughter say about this?"

"Her daughter will not know. I promised Usharna I would nominate someone other than you to be my successor. She died before I could."

"Who . . . who have you chosen to succeed you?"

"I have not made up my mind. Not entirely."

"You have, your Grace, or else you would not be telling me this." And suddenly, as if someone had turned a light on in a darkened room, Powl knew. "It's Rown, isn't it? That is why you have let him supplant me as the queen's confessor."

Northam said nothing.

"But why?" Powl insisted. "Why did Usharna stop you from nominating me?"

"She never properly explained," Northam said, and Powl saw he was telling the truth. "She did not like you. She did not trust you. She never said why."

Powl slumped in his chair, and Northam hated to see it. "You have great honor in the church," he said consolingly. "And you are a member of the queen's council. I will see to it that you do not lose the seat. The church needs hard working, dedicated, and intelligent men like you to help guide its way in the world. I hope you will believe me when I say that I wish it could be you who succeeds me. It had been my fervent wish. I want you to continue as my secretary, and . . . and I would like to resume our friendship."

Powl made no answer; he did not even look at the primate.

"If you think that might be possible," Northam added sadly.

Areava made time for Olio after her time with Hansen Beresard. He had specifically asked to be alone with her, the only one in the kingdom other than her husband who had the right to ask it, and she had granted it. He walked up and down her chamber nervously, wringing his hands.

"There is something wrong," Areava said.

Olio looked at her. "There is?"

She shrugged. "Why else are you pacing like a great bear with a burr up its behind?"

He shook his head. "No. There's nothing wrong." He

stopped. "Actually, that's not true. There is something wrong. I'm to be general of the army you're sending north in the spring."

Areava blinked in surprise. "What's wrong with that? You're a Rosetheme. I cannot go. Someone must lead it."

"I'm not the b–b–best choice."

"Are you afraid?"

"Of course I'm afraid," he said, not even offended by the question. "But that isn't why I don't want to be your general."

"I don't understand."

"I'm not the m–m–most qualified, Areava. I am not a soldier. I am at m–m–most adequate with a b–b–blade. I haven't an angry b–b–bone in my b–b–body. You don't want someone like m–m–me to lead the attack against Salokan."

"Then who do I want?"

Olio looked at her squarely. "You want someone like Sendarus."

"No," she said curtly.

"B–b–but Areava, look at the differences between us—"

"No."

Olio sighed and started pacing again.

"That is why you asked to see me?" she asked him.

"Yes. I don't think it's a good idea for m–m–me to lead the army. I think it does your cause m–m–more harm than good."

"The council doesn't think so."

"The council wouldn't know," Olio countered. "How m–m–many of them were on our m–m–mother's council during the Slaver War?"

"Umm, Orkid and the primate."

"Exactly. Only two, and neither of them soldiers. M–m–most of them know less about war and strategy than m–m–my tailor. Who was it who actually suggested I be general?"

Areava had to think about that. "Father Powl," she said at last.

"Your confessor?" Areava nodded. "You m–m–made your decision b–b–based on the advice of your confessor?"

"His advice seemed sound to everyone there."

"They did not want to put you in any danger."

"That only left you," she said reasonably.

"Not any m–m–more. There is now Sendarus."

Areava opened her mouth to say no again, but closed it before she could say the word. She realized Olio was right. Sendarus was the best man to lead the army, not her brother.

"Sendarus would not understand—" she began.

"Of course he would," Olio interrupted her. "He would leap at the chance to demonstrate his loyalty to the kingdom. M–m–more importantly, he would leap at the chance to p–p–perform some b–b–brave service for you."

"And you would not?"

Olio snorted. "I would die for you, if necessary. Not as willingly as your b–b–beloved, I grant, b–b–but I would rather that than see you harmed."

Areava smiled at her brother's words; she knew they were true. If she took the generalship from his shoulders and gave it to Sendarus, some would suggest it was because Olio was a coward, but the two of them would know better.

"Your idea has merit," she said.

Olio stopped in front of her. "Then you'll do it?"

"I didn't say that. But I will think about it."

Olio's shoulders drooped in relief. "It would b–b–be b–b–best."

"It is a great risk. What if the army should lose? They would blame my husband."

"Under Sendarus the army will not lose; he is no fool. Under m–m–me, it could, and then the p–p–people would b–b–blame you."

*   *   *

Father Powl wondered about the name of God. He wondered how many letters it had, and whether or not it had more than one syllable, and if it had more than one syllable where the stress was placed. He wondered most of all whether or not Primate Northam had written it down somewhere, had written down that most sacred word in case he forgot it. Or in case he died before his time.

Knowing what was to come, Powl was unable to sleep. His apprehension grew and grew until it was almost intolerable; when at last the flood came, it started with the hurried footsteps of Northam's attendant, a novitiate of some promise but little initiative. Although Powl knew where the attendant would go first, when the door rattled with the knocking, he flinched in surprise. Powl answered it, dressed only in a nightshirt, rubbing pretend sleep from his eyes.

"Brother Anticus. What time is it?"

"Early, Father." The novitiate looked at Powl with wild eyes.

"Brother, what is wrong?"

"It is Primate Northam."

Powl frowned. "Something is wrong with his grace?"

Anticus grabbed for Powl's hand, but Powl moved it out of the way. "Brother, please tell me what's wrong."

"You have to come see, Father. You have to come see." Powl let Anticus take his hand this time, and let himself be led barefoot along the cold stone passageway to Northam's chambers.

Northam was lying in his bed, his eyes staring straight up, wide open and slightly extruded, as if he had received a sudden vision of God. Powl went to the body and placed a finger just under the neck. There was no pulse. The flesh was quite cool, but not yet cold.

"Brother Anticus, I want you to get Father Rown. Tell no one else what you have seen, but get Father Rown now."

Brother Anticus scurried off, his breath already coming

in jerking sobs. While he waited, Powl made the primate decent—pulling his nightshirt straight, closing his eyelids, placing his hands across his chest. He did not know how much time he had, so he did only a cursory search of the room. When he heard two sets of approaching footsteps, he straightened and bowed his head in prayer.

"Oh, God, no," said Father Rown's voice behind him.

"Come in," Powl said, waving for the priest and Anticus to enter the room. "Close the door behind you," he ordered, and Anticus did.

Father Rown also felt for a pulse. When he felt none he turned, aghast, to Powl. "Do you . . . do you . . ."

"Do I what, Father?" Powl asked, holding his breath.

"Do you know who . . ." Powl frowned at him. ". . . I mean, do you know *what* the word is?"

"The word?"

"Did Primate Northam pass on to you the—"

"Ah, the name of God," Powl finished for him, and started breathing again.

"Yes, yes," Rown said, his face taut with tension.

"Of course he did," Powl said. "Did you think Northam would forget that?"

Rown sighed with relief. His round face seemed to fall into its normal shape, and his generous figure, released from tension, visibly relaxed.

"You must wake our brethren," Powl told Anticus. "Do not give them the news. Tell them to gather in the royal chapel."

Anticus opened the door and hurried out.

"You will give them the news?" Rown asked.

"No, Father, you will."

"Me? Why me?"

"Because as Primate Northam's successor my first duty is to inform the queen and her chancellor. I will do that now.

And it is also my duty to select a new secretary to replace me. I select you, Father Rown. Now go and do your duty."

Father Rown bowed in thanks, and in recognition of Powl's ascension into higher office. When he looked up again, he wore half a smile. "I will do my duty."

"I know it. Now I must do mine."

"You have been talking with my brother."

Orkid looked up from his desk to see the queen standing in the doorway to his office. She was looking particularly imperious and stern. He stood up so quickly he scattered piles of paper on to the floor.

"Your Majesty! I was not expecting you—"

"Was it yesterday, Chancellor? Or the day before."

Orkid was trying to pick up papers and figure out exactly what the queen was getting at. Two secretaries were on hands and knees picking up papers as well, handing them in fistfuls to the chancellor.

"I wonder how you approached the subject? Perhaps something about how cold Hume was at this time of year?"

And Orkid understood. He stood erect, his secretaries still scrambling around his feet. "You are angry with me."

"Of course I'm angry with you," she said without any ire at all. "This is something you should first have raised with me."

"You would have said no."

"My prerogative. You would have argued me around."

"Eventually, perhaps. But this way was quicker."

"It was wrong of you."

Orkid spread his hands. "My duty is to give you my best advice, and to ensure that your wishes are carried out. Approaching Olio so he could convince you himself was a shortcut I took to achieve both ends."

Areava turned on her heel and left. Orkid was not sure if he should follow or stay where he was. He looked at the mess on the floor, and decided he could do more good away from his office.

"Your Majesty!" he called after Areava. She slowed but did not stop for him. "Your Majesty, I am sorry if you feel that I have manipulated you—"

"You always manipulate me, Orkid. I'm used to that. What I am not used to is being manipulated behind my back."

Orkid nodded. "It will not happen again."

"Good."

They strode on, courtiers and visitors making a path for them. Royal Guards snapped to attention when they went past.

"There is something else," Orkid said eventually.

Areava breathed deeply. "There is always something else with you."

"It concerns Sendarus."

"Go on."

"If you are going to assign him as general—"

"You know I am going to assign him as general. That's what all this is about, isn't it?"

Orkid swallowed. "Yes, your Majesty. If I may finish. *When* you make him general, it might be wise to ensure his authority is respected among your officers."

"They will respect him or answer to me," she said curtly.

"Easier to enforce his authority in the first place."

Areava stopped suddenly, forcing Orkid to overshoot. He backtracked and met the queen's gaze.

"How, exactly, do you propose I do that?"

Orkid pointed to the Keys of Power hanging in plain view over her chest. "Give him the Key of the Sword."

Areava blinked. *At least,* Orkid thought, *she did not say "no" outright.*

"The Key of the Sword?"

"Yes, your Majesty. As ruler, you only need the Key of

the Scepter. Sendarus will be leading your army north against Haxus, in defense of the kingdom. Surely the Key of the Sword would be the perfect symbol of your royal authority and your trust in your consort."

Areava nodded slowly. "I like this idea." She resumed walking, Orkid in tow. "I like this idea a lot. Do you think the council would accept it?" Her expression became downcast. "With Primate Northam's passing, it is weighted toward the Twenty Houses."

Orkid shrugged. "Even so, if the idea has your blessing, I don't see why not."

"The Twenty Houses would be against it," she said slowly.

Orkid did not even have to think about how to answer that. "True, your Majesty. Another point in its favor."

18

WITHIN two days of each other, three armed forces moved out of camp and toward enemy territory.

The first to move was Rendle's raiding party, nearly four thousand strong. Divided into three columns, they rode single file along one of the three passes his scouts had discovered toward the end of winter. They moved quickly, perhaps dangerously, but carried only the limited supplies needed to reach the Oceans of Grass as soon as possible.

The next day Salokan started his invasion of Grenda Lear. His force was several times larger than Rendle's and took considerably longer to cover a similar distance, even though the ground was level and mostly clear of snow or mud. Hume's border posts were swept out of the way like solitary trees before an avalanche.

The same day, and before news of Salokan's invasion could reach his ears, Jes Prado had moved out his own force, heading straight for the Algonka Pass.

There were eagles overhead. Rendle cursed them, then turned his attention to the column struggling up the defile. He looked west, saw that the largest part of his force was now over the pass's highest point and descending to the

Oceans of Grass, still a good two days away. The eagles were waiting for accidents to happen, as some—inevitably—would. A hoof slipping on loose scree would send rider and mount into a long, uncontrolled fall, ending in broken limbs and maybe necks. He could not afford to leave anyone behind to care for the injured.

But almost all of us will get through as long as the snow holds off, Rendle told himself. He feared the cold more than anything else.

General Thewor, as he had since the invasion began, stayed close to Rendle, just waiting for him to make a mistake. Rendle could *feel* him, like bad luck, hovering behind him, but paid him scant attention.

"We have been lucky," the general said.

Rendle knew that, but was not going to let the comment go that easily. "We made our own luck, General. We moved when the time was right."

The general snorted but said nothing more. He knew he should have had command of this expedition—his cavalry made up more than half the riders!—but understood why Salokan had given it to this aging, petty mercenary. As long as they intended to ride through Chett territory, Rendle was still necessary; but the moment Lynan was in their hands and they were safely back in Haxus, or that part of Hume controlled by Salokan, Thewor himself would personally supervise Rendle's execution.

"Your men are slowing us down," Rendle said, pointing to a gaggle of uniformed riders who were trailing at the end of the column.

"They are not used to the cold," Thewor said defensively.

"The truth is they are not used to such hard work," Rendle said. "There is a great deal of difference between parade ground riding and real campaigning."

Thewor tried unsuccessfully not to blush. He shouted an

order and an adjutant rode back to the stragglers to hurry them along.

"Two more days, General. Keep them together for just two more days, then we hit the Oceans of Grass."

"They will get there."

Rendle grunted, but did not argue. He spurred his horse to catch up with the main column, and Thewor stayed as close behind as his shadow.

For a moment Salokan's eyes brimmed with tears. He thought it was caused by the majesty of the event, the serried ranks of his spearmen—dressed so finely in their sky blue tunics—marching in attack column across the border with Hume. There was no one there to attack, of course—his cavalry was four leagues away sweeping up any resistance and screening the movement of his army—but it was a great morale builder for the rest of the army waiting their turn to invade Grenda Lear. An hour later the colonels and majors would shout the command for the regiments to fall into marching order and the spears would be raised, the column spread out, and the rate slowed down to sixty paces a minute.

Salokan, for all his emotions, was far more pragmatic than most of his opponents gave him credit for. Except Rendle, he remembered. Rendle understood him the way the a frog understands the kingfisher: with respect, true knowledge, and a little fear. He wiped away the tears, knowing he would spill none for those who would die or be wounded over the next few weeks, and tried not to feel hypocritical about it.

We are all instruments of the state, he silently told the soldiers. *We all have our part to play for the good of Haxus, to wipe away with a brilliant victory the disgrace of our fathers' defeat at the hands of Grenda Lear.*

Soldiers with darker blue tunics were now marching past

him. They were conscripts largely, and would not last long if Grenda Lear had a chance to put its regulars into the field. But they were good for holding a line or digging and then occupying a siege trench; and if they were lucky, most of them would survive long enough to become veterans.

Twenty regiments of spear marched by him that morning, then ten of sword and shield, and finally his cavalry, full panoplied in fancy gear none of the troopers would ever think of using in real combat. And another five thousand light infantry had already fanned ahead to secure bridges and fords. Nearly thirty thousand soldiers in all. Not a bad-sized force with which to start an invasion of a kingdom several times bigger than his own.

But the enemy are spread out, he reminded himself, *and unprepared.*

Besides, if Rendle did his part, he would soon have another four thousand cavalry and Prince Lynan Rosetheme, a symbol Salokan would use to best effect. As well, he had ten thousand regular infantry and cavalry in reserve and encamped near his capital, though he hoped never to have the need to call on them. This war would depend on speed and luck. If things went well, he would soon control all of Hume. He would then add a sizable merchant fleet to his own, possess new grazing lands, and control access to the Algonka Pass. Perhaps he could even fortify the pass and control it outright. Imagine the tithes and taxes from that. His mind did some quick and not too fanciful calculations. He liked the numbers that rolled around in his mind. With that kind of money, he could double the size of his army and come close to matching Grenda Lear soldier for soldier.

And with Prince Lynan in my hands, perhaps I could force Chandra into an alliance. I could guarantee Tomar's independence from Kendra. He would like that, I think. Then I would match Grenda Lear in every respect.

But only if this first stage worked, he reminded himself.

He knew it best to remain pragmatic; if worse came to worst, he must know the time to retreat back to Hume to lick his wounds and wait for another opportunity.

Just now, however, having watched his wonderful army march past in all their glory and untested courage, it was hard to be pragmatic.

More tears came to his eyes, and this time he did not bother to wipe them away.

Prado's forces were moving slower than he liked. There was no problem with his cavalry, but the five hundred Arran archers were not used to marching long hours over alien territory and in winter. He had made sure they were all properly equipped for the cold, but the short days, the gray skies, and the melting snow all took their toll of morale. He knew the hardest part was still to come—the climb over the Algonka Pass, where altitude would add to their misery—but once in the Oceans of Grass things would improve, so he hurried them mercilessly. His troops hated him for it now, but would thank him later on. His captains—Freyma and Sal—knew from their own experience what he was doing and supported him completely, as did the older mercenaries who had gone through the Slaver War, so it could have been worse.

His scouts were already at the base of the Ufero Mountains, and so far there was no sign of any Chett movement. The threat of war had forced him to throw out his initial plan to raid into Haxus itself, but there was no reason why he could still not force Lynan and his protectors into action by raiding the Strangers' Sooq. If he could return to Kendra with Lynan's corpse, he would be a made man; Areava might even let him keep his force intact for action against Haxus at a later date. Whatever, he could not go after Rendle this spring as he had hoped, but maybe in the summer or spring of the following year.

Prado was eating his evening meal of thick vegetable soup when Freyma, looking excited, interrupted him.

"News from the pass?" he asked.

Freyma shook his head. "One of Charion's border riders stopped by to get a fresh horse. Salokan has made his move."

Prado did not hide his surprise. "Already? Any sign of Rendle?"

"No, not that the rider could tell. He only saw light cavalry, and they were dressed in Haxus colors. He said they were screening."

"So Salokan's infantry can't be far behind."

"That's the rider's guess. He only waited for a new mount to be ready and then was off again."

Prado put down his bowl. "We don't want to get in Salokan's way." He stood up and buckled on his sword belt. "As soon as the evening meal is finished, we set off again. I want to be at the pass in two days."

Freyma nodded; Prado knew as well as he that the troops would not like it, but they would like it less if they found themselves overwhelmed by an army from Haxus.

"Get Sal and come back here."

Freyma left, and Prado shouted for his orderly. A young man burst in. Prado gave orders for the horses to be readied and the tent taken down, then strode outside. He placed a map on the ground and pinned it down with two daggers. His captains appeared, Sal slightly out of breath.

"I want you to take a company and guard our right flank," he told Sal. "Don't engage the enemy. If you see them, send a rider to let me know their position and then retreat. If we have to, we'll follow the Barda River to the pass rather than take the main road."

"Do you think Salokan is trying to secure the pass?" Sal asked.

"He will if he has any brains at all, but it won't be his first priority. He has to bottle up Hume's forces first."

"He might send a small force to secure this side of it," Freyma said.

"If so, you'll shadow it, Sal. When we're ready, we'll take care of them and be across before Salokan can follow up. He won't send anyone after us until he controls the whole province anyway."

"Things are happening faster than anyone expected," Sal said.

Prado sheathed his daggers and rolled up the map. "Good for us," he said. "Enemies in a hurry make mistakes."

"You're thinking of Rendle," Freyma said.

Prado nodded. "I can hope," he said. "But no matter. If Salokan is here in Hume, then we'll have a free hand in the Oceans of Grass. If we take the Strangers' Sooq, only the Chetts will be able to respond, and we can handle any clan that comes against us."

"As long as it's only one clan," Sal said.

Prado stood up. "Most of them will still be at the High Sooq, a month's hard ride from the Strangers' Sooq. By then, we should know which clan is protecting Lynan and can make our move." He studied his two captains. They looked grim, but ready. All three knew the time had come to commit their force to action or withdraw over the border and stay out of the way until the war between Haxus and Grenda Lear was decided. If Freyma or Sal had been in command, the choice could have gone either way.

But with Prado in command, there was really no choice at all.

19

THE light coming through the trees spread in a golden
fan. Lynan cocked his head and listened for the sound of
birds and insects, but there was none. A breeze moved the
canopy high above. He took a hesitant step forward, his boot
settling in soft brown humus. He could smell the rotting
leaves and twigs. Bright fungi decorated the bases of tree
trunks. The air was cool and moist.

The faintest of sounds. Like the flight of a passing arrow.
And again. Not an arrow, but a bird's wing. Lynan stopped
moving, looked up among the trees. And again. No, not a
bird; the sound was too leathery to be a bird. A bat, then.

He saw something moving among the topmost
branches. A shimmer. He let his eyes unfocus, moved his
head slowly. There, a flurry of wings, but gone as quickly
as it had come.

And then a face, only a glimpse, but a face he knew. He
felt fear and desire. He wanted to run away, and he wanted
to wait. He could not make up his mind.

The smell of humus again, but something else underneath, something more carnal.

"No."

He decided to flee. He turned around and started running,

but it was like moving through water; his legs would not move quickly enough. The sound of flapping wings was much closer now, just behind him, then above him again. Then in front.

He stopped, his breathing ragged. The light seemed to dissipate, leaving only shadows. Branches and leaves flurried, and there she was. So young, so beautiful. Green eyes held his. He did not want to run away anymore.

"Where have you been?" she asked. "I have been searching the wide world for you. You belong to me."

"No," he said, but the desire in him was stronger than his fear.

"Yes. Look at your skin. So pale and cold."

"No."

"We can be together. Always."

"No."

"Come to me."

Lynan walked to her. Her arms spread out for him, embraced him. Her breath was ice cold and fetid. She kissed him on the lips, then on the throat, then on the chest. Her hands moved over his back, forced him closer. He saw her eyes change shape, and he could not look away.

"You want me as much as I want you," she said, and kissed his lips again.

"Yes," he said, and knew it was true.

She laughed, held him so tight all his breath was squeezed out of his body. Two black wings spread from her back, slapped together, and he felt himself lifted off the ground. Branches whipped by them. She laughed and they rose into the sky. He glanced down and saw the world disappear beneath them.

Lynan?

He looked at her, but she was distracted. She was searching for something below them.

Lynan?

It was not her voice. When she opened her mouth she did not say his name but cried in sudden fury. She let him go, and he fell from the sky.

"No!"

"Lynan!"

He shot out of his bed, eyes wide open but not seeing. Two hands grasped his shoulders and he jumped away from them.

"Get away from me!" he cried.

More voices, a man and a woman's. Flaring brightness.

"My lord? What is the matter?"

Someone was holding a brand. Someone with a red hand. "My lord? Are you ill?"

"Give me the brand," said another voice, the voice he had heard calling him. "Leave. He was dreaming. Do not tell anyone what happened."

"Yes, your Majesty."

The light retreated. He saw a hand place the brand in a bracket. Then he saw a face in the light. He knew her. A strong face, golden-skinned.

"Korigan?"

"Yes. You were having a nightmare."

"A nightmare?"

"Can you remember it?"

Lynan closed his eyes. Wisps of memory drifted in his brain—a dim forest, a pale woman, the smell of death—and then were gone. He shuddered. Korigan's strong hands helped him back to his cot.

"It was more than a nightmare, I think," he said. He faced Korigan. "Why are you here?"

"I heard you in your sleep," she said.

There was something in her voice that told Lynan she was lying, but he said nothing.

"Are you cold?" she asked.

"No."

"You should put some clothes on."

He looked down at himself, saw that he was naked. Worse, he had an erection. He scrabbled for the blanket and placed it across his lap.

"I'm sorry," he muttered.

"I've seen worse," she said, half smiling. "What do you mean, it was more than a nightmare?"

Lynan shook his head. "It doesn't matter."

"What was her name?"

"It wasn't like that," he said shortly.

Korigan sighed. "That is not what I meant. I know what happened to you, Lynan. I know about Silona."

He shuddered involuntarily, and Korigan came closer to him, put an arm around him. "It was Silona, wasn't it?" He nodded. "Have you dreamed about her before?"

"No."

"My people have stories of the old vampires who used to inhabit the Oceans of Grass." Lynan looked up in surprise. "Oh, yes, we had them, too. But they were hunted down and killed a long time ago. All the vampires on this continent were destroyed by our ancestors, all but one."

"Silona."

"She was the strongest. Even this far away we know of her. All humans dream of her at least once in their lives. For you, it is worse."

"She was calling for me."

"I was afraid this would happen."

He stared at her. "You *knew?*"

"No, I did not know. But I suspected. You have her blood in you. That would give her some hold."

"How strong a hold?"

"The closer you are to her, the stronger it will be."

Lynan started shaking, and Korigan held him even more tightly.

"Your people will not let her take you, Lynan. I promise you that."

Her breath was warm on his cheek. In the half light of the brand, her eyes were as golden as her skin. For the first time he found himself thinking of the Chett queen just as a woman, and for the first time in a long time he felt real human desire stirring in him.

There was a commotion outside. Korigan pulled away from him just as the flap to his tent opened and one of his bodyguards entered. The man looked at both of them with something like curiosity.

"Your Majesty, I'm sorry to interrupt—"

"You're not interrupting anything," Lynan said too quickly, and stood up. He remembered to keep the blanket in front of him. "What is it?"

"It's the clans, my lord. They're gone."

Makon's face was white. "Three main clans—the Horse, the Moon and the Owl—and four lesser."

"How did they leave without us hearing them in the night?" Lynan asked.

"Easy enough to do," Korigan answered. "They had days to maneuver their herds to the edge of the sooq. They have probably been sending detachments away for the last week."

"How many warriors have we lost?" Kumul asked.

"At least fifteen thousand," the queen answered glumly. "And they are only the clans who have publicly separated from us. Many others will be thinking along the same line."

"But why?" Lynan asked. "What made them do it now?"

"They have probably been planning this for some time," Korigan told him. "They had to wait until winter was almost over so that there would be some grass growing for them in their own territory, and they had to move before you gave the command for the army to move out."

"Kumul, how many of your lancers were from the missing clans?" Lynan asked.

Kumul shrugged. "I am not sure. Perhaps two hundred out of a thousand."

"And the Red Hands?" Lynan asked Makon, who commanded them in the absence of his brother Gudon.

"None have gone," Makon said proudly. "The Red Hands are sworn to protect you above all else."

"The loss in troops isn't that great, then," Lynan said, more to himself than the others.

"It is the loss in morale that concerns me," Korigan said. "The longer we wait here, the more chance dissension will spread."

"Let me go after them," Kumul said angrily. "I'll bring the clan heads back, and their clans will follow."

"You could not do so without violence. They will obey Lynan, but not you, and certainly not me now."

"Then I will go—" Lynan started.

"You cannot," Korigan said firmly.

"A king cannot chase his subjects, your Majesty," Ager added. "You would lose respect and authority."

"They have been very clever about it," Korigan said. "They have not disobeyed any command. They just left before a command could be given them."

Lynan sighed heavily. "We have no choice. To keep the rest of the Chetts behind me, we must move the army now." He turned to Makon. "Spread the word among all the clans: their remaining levy is due today." He then turned to Kumul. "Get your lancers together, all that are left. They will take the van. Let the clans see what we have built."

The two men nodded and left, glad to have something to do. Lynan faced Korigan and Ager. "Ready your people. We leave the High Sooq today."

"Do you travel with the White Wolf clan?" Korigan asked.

"For a while. The army will march east, and I will lead it."

"I will come with you," Ager said quickly.

"You are a clan chief now," Lynan said. "You have other responsibilities."

"I will come with you," Ager repeated, more firmly. "I will bring as many of my warriors as the clan can spare. The remainder will take the herd to our spring feeding grounds."

Lynan nodded, not willing to argue, especially when any extra warriors would be welcome. "Thank you, my friend."

Ager smiled and left, leaving Lynan with Korigan.

"It seems to me that I am always forced into action by the actions of others," he told her. "It would be nice to take the initiative once in a while."

"If you act quickly enough, you will regain it," Korigan said confidently. "No one could have predicted that Eynon, Piktar and Akota would move their clans away so soon. We will not make the mistake of trusting them again."

"Ah, but that's the hard part," Lynan said. "We will have to if the Chetts are to stand together, and it is only by standing together that any of us will withstand the storm that is coming."

Lasthear came to Jenrosa. "I must ride, and you must come with me."

Jenrosa obeyed without hesitation. The two women skirted the main part of the sooq and rode to the top of a hill. From there they could see the clans starting to disperse, and in the center the gathering of Lynan's army.

"My people have never seen anything like this," Lasthear said. "Your prince has wrought greater changes than he knows."

"Are you afraid?"

Lasthear laughed. "I am always afraid." She touched Jenrosa gently on the arm. "That is the nature of our calling. We see, hear, and smell things no one else can, and that brings us knowledge. Knowledge is fear."

"I don't understand. I always thought knowledge freed us from fear."

"Some knowledge, no doubt," Lasthear answered ambiguously but did not continue.

"Why did you bring me here?"

"To help in a seeking."

Lasthear opened a leather pouch attached to her saddle and withdrew an eagle's feather. "For seeing far," she explained. Then she withdrew something round and leathery. "A heart from a karak boar, for strength."

Jenrosa blinked. This was too close to shamanism to make her feel comfortable, but she said nothing. Lasthear held the feather and dried heart in her hand. She muttered a few words and her hand was surrounded by a faint yellow glow. When she took her hand away, the objects remained suspended in midair.

Now that's something the theurgia never knew, she told herself. *Shamanism or not, this works.*

"Now we cast," Lasthear said. "I want you to say what I say."

Jenrosa nodded, and as Lasthear recited her incantation, Jenrosa repeated the words; some of them were familiar, some not.

The objects started to smoke, then they burst into flame. The color of the flame changed from yellow to blue, and still Lasthear recited, and Jenrosa repeated.

"Now concentrate on the heart of the flame," Lasthear said. "We will see what we can see."

Jenrosa did as she was told. Almost immediately she saw a vision of a land not dissimilar from that around the High Sooq, but then she noticed some differences. The grass was greener, not so damaged by the winter. There were mountains in the background. And there were buildings, like those around the lake, and like those at . . .

"The Strangers' Sooq," Jenrosa said.

"Yes. But why are we drawn there? Keep concentrating."

The vision seemed to rotate as if the plane of the earth was revolving beneath them. Jenrosa noticed there was a figure in the middle, and wherever the figure went they seemed to follow.

"A Chett," Lasthear said. "Not very tall."

"Gudon!" Jenrosa cried with certainty.

Lasthear looked at her with surprise. "Yes, I think you are right. I did not see that."

Then Gudon looked up at the sky, directly at them.

"He senses us," Jenrosa said.

"No, he senses you," Lasthear said with awe. "Your casting is powerful indeed."

"What do I do?"

"The magic must be showing him to us for a reason. In your mind, tell him what has happened here."

Jenrosa recalled the flight from the High Sooq of the clans opposed to Korigan, then she put in her mind the picture of Lynan's army forming and marching out. She saw Gudon smile with what she thought was relief.

"This is remarkable," Lasthear said.

"Prado!" Jenrosa shouted.

"What?"

"Gudon brings news of Prado."

"He is casting to you?"

"No. I can see it in his mind. He is exhausted. He has been riding hard for several days. Prado was in Daavis when Gudon left there, and Gudon believes he is not far behind. He says Prado is coming to the Oceans of Grass, and he says Haxus is invading Hume."

In her mind, Jenrosa told Gudon that they knew of the invasion, but not of Prado. Then she told him that Rendle was also moving into the Oceans of Grass. Gudon replied, but she could not hear him properly. There was a pain somewhere in the middle of her head, and the vision started to fade. She tried to hold it, but the pain increased so suddenly she shouted in agony. The flame disappeared, leaving nothing but a wisp of dark greasy smoke that drifted into the sky and dispersed.

Jenrosa slumped over her horse. Lasthear reached out to hold her steady. "I have never seen anything like this," Lasthear told her. "You have a power that has not been seen among the Chetts since the last Truespeaker died."

Jenrosa barely heard the words. The pain in her head subsided quickly after the vision went, but she was more tired than she had ever felt before in her life. If Lasthear had not steadied her, she would have fallen out of the saddle.

Ager quickly organized the Ocean clan with Morfast's help. Their traditional territory was north of the White Wolf clan and southeast of Terin's South Wind clan, a situation which explained their ambivalent loyalty to Korigan's father—for centuries they had been the fly between two hard rocks, and everything they did was determined by the attitude of the chiefs of their neighboring clans. But now the ambivalence was gone; the Ocean clan was loyal to Prince Lynan, the White Wolf himself. Too many of the clan's warriors wanted to join the Chett army, and Ager had to persuade them that some had to stay behind to protect the herd in the uncertain and dangerous months ahead. He allotted a thousand warriors to stay with the clan and placed them under the command of someone Morfast had told him was well respected and wise, a man called Dogal, and the rest— another thousand—joined Lynan's army. They took pride in the fact that the crookback was their chief; he was after all a close friend and confidant of Lynan, and had proved himself the most formidable of warriors despite his deformities.

The army moved out first, nearly twenty thousand strong. It was arranged in banners of a thousand, each banner comprising ten troops, and each troop comprising one hundred riders from a single clan. Some of the larger clans, such as the White Wolf, contributed several troops, and they were distributed among several banners so that no clan would dominate. The banners were usually commanded by clan chiefs, including Ager, but one banner was commanded by Kumul and was made up of those riders he had started training as lancers, and another banner was made up entirely of the Red Hands—who proudly carried the short sword as well as the saber—and was commanded by Makon in Gudon's absence.

As Ager watched the army leave the High Sooq, he could not help the pride swelling within him. It was greater than the pride he had felt as a young captain serving under Lynan's father, the General, because he had played a part in its creation. He also felt a greater loyalty to this army. Even before he had become a chief among the Chetts, he had started thinking he had found his true home, that his wanderings had at last come to an end. After the Slaver War he had been attracted to the sea because it promised him a life without borders, and the Oceans of Grass promised something similar. Here, even a crookback could find respect and a kind of inner peace.

Lynan rode near the vanguard, his Red Hands surrounding him. They carried pennants, and Ager was surprised to see they were not the pennant of the White Wolf, but a new design. It was a plain gold circle on a blood-red background. Ager smiled to himself. *Clever,* he thought. *The Key of Union is our flag. And all those who fight against us, fight against that.* He wondered who had thought up that idea, knowing it would never have been Kumul. *Korigan, of course. She is cleverer and more dangerous than a wounded great bear. I'm glad she's on our side.* Ager shook his head. *At least, I* hope *she's truly on our side.*

Morfast jiggled his elbow, and he turned to see the clans now moving away from the High Sooq, his own among them. He swallowed hard, only now realizing what it meant to have the loyalty of so many. The responsibility both terrified him and filled him with a wild joy.

My people, he thought. He did not know if he would survive the next few months, but if he did, nothing would stop him returning.

As if she had been reading his mind, Morfast said, "They will wait for you. You are destined to die among them, not apart from them."

Ager grunted. He glanced at her with his one eye. "Are you a prophet, Morfast?"

She grinned and shook her head. "No. But you have to admit it sounded good."

Ager grinned back. "You'll never know how good," he said.

The Chett army had not gone far by the end of the first day, partly because it started off disentangling itself from the herds and wagons around the High Sooq, but mostly because it was the first time so many Chett warriors had been gathered together into a single force—nearly twice the size of the largest army Korigan's father had brought together during the Chett civil war. Kumul had done his best to sort out an order of march, and as the day progressed, they had actually started to ride with some kind of unity. That night, Kumul made sure they camped according to their position in tomorrow's order of march, and only arrived at the commanders' meeting well after it had started.

It was a large meeting, including all the chiefs and their seconds-in-command, as well as Lynan and Jenrosa. They were gathered around a large fire. This night there was little to discuss at first, mainly minor problems relating to the hurt pride of chiefs whose banners had been relegated to the rear half of the army. Lynan assured them that the banners would be rotated from necessity, since no banner could be expected to always hold the responsibility that came with being the vanguard or rearguard.

When the chiefs had stopped asking questions, Lynan asked if there were any other matters. Jenrosa stood up and said nervously: "Jes Prado will soon be on the Oceans of Grass," then sat down again.

All eyes settled on her, and she wished she was an ant and could crawl under the nearest rock. Several people started talking at the same time.

"Quiet," Lynan commanded, and everyone shut up. "Jenrosa, how do you know this?"

"She helped me cast," said a new voice, and Lasthear stepped forward. The magicker shook her head and half-smiled. "The truth is, she took over the casting."

"What do you mean?" Korigan demanded. She had not been keen on Jenrosa being trained by a magicker who was not from the White Wolf clan, but Ager had been persuasive and it was another way of tying the Ocean clan to her cause, so in the end she had agreed to it.

"I mean, my queen," Lasthear said respectfully, "that Jenrosa—without my assistance—actually communicated with another Chett, one who was at the Strangers' Sooq."

"So far!" Korigan said in surprise. "None among us has been able to do that since—"

"Since the Truespeaker died," Lasthear finished for her. "And indeed, the one Jenrosa communicated with was the Truespeaker's son."

Korigan jumped to her feet. "Gudon!"

"What's this about Gudon?" Lynan asked, staring at Korigan and Jenrosa in turn.

"He is fleeing Prado," Jenrosa said. "He was at Daavis,

spying on Charion as you requested, when Prado turned up with a large force of mercenaries. He is certain they are coming after you."

There were shouts from many at the meeting, angry that the queen of Grenda Lear would hire mercenaries to hunt down her own brother, and even angrier that she would send mercenaries to the Oceans of Grass.

"How long?" Kumul's voice boomed over the noise. Everyone fell quiet again.

"What?" Jenrosa asked.

"How long before Prado reaches the plains?"

Jenrosa shrugged. "Gudon did not know. He felt they were close behind. They may already be across the mountains."

Kumul turned to Lynan. "I knew we should have marched northeast to take care of Rendle. Now we have two mercenary forces to worry about before we even get to the east, and we are between them. We must ride hard to the Strangers' Sooq. It is closest to us. God knows we won't arrive in time to save it, but with luck we might get there before Prado moves out again."

"He may not be making for the Strangers' Sooq," another voice said, and an argument started about Prado's intentions.

Lynan kept quiet. He understood Kumul's frustration. Jenrosa's news had shaken him, too, at first. But there was an opportunity here, he could feel it. If only he could pin down the idea that was floating at the back of his mind.

And then he had it.

"We continue marching due east," he said quietly. Some of the chiefs were still arguing and did not hear him. Korigan did, though, and looked at him. "We march east and have Rendle in one hand and Prado in the other."

"What are you saying?" Korigan asked. "We have a large force, but as yet we have had no experience in fighting as an army. And you want us to take on two mercenary forces at the same time? Surely it would be better to concentrate on either Rendle or Prado first, and then turn on the other."

Lynan shook his head, a smile crossing his face. "No, that would not be better."

By now everyone realized Lynan was speaking, and they shut up to listen to him.

"Did I hear you say we just continue riding east?" Kumul asked.

"Yes."

"That's stupid, lad," Kumul said bluntly. "You'll put us smack between our enemies."

Lynan's smile disappeared. He stared at the giant, his pale face shining in the light of the fire. "I will take your advice, Kumul Alarn, but I will not take your insults."

Kumul's face blushed bright red. All around him held their breath. Even Lynan did not know what his old friend would do. Jenrosa stood up and moved to stand by Kumul, but suddenly Ager was by her side, holding her back.

"Do not divide us further," he hissed in her ear.

Kumul looked down at his hands. He was confused by his own anger and sense of humiliation. He then looked up at Lynan, saw the youth's implacable stare and understood he, too, felt humiliated.

"I am sorry," Kumul said brusquely. "I had no right."

Lynan swallowed. He could not let it end like this. There would be too much resentment on both sides.

"Kumul, Ager, and Jenrosa, we need to talk. Everyone else, please return to your banners." He saw Korigan hesitate, but he nodded to her and she left.

The four remaining came together, standing, all trying to figure out what had just occurred between them and not liking the answer. They were dividing; after all they had gone through together, they were dividing.

"Kumul," Lynan started, "I have good reasons for letting the army continue as it is."

"I think you are unwise in risking the army getting caught between two enemies," Kumul replied.

"I understand that. I will not let it happen."

Kumul nodded perfunctorily, not happy with the answer but afraid to question Lynan again.

"I am not against you, Kumul," Lynan said.

"I did not think you were—" Kumul blurted.

"Yes, you did. You think that I have turned against you in favor of Korigan. You think I am punishing you for treating me like a child." He stopped. He wanted to say, *And you think I am punishing you for being Jenrosa's lover,* but he could not say the words. Instead, he said: "That was partly true that night I made the decision to go to the High Sooq. It is not true now."

"I accept that," Kumul said, his anger tempered by Lynan's honesty. "But am I to keep quiet when I disagree with you?"

"I hope not. Whether you know it or not, I still rely on you, old friend. I need you. But I do not need to be lectured by you."

Kumul swallowed. "I am ever at your side."

Lynan turned to Ager and Jenrosa. "The same goes for you, as well. I have not forgotten what you have all done for me. I have not forgotten the bonds of friendship. But one of the things you taught me was the responsibility of leadership, and now that I am a leader, I am responsible for more than our friendship. In the future I may say and do things that may make you forget that friendship, but I will never forget it."

Ager and Jenrosa nodded.

"I need to talk to Kumul alone," Lynan said, and they left. Lynan and Kumul looked at each other shyly. They opened their mouths to speak at the same time, then closed them together. That made them both grin.

"I count on you more than I can say," Lynan said quickly.

"You have been my father, older brother, and teacher all at the same time. I always took it for granted that you would be by my side."

Kumul tried to swallow, but his throat was suddenly constricted.

"I know about you and Jenrosa," Lynan continued. "I was surprised." He laughed bitterly. "I was hurt."

"Lad, I did not mean—"

"I know," Lynan said, holding up his hand. "It was self-pity on my part, something I'm very good at, as you well know. I am sorry for that. I want you to know that you both have my blessing." Kumul looked up sharply. "Not that you require it, of course—"

"I am glad of it," Kumul said.

Lynan sighed. He felt as if a great load had been lifted from his shoulders. "Well and good," he said. "Well and good."

20

"DON'T look so grim," Sendarus said.

"Easier said," Areava replied, her arms around his neck. "I'll be without you for God only knows how long."

"Not long. We will throw Salokan back into Haxus by summer. By the start of autumn, I will be back in your bed."

"Our bed."

"Oh, no. You are the queen."

"The queen of beds."

"The queen of hearts," he said, and kissed her.

Areava laughed. "Oh, you are like butter."

He kissed her again, and they did not come up for air for some time. At last, they heard the sound of troops marching outside.

"Your army is gathering, General," Areava told him.

Sendarus nodded sadly. "Well, the sooner we leave, the sooner we'll be back." He patted her belly, already starting to swell. "I want to be here when our child is born." There was something like reverence in his voice.

"Then you will have to handle Salokan speedily. Babies don't schedule their birth for the benefit of generals or queens."

"When do you think?" he asked seriously.

"Early to midsummer."

"Close, but I will be here." He let her go and went to the window overlooking the courtyard. "Cousin Galen is waiting for me. The knights look splendid in their mail."

"It's good to know the Twenty Houses are good for something," Areava said.

"They don't trust me, you know. They hate the fact that an Amanite is leading them. They wanted Olio."

"They wanted someone they could manipulate. Olio would have surprised them, but with you, they won't even try. You'll be lucky to get a courteous word from them."

"As long as they obey orders, I'll not complain."

Areava joined him. "Oh, they'll obey your orders." She placed a heavy chain over Sendarus' neck. He looked down and fingered the Key of the Sword.

"You are leading my kingdom's army into battle against our oldest and most determined foe. You have every right to wear it."

Sendarus could not help puffing up a little with pride. The Key shone in the early morning light.

Areava placed her hand against his cheek. "You must go."

Sendarus held her hand and looked down on her. For the first time she saw something akin to fear in his eyes. He opened his mouth to say something, but seemed to change his mind; he pretended to smile, let go of her hand, and left.

Areava waited by the window until Sendarus appeared in the courtyard. Orkid was holding his horse for him. Sendarus mounted quickly, glanced up at the window, and waved at her. She wanted to wave back, but her hands were clasped tightly over her heart and could not move. She wished Olio was by her side, but he had not been seen all day. And then she thought of Primate Northam, wanting badly to talk to him, and then she remembered he was dead. *A week ago!* she thought in surprise. It seemed those that

loved her most were no longer around her, and she wished
she was not queen at all but merely a woman with a husband
who was nothing more important than a carpenter or a shop
keeper.

Galen Amptra sat on his horse in the courtyard in full
armor and with his helmet on. He wished to hell Sendarus
would get a move on so they could parade out of the city and
then get into more comfortable traveling clothes. Mail
hauberk and shin guards were all well and good in the middle of a melee, but a bloody torment on a sunny day when
the greatest threat was heat stroke.

He chided himself for his impatience. He had no wife,
and currently no mistress, to tarry with before setting out on
campaign. And Sendarus, of course, had Areava, possibly
the most beautiful woman in the kingdom.

No, not really, Galen told himself. *She has the features
for beauty, but no concern for them. It is her power and her
assuredness that makes her beautiful. No wonder Father is
afraid of her.*

Sendarus appeared from the palace, his new mail shining
brilliantly in the sun. In his hand he held a helm of the peculiar kind worn by Amanite infantry; it covered almost the
whole head, leaving only the eyes and mouth exposed. *He'll
learn soon enough,* Galen thought. *A cavalryman needs to
see and hear more than he will inside that pot.*

Sendarus turned to review the knights before mounting,
then with Orkid's help got into his saddle. Galen's breath
caught in his throat when he saw the Key of the Sword resting against Sendarus' mailed chest. Areava had told the
council Sendarus would have it for the campaign and that it
was no use their objecting, but seeing the crossed swords
and spear worn by an Amanite made Galen wish he had. The
nobleman could feel the blood rushing to his face but could
do nothing to control it. He looked around and saw that he

had not been the only knight to see the amulet hanging from Sendarus' neck, and several were talking angrily among themselves.

Sendarus waved to a window in the palace, and Galen turned. He caught a glimpse of Areava, and seeing that pale, severe face cooled him more quickly than a winter rain. She had given the Key to her husband. Sendarus might be an Amanite, but he was no thief.

Areava is betraying us! he thought angrily, but immediately banished it from his mind. It was he who was thinking treason, and the revelation shocked him. *She is my queen. Sendarus is her lawful husband and general of this army. He has a right to wear one of the Keys.*

His reasoning was solid, yet his heart still fought against it.

There was not enough time to properly invest Father Powl as the new Primate of the Church of the Righteous God, but as senior cleric he was still the only one who could properly bless the army. He stood on a makeshift dais near the city's north gate, the wide dirt road leading from it disappearing into the hills that backed Kendra. It was a difficult route for the army to follow, but the most direct to Chandra and then Hume. Infantry stood in their regiments waiting for the commander. It was nearly mid-morning, and though the air was cool, the sun was warm and some of the men were getting fidgety. Father Rown, standing to the right and slightly behind Powl, pointed down into the city. At first all Powl saw was the glimmer of the sun off armor, and then he heard the steady hoofbeats and clinking of mail that told him this was the heavy cavalry from the Twenty Houses. Now he could hear people cheering them as they rode through the streets.

The soldiers waiting by the gate were craning their necks to catch a glimpse of the spectacle. After all, the knights of

Kendra had not marched to war in over fifteen years, and once Haxus was thrashed, they might never have cause to ride again. The first troop comprised the youngest nobles, each carrying the pennants of their houses. Next came Sendarus, his mail shining as bright as the sun, and on his chest the golden Key of the Sword—the infantry cheered to see it. Then came the knights themselves: three regiments, all kitted up, their stallions pulling at the reins. Father Powl blessed each regiment as it rode by, and then they were out the gate and heading into the hills, their going marked by a slowly drifting cloud of dust.

When the last knight had gone, the infantry wheeled, saluted the city, received their blessing in turn, and followed the cavalry out of the gate. The tramping of their feet echoed all the way down to the harbor. By mid-afternoon, the last soldier had gone, and a breathless silence fell over Kendra.

Father Powl remained on the dais long after every one else had gone. He had just performed his first official function as Northam's successor. Not as primate, perhaps, but nonetheless the recognized heir. If he had been a power in the land before, it was nothing to what he could achieve now.

And the cost, really, had been so small, he thought. And then he remembered he still had not found the name of God. He had spent half a day in Northam's chambers searching for some clue, some secret scribbling, but to no avail. Still, he had the rest of his life to find it, and he was confident he would.

Olio did not watch the army go. He felt a mixture of guilt and shame and relief that it was Sendarus and not he who was leading the army, and although he knew it was for the best, he could not help the sense of failure that filled him. His second failure, taking into account the way he had handled the healing work at the hospice.

He was an encumbrance, he was sure, to his sister. She was trying so hard to be the best queen for her people, and here he was, her stuttering, slovenly brother who could do nothing right.

He shook his head in shame. This was no way for a prince of the realm to behave. He would go to Areava and ask for some other commission. There must be something he could do for the kingdom, something that would allow him to prove his worth.

He wandered the halls of the palace, absorbed in his own thoughts, eventually finding himself in the west wing. Priests walked around him, nodding but saying nothing. He passed the royal chapel, hesitated, but decided not to go in. He entered the library, then just stood and looked around at the shelves of books that rose around him like walls. He fought off a twinge of claustrophobia. One book was open on a reading desk and he went to it. Half of one page had writing on it, done in a careful and elegant hand, but the rest of the page and its opposite were blank.

"I pray for guidance," he read aloud, "and for the souls of all my people; I pray for peace and a future for all my children; I pray for answers and I pray for more questions. I am one man, alone and yet not lonely. I am one man who knows too many secrets. I pray for salvation."

He traced the last word with a finger. *Salvation for whom?* he wondered.

"It was his last entry," said a voice behind him. He turned and saw Edaytor Fanhow. The prelate's plain face looked as downcast as Olio felt.

"Whose last words?" he asked, and realized the answer even as he asked the question. "Northam's?"

Edaytor nodded. "The book will stay open until Father Powl is invested as the new primate, and then he will continue it. Each day the primate writes a passage or a prayer, or maybe nothing more than an observation. It is called the Book of Days." He pointed to a shelf near the desk. Every volume on it was black-bound, without any title or description. "They go back to the first primate. Anyone can read them. They are to provide guidance, solace, wisdom."

"These are sad words," Olio said, pointing to the script.

"I think he was a sad man," Edaytor said. "I think he never knew how much he was loved and respected."

" 'Alone but not lonely.' I think he knew."

Edaytor studied the prince. Olio steadily returned the gaze.

"I think you are ready," Edaytor said eventually.

"I think I am, too. My nightmares are less frequent. I have . . ." Olio could not find the words to describe how he knew he was ready to resume using the Healing Key.

"You have grown up," Edaytor said. "A priest from the hospice tells me they have a sick girl. They do not know what afflicts her, but she is dying."

"Tell me, my friend, would you have told me this if Primate Northam was still alive?"

"He would not have stopped us, I think. Not now."

"Will you tell Father Powl about our arrangement with the hospice?"

"He will have to know when he is primate."

"We will go to him together, then."

"Yes."

"A sick girl, eh?"

"Yes."

"I will go the hospice immediately."

"You are a good man, Prince Olio Rosetheme."

"And I am neither alone nor lonely," he said, smiling at the round prelate, the sudden truth of it giving him more joy than he expected to feel that day.

*　　　*　　　*

Orkid found Areava alone in the throne room. She was wandering among the columns that separated the red-carpeted nave from the aisles. At that moment she seemed to him like a little girl who was lost in a forest. Her face was downcast, her cheeks wet with tears. Her guards stood at attention at the entrance and the rear exit to her private chambers, their eyes straight ahead, ignoring her pain because there was nothing they could do to alleviate it.

Her tears are for Sendarus. I wish they were for me.

"Your Majesty?"

Areava looked up, but her eyes were unfocused. "Why did Berayma have to die?"

Orkid's heart skipped a beat. He knew she believed Lynan had committed the murder, but for a moment it seemed to him she was seeing deep into his own heart.

"No reason that we may ever understand," he said slowly.

"If he had still been king, I would be leading our army north. My mother gave me the Key of the Sword. That is where I should be now, with my regiments, not here in this empty palace."

"The palace is never empty while its queen is in it."

She stared at him, not understanding. "Maybe I am not queen. Maybe this is all a nightmare."

"Sendarus will return soon, your Majesty. The nightmare will not last forever."

"I want to believe that. But you know that some nightmares never end, don't you, Orkid? Some nightmares last a lifetime."

He went to her and took her hand. "Not this nightmare. I promise you."

She sighed deeply and with her other hand held up the Key of the Scepter so that a ray of sunshine coming through one of the high windows fell upon it. "See how it shines? It is the only bright thing in Kendra today, and yet it is this Key that weighs me down."

Orkid glanced at the Key, then quickly looked away. All he could see on it was Berayma's blood. Why had she not cleaned it yet? Could she not see it as well?

"It is the symbol of the kingdom, Areava. You *are* the kingdom."

"But today I would rather be its lowliest subject."

They heard one of the guards come to attention; Harnan Beresard appeared at the rear exit, his small writing table under one arm.

"You are being called to your duties," Orkid said with some relief.

"And I am keeping you from yours. We will talk later."

"I am always at your service, your Majesty."

She nodded and patted his hand. "And for that I will always be grateful, my friend."

Dejanus had watched the knights leave from the main palace gate. He could not help the sneer on his face as Sendarus rode past, and did not care if anyone saw it. He was angry that he had been passed over for the command of the army a second time. He could understand that the queen and her council would make Olio a general—he was, after all, a Rosetheme—but not this upstart from Aman. Queen's plaything, pretty boy, and now general. Dejanus almost shouted in rage when he saw that Sendarus also wore the Key of the Sword.

After the regiments had passed, he stomped into town in a red rage, looking for something or someone to take it out on. He passed the Lost Sailor Tavern, stopped, and went back. Business was slow, most citizens on the streets heading to the north gate so they could watch the army leave for the war. But, he noticed with satisfaction, his pretty inform-ant was on duty. What was her name again? That's right,

Ikanus. He found a corner table and signaled to her. She came over, nervous and diffident.

"My lord?"

"What news?" he snarled.

"Nothing much—"

"What news!" he repeated, and slapped the table. Ikanus jumped. The few customers in the inn looked across warily and, on seeing Dejanus, quickly looked away again.

"Y–you know of the hospice?" Dejanus shook his head. "There is a hospice in this quarter run by the church."

"And why should that interest me?"

"I have heard that it is visited frequently by the magicker prelate and one other."

"The prelate? Edaytor Fanhow?" Ikanus nodded. "And which other?"

"N–no one knows, my lord. He wears a cape and hood, but is always in the company of the prelate. They stay for a while and then leave together. People say the prelate's companion is a great magicker, for many who go there are dying, and the next day return home completely healed."

"How many?" Dejanus asked, curious despite himself. He had been looking for an excuse to beat Ikanus.

"I d–do not know. They are mostly children."

Dejanus sat back, deep in thought. This was news indeed. A magicker who cured the dying? He had never heard of any so powerful. And why was the prelate trying to keep it so secret?

Unless . . .

No, it was too incredible. He scratched his beard. Or maybe not. It would go a long way to explaining the recent unusual behavior of a certain member of the court. He had heard only rumors, but now they were starting to make sense.

"Is there anything else, my lord?" Ikanus asked.

Dejanus shook his head, and she turned to leave. "Wait!"

he ordered, and gave her a silver coin. "A flagon of Storian red."

"I cannot change this . . ."

"Keep the change. You have done well."

She did a sort of curtsy and hurried off. Dejanus watched her go, admiring the way her backside moved. Maybe he would linger a while, at least until she was off duty. She might even earn another silver coin before the night was out.

21

THE four riders stopped on the windward side of the hill and for a moment enjoyed the soft westerly breeze that cooled their sweat.

"It has been many years since Gudon rode the White Wolf territory," Lynan said to Korigan. "Are you sure he knows the field you've told me about?"

"I am certain. We call it the Ox Tongue; in area it is almost as large as the High Sooq, and is almost always sprouting new grass this time of year."

Lynan turned to Jenrosa. "Are you ready?" he asked.

Jenrosa took a deep breath. "No. But we can't wait." She glanced at Lasthear, who pulled another feather and boar heart from her saddle pouch, held one of Jenrosa's hands, and started the incantation. Within moments, a ball of blue fire appeared.

"Can you see it?" Lasthear asked Lynan excitedly.

Lynan could not speak. Inside the fire he could see the Strangers' Sooq, and even as he watched, the focus changed and there was Gudon, his face looking up into the sky.

"Incredible," he said. Korigan echoed the sentiment.

Jenrosa laughed in surprised delight. "He knew I'd be in touch again," she told Lynan. "He's asking if you are here."

She frowned in concentration. "He is glad you are both well. What do you wish him to do?"

Lynan told her. She relayed his instructions, then suddenly swayed in the saddle. The flames disappeared. Both Lynan and Lasthear reached out to steady her, but this time Lasthear seemed more tired than Jenrosa. "I gave her as much help as I could. It was exhausting."

"Thank you," Jenrosa told her. "You did help. There is almost no pain at all in my head. But I grew tired more quickly."

"We do it too soon after the first time," Lasthear explained. "Even for one with your raw talent, there is a cost."

Lynan looked closely at Jenrosa. She smiled weakly and said: "It is done. Gudon will do as you ask."

"If Terin does his part, all is ready," Lynan said.

"Terin will do as you have asked," Korigan assured him. "Now it is up to us."

Igelko had led Terin and his troop of four riders straight as an arrow. From their vantage point atop a crest they could see a scouting party for Rendle's mercenary force, although in this case they were Haxus regulars.

"I count seven," Igelko said. "There are another three somewhere."

"One on each flank, one bringing up the rear. Good."

They scrabbled down the crest to where their horses waited. They mounted quickly and rode back to the mouth of the shallow valley Rendle's scouting party was exploring. They reined in a short while later, letting their horses lazily crop at the spring grass.

"How long?" one rider asked.

"Any time now," Terin answered. He was younger than most of his warriors, but they were proud to have him as their chief. He was a great hunter and horseman, and his decisions concerning the clan, including tying its fortunes to

Queen Korigan's ambitions, had brought the clan increasing honor. And in the last few days he had shown his skill as a warrior by leading his warriors against the rearguard Rendle left behind to protect the passes his force had come through.

"Don't look, but the first is now in sight," Igelko hissed. Terin risked glancing from the corner of his eye. His troop was in plain sight, and yet the Haxus rider still did not see them. Carrying out Lynan's latest instructions—brought to him by rider only the day before—would be harder than he thought.

"These enemies are as blind as karak in the dark," another rider said. "They would be easy prey,"

"We will have our turn," Terin said under his breath. "But not here, and not now. You know what we have to do."

More of the regulars appeared, and then at last one of them gave the alarm.

Terin and his riders pretended to be startled. They spurred their horses to a gallop and rode away from the regulars.

This is a fine game, Terin thought, and laughed in the wind.

The sergeant leading the scouting party was the first to see the Chetts. He shouted a command and his party gathered around him.

"What do we do?" one of his men asked.

"Go back and warn the general . . ." he started to say, but then noticed the Chetts were galloping away from him. "No! There are only five of them! We must catch them! Rendle will reward us for taking a prisoner!"

With that, he dug his heels into his horse and started off in pursuit of the fleeing enemy, his men close behind. It did not take him long to realize they were catching up with the Chetts, and could only think it was because they must already have ridden hard and their horses were nearly blown.

"Not long now!" he shouted, and his men cheered in anticipation of a fight heavily in their favor, and the prizes Rendle would shower on them for being the first to bring back a Chett captive.

They rode along the whole length of the valley, then over a shallow rise, then down into another valley. Although they drew closer and closer to the Chetts, it was taking longer than the sergeant thought it would to reach them. Up ahead was another rise, and he was sure it would be the last effort for the Chett mares. Then he saw the cloud of dust over the rise. For a moment its significance did not register. When it did, he reined in hard, the bit digging hard into his horse's mouth.

"What's wrong?" one of his men cried. "We almost have them!"

The sergeant pointed to the dust cloud. "Use your eyes, you dolt! The whole clan and its herd must be over that rise. We'd be massacred."

"God's death! They'll alert their outriders!"

They turned their horses around and quickly spurred into another gallop. The sergeant was now frantically worried that if they were pursued their own mounts would tire.

After they reached the point where he had first seen the Chetts, he risked looking over his shoulder, and when he saw there was no one after them, he slowed down to a quick walk. They were only a league or two from the main force now, and so were almost certainly safe. Still, he had to resist the urge to gallop the rest of the way, and he never stopped looking over his shoulder to check that a horde of murderous Chetts were not rushing down on them.

"They've gone back," Igelko told Terin, then leaned over his saddle to catch his breath.

"How far to their main force?"

"Four leagues, maybe less. Rendle will have a thousand soldiers here by midday."

Terin grinned. "Right. Get a fresh horse. You'll have no time for rest, I'm afraid."

Igelko nodded wearily. Terin then gave orders for the riders who had been pulling the long rakes made up of sinew and karak bones to dismantle them. They had put enough dust in the air for it to last at least until the afternoon. "The enemy has taken the bait. We ride south for another ten leagues and repeat the performance."

"How long do you think they will follow us?" Igelko asked. "Even Rendle must get tired of chasing dust all day."

"They'll keep it up for a few days, and that's all we need."

Igelko found the energy to grin back at his chief. "Then we don't run anymore."

Terin slapped him on the chest. "Then we fight, my friend. Then we fight."

Gudon scoured the markets in the Strangers' Sooq for the clothes he wanted. He found a pair of barge pants and an old wagon driver's shirt that would make do. He traded his own clothes to purchase them, and the merchant was so surprised he threw in a handful of coins as well.

"You are very generous," Gudon told him.

"I am cheating you, stranger," the merchant said, shaking his head, then held out another few coins. "Here, have these as well. My conscience needs the salve."

Gudon accepted them gratefully, although he did not need them; but there was no need to make the merchant feel bad.

The two shook hands, and Gudon quickly changed into the barge pants and old shirt. He inspected himself in the reflection of an old mirror the merchant held up for him.

"You don't look much like a Chett anymore," the merchant told him.

"Ah, but I do look like a barge pilot who has run out of luck," Gudon replied.

"You are crazy, my friend."

A short while later he was having a drink in the sooq's best inn. A tall, ascetic-looking man joined him.

"I see you found what you are looking for," the man said.

"The merchant thought I was crazy."

"You are."

Gudon shrugged. "Perhaps, Kayakun. Crazy or not, only I can do this."

Kayakun did not argue, but ordered a drink for himself and a refill for Gudon.

"You think Lynan can pull off this plan of his?"

"You met him. What do you think?"

"He is a boy."

"He is a great deal more than a boy. I have seen him change beyond recognition. He has won over most of the clans. He is the White Wolf returned to us, Kayakun."

Kayakun regarded his friend carefully. "If true, it is a marvel indeed."

"You sound skeptical."

"I have spent over ten years in this town, spying for Korigan and her father before her. I have seen many marvelous things, heard many amazing stories. But the White Wolf returned?" He shook his head. "I am sorry, but now legends only sound like tales from the wine pot."

"You will see for yourself before long."

"As long as this boy's plan works. You are taking a terrible risk."

"Have you any word?" Gudon asked him, changing the subject.

"There are birds flying high over the pass. Prado's men will be here by tomorrow morning."

"Then his scouts will be here by tonight."

"They will not enter the town alone. You have one more

night's good sleep. You will need it. Only the gods know when you'll sleep safely again."

Prado woke with the sun. Freyma and Sal were already up, stirring the troops. He looked behind him at the pass, remembering with bitterness that the last time he passed across it was as Rendle's prisoner. Next time he crossed it would be with a basket carrying Lynan's head. In front of him lay the Oceans of Grass, a great yellow expanse still recovering from the winter. In less than a month the First Light caravan—the first caravan to make the crossing after winter—would be making the journey here from the east.

No, not this spring, he corrected himself. Not with the war. God only know how long it would be before the next caravan made the crossing.

Freyma appeared by his side. "Do we move with the archers?"

Prado shook his head. "No, they can catch up. By now those in the Strangers' Sooq will have seen our scouts and know we're coming. I'd like to get there before they can organize any proper defense." He looked around at his mercenaries. "See how eager they are?"

"After marching all winter, they can hardly wait to get their hands on something to make it all worthwhile."

"They'll fill their saddlebags at the sooq. And that's only the beginning. Tell them to mount up. We ride now."

"They're hungry. Surely they can eat a little before—"

"Tell them in three hours they can eat breakfast in the comfort of an inn."

"Yes, General," Freyma said, and left.

There was panic in the Strangers' Sooq. Many merchants loaded their horses and wagons with all the goods they could lay hands on and tried to get as far away as possible from the town. Most realized there was no time to flee, and instead boarded up their homes and readied buckets of water and damp blankets to put out any fires. A few tried to set up an ambush, but there were not enough warriors for them to offer anything but the opportunity for a massacre. The oldest among them remembered the Slaver War and how the sooq had been captured and then recaptured several times, but neither side had ever destroyed the town—it was too valuable a prize to raze to the ground—and so placed their trust in the gods and hoped that whatever blood was spilled did not come from their own families.

When Prado's main column did arrive, it raced through the town at full gallop. The riders whirled swords above their heads looking for an opportunity to use them. When they got to the end of town, they slowed to a canter and split into two lines, each one reversing their course and taking time to inspect each dwelling. By the time Prado himself arrived a few minutes later, the Strangers' Sooq was mostly under his control. A group of young men tried to ambush him and his bodyguard, but they were cut down before they were close enough to land a blow. Prado ordered that their heads be cut off and put on pikes planted in the sooq's trading ground, then claimed the best inn for his own headquarters.

Prado next ordered the town's elders to be brought before him. He interviewed them carefully about the whereabouts of Lynan, but all they could tell him was what he already knew: he had come in the company of a merchant and left in the company of a Chett, a giant, a crookback from the east, and a young woman. No one had seen or heard of him since.

Prado was disappointed but not surprised. He had one of the elders tortured to make sure his story was true, but the facts did not change. Prado let them all go.

"What now?" Freyma asked, rubbing his pock-marked cheeks. He had forgotten how the dry air on this side of the pass made his skin itch.

"We wait. Let those who live here know that I will pay good money for information about Lynan's whereabouts. Word will come."

"How long can we wait?"

"Twenty days at the most. After that, we can expect a visit from a couple of clans at least. But someone will come in with information. In the meantime, organize a collection. Every house must deliver one half of its goods. When the collection is complete, distribute the booty among our riders and archers."

"That will make the reward for information about Lynan more valuable," Freyma observed.

"Exactly."

It was at the end of the collection that Prado's break came. He himself was riding to inspect the loot when a short, ragged-looking Chett darted from a nearby house. Prado drew his saber, thinking for a moment that he was about to be attacked by a single madman, but then another Chett, well-dressed, carrying a stick and as angry as a wounded karak, came after the first Chett, caught him, and started beating him to the ground. Prado and his men laughed at the scene, some betting each other whether or not the smaller Chett would die before his attacker's fury evaporated. The runaway managed to get to his feet despite the blows, looked around desperately for help, and on spying Prado darted toward him crying, "My lord! My lord! Protect me, please!"

The other Chett chased after him, shouting, "Scoundrel! Thief!"

This made the mercenaries laugh twice as hard. Prado kicked the first Chett away, and he landed hard on the ground again; his pursuer nodded his thanks and raised his stick to resume the assault.

"Stop!" Prado yelled suddenly.

Everyone did.

"Pick the little bastard up and bring him here," Prado ordered. Two riders jumped off their horse and collected the Chett. Prado peered at the captive's face. "I know you."

The Chett's eyes, already wide with fear, seemed ready to pop out of their sockets.

"No, master! We have never met. I would not forget such majesty—"

Prado slapped his face, hard. "You worked on the Barda River."

"Me? I am a Chett, master! Why would a Chett work on this river—"

Prado slapped his face a second time. "Barge pilot," he said.

The Chett seemed to collapse in the arms of the two riders still holding him, and started whining like a whipped dog. "Oh, master!"

"We were on your barge and you drove us into a jaizru nest. Because of you, I lost two of my best men. And I lost my prisoner."

Prado dismounted, drew his dagger and placed it against the neck of the Chett.

"I know where he is!" the Chett squeaked just as Prado was tensing to slash open his throat.

Prado put his face right against the Chett's. "Who? You know where who is?"

"The prisoner."

"Prince Lynan?"

The Chett swallowed. "*Prince?* I did not know the little master was a *prince!* Had I known I would have asked for more money—"

Prado roared in fury, and for a moment everyone around him thought he would cut the Chett's throat, but instead he settled for slapping his face so hard the little man lost consciousness. Prado spat on the ground. "Take him to my quarters," he ordered.

The tall Chett who had been chasing the prisoner opened his mouth to protest, but Prado stared him down. "Leave well enough alone," Prado muttered, and Kayakun bowed and scraped and backed away until he reached the safety of his own home.

22

FOR King Salokan, ruler of Haxus and soon, in his own mind, to be ruler of Hume as well, things were going about as well as expected. He had swept through northern Hume like a winter storm through a fishing fleet, scattering all before him. Even Charion's border guards, well-trained and usually alert, had been surprised by his advancing before the spring thaw. And now, in the distance, he could see the walls of Daavis itself. Once the provincial capital was in his hands, and he had no doubt that would happen within the next month—well before Areava's army could relieve the city, he would settle down to withstand any counterattacks and send out small units to harass the enemy's line of supply. And the next spring? Maybe Chandra would fall to him as well, and after that who could tell? Salokan, ruler of the whole continent of Theare. Well, why not?

"Oh, what a beautiful war," he said aloud, clapping his hands together. He wished his father could have seen this. But no, he told himself, the old fool would have been in charge still and fouled the whole thing up.

From his vantage point at the end of the plain that spread north from Daavis, he had watched his army's columns ribbon their way toward the city. First the cavalry to secure the roads and the little river towns that dotted the Barda east and west of the capital, then the infantry to protect the sappers as they dug trenches. Finally, two hundred carpenters and smithies, conscripted from villages and towns in northern Hume, would arrive to build flat-bottomed barges to help secure the river and siege engines to help storm Daavis if Salokan decided an all-out assault was necessary.

In the middle distance he watched a few enemy companies retreating in good order, halting occasionally to slow down the pursuit. Even now there was an action between a battered Hume regiment of foot and one of his light cavalry units; the enemy regiment had stalled too long and were now surrounded by the cavalry who hung back and shot arrows into them. Salokan watched the action, picking at a roasted chicken and sipping on a fine wine his aide brought him for lunch, until the last enemy dropped. He then sighed as the cavalry dismounted to butcher the wounded and loot whatever possessions took their fancy. He hated to see this casual slaughter. War should be between the nobles and their retinues, as it had been once, but Grenda Lear had changed all that during the Slaver War, actually going so far as to train and pay their levies. That war had seen the first truly professional national army—one reason why Haxus and the mercenaries had been so decisively beaten—and now Haxus had one, too. From now on, war meant the common people killed each other while the nobles sat back to watch things from a relatively safe distance. Little honor, Salokan thought, although victory still brought glory, as well as considerable booty.

By the afternoon his forces controlled all the area around Daavis and a good portion of the northern river bank. His sappers had set up prebuilt wooden walls to protect them from enemy archers and prying eyes while they started digging trenches. His infantry were setting up a semipermanent camp, with shit holes, piss trenches, cooking pits, and even two main streets; in the corners farthest from Daavis they would set up a hospital for the most severely wounded and a special, semidetached section for Salokan's own quarters and his personal bodyguard. The king waited until he saw his own tent going up, then slowly rode through the plain to the camp. He ambled by clumps of slain soldiers, their bodies pierced by arrows, cut by swords, battered by clubs and maces, and now gnawed on by dogs and pigs from nearby farms; insects burrowed into their skin. Occasionally, a dispatch rider would gallop up to him with reports; he would listen attentively, thank the rider, and continue on his way. He finally reached the camp just as the sun was setting. He could see the Barda River, quietly ruffled by the gentlest of breezes, smell smoke from cooking fires, hear the sounds of confident soldiers and occasionally groans from the wounded, feel in his bones a victory that if not yet imminent was nonetheless inevitable.

"Yes," he said as he sat in front of his tent and overlooked his camp and the walls of his enemy's final refuge in the north, "this is a beautiful, beautiful war."

Queen Charion insisted on patrolling the walls herself. Her bodyguard fretted as they tried to keep up with her, but despite her short legs she could move like the wind when she had a mind, her energy fueled by her rage.

"What is being done for our wounded?" she demanded. Her brown eyes looked as hard as polished wood.

Farben, who thought war was an inconvenience designed primarily to disrupt his orderly life, hurried to her side. The effort made him short of breath. "There are too many for the priests and magickers to deal with all at once. Those that are in most need of treatment are being seen to first."

"And our garrison? Now that all our forces have pulled back to the city, how many have we to man the walls?"

Farben looked helplessly at an officer, who could only

shrug back. "It is too early to tell, your Highness, although it seems we will have enough to man the walls, and some left over to act as a reserve."

"If we need to, thin the walls to beef up the reserve."

"Your Highness?"

Charion sighed, stopping suddenly so that her bodyguard was forced to stop to avoid bumping into her. There was a shambles behind her as they sorted themselves out, Farben somehow finding himself squeezed to the front so he was standing next to his queen. A breeze blew her long black hair and strands of it tickled his face. She nodded along the length of the wall. "These walkways make sure we can re-inforce the wall at any point an attack is being made. I want a soldier at every parapet, ten at every gate, and one every ten paces in between. When an attack comes, we thin the de-fenses on the walls to the left and right, leaving the opposite wall at normal strength."

"Why not pull the reinforcements from the opposite wall?" Farben asked.

"Because that's what the enemy will want us to do, you fool," Charion spat. "He will try feinting at one point, then attack at the opposite. If he attacks too close to the original feint, then it can be countered too quickly."

"Oh."

Charion regarded him with something like desperation, then resumed her walk. "Supplies?"

"All stored. We have four distribution centers for food. We've cleaned the underground aqueduct to the river and have filled all the city wells. We have enough sheep and cat-tle to provide fresh meat and milk and butter for three months, enough dried vegetables and fruit for six months or longer."

"We have to get rid of our waste and our dead. Disease will kill us faster than the enemy's arrows."

"We have cleared the main park for pyres. All the dead

will be brought there for burning. Solid waste will be collected and thrown over the north wall between us and the enemy camp. Liquid waste will be collected and allowed to dry so we have applications for fresh wounds."

"Good." Again she stopped suddenly, but this time the bodyguard was better prepared. There was less confusion, but somehow Farben, who thought he had been the centre of Charion's attention for long enough, still ended up standing next to her. She looked toward the enemy camp, already half-built. "They will send a messenger tomorrow morning asking for our surrender. When we refuse, they will spend a few days testing our defenses; at the same time they will build their siege engines. In ten days' time, or close enough, they will ask for our surrender a second time. When we refuse again, Salokan will start the assault in earnest. We must convince the enemy that our strongest points of defense are our weakest, and we must convince the enemy that our weakest points of defense are our strongest." She grasped Farben's arm. "Make sure my generals understand this."

Farben nodded.

"We must last six to eight weeks. That's how long it will take Areava's army to reach us. Eight weeks if the thaw is severe and floods the rivers between here and Kendra. Six weeks if the thaw is moderate."

"We will last six weeks," Farben said with more confidence than he felt. The enemy camp seemed to be almost as big as Daavis itself.

"If we don't," Charion said, "we lose *everything*."

As he always did, Sendarus rode by himself at the head of the main column. He did not get on with the knights from the Twenty Houses, forcing him to be aloof and alone. During the day he did not mind so much; there was much to be done—reports to read and write, decisions to make and review—but at night he could do little except inspect the sentry posts or lie on his blanket and stare up at the sky, wondering if Areava was doing the same thing.

After the army had made it over the ridge behind Kendra and entered Chandra, he started enjoying the countryside. He had never been this far north before, and to find a landscape that was so flat, so filled with the regular shapes of fields and orchards and pasture, was something new for him. At first, he could only think about how lucky were the people who inhabited such lands—rich soils, wide and navigable rivers, a benign climate—but then he remembered that the wealth of the land made it the target of every invading army and brigand. His own home of Aman may have been hilly and forested and cursed with soils too heavily leached by winter rains ever to be truly fertile, but only one army had ever had ever invaded its borders, and that had been centuries ago when the growing kingdom of Grenda Lear decided it needed Aman to secure both its southwest border against the southern Chetts and its timber supply for its expanding navy.

Four weeks after leaving Kendra they were nearing Sparro, Chandra's capital, where they would meet up with forces that had sailed north from Lurisia along the coast, and the extra light infantry Sendarus' father had promised from Aman. Sendarus felt their progress was good, and that they might even make Daavis before Salokan's army. Then the messenger came from Sparro, telling Sendarus that Salokan had already invaded Daavis and that time was running out.

He called an emergency meeting with the leading nobleman and his captains. When he told them the news, there was a stunned silence.

"Salokan must have marched before the end of winter," Galen Amptra said.

"I agree," Sendarus said. "There is no other way he could have reached Daavis so soon. He must have taken the bor-

der posts completely by surprise, and his army is obviously
larger and more professional than we guessed."

"He has learned from his father's mistakes," a captain of
infantry said, a man old enough to have fought in the Slaver
War.

"What do we do now?" another captain asked. "We cannot cross the Barda at Daavis. Salokan will be controlling
the river on either side of the city for some distance."

"We must cross at Sparro," Sendarus said, and was
pleased to see Galen nodding in agreement. "But it will
mean a longer march."

"Six or more weeks," Galen said.

"It will have to be less than six weeks. We cannot risk Salokan taking the city. If he does, we lose the north, and must
base our supply in Sparro; that will be too far from the front
for my liking."

"How do we do it in under six weeks?" the first captain
asked.

"We must find a way," said Duke Magmed, a young and
proud nobleman who had only recently inherited his title
and was keen to prove his worth.

"We get our cavalry and light infantry across the Barda
first," Sendarus said. "They will immediately march toward
Daavis, engaging the enemy as soon as possible but avoid-
ing a pitched battle. With luck, this will force Salokan to
break off the siege and retreat to protect his supply lines.
Our heavy infantry and engineers will not be far behind the
advanced force—two days at most if we push them. As soon
as the army is reunited, we attack."

"A good plan," Galen said emphatically. He admired the
consort's grasp of strategy, and the speed with which he had
come up with a plan that had the best chance of saving the
kingdom from disaster. He turned to face the other noble-
men present. Although not yet titled himself—every day he
gave thanks to God that his father still lived—the fact that

the Amptra family was the most senior in the kingdom after the Rosethemes themselves gave him command of the knights. "This we will do. Our cavalry will move across first." He glanced at Sendarus for confirmation.

Sendarus, who originally had planned to send across a company or two of light infantry from Aman—soldiers trained to run all day if necessary—understood the meaning behind Galen's eyes.

"That was my intention," he lied, and the nobles rumbled their approval.

Sendarus made sure every captain understood his orders and his position in the order of march, then dismissed everyone but Galen.

"Thank you for your support tonight," he said earnestly.

"You deserved it," Galen replied neutrally. "You came up with the right plan of action."

"And if I had not? What would you have done?"

Galen did not answer.

"Are you silent because you think I would be offended?" Sendarus prodded.

"I am silent because I do not know what I would have done."

"Do you hate me, Galen Amptra?"

"I am suspicious of what you represent, but no, I do not hate you."

"You are remarkably honest with me."

"What purpose would be served by dissembling?"

"My thoughts exactly. Which is why I will now ask you what you will do when we meet the enemy."

"What do you mean?"

"Will you follow my orders then, too, or will you do what the cavalry of the Twenty Houses has always done?"

"And what is that?"

"Charged without thought for consequence."

Galen blushed. "During the Slaver War—"

"During the Slaver War, General Elynd Chisal refused to use your knights because he could not rely on them to do their part. Will I suffer the same?"

Galen did not answer immediately, but this time Sendarus waited. Eventually, the nobleman shook his head. "No. You will not suffer the same. You have proven your worth as a leader today."

"Not on the battlefield."

"I would never doubt the courage of an Amanite on the battlefield," Galen said without hesitation. "When we meet Salokan, we will not engage in a pitched battle."

"Good. In that case I will have no hesitation in giving you command of the vanguard. I cannot desert the main body of the army to rush ahead."

Galen nodded. "I am . . . honored."

"When we do force Salokan into battle, I will ensure your knights are given a role fitting their nobility and strength. And when we return to Kendra, I will tell Areava of the part you have played in the kingdom's defense."

Galen viewed the consort in a new and surprising light. Perhaps the very thing that had threatened to drive the nobility and the crown irrevocably apart might instead be the key to their rapprochement. Tonight was proving to be a succession of unexpected turns.

"Thank you," he said solemnly.

"Don't thank me yet," Sendarus said. "We both have to survive the next few weeks first. Now get some rest. You move out at first light tomorrow."

23

GUDON'S hands were tied to the pommel of a saddle. His horse was too big for his legs, and the muscles from his groin to his knees ached as if they had been permanently pulled out of shape. Prado would occasionally favor him by riding by his side and slapping and punching him, saying, "Tell me again where Lynan is," and Gudon would concentrate to repeat the story without making a mistake, concentrate through the pain that filled him like a winter mist fills a valley.

"He found refuge with the queen."

"Which queen?" Prado always asked, his scarred face scowling.

"Korigan, who succeeded Lynan."

Prado, confused the first time he had heard the story, punched Gudon in the kidney. "How could she be the daughter of Lynan?" he roared in Gudon's ear.

"Lynan is a Chett name," Gudon had explained. "Lynan was the name of the first king of all the Chetts. Korigan is his daughter."

"Why did Lynan find refuge with Korigan?"

"Because her clan is the White Wolf clan, and their territory is closest to the Strangers' Sooq." Gudon bit his tongue to make sure he did not tell the whole truth: the Strangers' Sooq was *in* her territory.

"Where is the White Wolf clan?" Prado would ask.

For Gudon, this was the hardest part. "Maybe still at the High Sooq."

And this is where Prado would always hit Gudon again. The last time he cut him with a knife, cut his ear right open so blood poured down his cheek and neck. "And if it isn't at the High Sooq?"

"Then the clan is on its way to the Ox Tongue, the best spring grass in its territory."

"Where is the Ox Tongue?"

And Gudon would stare at Prado and say, so quietly that the mercenary had to lean forward to hear his words, "It is a secret way. You must know the hills and valleys in between. I can show you the way, master, but please, please, let me live."

Prado always laughed then, and slapped the Chett on the back in an almost genial way. "Maybe I will. Maybe I won't. Show me the way to the Ox Tongue and I will think about it."

So Gudon showed Jes Prado and his two thousand cavalry and his five hundred archers the way to the Ox Tongue.

Thewor was getting out of hand. Rendle decided it was time to kill him.

"How many bloody days are we going to chase a dust cloud, General?" Thewor demanded for what seemed the hundredth time, and for what seemed like the hundredth time, Rendle said, "The dust a herd pushes into the air can be deceptive. It can be a small herd close by or a large herd far away. We are chasing a large herd."

"Then we are chasing a large clan!" Thewor shouted. "We will all be killed!"

"No, they are afraid of us, that is why they are moving

away. If they were not afraid of us, we would already be dead. My people are now scouting, and they will not make mistakes like your scouts did. This time we will not only see the Chetts first, we will find out where their main group is and we will attack them. From prisoners, we will find out where Lynan is and complete our mission. It is even possible Lynan is with this clan, since they are so close to the east."

"You are guessing, General," Thewor said with a sneer. "You are an amateur at this game."

Rendle gave the hand signal to his escort, and each of them slowly, carefully, edged their horses closer to a regular officer.

"You are not only an amateur, General," Thewor continued, "you are a *dangerous* amateur."

"And you speak too much," Rendle said.

As Thewor opened his mouth to protest, Rendle drove a dagger up through the bottom of his throat. The point drove on, stabbing into the roof of Thewor's mouth. Blood sprayed Rendle. He gave the dagger one good twist and pulled it out. Thewor, already dead, dropped from his saddle.

Not believing what they had seen, each of the regular officers hesitated a moment too long in reaching for their own swords, and in the next second they, too, died and dropped to the ground. All except one. The youngest officer. His mercenary guardian, under instruction, had clubbed him unconscious. He was kept in his saddle and, when Rendle was ready, was woken with water thrown in his face. He opened his eyes and looked around, remembered what had happened, and promptly fainted. Rendle sighed and ordered more water thrown in the young officer's face. When he woke the second time, Rendle grabbed a handful of his hair and shook him so hard his eyeballs almost fell out.

"Stay awake," Rendle ordered. "Your name is Ensign Tyco, is it not?"

"Yes, General."

"You are now in command of all the regular forces, do you understand?"

"Sir, yes, sir. But Captain Yan is with the supply horses. He outranks me—"

"Find this Captain Yan and kill him immediately," Rendle told one of his men, then turned back to Tyco. "You are now in command of all the regular forces. You will do as I tell you. You will not talk to me unless I talk to you first. Do you understand?"

"Yes, sir."

"Good. In the name of King Salokan of Haxus, I promote you to captain."

"Thank you—"

"Ah!" Rendle warned, and Tyco shut up. "You are to stay close to me, but not so close my men get nervous. Do you understand?"

"Yes, sir."

"Now you may thank me."

"Thank you, General."

"You will make an excellent captain, Captain. Now hang back."

Tyco reined back on his horse so he fell behind, still trying to absorb everything that had happened in the last few minutes and still dazed from the clubbing he had received. He looked over his shoulder and saw only a few hundred paces away the bodies of Thewor and all his fellow officers. He shat himself.

"We are close now," Korigan said to Lynan. "Maybe a day's ride, depending on how soft the grass is between here and the Ox Tongue."

"Have our scouts sighted the mercenaries yet?"

"Terin has sent word of Rendle's force. They are within a half day's ride. We have no word yet about Prado."

Lynan said a silent prayer for Gudon. He knew he had asked his friend to perform a mission so dangerous he might not survive it. But it had been the right thing to do, he told himself, and wished that was enough.

"They will be close, too. We will ride for half the night and then camp; but no fires. That will take us within half a day of the Ox Tongue."

"Will that be close enough?" Korigan asked.

"It will have to be. I won't risk Rendle's or Prado's scouts stumbling on us before we're ready to show ourselves."

A flash of red caught his eye, and he glanced up to see his pennant waving in the wind. It was quite a beautiful flag, he thought, and simple. A gold circle on a dark red field. A circle for unity, for eternity, for strength. And red for blood, of course, and maybe courage. It seemed to him then to be a potent symbol, and wondered if anyone else saw it that way. Would his enemies recognize it for what it was, and what it represented? Would they see that pennant and know that Lynan Rosetheme rode under it?

He looked around, saw the Red Hands determinedly looking forward, proud of their distinction among their own people, with Makon at their head and never far from Lynan's side. He saw Kumul ahead and to the left, leading his lancers who tried so hard to ride in proper column; in the last few days they had actually started to get it right, and it was strange to see a forest of lances sticking up into the sky above the Oceans of Grass. He saw Ager leading the warriors of his own clan, and also saw how the Ocean warriors kept an eye on the crookback, so proud to have him for their chief. He saw Jenrosa riding among a swarm of fellow magickers, all asking her questions, and also saw how frustrated she was that it was not her asking the questions, and afraid of what she might be becoming—a feeling Lynan understood so well himself. And he saw Korigan, the noble queen, the golden queen with the golden eyes, and wondered what it was he felt toward her; he recognized respect, and he recognized desire, which made him feel ashamed because he did not recognize love as well. Perhaps with time, he told himself. And he saw all around him the rolling tide of the Chett army, riding into a future never predicted for them but eager to discover what it held.

Igelko found Terin north of the Ox Tongue, keen to be off. "Rendle is stopping for the night. His riders are very tired, especially the Haxus regulars."

Terin nodded. "Well, they'll have their reward soon. Maybe tomorrow." He looked down at the ground. "Look at this grass, Igelko. Have you ever seen such rich spring pasture?"

Igelko shook his head. "Certainly not in our territory. It explains why we have a thousand cattle and the White Wolf clan has four thousand."

"Indeed. It is good to be allied with such a clan."

"Certainly better than being their enemy. It is interesting; watching the enemy riders, I saw none of them take the time to actually look around and see the land itself. Not one of them understands what it means to ride on the Oceans of Grass."

"They will learn," Terin said grimly.

It had been hard for Gudon to keep the reserve of strength he knew he was going to need. He had to block away the pain of his bruises, his slit ear, and the broken cheek bone and cracked rib. He concentrated on keeping his breathing even, on closing his eyes and relying on his other senses, particularly his sense of smell. In fact, it was his hearing that told him he was close to where Lynan wanted Prado to be: the horses were making less sound, which meant the grass under hoof was greener, more supple. Then, almost immediately, he could smell the scent of crushed spring grass as well.

He opened his eyes. Prado's force was moving into the narrowing valley that marked the entrance to the Ox Tongue. The sun was down and the air was getting cooler. Prado called a halt and came along side Gudon.

"Well, my little barge pilot?"

"We are very close. Maybe another day's ride."

"Which way?"

"I will guide you."

Prado grunted and grabbed Gudon's jaw. Gudon could not help his cry of pain and was ashamed of it. "You could just say—'Ride north' or 'Ride east.' Then you could rest."

"I will guide you," Gudon said around Prado's hand with some difficulty.

"I could find it by myself if I am within a day's ride."

"And Korigan could find *you*," Gudon countered.

"She is still weeks away." Prado released the Chett with a sneer. "Tomorrow, then." He turned to his captains. "We camp here. I want sentries doubled tonight, two hundred paces from the nearest fires."

One of the sentries disturbed Rendle's rest. "Campfires! Campfires to the south!"

Rendle tugged on pants and rushed out of his tent, following the sentry to a knoll some three hundred paces from the camp. There, in the far distance, he could see the night sky shimmering slightly.

"We have them at last," he said, and grinned. "I had begun to think we would never catch them." He thought furiously, then slapped his thigh. "We cannot risk losing them again."

He strode back into camp, shouting for all to arise. He would march them through the night and surprise the enemy just as dawn touched the sky.

*　　*　　*

Gudon waited until two hours before sunrise. He stood up carefully, quietly. His guard, sitting ten paces from him, was dozing quietly, his chin on his chest, just as he had for the last five nights. Gudon tugged gently, insistently, on the stake to which he was tethered, stopping whenever the guard snored or snuffled. At last it came free, and he was able to slip his bonds over its end and then use his teeth to loosen them from his wrists. He crept up to the guard and with one swift movement put one hand over the man's mouth and with the other took the guard's own knife and slipped it between his ribs. The guard jerked once, then slumped. Gudon laid him out gently, took his sword as well, and started to make his way out of Prado's camp, trying not to wince as his cracked rib dug into his side.

He had watched where the sentries were posted and knew he would have to take care of one of them. This was the difficult part. The sentries were relieved on the hour, so they were always fresh. He found a hollow and waited for the next turnaround, afraid that the dead guard would be discovered at any moment and the alarm raised. At last he saw a man coming his way, yawning and stretching his arms. He wore a simple cloak over his riding breeches and shirt, had a pot helmet on his head and carried a spear. Gudon waited until he had passed, then crept up behind him and killed him the same way he had killed the guard. He brought the body back to the hollow, took the helmet, cloak and spear, and took his place. Five minutes later he was approaching the sentry.

"What happened to Garulth?" the sentry asked.

"I lost a bet to him," Gudon said gruffly. "I have his watch tonight."

The sentry was not convinced. "You know what Freyma says about the roster. It cannot be changed. Who are you?"

Gudon swore silently and changed the grip on the spear

so he could throw it, but even as he did so knew it was too late. The sentry had his own spear held out and was half-crouching, only a breath away from calling out to the camp.

The sentry stiffened suddenly, seemed to teeter for a moment, then fell forward onto his face. Gudon could only barely see the outline of an arrow sticking from his back. Relief flooded him, and he ran forward as fast he could with his injuries, throwing away the helmet and spear. He had gone fifty paces when two figures sprang out of the darkness, one of them hissing his name. He stopped, turned, and saw a Chett woman.

"I'll bet my mother's fortune you have a red hand," he said quietly, and although he could see no color, she obligingly held up her hand so it was silhouetted against the paling sky.

Prado learned three things within minutes of each other. He learned the first when he heard a cry from within the camp that the barge pilot's guard had been slain, and that the barge pilot himself had escaped. Before he could investigate, he learned the second when one of the sentries in the west called out that he had discovered the bodies of two of his fellows, and that one of them had been killed by a black Chett arrow. This time he managed to reach the scene of the deaths before he learned the third: sentries in the north calling out what they could feel through their feet: the approach of many, many riders.

Freyma and Sal rushed up to him, their expressions grim. Prado could see fear in their eyes, but they were professionals and would not panic. "Set our archers in front, their line placed one hundred paces north of our camp," he snapped to them. "Put our recruits directly behind them. Veterans on the flanks except for a small reserve that will stay with me behind the recruits."

His two captains nodded and ran off to carry out his instructions. All around him men still stirring from sleep were beginning to feel that something had gone terribly wrong. They looked at Prado, saw him striding by purposefully but without hurry, and felt reassured. He reached his own tent, hurriedly finished dressing, left the tent, and got on his horse being held for him by a nervous-looking recruit. Prado patted the boy on the shoulder, then stayed where he was, making sure everyone knew he was there and was not afraid.

The veteran mercenaries grouped themselves without much fuss, but Freyma and Sal had more trouble settling down the recruits and organizing them into two companies behind the archers; their mounts could feel their owners' fear and were stamping and nipping at their neighbors. Prado wished he had had the time he needed to give them some training in Hume, but the threat of invasion from Haxus had forestalled that. The archers themselves were quite green, but supremely confident of their ability with bow and arrow. In front of their line they planted sharpened stakes they had carried with them all the way from the Arran Valley, then they strung their bows, carefully checked the flights of their arrows—placing each of them point first in the ground near their right or left hand, depending on which they used to draw the bow—and finally tested the wind with licked fingers and tufts of grass thrown into the air. The steady professionalism of the archers helped settle down the recruits behind, which in turn helped them settle their horses.

When all that could be done was done, the mercenaries waited. Some fidgeted, some slumped in their saddles and closed their eyes to pray to their god, some checked and then rechecked their weapons and—if they had them—the straps on their shields and helmets. Most just sat in their saddles or stood straight, gazing as far as they could into the distance for the first sign of the enemy.

Freyma and Sal reported to Prado for their final instructions. "Freyma, you stay with the recruits. Keep them to-gether. When the enemy is within fifty paces, make sure they let the archers come through. If the Chetts dismount to get through the stakes, dismount the recruits and counter-attack, but make sure they do not pursue the Chetts if they break and flee. Sal, stay on the right wing. Wait to see if the Chetts are trying a flank attack. If they are, keep the attack away from the center. If not, wait until the enemy's first as-sault has wavered, then move out, taking them from the rear. Drive them onto the stakes if you can. Put Lieutenant Owel in charge of the left wing. She is to copy you, and not to act independently unless I give her an order in person. Any questions so far?"

Freyma and Sal shook their heads.

"If I think the Chetts are retreating from the battle, I will give the order for a general advance. If that happens, stay in sight of each other, then break off the pursuit at midday and return promptly to this camp. Good luck."

His captains saluted and left. Prado breathed deeply, wondering if there was anything else he should do or take care of, but without knowing who was attacking or in what strength, his choices were limited. Still, he had some idea. Korigan's clan had been close, and the barge pilot had led them here knowing that. He had heard stories about the White Wolf clan and knew it was one of the larger ones, but his two-and-a-half thousand mercenaries, mostly veterans, would be able to handle them. The important thing to re-member was not to break the line and chase the Chetts if they looked like retreating—as often as not it was a Chett ruse to lure their enemies out of formation. Prado knew the Chetts well enough to know when they really panicked and started to flee.

The outer sentries appeared, running as fast as their legs could carry them. "Half a league!" they called. "Half a

league!" One of them came straight to Prado and breathlessly said: "Three thousand! Maybe more!"

Prado nodded. That sounded about right for one of the
larger clans, and even allowed for another thousand left behind to protect the herd or sent on a long flanking maneuver;
he would have to be wary of the last.

"Haxus cavalry," the sentry said then.

Prado looked at him in surprise. "What?"

"Haxus cavalry . . . uniforms . . . Haxus pennants . . ." ·

"Three thousand Haxus cavalry *here?*" He could not believe what he was hearing.

"Yes, but many in no uniform . . . not Chetts." Prado
waved off the sentry, who scurried away, and stared north-
ward disbelievingly. He could not see the enemy yet, but he
could hear them.

Prado knew instinctively who it was. Three thousand or
more, most Haxus, but some not in any uniform. Mercenaries. Rendle. There was a moment, the briefest of moments,
when he *knew* everything had gone wrong, but then realized
he was in the perfect position. Rendle could not possibly
know he was not attacking Chetts. In fact, he was almost certainly on the Oceans of Grass for the same reason as Prado—
to secure Lynan. Maybe Rendle even thought Prado's force
was the White Wolf clan and that he would find Lynan here.

*And if he thinks he is attacking Chetts, he will drive
straight up the center, hoping to scatter us,* Prado thought.
*And he will have another column out wide to drive in one
flank. But which one?*

Rendle always did things a little differently, Prado remembered. Nothing revolutionary, just unconventional.
Rendle's flying column would be sent from his left wing.
That meant it would come in on Prado's right flank. How
much time did he have?

He called over one of his veterans. "You will find Captain Solway with the right wing," he told him. "Tell her that

the enemy is not the Chetts, but Rendle. Tell her to move out wide and ambush a flank attack Rendle will be sending against our right."

The veteran spurred his horse and galloped away. Prado heard sounds from the front and looked up. There, in the distance, a straight line of cavalry. Little dust. It was too far to be sure, but the enemy were riding close together, too close for Chetts.

"Rendle," Prado said quietly, smiling slightly. "I knew we would meet again."

Rendle knew he was close to the time when he would lose control over the attack. His cavalry was advancing at a steady canter, the line mostly holding, but he could now see the enemy ahead. He was worried they were not panicking. He was worried they seemed to be dressed in formations far too tight for Chetts. But there weren't many, and he had another thousand riders behind the line of hills on his left moving to hit the enemy in the flank at the same time he hit them in the front.

A thousand paces. He swung his sword over his head. Just as he brought the sword down to point it straight at the enemy, just as he spurred his horse from a canter into a gallop, just at the moment he finally lost control of the assault, he saw the foot archers.

On receiving Prado's surprising instructions, Sal had formed her cavalry into a wedge and galloped it east for three hundred paces and then turned them north. As they surmounted a small rise, they saw before them at least a thousand cavalry running in front of them, the heads of their mounts starting to droop, and she cried in surprised delight. She did not need to give any command—her whole force shouted with her and charged.

*   *   *

Prado had half expected the enemy to wheel to either side of his front line, risking their horses on the slopes on either side of the valley to enfilade him, but when he saw them break into a gallop, he knew they had left it too late for anything fancy. His archers loosed their first salvo. The arrows whistled as they rose and then fell about midway among the charging cavalry. Horses and men fell to the ground, tripping those behind them. A few seconds later the second volley fell, and the enemy ranks started to peel away, the formation losing cohesion. A third volley, and this time Prado could see individual arrows striking riders in the head and chest and thighs, and horses in the neck and shoulders. He could see some riderless horses canter and buck from the fray with arrows sticking from their haunches.

The Arran archers picked up their unused shafts and retreated. For the most part they got through, but some of the younger recruits could not control their mounts properly and one or two of the infantry were trampled. The enemy charge reached the stakes. Horses reared, throwing their riders, some of whom ended up skewered, most of whom ended up in heaps on the ground—dazed, broken, or dead. The following ranks of enemy cavalry split, some going left, some right, most trying to retreat. Many riders jumped off, drawing their swords and advancing through the stakes, chopping at them, forcing their way through, desperate to actually land a blow on an opponent. Freyma ordered the first rank of recruits to dismount and counterattack. A confusing melee started just behind the line of stakes, swinging one way and then the next. As more of the enemy got through the stakes, the line was pushed closer and closer to Freyma's position. Rather than send more of his recruits in, Freyma ordered his rear ranks to ride between those fighting on foot and the stakes. They hewed into the enemy from behind, mercilessly cutting them down.

Prado meanwhile was searching for Rendle, finally

catching sight of him on the left flank, leading the battle between his mercenaries and Haxus regulars against Owel's troops. Owel had not had time to charge, and the impact of Rendle's assault had forced back her formation. Prado checked one more time to make sure Freyma had things under control in the center, then raised his sword and spurred his horse into a canter. His veterans formed a line on his left. As soon as it was straight, he lowered his sword and they charged, hitting the enemy just as Owel's force was on the verge of fleeing.

Prado swung at any head that came within reach, but concentrated on bringing his line right behind Rendle's force. He saw Rendle realize what was happening and trying to wheel his cavalry around to meet the new threat. Prado screamed his name, dug his heels into his horse's flanks, and charged again.

Even though Sal's force was outnumbered two to one, the charge of her troops had sent the enemy reeling in shock. In a few minutes they had cut down a quarter of them and divided their force in two. The rear half turned and fled the field while the vanguard, knowing they had no hope of regaining the initiative here, spurred their horses to even greater effort and desperately tried to reach the main battle in the hope they could find reinforcements. Sal quickly ordered a company to chase the fleeing riders to make sure they did not double back and take her force in the rear, then reformed her line and pursued the vanguard.

They had almost caught the enemy's tail when both groups burst into the valley. There were dead horses and riders everywhere. Sal quickly saw the battle had developed into two main struggles—one on the far flank and one in the center. The enemy she was chasing saw that the only hope they had was to get involved in one of the larger actions, and charged straight into the flank of the recruits in the center.

The recruits, who had just gained the upper hand, fell back in confusion. Freyma desperately tried to steady the line, but there were too many gaps. The archers tried to flee, but many were cut down.

Then Sal struck the enemy's rear and the battle broke up into skirmishes between four or five combatants and in some places individual contests. Freyma gathered together all the recruits he could and formed a new line just in front of their camp. The surviving archers, seeing what he was trying to do, formed up behind him. Sal saw as well and started calling her own riders back. The enemy was exhausted and their horses blown; their leader tried to get them to form a line as well, but they were too slow. Arrows started falling among them, scattered and largely ineffective but demoralizing nonetheless, and they started to pull back through the stakes to safer ground, and there they were rejoined by their comrades retreating from the battle on the left flank. They knew they had lost, but they also knew their opponents were too tired to pursue. Some among them were crying for another charge, but they were shouted down; for most of them, it was clear that the battle was over.

All the pain, all the planning, all the waiting, were made worthwhile when Prado saw that Rendle recognized him. The man turned whiter than a sheet, cursed Prado, and charged toward him.

It seemed as if all the fighters there knew to avoid this contest and peeled away. The two leaders met at full gallop. The flank of Rendle's horse crashed into the head of Prado's mount, but even as his horse went down, Prado felt his sword strike flesh. He landed heavily, somersaulted, and staggered back to his feet. His horse lay on the ground, its neck broken. Rendle wheeled his horse around and charged again, raising his sword high. Prado stood his ground and blocked his enemy's slashing attack. As Rendle barged past,

Prado grabbed hold of his jerkin and pulled down savagely. Rendle shouted as he lost his balance, his torso twisting back over his horse's hindquarters, and used his thighs and knees to remain mounted. Prado saw his chance and swiped savagely with his sword. His blade sliced into his enemy's neck. Rendle gasped, coughing blood; his horse reared and bolted, the sudden action forcing Prado's blade deeper. Rendle's head jumped off his neck, and his horse galloped on, its decapitated rider slowly sliding off the saddle; one foot caught in the stirrup and the torso bumped along the ground as it was carried away.

Prado heard a groan, and realized it came from his own lips. He looked down and saw a deep slash in his right thigh, blood oozing over his breeches. He looked up again and saw Rendle's head not far from him. He stumbled over to it and used his sword to impale it through the neck. He raised the grisly trophy over his head and waved it in the air, shouting his victory for everyone to hear.

First, it was only the enemy riders nearby that cried in despair and fled, but it was enough. In a few minutes the slopes were occupied only by Prado's troops. They watched as the enemy gathered and milled about two hundred paces north of the stakes, unsure of what to do, wary of any pursuit, but Prado knew his own side was too exhausted to follow. Some of the enemy turned their horses and kicked them into a slow trot, and soon the rest of them were following.

Freyma rode up. "Shall we start the chase?"

"Have we any fresh horses?"

Freyma shook his head.

"Our casualties?"

"Moderate. Maybe four hundred dead, twice that many wounded. I figure two thousand of the enemy are dead or wounded here. Sal says there are at least three hundred of them dead on the other side of the hills to the east."

"Kill any of their wounded left behind."

Freyma left to carry out the order, and Prado looked to
the retreating enemy again. They were now half a league
away. He counted a thousand or so, many of them slumped
over their saddles. They were leaderless and at least two
weeks from sanctuary; many of them would not see their
homes again.

He searched among his own troops. They were worn out,
but he still had enough to carry out his first mission. He
raised his sword again, peered at Rendle's bloody face and
grinned at it. "I was just going to cut your throat, you bastard." He laughed crazily.

And now for Lynan, he thought.

That was when he heard the screams of dying men in the
distance. His first thought was that some of Sal's riders had
come late on the field and pursued the retreating enemy after
all. He looked up and what he saw did not make any sense.
The enemy were riding as hard as they could, but toward
Prado and his troops!

"God's death, what's happen—"

"Prado!"

He spun around to his left and looked up the slope. There,
standing as free as you please, and grinning from ear to ear,
was the blasted barge pilot.

"You sent me into a trap!" Prado shouted at him. He
shook Rendle's head at him. "And see what has come of it!"

"That was not my trap, master!" the Chett replied. He
spread his arms wide. "*This* is my trap!"

And suddenly the barge pilot was no longer alone. It
seemed as if the skyline itself was changing shape, turning
into a line of cavalry that stretched along the whole length
of the valley.

"My God," Prado whispered hoarsely.

Kumul gazed out over the battlefield and shook his head.
"It is a day of wonder when the mercenaries do our work for

us." He glanced sideways at Lynan. "Your father would be very proud of you, lad. I was wrong—again."

Lynan smiled at Kumul and reached out to grip his shoulder. "You taught better than you knew."

Kumul shook his head. "No. I never taught you this well."

"Excuse me," Korigan interrupted impatiently. "But can we kill them now?"

Kumul laughed. "My lancers first."

Korigan bristled. "I am a queen! It is my right to lead my people into battle!" she declared.

For a second they tried to stare each other down, then a plaintive voice said, "I am without a horse."

Lynan dismounted and held out the reins to Gudon. "My friend, would you do me the honor of leading the first charge of my army?"

Gudon stared wide-eyed at Lynan, and the prince had to place the reins into his hands.

Korigan and Kumul looked at Lynan, then at Gudon, and then at each other again. "It is fitting," Korigan said.

"Yes," Kumul agreed. He turned to one of the Red Hands, nodded to his horse. The Chett dismounted and quickly brought his horse up to Lynan, who thanked him and mounted. The Red Hand hurried away to find another ride; he certainly was not going to miss out on the battle.

"Your orders?" Lynan asked Gudon, now astride Lynan's horse.

Gudon, still in considerable pain, grimaced. Below them, Prado had hurriedly formed his lines, but his troops were obviously exhausted and frightened; they thought they had won a great battle and instead had only made their own deaths more certain. He remembered the terrible atrocities and crimes they had committed against his people in the past and hardened his heart.

"Kill them all," he said. "Kill them all except Prado."

*   *   *

"I don't recognize the pennant," Freyma said, pointing to the blood-red flag with its golden circle. "It's not the Sun clan, is it?"

Prado shook his head. "No. This is not their territory." He knew what it meant, but did not want to tell the others. In a strange way, the implication terrified him even more than his own imminent death. He saw the whole of the continent of Theare falling into a maelstrom of violence and death. The Chetts were organized, and they were marching east. The pennant waving atop the western slope promised years, maybe decades, of constant, bloody war. Even mercenaries needed some years of peace to enjoy their spoils.

"I should have stayed on my farm," Freyma said, but there was no self-pity in his voice. He said it as a statement of fact.

"We all should have stayed on our farms," Prado replied. "Even them," he added, nodding to the survivors of Rendle's army who had joined his force in common defense. He could hear some of his recruits starting to sob, and surprised himself by feeling sorry for them. He wished suddenly that he had taken the time to have children. *Well,* he admitted to himself, *children I knew about.*

"Here they come," Freyma said.

There was no shout or cry. The Chett cavalry eased over the slope, ambled their way to level ground.

"They have lancers," Freyma observed. "That's a surprise."

"Do you see who leads them?"

"That's Kumul fucking Alarn, isn't it?" Now there *was* surprise in Freyma's voice.

"I see our barge pilot is calling the shots."

"Imagine him making king."

"Imagine," Prado said tonelessly.

The Chett cavalry took a moment to straighten their line. They were no more than two hundred paces away. Prado ordered the archers to shoot. A dismal shower of arrows whistled overhead and fell among the enemy. Most stuck in the ground, one or two found flesh and eyes. Another flight, with similar results.

"Now," Prado said under his breath, and even as he said the word, the Chetts started their charge. He never thought he would see the day when the Chetts would keep close order, although it was only the lancers. The horse archers were already spreading apart and moving around his force's flanks. The lancers went from a walk to a canter to a gallop so smoothly he could not help admire it.

"Good-bye, Freyma," Prado said.

"Good-bye, J—"

An arrow seemed to sprout from Freyma's left temple. He fell out of his saddle. Another arrow claimed Freyma's horse. Someone moved into the gap.

"Charge!" Prado cried, and his own thin line started its countercharge. Armed mainly with swords, they knew most of them would be skewered before they had a chance to come to grips with the Chetts, but also knew that if they tried to flee they would only be skewered from behind.

Prado kneed his horse until he was almost in front. He aimed his sword at the barge pilot's head, promising himself to take out the little bastard before he died. The rider charging beside Gudon caught his attention; he was as pale as mist and as small as the pilot, and he had a scar . . .

No, it couldn't be!

Lynan focused on one enemy, a rider with a helmet and a long sword, and for the whole charge kept his sword point aimed at that man's chest. Seconds before they would have collided, his target was taken by a lance and disappeared from view. Lynan swerved to his left, half saw a sword slashing toward him and deflected it easily. His horse veered to avoid a biting stallion and lost its momentum. Lynan wheeled around, searching for the nearest enemy. A young man, no older than he, rode into view, swinging a sword with more energy than skill. Lynan dodged the first blow and drove the point of his own sword into the man's neck. He did not wait to see the results. He spurred his mare into a canter and attacked one of two riders ganging up on a wounded Red Hand. He dispatched the first by stabbing him in the back. The second twisted aside to counter the new threat, and the Red Hand took off most of his face with a slashing cut. More enemies joined the fray, and Lynan found himself in a confusing tumble of men and horses. A Red Hand died in front of him, a dagger in her heart. A wizened mercenary coughed blood, disappeared. A man in the uniform of Haxus was huddled in his saddle with his hands closed over his head, screaming something; Lynan sank his sword into the man's stomach and the screaming stopped. He saw a sword coming toward him out of the corner of his eye and quickly brought his own weapon up to block it; he deflected the killing stroke, but the flat of the other sword thwacked against the crown of his head. Lynan saw stars, felt himself swoon in his saddle. Someone nearby screamed. Hands plucked at him, trying to keep him upright.

And then his senses cleared so quickly it felt as if someone else was suddenly occupying his body. Red Hands were all around him, protecting him at the expense of their own defense.

"Enough," he said, and kicked his heels into his mare's flank. She leaped forward. Lynan saw a huge mercenary loom in front of him, carrying a long saber in one hand and a spiked mace in the other. He grinned at Lynan, raised his sword, and slashed downward. Lynan blocked the blow and used his own sword to flick it away. The saber flew out of the mercenary's hands. The impetus of his charge took Lynan past the man, but he swung his sword backward and caught the man in the neck. He twisted his sword free and spurred his horse again into the fray, breaking through the enemy line. He was surrounded by mercenaries. His sword whistled as he thrashed left and right, not aiming at any one target. He kept on moving, plowing through any opposition, not able to control the white fury that had taken over his mind and body. One moment he was surrounded by screaming men, panting horses and the almost overwhelming smell of blood and shit, and then he was in the clear.

There was a line of foot archers in front of Lynan, desperately loosing arrows at the Chett horse archers picking at them from both flanks. They did not see Lynan. He charged into them, hewing at heads and arms. The archers scattered, crying in fear, and Lynan rode them down until once again he found himself in the melee and surrounded by the press of fighting and dying men and horses.

He attacked a rider in the uniform of a Haxus officer, someone not much older than a boy. The officer tried desperately to ward off Lynan's attack, and he started to cry. "Please . . ." he whimpered, blocking another thrust. "Please . . ." But Lynan only smiled at him and attacked again, his sword slicing through the officer's wrist, then onto into his thigh. The officer wailed as Lynan plunged his sword into his chest, then gurgled and died.

Lynan roared, driving his horse on. Three more enemies. They saw him coming and split to take him from the front and both sides at the same time. Lynan slashed at the one on his right, his sword sinking deep into the man's skull. Something stuck in his waist, and he looked down to see a dagger there, half its length inside of him. He let go of the reins and punched the mercenary on his left in the face. The face crumpled and the mercenary fell back. The mercenary in front gaped in horror and tried to back his horse away. Lynan pulled the dagger out of his side, saw a trickle of dark, dark blood run down his shirt, then threw the weapon at the retreating mercenary, striking him between the eyes.

He wheeled his horse in a tight circle, searching for another enemy, but there was no one left to kill. There were no more mercenaries, no more riders in Haxus uniform, no more archers. A troop of his Red Hands galloped up to him, crying his name, their desperate concern obvious on their faces.

"I am all right," he assured them, then remembered he had been stabbed. He looked down at the wound, but although he found the flat, diamond-shaped cut in his shirt, there was only the faintest mark on the skin underneath.

Prado received a second wound that day, a hard blow to the back of his right hand. The barge pilot had done that. Prado had been surprised the little Chett could fight at all, let alone outfight someone like himself, a mercenary with a quarter century of combat behind him. As soon as they met, Prado had swung for his head, but the Chett had ducked as lithely as a young boy and brought down the hilt of his own sword on Prado's hand, breaking a few bones and forcing him to let go of his weapon. After that things had become confusing. He remembered being knocked off his horse, two men with red hands falling on him and tying him up. He lost consciousness for a while, and when he woke, the battle was over. The barge pilot had reappeared, made him stand up, and forced him to look over the battlefield.

"We've counted them," the barge pilot told him. "We have removed our eighty dead and already burned them. That is their pyre over there. All the other bodies you see are those of our enemy. Nearly six thousand of them. You are the only survivor." The Chett leaned closer so he could whisper in Prado's ear. "But not for long."

Prado was turned around again. There were five figures approaching. He recognized Kumul and Ager and Jenrosa and—he still could not believe the change—Prince Lynan, but the fifth was a tall Chett female he knew nothing about.

When they were near enough, the barge pilot bowed deeply. "Your Majesty."

Lynan smiled. "Well done, Gudon. How do you feel?"

The Chett called Gudon breathed deeply and joined his companions. "Rejuvenated," he said.

"What now?" the Chett female asked the prince. "How do you want him to die?"

"Gudon?"

"I have finished with him, little master. He knows I am the one who brought him down. It is enough."

The prince stood directly in front of Prado. The mercenary could not meet the eyes in that pale face and had to turn away. Fear curdled in the pit of his stomach, fear of something much worse than death. Lynan turned to Kumul. "When we were finally reunited in the Strangers' Sooq, I remember you said something about Jes Prado."

"I said I would fillet the bastard," Kumul returned.

Prado went white. He had expected to be paraded before the victors and then beheaded. But not . . .

"He is yours," the prince said. "But when you are finished, make sure his face is still recognizable."

It took the rest of the day and the whole of the next to gather all the enemy dead together and burn their remains. An expedition was sent to Rendle's distant camp to take care of any guards left behind and to bring back all the booty they could find. They returned with horses, weapons, and the news that on sighting them one of the guards—a Haxus regular—had released several carrier birds, all of which had escaped.

Together, the two mercenary forces delivered a great deal of potentially useful booty; horses mainly, but also weapons, stocks of food, including some hay for the horses, and good clothing, including new leather boots and jerkins. Everything was loaded onto most of their surviving mounts, and a few of the less seriously wounded Chetts were charged with escorting them back to the High Sooq for distribution among all the clans; all except some of the stallions which Kumul insisted on keeping.

"Our mares do not make good chargers," he told his companions. Lynan and Korigan smiled at each other. "What's so funny?"

"You said 'Our mares,'" Lynan explained.

Kumul grunted. "With these bigger eastern stallions we can start breeding a proper war horse."

"We will take your advice on this," Korigan said, and Kumul bowed slightly for the favor she was showing him.

"What did you want with Prado's head, lad?" Kumul asked Lynan.

"Did we find Rendle's remains?"

"Yes, on the slope," Korigan answered. "His head was already off his shoulders. It got trampled on, but it is recognizable."

"Good. Put both heads in a basket. Fill the basket with salt and bring it to me."

"Very well," Korigan said, her voice flat, and gave the order.

Early the next morning the basket was presented to him. He opened it and placed in it the Key of the Union. Those around him gasped in surprise.

"What are you doing?" Ager asked.

Lynan called for Makon, who appeared moments later, bowing deeply. "Your Majesty?"

"In Gudon's absence you performed well as leader of my Red Hands."

"Thank you, your Majesty."

"I have another important task for you. You must not fail in it. You may take a company of the Red Hands to help make sure you are not interfered with."

"What is the task, my lord?"

Lynan showed Makon the contents of the basket. "You are to take this to Eynon, chief of the Horse clan."

Makon could not hide his surprise. "To Eynon? Including the Key of the Union?"

"You are to tell Eynon that the heads are those of the mercenary captains Prado and Rendle, and are a present to him from Lynan Rosetheme, the White Wolf returned. And as a symbol of my trust in him, I also send the Key of the Union, so that he may find me to return it."

No one said anything as Makon sealed the basket and tied it with sinew. "I will leave immediately."

When Makon was gone, Lynan looked at the faces of Korigan and Kumul, expecting the greatest outrage from them, but both seemed calm.

"Neither of you have any objection?"

Kumul shook his head. "I do not doubt you know what you are doing," the giant said.

"And I admire the strategy behind the move, your Majesty," Korigan said. "You play this game of kingship very well indeed."

"Ah," Lynan said quietly, "that's because I do not think it is a game."

24

A REAVA had wanted to keep the investiture ceremony brief, but Orkid argued she should use it as an opportunity for a celebration.

"Celebration!" Areava had exclaimed. "We are at *war*, Chancellor. Primate Giros Northam is *dead*. My husband is hundreds of leagues away risking life and limb—"

"Exactly, your Majesty. Which is why your people need to see you are confident about the future, that you are not obsessed with all the problems besetting the kingdom—"

"Of course I'm obsessed by them!" she snapped.

"—and indeed you are thrilled to have the opportunity to throw a party for the city."

"A party?"

"A celebration, your Majesty. Use Father Powl's investiture as an excuse to show the kingdom that you are in charge and that, despite the war, the kingdom goes on."

Areava had agreed reluctantly, and was unsure if she had made the best decision. Until now. Looking down on the palace courtyard, she saw the beaming faces of her people as they enjoyed the early spring sunshine, the free food and drink, and the sign that even with a war the kingdom and its monarch were strong and confident enough to hold such a glorious and pomp-filled event. Father Powl, splendid in the official robes of Primate of the Church of the Righteous God, strolled among the citizens of Kendra, dispensing blessings and thanks to all the well-wishers.

Areava stayed aloof, but was pleased to see her people enjoying themselves so much. For a while Olio joined her on the south gallery. He placed a hand on her belly.

"Six months, the magickers tell me," she said, and her face became sad.

"He m–m–might m–m–make it b–b–back in time," Olio said.

Areava shook her head. "No, not now. Salokan has taken us all by surprise. Sendarus will not be back until after his daughter is born."

"Daughter?"

"Yes. It is a girl."

"You will call her Usharna?"

Areava's face lost some of its sadness. "What else could I have called a daughter?"

"Oh, I don't know." He grinned suddenly. "Olio would have b–b–been nice."

Areava seemed shocked. "That would only have confused the poor darling. Having an uncle with the same name as herself. What would she think?"

"That her uncle was extremely lucky to have b–b–been named after her, of course."

Areava laughed. "That's true. If she is anything like me, that would not surprise you, I think."

Olio kissed her cheek suddenly. "Everything about you surprises me, sister." He held her hand briefly. "Are you coming down?"

"No. I prefer to watch from up here. But you should go down. They need a Rosetheme to mingle with them."

"They would p–p–prefer you, I think."

Areava shook her head. "You are quite wrong, brother.

They prefer *me* to be up here. That way everyone is in their place, and they know all is right with their world."

Orkid waited until the new primate had finished receiving everyone's congratulations, and then caught up with him as he walked back toward the west wing to change out of his ceremonial garb.

"The balance of power shifts once again," Orkid said.

Powl looked at him without expression. "That is the most interesting greeting I've heard in some time."

"Now that Primate Northam has gone—God care for his soul—"

"God care for his soul," Powl recited.

"—I feel the council has moved somewhat away from the queen in sympathy and toward the Twenty Houses and some commercial interests in the city."

"Not for my part, Chancellor."

"I have always believed you were on the queen's side. That is why I approached you earlier to establish a special liaison between us."

"For which I was grateful. Regrettably, events have meant we were never able to take advantage of that."

"Those events may still occur, but are *you* still interested in maintaining a special relationship with my office?"

"Unreservedly, Chancellor. Do you feel it will be important in the near future?"

"It is hard to tell, your Grace." Orkid said the title with something like deference, which did not go unnoticed by Powl. "The state of war distorts the normal picture. For the moment we are all on the same side, but who knows what will happen after the war is over?"

"Surely that depends on whether or not we win?"

"Oh, we will win," Orkid assured him. "Maybe not tomorrow, or next week, but inevitably, inexorably, Haxus will pay for its sins."

Powl stopped and looked at the Chancellor. " 'Sins,' Chancellor? That is an interesting word to choose. Do you believe whether or not something is a sin is determined by the origin of its perpetrator? Salokan sins because he is from Haxus and is invading Grenda Lear, for example?"

"Surely what is moral in one country—if it is *truly* moral—must equally be moral in another country?" the chancellor countered.

"That was my point," Powl said, resuming his walk. "I would not like to think we had been reduced to the level where we believed that sin was somebody doing something we didn't like, irrespective of intention or method."

"Are you arguing *for* Salokan's invasion?" Orkid asked, not even trying to hide the surprise in his voice.

"By no means. I am merely offering, say, guidance, on your earlier choice of words. Let's leave 'sin' out of it for the moment. You believe we will win the war?"

"Yes, and moreover I believe that once that happens we will see the queen's council split into two factions, one that supports her Majesty and one that supports the Twenty Houses and certain moneyed interests who would benefit from a weakened monarchy, especially if Haxus is taken and there are new lands and new opportunities to exploit."

"It is the tradition of *my* house to support the monarch in all she—or indeed, he—does."

"A tradition you intend to continue."

"Without doubt."

"I am glad to hear it, for you see there is a way to ensure the balance on the council is restored."

"How is that?"

"With Northam gone, you inherit his seat."

"Ah, I see," Powl said. "Which means my seat becomes vacant, to be filled by the queen's new confessor."

"Exactly," Orkid said. "And you choose the queen's confessor."

Powl stopped. "Yes, that's true, isn't it?" He looked strangely at Orkid. "Lucky for our side."

Olio and Edaytor entered the hospice through the back door. The priest welcomed them and led them into the kitchen, bowing and scraping the whole way.

"You're new to this, aren't you?" Olio asked.

The priest gave a sickly smile. "Your Highness sees my deficiencies with an eagle eye."

"You m–m–misunderstand m–m–me, Father. I m–m–merely m–m–meant that we are in the habit of treating these visits of m–m–mine with some informality. Indeed, I would p-p-prefer it if you could avoid calling me by my title."

"Without your title, your Highness?" the priest said uncertainly.

Olio patted him on the shoulder. "It will take some p–p–practice, I can see."

"I was given a message today that you had a dying child for the prince," Edaytor said with some impatience. He did not like the fact that the regular priest had been changed suddenly by the new primate. He and Olio really did have to meet with Powl and sort some things out.

"A child, Prelate?" The priest seemed confused. "No. I have a man in his sixties. He has a bad heart . . ."

"We are wasting our time here, your Highness," Edaytor said abruptly, then said to the priest, "his Highness only deals with those who are dying before their time, from illness or accident."

The priest seemed horrified. "But the patient is a good man with many small children—"

"Nevertheless," Edaytor interrupted, "it was not part of the original agreement . . ." He let the sentence die. He had already said too much to someone who had not been involved in the original establishment.

"P–p–perhaps this one time, Edaytor?" Olio said. He

hated the thought of letting a man die who had small children.

"Your Highness, you cannot cure every ill afflicting Kendra," Edaytor said somewhat impatiently. "We have discussed this before. If you truly wish to help your people, you have to use your power sparingly and only where it will do the most good. We must go, and we must go now."

The priest was confused, and became even more confused when the prince and the prelate left without seeing his dying patient. When they were gone, he hurried back to the kitchen and wrote down everything that had been said between the three of them. He took some time over it, trying to remember every single word and nuance. In this regard, Primate Powl's instructions had been explicit.

It was late at night and Dejanus was about to leave his office to go to his own rooms when one of the guards knocked and opened the door, letting in a small, rat-faced man who seemed uncomfortable in the presence of so many people with so many weapons.

"He says he has some information for you," the guard said, his voice doubtful.

Dejanus nodded and the guard left. "Hrelth." He said the name like a swear word, and came to stand over the man. "How pleasant to see you again."

Hrelth bowed. "Your Magnificence, you asked me to come if I had any news about Prin—"

Dejanus's hand shot up to cover Hrelth's mouth. "And I also asked you to never come to me in the palace, remember?" he hissed. "Only talk to me at the tavern!"

Hrelth shook his head; Dejanus resisted the temptation to twist it off his shoulders. He let the man go and went to the door. He opened it quickly, and did not like the way the guard was so determinedly at attention. "Find some wine," Dejanus snapped. "Couldn't you see my guest was thirsty?"

"Sir!" the guard shouted and ran off on his errand.

Dejanus closed the door behind him and turned back to Hrelth. "All right, quickly. What news of the prince?"

"He and Edaytor Fanhow went to the hospice you asked me to watch. They went in the back door, stayed for only a few minutes, and then left again. The prelate escorted Prince Olio all the way back to the palace and then left for his own home."

"And they were at the hospice for only few minutes? Are you sure?"

Hrelth nodded vigorously. "And there's something else."

"Something else?"

"I was heading back when I saw the priest from the hospice running to the palace as well. This was about ten minutes after the prince had returned."

"He probably lives in the west wing," Dejanus said reasonably.

Hrelth shrugged. "Maybe. That is certainly where he went, but less than ten minutes later he was rushing back to the hospice again."

"Really?" Dejanus mused.

Hrelth nodded again. "I'm sorry for coming to the palace, your Constableness, but I thought you would want to know . . ."

"Yes, yes. You were right."

The door opened and the guard came in with a flagon of wine and two mugs. Dejanus looked askance at the mugs—he was used to better now that he was constable—but at least they were clean. The guard left to take up his post again.

"So, you think the harbor patrols are doing a good job?" Dejanus asked.

Hrelth looked quizzically at him for a moment, then understanding dawned in his eyes. Dejanus wanted to kill him again.

"Yes, that's right. Very good. Good patrollers on the harbor."

Dejanus poured him a mug of wine and handed it over. Hrelth drank most of it in one gulp, then whispered, "Err, we have not yet discussed my retainer, sir."

"You just drank a mug of vintage Storian wine. How much do you think that's worth?"

"It was very nice, sir," Hrelth admitted, "but it doesn't feed my children."

"You don't have any children."

Hrelth thought about that for a moment. "Err, that's true."

Dejanus opened his coin pouch and threw the rat two pennies. "Enough to feed you for a week, at least, or keep you drunk for two days."

Hrelth did a little bow and scampered off.

Dejanus poured himself a wine and sat behind his desk again.

So two of us at least are collecting information about Prince Olio, he thought. *And what is the new primate's interest in all of this?*

Dejanus had no answer to that question, but it did not worry him overly. The primate was a new broom and probably just wanted to make sure of things before sweeping everything clean. Still, it would not hurt to keep an eye on Powl. Maybe, just maybe, he could prove useful as an ally, and then there would be two of them on the council secretly opposed to Chancellor Orkid Gravespear. Now that was worth thinking about.

25

IF Salokan had known beforehand that Daavis was going to be such a tough nut to crack, he might have reconsidered his strategy. His generals continually assured him that the city's fall was imminent, but as far as he could see the only thing that was imminent was another failed and bloody assault. He was tired of seeing long streams of Haxan wounded making their way to the hospital corner of the camp while the walls of Daavis stood there scorched and battered but still standing. He had no idea what casualties Charion's forces were suffering, but he was damn sure it was considerably less than those she was inflicting on him.

"When I take the city," Salokan said aloud, "I am going to hang Queen Charion from the main gate. I will hang her by her feet. Alive. And naked."

Some nearby officers chuckled appreciatively, secretly relieved he was not yet talking about hanging them upside down and naked from the walls of Daavis. If the city did not fall soon, they knew they could expect little in the way of kindness from their king. The problem was no one had expected Charion to be so effective in rallying the defense of her capital.

Salokan studied his officers, accurately reading their

minds. *I need an advantage,* he thought. *I need something Charion does not have.* He sighed heavily. And, of course, that something was Lynan Rosetheme. Then he could parade the exiled prince up and down the country raising the province against its own diminutive queen now bottled up in Daavis. Symbols were important, he knew, just as he knew his army's continued lack of success against the city was also a symbol: a symbol of his failing invasion of Grenda Lear.

It was not supposed to turn out like this, he told himself. By now he was supposed to be inside Daavis preparing for the inevitable counterattack, with Lynan in one pocket and Charion in the other.

There was a cry from behind him, and he looked around to see some soldiers pointing to a flock of pigeons coming from the west and heading northeast.

"That's strange, isn't it?" he asked allowed but of no one in particular. "There are no pigeons on the Oceans of Grass, are there?"

"No, your Majesty," said an aide, then cleared his throat. "They could be ours."

Salokan looked at him, startled. "What do you mean?"

"I mean they could be the pigeons we sent with Thewor for Rendle's expedition."

"They couldn't all be carrying a message, could they?" someone asked.

"I think they are all bearing the same message," Salokan said bleakly.

Farben shook his head as if to clear his ears. "I'm sorry, your Highness, but I'm not sure I understood you correctly."

"You understood me, Farben. Don't lie."

"But we don't have enough soldiers."

"See, I knew you understood me. We *do* have enough soldiers."

"But we are safe inside the city walls," Farben argued, knowing even as he did so that he was arguing for a lost cause. "Salokan's forces are bleeding to death out there. Why risk such a venture?"

"Because anything we can do to demoralize the enemy increases the chances of them breaking off the siege."

"But Areava's army will be here soon! They can do the fighting! Our soldiers are weary, most are injured in one way or another . . ."

"Our soldiers would jump at the chance of striking back at the enemy," Charion declared. "You do not know them as I do."

"Undoubtedly, your Highness. Is there nothing I can do to dissuade you from this course of action?"

Charion shook her head. "And tell them that I will lead them personally."

Salokan himself organized the next assault. He planned for the catapults to concentrate their bombardment on the northeast wall, near the camp. The enemy would assume either that wall or its opposite, the southwest wall, would be attacked in force. Two regiments of foot would take scaling ladders and assault the southwest wall to reinforce that impression. Then the main attack, consisting of five regiments of foot, would attack the north wall, with no warning. With luck, they would reach the parapets and clear the walkway to the southwest wall allowing the decoy regiments to join them. With seven regiments in the city, they should be able to open the main gates to let in the rest of Salokan's force, including his cavalry.

At first it went well. The catapults hurled their stones accurately from the second shot, and a short while later, for the very first time, a part of the wall was seen to crack from parapet to base. Salokan then gave the order for the attack on the southwest wall to start, and that, too, went better than

expected. Several ladders managed to stay against the wall
long enough for some of the infantry to actually reach the
parapets. When Salokan determined Charion would have
committed her reserves to the southwest, he ordered the general attack on the north wall. It was then that things started
to go wrong.

There were far more defenders atop the north wall than
he thought would be possible, unless Charion had double-
guessed him. He refused to believe that; too many of his
troops already believed she was preternaturally lucky. Scaling ladders were pushed off as soon as they were put up. A
hail of arrows and rubble pierced and pelted his troops. Just
as he was about to call back his forces to reform and attack
again, he heard the great main gate start to creak. His heart
leaped with joy! He was certain it could only mean the two
regiments attacking the southwest wall had made it over despite the odds against them and were now opening the city
to Salokan. He hurriedly shouted new orders and his generals scurried to obey them. The five infantry regiments
dropped their ladders and lined up on the causeway in front
of the gate while his cavalry eagerly readied their columns
behind the infantry.

But instead of his forces being greeted by two friendly
regiments inside the walls, they were met by a cavalry
charge. Salokan watched in horror as his waiting foot regiments were cut down like wheat before a scythe. His army
panicked and started to spill off the causeway, and still the
Hume cavalry came on, hewing left and right. What was
worse, leading the enemy attack was Charion herself, shining in polished mail, her saber whirling, glittering in the air,
seeming twice her size in combat.

Salokan screamed for his own cavalry to engage the
enemy, but his infantry was in the way. Between the charging horses in front and the pressing mass behind, a large portion of the foot regiments could not move at all and the

soldiers were simply stabbed or slashed or suffocated where they were, the dead left standing because there was no room for them to fall down. And then, just as suddenly as it had come, the attack ended and the enemy retreated, the gates closing behind them before the Haxus cavalry could get through their own infantry to reach them. Salokan sat on his horse in shock, staring at the heap of Haxus dead on the causeway, almost overwhelmed by the cries and groans of the wounded and dying.

It was a small river town, made up of little more than a single street ending in a wharf and with houses on either side. There was a small inn, a ramp near the dock, a stable. A few townspeople were engaged in their business despite the early hour. One stall was open, selling freshly-baked bread. And there were soldiers.

"Infantry?" Magmed asked.

"I think so," Galen agreed. He pointed to the stable. "It doesn't look large enough to hold more than a dozen horses, and I see no camp nearby."

"How many enemy?" he asked eagerly, anticipating a battle, and pleased to be away from the upstart Sendarus. Galen Amptra might not yet own his father's title, but he was at least a member of the Twenty Houses.

Galen shrugged. "Hard to tell. If what we see now are just the sentries, then they have fifty down there at least."

"Just a garrison."

Galen was not so sure. From their position behind a fringe of trees on a nearby hill he could see no other sign of the enemy, but it worried him that there was no cavalry nearby. It made little sense to garrison a town with just infantry, who could be cut off and isolated by any enemy force with even the smallest mounted arm.

"I think we should explore a little more," Galen said.

"We could take the town in a single charge," Magmed said. "Give the signal and . . ."

"And we could find ourselves engaged in a large-scale battle without hope of reinforcements."

Magmed waved his hand dismissively. "What of it? The sooner we beat off this Salokan, the sooner the war will be over."

"We are under instruction," Galen said. "Our orders are clear."

"From that Amanite upstart," Magmed said, his disgust obvious.

"From our queen's consort," Galen told him sternly, "and from the holder of the Key of the Sword. Would you go against him?"

Magmed snorted derisively but said nothing. Galen shook his head. Too many of the nobles were nothing but bluster. They had gotten so used to being dominated by the throne, and so used to doing nothing but complain about it, that when they had some freedom of choice they did not know what to do with it. Well, Galen did know what to do with it; he would do everything in his power to work for the good of the kingdom, and that meant reconciling the Twenty Houses with Areava. He wished others saw the situation as he did, including his father, but maybe if he showed through example, he could help change things around.

"I think we should explore a little more," Galen repeated, and went down the other side of the hill to the waiting knights to put together a scouting party.

They waited, most of them impatiently, for the rest of the day. The scouts returned as evening fell, and the news was as Galen expected. There was a larger enemy force nearby—a large camp not five leagues from the town with at least one regiment of cavalry and two of foot.

"They patrol between the camp and two river towns, including this one," one of the scouts told Galen. "Destroy the camp, and you can secure both towns."

"And you saw no other enemy forces?"

"Only patrols from the camp. They were not expecting trouble, and did not see us. They are lazy soldiers."

Not that lazy, Galen thought. *Look how deep into our territory they already are. But overconfident, perhaps.*

"So we attack the camp!" Magmed declared. "And then we can attack the towns!"

"No," Galen said emphatically. "If we attack the camp, we risk being repelled. We have to make sure we destroy the three regiments, not simply damage them. To do that we have to bring them out into the open."

Magmed, who was not stupid, saw the wisdom in Galen's words and where they led. "So we attack one of the towns first with only some of our knights."

"Drawing the regiments out," Galen said, nodding. "Then when the enemy is clear of the camp, we attack with the main part of our force. Wiping out the regiments should distract Salokan from the siege long enough for Sendarus to catch up with us. Then we can engage in a general battle with the main Haxus force."

Salokan knew that the actual physical damage done to his army by Charion's sortie was comparatively light—a few hundred dead, no more—but the damage to his army's morale was considerably greater. Not only had they not yet breached the walls of Daavis, it seemed that Charion felt so little threatened by the siege that she could storm out of the city any time it took her fancy and wreak havoc.

Salokan knew that something had to be done urgently if Daavis was to be won . . . indeed, if the campaign and thus the war was to be won. It seemed obvious to him that Rendle had failed in his mission—he should have delivered Lynan by now, and there had been that strange flight of pigeons from the west that bespoke unknown disaster to him—so everything now rested on taking the province's capital. Subtlety had to be thrown aside and brute force applied to the problem. He ordered the catapults to work on the northeast wall where the crack had appeared. At the same time his sappers mined several tunnels under the same section of the wall, too many for the enemy to detect all of them in less than two days. In the night he mobilized his entire army—including the cavalry, which he dismounted—dividing them into three divisions, and moved them into position. They were given extra rations of wine that night.

His generals complained to him that if the morning's assault was unsuccessful the entire army would be too exhausted to launch another attack for many days. Salokan told them he understood that, but that he also understood that the army could not be expected to endure continued failure.

"I believe we must win this battle now, or risk losing everything," he told them, and they could not argue him out of it.

The next morning dawned fine, with the promise of a warm day ahead. Salokan was sure it boded well. Then the rider from the east came with the news that Kendran heavy cavalry had destroyed the best part of three of his regiments and recaptured two river towns. The enemy relief column, it would seem, was less than a day's hard ride away. Soon after, two boats sailing upriver from the towns carrying the remnants of the garrisons that had managed to escape, brought the same news. Salokan was numb with shock. If the assault on Daavis failed, he would be caught between the city and a comparatively fresh army. If the assault succeeded, he would have less than a day to rebuild the walls and stock up for a long siege. Salokan had no choice, and the realization almost crushed him. His generals came to see why he had not ordered the assault and were sent back with instructions to break the camp and prepare for a retreat.

If they moved fast enough, the army could reach Haxus and some measure of safety in less than a month. But what then? Would the army of Grenda Lear come after Salokan? Almost certainly. He knew Areava would neither forget nor forgive his incursion. The king understood suddenly that he had started a war he might lose.

26

THE Chett army came to the Strangers' Sooq. The inhabitants came out to stare, for they had never seen anything like it before, not even in the days of Korigan's father. They did not cheer, but stood open-mouthed, amazed, seeing something they did not ever think they would see. An army of their own. For the first time many of them started thinking of themselves as Chetts and not simply as members of a clan. Their horizons had expanded, and the most far-sighted of them realized this meant their ambitions could expand, too.

As surprising as the army was its leader. Small, marble-white, scarred. He was like an ancient idol come to life, and as unapproachable. They did not know him well enough to welcome him, but just by seeing him, they felt they knew him well enough to be afraid of him. They already knew of Korigan—their own queen—and in the next few hours learned about Lynan's other companions: the famous Kumul Alarn, the crookback Ager Parmer, the powerful magicker from the east with her entourage of Chett magickers, Gudon of the Red Hands—who resembled a certain barge pilot Jes Prado had taken prisoner only a few days before. It seemed as if the stuff of legend was coming alive in front of their very eyes.

The army and its leaders rode silently through the main street of the sooq, eventually halting before a single man who stood in their way. The inhabitants were surprised to see it was Kayakun, the most reticent and retiring merchant in the town. He stood before the terrible, pale Lynan and bowed, but not too deeply. They watched as Lynan dismounted and went to Kayakun and embraced him. Lynan was joined by Gudon, and then Korigan.

The people of the Strangers' Sooq did not know what to make of it all, but they knew it was something they would remember for the rest of their days.

Jenrosa was squatting in the dirt. Lasthear sat opposite her. In between them, they had leveled the ground with the palms of their hands. Words appeared in the dirt, then an eddy would come and the words would disappear, and new words would take their place.

"I read *Charion*," Lasthear said.

"And *slaughter*," Jenrosa added.

"The city of the river."

"The retreat of an army."

Lasthear again leveled the ground between them. "But whose army?" she asked aloud, and words appeared again, were erased, and were replaced with more words.

"I am done, I am done, I am done," Jenrosa read.

"The hanging sword," Lasthear said.

"All march north."

"All march north."

The pair waited, but no more words came.

Jenrosa sighed heavily and leaned forward, her head in her hands.

"Is there pain again?" Lasthear asked.

"A little. It gets easier every time. Tell me, did we read what has happened or what will happen?"

Lasthear looked at her apologetically. "I am sorry. I wish I knew, but no one has performed this magic since the Truespeaker's day."

"I am not the Truespeaker," Jenrosa insisted.

"You continue to deny it, but every day I see you do things that only a Truespeaker could do."

Jenrosa stood up unsteadily.

Lasthear watched her with concern. "What are you afraid of?"

"Why am I able to do so much so quickly? I could perform nothing but the simplest tricks before I came to the High Sooq . . . before I met you."

"Because you had no one to guide you, no one to show you the way, to let your natural talent mature."

"But the theurgia—"

"Imprisoned you with their ceremonies and procedures and complex incantations. The way of magic is always simple, and always dangerous. From what you have told me, the theurgia want to convince you that magic is always complex and difficult, and about as dangerous as learning how to bake bread."

"You make it sound as if the theurgia were created to control magic, not use it."

"Maybe they were," Lasthear said seriously. "Originally, at least. Do you wish to do more now?"

Jenrosa shook her head. "No. Not today."

"Then we will meet again tomorrow."

"Yes," Jenrosa said without enthusiasm.

Lasthear stood up. "I told you the way was dangerous. I told you that courage was necessary."

"You did not lie to me," Jenrosa admitted. "What about the words in the sand? Should we tell someone?"

Lasthear considered the question, then said, "Perhaps

you should tell Lynan. He may be able to make sense from them."

"The hanging sword?" Kumul asked. He shrugged. "I have no idea."

"Most of the rest of it makes a kind of sense," Ager said. "Charion's name is the key."

"I agree," Lynan said. "The city of the river is Daavis. We know from Gudon that Salokan intended to besiege the city. Where there is battle there is always a slaughter. And if armies are moving north, then Salokan lost and is retreating. He is the one who is crying 'I am done.' "

"So you think the siege of Daavis was broken," Korigan said, "and that the Haxus army is retreating north, probably being pursued. By Charion?"

Lynan shrugged. "I don't know. I think 'the hanging sword' may be the key to that."

"That's it!" Jenrosa said suddenly.

The others looked at her. "What's it?" Ager asked.

" 'The hanging sword may be the *key* to that,' " she said excitedly. "The Key of the Sword!"

"The 'hanging sword,' of course!" Lynan said. "It hangs around Areava's neck."

"So Areava is pursuing a defeated Salokan north to Haxus after raising the siege of Daavis," Gudon said, putting it all together.

They all looked at each other. "I think so," Lynan said, then he saw that Jenrosa seemed doubtful. "What's wrong?"

"It's so *complete*," she said. "I don't know that magic works for us that easily."

"But what else could it mean?" Kumul asked. "It makes sense, based on what intelligence we have of goings-on in the east."

"I don't know. But by itself, magic cannot tell you everything."

"I could always ride east again and see what I can see," Gudon said, but with little enthusiasm. The wounds inflicted by Prado were still healing, and would not be helped by a long ride across the Algonka Pass and into Hume.

"No, thank you, my friend," Lynan said. He glanced at each of the others in turn, took a deep breath, and said, "It is time I went to see for myself."

"Not by yourself, you won't," Kumul declared. "I'm coming with you, at least."

Lynan smiled. "I wasn't thinking of going by myself. Indeed, I was thinking of taking the whole army with me."

It was late at night when Ager returned to his clan's camp. He was about to enter his own tent when he noticed that a lamp was still burning in Morfast's tent. He went over, found the flap was untied, and opened it.

"Morfast?" he called from the threshold.

"You can come in, you know," she answered. "You are my chief."

Ager entered. Morfast was lying in her cot, still dressed, her hands behind her head.

"Why are you still awake?" he asked. "Is something wrong?"

"I had never been in a battle before," she said.

"From your scars I thought—"

"I've fought many Chetts, for one reason or another," she said. "But that was different. Much more personal."

Ager scratched his head. "The opposite for me. I've been in very few fights that weren't part of some larger battle. In fact, none before I met Lynan."

"Your prince has changed the world for both of us, then."

"Does that upset you?"

Morfast frowned in concentration. "I'm afraid, I think."

"And you've never been afraid before?" he asked, quite willing to believe it.

"Of course I have been, but for myself. When you slew Katan, I became afraid for my clan. Now I'm afraid for all of us."

"There's a great deal at risk, but I think that would have been the case whether or not the Chetts tied their fortunes to Lynan."

Morfast said nothing, and Ager started to feel uncomfortable. "Do you regret asking me to be your chief?"

"No!" she said quickly. "Never that! You cannot know how much it has meant to the Ocean clan. We are proud to have you for our chief."

"Even though I am so closely linked to Lynan?"

"That is fate, but knowing that does not stop me being afraid. I cannot see where our future lies anymore. Once, it was easy. We would protect our clan, mate and raise children, live and die on the Oceans of Grass. Now, I do not think I will die on the Oceans of Grass, and that saddens me."

"You and your people can return to your territory, you know. I will not be angry—"

"Me and my people?" she said angrily. She sat up and stared at him. "You mean *your* people, don't you?"

"Well, yes . . ."

"You still don't understand, do you? We made the decision to continue as a clan under you. It cannot be taken back, and we will never regret it."

Ager felt humbled by her words, and ashamed. "I am sorry, Morfast. I am proud to be your chief, prouder than words can express. But being chief of the Ocean clan means I must also consider what's best for them, and going east with me may not be what's best for them. I am thinking that most of you should rejoin the herd in the clan territory, leaving behind only that contingent conscripted in the army. Other chiefs ride with the army, but with no more than a few hundred of their warriors."

"It comes back to Lynan, Ager. You are not just a chief; you are one of the White Wolf's companions. We understand that, and can no more desert you than you can desert Lynan. Do not talk again about sending us back to our territory."

Ager looked away from her. "Is it just the future that makes you afraid?" he asked.

He heard her hold her breath, and found himself hoping—and at the same time fearing—she would say the words he wanted to hear.

"You already know the answer to that question," she said.

It has come to this, he thought. *And I do not know what to say.*

Morfast reached out to take his hand and pulled him to her cot. He sat down beside her. She gently turned his face so he was looking at her, and kissed him.

Jenrosa was alone in the middle of a wide green plain. It was not on the Oceans of Grass, the vegetation was too green for that. She was in the east. All around her were the signs of what had been a great battle: spears in the ground like bare saplings, abandoned helmets and shields and weapons, streaks and puddles of blood, the smell of shit and rotting flesh, the sound of flies and ravens. But there was no human, alive or dead, as far as she could see. It was the moment just before evening, and the plain was brushed in a golden light.

Something glinted on the ground not far from her. She walked over to it. Curled in the grass like a snake was a golden chain. She picked it up and saw that it carried an amulet. It was the Key of the Sword. She sensed something nearby. She spun around and saw Lynan. He was standing straight as an elm. He was dressed simply in tan riding breeches and an open jerkin. His eyes were staring at the horizon. Around his neck hung the Key of Union.

She went to him, stood before him, but he looked right through her.

"Lynan?"

No sign of recognition. He did not know she was there. The chain she was holding suddenly became very heavy, and she knew what she had to do with it. She carefully put it over Lynan's head, then stepped back.

Lynan's body started to shimmer and blur. His eyes changed color, his hair grew longer, his clothes metamorphosed into bark and twigs and leaves. And then he was gone. Standing in his place was Silona. Only the Keys of Power remained unchanged.

Jenrosa tried to run away, but she was frozen in place. Silona's eyes closed, then opened. She looked straight at Jenrosa and recognized her.

"You," the vampire breathed, and reached out a hand.

Again Jenrosa tried to run away, but something held in her in place. Silona's fingers curled around Jenrosa's hair, and her mouth opened. A long, green hollow tongue flickered in and out.

Jenrosa screamed.

She woke sitting up, Kumul sitting next to her, his arms around her shoulders.

"God's death!" Kumul cried. "What's wrong?"

Jenrosa was panting for breath. "It was her. Silona."

Kumul's face went pale. "Where? Is she in the camp?"

She shook her head. "No, no. In my dream." She started shaking and wrapped her own arms around Kumul to try and stop it.

Kumul hugged her tightly. "It's all right," he said soothingly. "I'm here. No one can harm you." After a while, he asked, "Can you tell me about it?"

She haltingly described the dream, still fresh in her memory.

"No wonder you woke up screaming," Kumul said.

"What if it wasn't a dream?" she said. "What if I was seeing something in the future?"

"You have no reason to believe that," Kumul told her, but she heard the doubt in his voice.

She closed her eyes, and the image of Silona was still there, reaching out to her. "Oh, Kumul, I wish that was true," she said, and started to cry.

Lynan and Korigan were in his tent squatting on the ground and looking over a map that rested between them. The Algonka Pass marked the westernmost edge of the map, the Sea Between the easternmost edge, and in the middle were the provinces of Hume and Chandra.

"If we have correctly interpreted the words Jenrosa and Lasthear read with their magic," Lynan was saying, "then Salokan will be making directly for his border. His rate of march will be determined by how closely he is being pursued by Areava and her army."

"The problem is, we don't know if the magickers are telling us about something that has happened or will happen," Korigan said.

"That is why we have to cross the pass as soon as possible. If we send scouts a day or two ahead of us, they should find signs of a retreat easily enough, if there is one. Then we will know where to strike next."

"You are looking for another battle, then?"

Lynan nodded.

"With whom? Areava or Salokan."

"We both know, I think. Areava's forces will be spread out—scouts well north, a vanguard, then the main body of infantry. Her cavalry will be out wide on her northwest and northeast flanks to make sure Salokan doesn't double back. She will not be expecting a threat directly to her western flank. We could decide the whole issue if we defeat her centre, then destroy her detachments in detail."

"What issue?" Korigan asked.

Lynan's breath caught in his throat. He had not said it before, but knew in his heart there was only *one* issue that would guarantee he and his friends could return safely to Kendra. "The issue of who will rule the kingdom," he said slowly, and with the saying of it was surprised to feel a great weight lift from his shoulders.

"Have you told Kumul of this decision?" she asked.

"No."

"You will have to, sooner or later."

"Sooner, I know. Before the battle. He has a right to know what he is fighting for."

"If it helps, I think he knows already. He just can't admit it to himself."

"He has always served the throne of Grenda Lear."

"By serving you, he still does," Korigan said.

Lynan looked up, met Korigan's gaze. "Thank you," he said.

They both stood, still looking at each other.

"I had better go," Korigan said.

"Yes."

They both reached for the flap at the same time and their hands touched. For a moment neither moved, but then Lynan opened the flap and the contact was broken. Korigan left without saying another word.

Kayakun picked up the wine jar and refilled the two goblets, took his own, and drank deeply. "I cannot believe it is the same boy."

Gudon belched, pounded his stomach with a fist and belched again. "Where did you say this piss came from?"

"I didn't. It's from some new vineyards in eastern Hume."

"It is too warm there for good wine to grow," Gudon declared.

"That hasn't stopped you from helping me drink two flagons of the stuff."

"Two?" Gudon asked, surprised. "Already?"

"We're ready for our third."

As if Kayakun's words were a signal, one of his servants reappeared with a full jug and took away the empty.

"As I was saying, I can't believe it is the same boy."

"We're talking of Lynan now?"

"Of course."

"I only ask because in the last few hours we've discussed the defeat of the mercenaries, the weather, politics in Grenda Lear, the lineage of some merchant who offended you ten years ago, the weather, a new brood mare you purchased in the winter, and the bloody weather. I've lost track of where we're up to."

"We're up to Lynan. The boy. The man. Whatever he is." Kayakun glared at Gudon through half-closed eyes. "Come to that, *what* is he?"

"The gods only know."

"That isn't an answer."

"He is the White Wolf returned—" Kayakun waved dismissively at that, "—he is heir to the throne of Grenda Lear, he is a warrior and a general, he is a leader, he is a prophecy in the making." Gudon put his goblet down and said heavily, "And he is a boy. Nothing more than a boy."

"You like him, don't you?"

"I love him. Truth, he is a son and a brother all at once to me. I saved his life. He has saved mine. He makes me proud. He terrifies me."

"Have you told anyone else this?" Kayakun asked.

"Oh, that's clever," Gudon said, wagging his finger. "Ply me with bad wine and then interrogate me. What do you want?"

"I want to know whether or not this Lynan is leading our people to disaster."

"I think he will save us from disaster."

"What do you mean?"

"He saved Korigan's crown at the High Sooq. Maybe even her head. He has united most of the clans under his pennant, and may yet unite all of them. If he wins the throne, our independence will be guaranteed and our isolation ended."

"He can't do both. Our isolation is our independence."

"That's glib, Kayakun, but not true. Independence comes not from being left alone, but from being equal with all the other peoples that make up the kingdom of Grenda Lear."

"And if he loses? What attitude will Areava take toward us then, sitting on her throne in far-away Kendra?"

"I'm too drunk to answer that."

"And tomorrow you'll be too sober to answer it."

Gudon giggled. "Oh, now that *is* clever."

Kayakun leaned forward until his face was less than a hand's span from Gudon's. "I'm serious."

"Then you haven't drunk enough of this wine."

"I'm *serious*," Kayakun repeated.

Gudon sighed deeply. "All right, I'll answer your question. If Lynan loses, Areava will not attack us. But she will make sure that our isolation becomes permanent. We will be imprisoned within the Oceans of Grass."

"That sounds like a reward, not a punishment."

Gudon scowled at him. "Kayakun, that is the most stupid thing you have ever said."

The Chett army stayed at the Strangers' Sooq for over a week. In that time, most of the grass around the sooq was eaten by all the horses, but since no caravan would be coming this spring, it was no great loss.

Lynan, Korigan, and Gudon spent the days gathering supplies and the wagons necessary to carry them across the Algonka Pass and into the eastern provinces; Lynan wanted to avoid his army living off the land and alienating the very people he wanted as his subjects. Kumul and Ager resumed their training of the army and invented pennants for each banner, pennants that had nothing to do with any existing clan. Jenrosa spent all her time with Lasthear, trying to master her skills, hoping there was a limit to them and that in the end she was nothing more than another magicker; she had no more dreams about Silona, but could not forget the one dream she had had.

At the end of that week the warm winds of the coming summer were already blowing across the Oceans of Grass. For Lynan it was a sign, and he ordered the army to move out.

The banners, proudly carrying above them their new pennants, left the Strangers' Sooq as quietly as they had come.

27

GALEN did not enjoy being in the middle of the argument, but he knew whose side he was on, and that surprised him. "It may be your province, your Highness, but our queen gave command to Prince Sendarus; indeed, not only did she give him command of her army, she also gave him the Key of the Sword, and whoever wears that has supreme military authority within Grenda Lear."

Charion's eyes narrowed and she glared at the nobleman. "I am also a queen," she hissed. "I want Salokan's head, and I want it now. I don't see why this—" she waved deprecatingly at Sendarus, "—gentleman will not lend me his cavalry so I can pursue the bastard!"

Prince Sendarus closed his eyes and wished desperately he was back in Kendra with his wife. This black-haired witch's bad temper and abuse made him want to drop her from the top of her own city's walls.

"I'll explain again," he started calmly, "and this time I expect you to listen, because it is the last time. I am going to pursue Salokan, but I will wait until all my infantry has caught up with me here at Daavis. In the meantime a portion of my cavalry and light infantry will keep in touch with Salokan's rearguard, ensuring he does not double back to catch us unaware, and the rest of my force will help repair any damage done to your capital and help bring in fresh supplies."

"But what if Salokan reaches Haxus before—!"

"Be that as it may," Sendarus interrupted, his voice rising, "my first priority is to secure *this* city. When I am satisfied that Daavis is safe, we will hunt down Salokan and destroy his army to the last soldier."

Charion put her hands on her hips and looked ready to spit, but she had run out of arguments and insults. Obviously, this upstart prince was not going to let her pursue Salokan—undoubtedly because he wanted all the glory for finishing off the foreign king for himself—nor was he going to let her assert her right to determine events in her own country.

"Very well," she said tightly. "I will await your pleasure. When your lost regiments finally discover how to find this city—ten square leagues in size and sitting astride the continent's widest river—I look forward to once again taking up the war."

She spun on her heel and stalked off before Sendarus could reply. He wiped his brow with the back of his hand. "I don't think this would be a good time to ask her about billeting," he said.

"That's the truth," Galen said. "I think that went as well as can be expected."

"You've had dealings with her before?"

"Only once. I attended an embassy to her from Usharna; I escorted Berayma. Berayma was . . . overwhelmed . . . by her."

"She would overwhelm a great bear, I think."

They started back to their camp north of the city.

"I haven't had time yet to congratulate you and the knights for your victory over the Haxus regiments south of here. I think it was that which finally convinced Salokan to turn tail. If he had not heard news of your victory, he might well have taken Daavis that morning. Charion will never admit it, of course, but her secretary Farben told me that the city's defenses were not far from collapsing."

"I think I am speaking for all the Twenty Houses when I say we are only too glad to contribute to the security of the kingdom."

"Areava will hear of it, I promise," Sendarus said.

Salokan knew he was defeated, but he was not panicking. His army was retreating in good order, not in a rout, and he wanted to keep it that way. He selected his best troops for the rearguard, with clear orders to slow down any pursuit. Over the last eight days there had been some skirmishes with Grenda Lear cavalry, and on two occasions with fast-moving and lightly-armored infantry, but nothing that seriously interfered with the retreat. The problem was that the enemy cavalry and light infantry was not trying to slow down the retreat at this point, but simply to stay in touch so that when the main Grenda Lear army came up, it could go straight for the throat of the Haxus army. He knew that if he wanted to survive long enough to reach his own kingdom—where he had reserves and well-established supply lines—he would have to do something unexpected, something that would throw the enemy off his scent or make them think twice about dogging him so closely.

His troops were tired and demoralized, but they would be considerably more tired and demoralized if the enemy caught them on a field not of their choosing. Thus it was that on the eighth night of their retreat, as soon as the evening meal had been finished, he ordered the army to march on instead of settling down. He pushed them on until midnight, and then, instead of letting them rest, he made each regiment build a rampart from packed earth with two ditches in front, one filled with wooden stakes and the other with their last reserve of cooking oil. The ramparts were not continuous, but built checkerboard so that gaps between the first line were covered by those ramparts making up the second line. Finally he had the ditches and ramparts covered with branches and turf. The work was done by dawn; he let them sleep until noon, then stirred them and made them line the ramparts, with strict orders not to make a sound.

The enemy, who had expected to make contact with the Haxus rearguard by mid-morning—based on the expectation that they themselves had not camped too far from Salokan's forces—found that their quarry was missing. Their commanders panicked and pushed them to catch up. In the early hours of the afternoon they did catch up. Spectacularly.

The Grenda Lear cavalry hit the hidden defenses first; some tripped in the first ditch, but most of the horses jumped it only to land in the second ditch filled with stakes. The screams and cries of impaled horses and men were dreadful, and when brands were thrown from behind the ramparts into the first ditch, setting alight the oil, the terror of the survivors sent them hurtling carelessly into the Haxus troops waiting behind the ramparts. It was a bloody slaughter.

Dazed, unsure what had happened to their mounted comrades, the light infantry hesitated. Salokan ordered his own cavalry to charge. The Grenda Lear infantry, tired and shaken, were virtually wiped out. A few managed to flee, but Salokan knew he had no time to waste in fruitless pursuit and ordered his troops to resume their march north; it had been a long day for them, but invigorated by their victory they complained not at all.

"How many?" Sendarus asked as he strode to his horse, strapping on his sword belt. An early morning mist whirled about his feet, but a bright sun was already burning it away.

"Four companies of our horse, almost all our light infantry," Galen said. "How far behind are our heavy infantry?"

"At least another day. The remainder of our cavalry, including all your knights, and all our archers are here; that will have to do."

"Do we march north, then?"

"We have no choice. We don't know what Salokan is planning. Maybe he received reinforcements and is on his way back. In its present state Daavis could not withstand another siege. We have to stop him before he gets here." An orderly hurried up with his chain shirt and helmet. "Choose a messenger, Galen, and give him three horses. He has to reach our regiments of spear by midday. Tell them to follow us at double pace."

"They'll be exhausted and almost useless if they have to fight straight away."

"Nonetheless, I want them with us, even if only as a reserve. Salokan will think twice about using his own cavalry if he sees a few thousand spears pointing in his direction."

Galen nodded and left. Sendarus finished dressing and mounted his horse.

"You wouldn't be leaving without me, would you?"

It was the last voice he wanted to hear at that moment. "Your Highness, you're up early. Word travels quickly."

"Word of disaster always travels quickly," Charion said levelly. She was dressed in full armor and mounted on a hack, not her usual ceremonial pony. "Are you aware that in the whole campaign so far, the only serious loss we've suffered has been the destruction of your cavalry and light infantry?"

"Only four companies of horse, your Highness," he said between his teeth. He could imagine the message she would already have sent to Areava by carrier bird. He would have to send one of his own to put things in the proper perspective.

Which is? he asked himself. *Remember, you rescued Daavis. That's the most important thing.*

"I still have four regiments, including three of the knights," he told her.

"I can give you another regiment, plus two regiments of infantry."

"What does that leave you to protect the city?"

"Most of my archers, and a goodly number of swordsmen."

Sendarus wanted to tell her what she could do with her offer, but bit his tongue. Any extra troops at this point would be welcome, and another regiment of horse would bring his cavalry back up to full strength.

"Thank you. I accept."

"And I will lead them myself," she added.

Sendarus glared at her, but she did not look away.

"That's the price," she said.

"You will be under my command," he said.

"Of course. You wear the Key of the Sword. Galen Amptra explained the situation to me very clearly yesterday. Do you agree?"

Sendarus could not say the word, but nodded.

"Good. My troops will be ready in an hour."

"We leave in half an hour," he said and wheeled his horse away from her.

Salokan's generals, their confidence boosted by their recent victory, urged him to turn back.

"We've proven we can take on and defeat Areava's army. Let's finish the job and take Daavis."

But Salokan did not listen to them. He understood the difference between winning a skirmish and winning a battle. He also understood that even if he met Areava's main force and defeated it, his own army would probably be so damaged it would not be fit to start another siege or execute a successful city assault. He had already swallowed his pride.

Besides, if Grenda Lear tried to invade Haxus in retaliation for his invasion, he thought he had a better than even chance of beating them back, and then the option of returning to Hume with a fresh army would be a real possibility. An autumn campaign held the advantage of leaving a winter between any counter move from Kendra. Maybe he should have thought of that before starting his late winter offensive.

Well, I lose and learn, he told himself. Unlike his father, who lost and then lost again. Whatever happened, he was not going to do that.

28

FATHER Powl was in the primate's chambers—*his* chambers, he constantly reminded himself—kneeling at his prayer stool. His eyes were closed and his mind scurried like a cockroach through all his memories of Giros Northam, all the words he had ever spoken, all the lessons he had ever imparted, all the clues he had hinted at about the greatest secret of their religion.

"God has a name," Northam had once told him, "and the name is everything that God can be."

And another time he had told Powl, "A single word reveals all there is to know about God."

So the name of God is a single word?

His gripped his hands so tightly together the fingers were pinched white, and he prayed so fiercely the veins in his temples stood out like tracery in a stained-glass window.

"One secret, Lord, is all I ask," he prayed. "One secret to show me all your wonder. One secret to let me carry on your work. All these years I have been your faithful servant."

He waited for a voice, a whisper, a sign, anything at all that would point him in the right direction, but all he heard was the silence of his own great sin.

"Oh, Lord, I am a weak man, I confess. But I would be strong for you if only you would let me."

He tried to picture in his mind what God would be like. When he was a callow youth, God had come to him so many times in his dreams his face was more familiar than those of his fellow novitiates. Why now, when he was temporal head of God's own religion, was his face turned away from him? Was his sin that great?

"Show me your face, God, so that I may call you by your name."

And an answer came so suddenly his eyes opened in surprise. "When you call me by my name, you will see my face."

The voice had been his own.

Dejanus pinned down Ikanus' arms as he thrust into her. He did not look into her face, but stared straight ahead. The woman grunted underneath his weight, and he wondered if it was in pleasure or in pain. She never said, but accepted him like the whore she was.

When he came, he collapsed on top of her, panting like a dog after a chase. Ikanus slid out from underneath him and quickly dressed.

"What's the hurry?" he asked.

"I am still on shift."

"The landlord won't mind. He knows who I am."

Ikanus did not answer, but hurriedly left the small room on the first floor of the Lost Sailor Tavern that the landlord had set aside for just such meetings.

After he caught his breath, Dejanus sat up and took a long swig from the flagon he had left on the floor. It occurred to him that Ikanus did not like him very much. Well, it did not matter, as long as she kept her mouth shut and her legs open. He grinned at that.

Oh, you're a clever prick, he thought to himself.

He lay back down on the bed and finished drinking the wine.

Father Powl pulled out *On the Body of God* from the bookshelf by his bed. He had been through it a dozen times in the last few months. He carefully turned each page, scanning for any mark, any sign, that Northam may have left and that he had missed. He did not read the words, the words meant nothing to him anymore, but he hoped there was some meaning in the book itself, in the way it was set out or designed—in a misplaced curlicue or a hanging sentence or an odd illustration.

Please, God, let me find the sign.

He finished the book and threw it aside, and from the shelf got *The Meditations of Agostin.* This was a much larger book, but he scrutinized each page minutely. When he was finished with that, he went through *The Seven Penances of a Great Sinner,* and then the life of Margolayus, the first primate, and every other book that Northam had thought special enough to keep in his own chambers.

Occasionally, he did come across a marginal note in Northam's hand, usually next to some underlined phrase in the text, but in every case it was nothing more than some pitiful revelation, like *Now I understand!* or *See Seven Penances part the first* or even *Remember this!*

At one point he had listed all the marginalia and the underlined phrases, thinking there may have been some code hidden in them, but in the end he knew they were just what they seemed, trite observations from a lazy meditation.

Oh, Giros, I never knew your mind was so small. How I remember looking upon you as the wisest of the wise.

He hurled the last book across the chamber in anger. He placed his head in his hands, filled with self-pity. He wanted to burst into tears, but knew he could not cry. He had not cried for so long he did not think he knew how anymore.

He remembered seeing tears in Northam's eyes on more than one occasion. The old primate had a strong empathy for those who suffered.

Not so wise, perhaps, Powl thought. *But a good man.* And suddenly he wondered if he himself was either wise or good.

He heard hurried footsteps outside, and someone knocked on his door.

"Yes, what is it?"

The priest from the hospice entered, opened his mouth to say something, but then saw the books strewn all over the room.

"What is it?" Powl repeated testily.

"Your Grace, you wanted to know when next Prince Olio came to the hospice. He is there now, and treating one of the patients."

"Which patient?"

"A young man who was beaten in a robbery two days ago. He is dying."

Powl scowled. He did not want to be bothered with this right now, but knew it might be days or even weeks before the prince visited the hospice again.

"Was the prelate with him?"

The priest shook his head. "But his Highness said he would wait for him before starting the healing. Your Grace, I have to get back. Will you come with me?"

"I will come with you," Powl said.

Olio stood over the unconscious man. He could not believe someone could have been bashed so badly and still be alive. The nose was broken, the eyes swollen and black, one cheek fractured, the jaw broken. Olio lifted the sheet and saw that one rib was ridging the skin at an odd angle. The man breathed in spasms, which meant another rib had probably pierced a lung.

Olio stood back, peered out the room's window. *Come on, Edaytor, where are you? This one is dying; he needs us.*

He noticed that the Key of the Heart was warm against his skin. He took it out from underneath his shirt and held it in his left hand. He reached out to the battered man with his right hand, but pulled back before he touched him.

Wait for the prelate, you fool, he told himself. *You're not strong enough for this.*

He looked out the window again. There was a pool of light on the street. Olio saw a drunk sitting in the street, a flask of wine in one hand and an oil lamp in the other. *If he doesn't go home soon,* Olio thought, *his lamp will run out and he'll never find his way back.*

That was what had happened to this patient, he realized. The lamp of his life was sputtering out, and he was so deep into the darkness he could not find his way out. Not without help, anyway.

"B–b–but quickly, Edaytor, or even we m–m–may not be able to help him. Even I can't b–b–bring p–p–people b–b–back from the dead."

He was still grasping the Key in his left hand, and it started to tingle.

Is it possible? Can I do it alone?

He reached out again. His right hand rested lightly on the man's forehead. Almost instantly, Olio felt the rush of power from the Key through his body and into the man. Olio was so surprised he jerked back, breathing hard. How could this be possible? He remembered Edaytor telling him that some magickal items—especially items of great power—took time to attune themselves to their owners. Perhaps the Key had finally done that with him. After all, he knew his mother had been able to wield it without any assistance from a magicker.

He placed his hand on the patient again, and this time let the power flow through him. He became aware that the air around him was charged with a flickering blue energy, like miniature lightning, which whipped out, disappeared, and whipped out again.

Suddenly it was done. Of its own volition, his right hand dropped from the young man and hung limp by his side. He could not help the groan of exhaustion that escaped his lips. He let go of the Key, now cold, and used both hands to grip the side of the patient's bed to stop himself from falling over. He looked up and saw that there was still a feint remnant of the blue energy. It surrounded his body like a soft mist. A few moments later it was gone, too.

The patient's eyes flickered open, stared at Olio in confusion. "Who are you?" he croaked.

Olio patted his shoulder. "A friend," he said. "How are you feeling?" Olio could not see any sign on his face of the beating he had received.

"Tired. Never been this tired before."

"Then close your eyes. Sleep. When you awake again, you will be able to go home."

"Where am I?"

"Don't worry about that now. Just sleep."

Olio could see the patient wanted to ask more questions, but his eyes shut despite his efforts to keep them open and he fell asleep almost instantly.

Olio quietly left the room. If he had looked one more time out of the window, he would have seen that the drunk and his lamp were gone.

Dejanus, too, was sleeping peacefully. And naked except for his boots. Hrelth was afraid to wake him. It occurred to him he could slip his knife between the giant's ribs and be rid of him. He was a cruel master, nothing like Kumul who had treated him firmly but with respect.

But Hrelth would do no such thing. He had lost his courage years ago, fighting for Usharna during the Slaver

War. It was not the only thing he had lost in that bloody conflict. His own brother had died while standing right next to Hrelth in the spear line, an arrow through his eye. He wished he could forget. Maybe, if he did, he would remember what courage was like, and then he would stick Dejanus good and proper.

The constable snorted, and Hrelth jumped in the air. His feet made only the slightest noise when they hit the floor, but it was enough. Dejanus had swung out of bed with one lithe movement, pulling a dagger out of his boot at the same time. The effect was spoiled somewhat when he kept on swinging and fell on his side. *Maybe I could have knifed him after all,* Hrelth thought, and cocked his head to look at him straight.

"Your Constableness? Are you all right?" He saw the empty wine flagon on the bed. "You've been drinking."

Dejanus growled and lifted himself into a sitting position. "What do you want, you gutter rat?"

"You said you wanted me to tell you when Prince Olio came to the hospice. I just saw him there."

"What was he doing?"

Hrelth swallowed. If there was one thing that scared him more than Dejanus, it was magic. But Dejanus was here, and the magic was out *there*.

"He was using the Key of the Heart, my lord."

Dejanus blinked. "You saw that?"

"Yes. Through a window. It was dark in the room, and suddenly it was filled with a strange blue light. I saw Olio."

"Was Prelate Edaytor Fanhow with him?"

"I did not see him."

Dejanus stood up unsteadily and reached for Hrelth's shirt. Hrelth stepped back instinctively. Dejanus growled and reached forward again. This time Hrelth let himself be captured. Dejanus pulled him so close Hrelth could smell the wine on his stale breath, and something else as well.

"Are you sure the magicker was not with him?"

Hrelth nodded.

Dejanus looked at him for a minute, and Hrelth wondered if the constable was going to kill him for waking him up. Instead Dejanus just pushed him away. Hrelth stopped when he slammed into a wall, his head hitting it with a loud thump.

"Wait outside," Dejanus ordered. "I'll get dressed and you can take me to the hospice."

Hrelth did not wait for the giant to change his mind. He ran out of the room and downstairs. When he got outside of the Lost Sailor Tavern, he wanted to keep on running, but he knew what Dejanus would do to him if he ran out now. Feeling miserable, he found his lamp and held it close to him in the cold night.

Edaytor arrived at the hospice out of breath, his face covered in a fine sheen of sweat. Olio was waiting for him in the kitchen, sitting behind a large wooden table.

"Your Highness, I am sorry I am late. Your messenger could not find me at first, and had to visit two of the theurgia before he did." Edaytor tsk-tsked. "I was caught in a conversation with that damned magister of the Theurgia of Stars. Most boring man alive, but very influential . . ."

Olio was staring in his direction, but Edaytor got the feeling he was looking right through him. He saw the prince was holding a goblet.

"You haven't been . . . ?" He could not finish the question.

Olio shook his head as if coming out of a deep trance. He blinked and looked at Edaytor as though he was seeing him for the first time. "Edaytor? When did you get here? And why are you so late?"

"What is in your goblet?" Edaytor asked, not to be put off.

Olio held up the goblet. "Water," he said, nodding to a small cask on the table. "Just water. Did you want some?"

Edaytor sniffed the air. He certainly could not smell any wine. "I was just saying how sorry I was for being late . . ." He stopped and sniffed again. There was something else in the air, something extraordinary, something he had smelled only once before in his life.

"Is the patient still alive?" he asked absently.

"Oh, yes," Olio answered.

"Then maybe we should start. Where's the priest?"

Olio shrugged. "He was here when I arrived. I don't know where he is now."

"I see." Edaytor left the kitchen and went into the special room set aside for the patients he and Olio were to heal. There was a single man there, young, robust, and sleeping. Sleeping peacefully.

He returned to the kitchen. "That priest has put the wrong patient into the room."

"Actually, he didn't."

"I don't understand. The man in the room seems perfectly healthy to me."

"He is," Olio said levelly.

"I must be getting old or senile," Edaytor said. "I don't understand what is going on here."

He left the kitchen for the special room again. He bent over the man in the bed. There certainly seemed to be nothing wrong with him. Edaytor took a deep breath to clear his mind. And was struck by that smell again, but this time it was much stronger. He quickly looked around him. Where could it be coming from? It was almost as if the whole room was charged with—

No. He couldn't have.

He returned to the kitchen. Olio was looking at him almost sheepishly.

"You used the Key by yourself, didn't you?"

"Yes."

Edaytor pulled out a seat and sat at the table next to Olio. "What happened?"

"I'm not quite sure. I was standing over the p–p–patient, waiting for you to turn up, when it just happened."

"It can't just happen, your Highness," Edaytor said. "Magic doesn't work like that."

"M–m–maybe there's more to the Key than just m–m–magic," Olio said.

"Why didn't you stop?" Edaytor asked, his tone abrupt. "Why didn't you wait for me?"

"Why are you so concerned?"

"I've warned you about the Key's power. You know what it can to do to you even if you use it with a magicker's help. Why did you do it?"

"Because I could," Olio said simply.

"Your Highness—"

"I'm tired of this interrogation, Edaytor."

"I see," Edaytor said slowly.

"Are you so angry because you were left out?" Olio asked.

Edaytor blushed with sudden anger. "I don't deserve that."

Olio, who realized how hurtful his words had been, blushed then as well. "I am sorry, m–m–my friend. I did not m–m–mean that. But p–p–please understand, I did not have that m–m–much control over m–m–my actions in that room. I knew I could stop it if I really concentrated, but I didn't want to stop it. It seemed as if I was m–m–meant to be there at that p–p–precise time to carry out that p–p–precise task."

The prelate did not know what to say. He was afraid for the prince, for he was not trained in magic and the Key of the Heart was a much more powerful item of magic than any even he had come across before. Perhaps it could influence the prince to such an extent he was no longer entirely responsible for his own actions.

There were footsteps outside, and a moment later the priest entered the kitchen.

"Ah, Father!" Olio stood up in greeting. "I was wondering—"

Someone else came in behind the priest.

"P–p–primate P–p–powl," Olio said quietly. "Delightful."

Edaytor stood up, too. "This is a surprise," he managed to say.

Powl smiled humorlessly at them. "I have no doubt. Please, your Highness, Prelate Fanhow, sit down. You both look exhausted."

The two men sat down. The priest mumbled an excuse and left the room. Powl remained standing, looking carefully at the two men. "I think I deserve an explanation at last," he said.

Olio and Edaytor exchanged quick glances.

"We had always meant to come to you," Edaytor started, "but the right opportunity never seemed to come up."

"It has now," Powl countered.

"So it seems. Your Grace, we—that is, the prince and I— or rather the prince by himself, now—we—him, I mean, now, but before with me or with someone like me—I mean a magicker, of course . . . Where was I up to?"

"What he m–m–means to say," Olio said, "is that we entered an arrangement with your p–p–predecessor that allowed m–m–me to heal the dying using in combination the p–p–power of the Key of the Heart and the ability of a m–m–magicker, usually the p–p–prelate."

"I was not far wrong, then," Powl said. "I assumed the Key had something to do with it, but assumed you, your Highness, merely provided it while the prelate here did all the real work."

"What are you going to do now?" Olio asked.

"What do you mean?"

"Will you close down the hospice, or tell Areava about what we are doing?"

Powl's surprise was obvious. "Close down the hospice? Why? And doesn't Areava already know?"

"The hospice was started under the understanding that the prince's involvement would be kept secret," Edaytor explained. "My concern was that the prince would be mobbed if word got out that he could heal the sick."

"It is indeed a wonderful miracle," Powl admitted. "But surely some kind of official office could have been established to deal with that—"

"Olio cannot perform the healing too often, or he suffers for it."

Powl waited for more information, buy Edaytor would say no more.

"Suffers?" the primate prompted.

"It tires me," Olio admitted.

Powl bowed his head and thought for a moment. "It does more than tire you, doesn't it?" he asked eventually. "Two of my novitiates found you on the street once, remember?"

Olio sighed unhappily. "Ah, that was you in the room that time?"

"Indeed. Don't worry, your secret was safe even from me: Primate Northam refused to tell me what you had been doing. Your drunkenness, however, was a secret from no one except your sister."

"She learned of it, nonetheless," Olio admitted.

"And now? How do you handle the strain now?"

"Well, I think," the prince said a little too quickly. Powl saw Edaytor look down at the floor.

"There's something else, isn't there?"

"I cured a p–p–patient b–b–by m–m–myself tonight for the first time."

"You used the Key's magic without the prelate's help?"

Olio nodded.

"This is astounding," the primate said, more to himself than the others.

"What will you do?" Olio asked.

"Do? Nothing, I think. What can I do? I will not stop you carrying out your work at the hospice, as long as you guarantee me that you will never place your own life at risk here."

"I do p–p–promise that," Olio said.

"Well, then, we have come to an understanding. I hope both of you feel you can trust me more readily."

"Yes, of course," Edaytor said quickly.

"I am sorry we did not do so earlier," Olio added.

"Well and good. I will leave you two alone, then." Powl put a hand on Olio's shoulder. "Your Highness, if there is ever a time you need assistance or some comfort, I am always at your service. I know you held my predecessor in high regard and with great affection, but although he is gone and I am now in his place, the function and purpose of the office of primate had not changed."

"Thank you," Olio said sincerely. "I will not forget."

Dejanus held out a full flagon of cheap wine. "Well, Hrelth? This or a penny?"

Hrelth, still hugging his lantern, knew the wine would warm him better and reached for the flagon. Dejanus laughed and pulled it away.

"First, you take me to the hospice. It is dark and you have a lamp."

Hrelth said nothing but scampered down the street, followed by Dejanus. He had to stop every twenty paces or so for Dejanus, who was still feeling the effects of his drinking bout, to catch up.

Eventually they reached the street where Hrelth had set

up watch. He pointed to a dark window. "That is where I saw the magic."

Dejanus checked no one else was on the street and went to the window. He cupped his hands on either side of his face and peered through the glass. He could only dimly make out the shape of a bed and someone lying in it. He grunted and moved back to where Hrelth waited.

"There's no prince there now," he said, unhappy he had crawled out into the cold night for nothing.

Hrelth suddenly put a finger to his lips, then pointed farther down the street. A sliver of light appeared, and a dark shape emerged. "Thank you, Father," the shape said to someone still inside. "Good work tonight."

"That's the primate's voice," Dejanus whispered.

Hrelth was not sure if he was supposed to comment or not, but decided that saying nothing was the safest course.

The sliver of light disappeared, and the dark shape left behind turned and started walking away from the couple watching him.

"I must follow," Dejanus decided suddenly. "The primate and I have things to talk about." He handed the flagon to Hrelth. "You stay here and keep an eye on the hospice. I'll be back later."

Hrelth took the flagon gratefully and squatted down in the street.

Areava was woken by a sudden spasm of pain. At first she thought it had just been a dream, but then she noticed her sheets were wet. Another spasm made her gasp in surprise.

"God, it's happening!" she cried. "Too soon! Two months too soon!" She put her hands over her belly, expecting to feel the baby moving. The shape felt different, but there was no kicking or wriggling.

She waited for the pain to pass and got out of her bed. It

was harder to do than she would have thought possible. She half-walked, half-waddled to the door to her bedchamber and pulled it open. Two surprised guards snapped to attention. They caught a glimpse of her Majesty in a nightgown and averted their eyes.

"Get Doctor Trion," she told them, her voice heavy, and disappeared back inside.

Powl had almost reached the palace gates when a dark shape suddenly loomed in front of him. He was too surprised to be afraid. There was not enough light by which to see a face, but there was no mistaking the bulk.

"Good evening, Constable," Powl said. "What are you doing out at this hour?"

"I might ask the same thing of you," Dejanus returned.

Powl could smell the wine even from two paces away, and was irritated by the sharp reply to what he thought was a perfectly amiable greeting.

"Visiting one of my priests, if you must know," Powl answered.

"I am the constable. It is my job to know . . ." Dejanus spread his arms as if he was trying to encompass the whole city. ". . . everything about everything."

'That's ambitious," Powl said dryly.

"I am an ambitious man. Indeed, we are both ambitious men."

Powl started, immediately suspicious. "What are you talking about?"

Dejanus laughed; the sound was like rocks rolling down a hill. "We have something in common. We both have secrets."

Powl caught his breath. "I have no secrets."

Dejanus put a huge arm around the primate's shoulders and bent his face down near his. Powl winced at the smell of his breath. "Everyone has secrets. I bet even God has secrets. But I know some of yours. Do you want to know some of mine?"

Powl removed the man's arm and said coldly, "I have no secrets that you could know about. And I am certainly not interested in yours."

Dejanus, even in his semi-drunken state, could hear the growing alarm in the priest's voice. So what *was* going on in that hospice? He put his arm around the priest again and drew him in.

"Believe me, your Grace, you would be very interested in my secrets. My secrets can tear down monarchs and put new monarchs in their place. My secrets can curdle milk and kingdoms. My secrets are so heavy that when I die I will sink straight to the underworld."

Powl was now afraid. What was this oaf talking about?

"You are playing at the high table now, Primate Powl. You need friends."

"I have friends," Powl said angrily and twisted away. "I am the queen's confessor, and I am a close associate of Chancellor Orkid Gravespear."

Dejanus scowled at the priest, and then started laughing again. "You are no longer confessor to anyone but yourself, your Grace, and Orkid Gravespear has secrets as dark as mine."

Powl pushed past the constable. He heard the man's laughter follow him all the way to the palace gates.

The midwife used her hand to explore the queen's body, keeping her eyes always averted. She was not so coy with any other patient, and the truth was Areava would have no objection to her using all her senses, but she felt that the majesty of the monarch should be preserved whenever possible.

"There is some dilation," she said. "How often are the spasms apart?"

"I've only experienced them once," Areava replied.

"Well, this is your first child, so we can expect a long labor," Doctor Trion said.

He rested his palm against Areava's forehead. "Good, good," he muttered to himself.

"What do you want me to do?"

"Do? Why, your Majesty, you wait. And then you suffer. And then you are a mother."

"The baby is too early."

Doctor Trion tried to hide his concern. "I have delivered many early babies. Some are impatient to see the world for themselves, and since this is a Rosetheme, and you tell me it is a girl and I believe it, I do not think anyone in the kingdom will be surprised she wants to make an unexpected appearance."

"I want my brother here. I want Olio."

"I will see that someone gets him," Trion assured her.

Hrelth had finished most of the flagon of wine Dejanus had given him. His fingers and toes were now quite warm, and his cheeks felt flushed. He stretched out a little. His head lolled back and his eyes closed. He did not see the prince and prelate leave the hospice. He did not wake when a rat crawled over his legs. His hand twitched, knocking over his lamp. The lamp rolled down the street and bumped into the hospice wall. The glass cage cracked, and burning oil spilled out. Yellow flame spurted up the wall, caught and consumed dry leaves on a window sill, travelled up a thatch fill to the roof, growing all the time, and then caught the tail end of the onshore breeze that riffled among all the rooftops of the city's old quarter.

29

KUMUL lay awake in the early hours of a new day, his first in the civilized lands east of the Algonka Pass for many months. It was hard for him to believe that spring was almost over. He had forgotten how long it took a large army to march any distance, even one as mobile as the Chetts'. In some ways it seemed a lifetime ago when he and his friends had crossed into the Oceans of Grass. Since then his prince had grown into adulthood and become a leader among warriors; the world he had lived in all his life had been turned upside down; the sureties of his past had become the uncertainties of his future. Most of all, he thought with wonder, Jenrosa Alucar had fallen in love with him.

How and when he had fallen in love with her was a mystery to him, and in that way seemed typical of all the other changes in his life. Before he had not been sure whether or not those changes were for the best, but now—in the cold early morning of a new day, and perhaps a new era for the whole kingdom of Grenda Lear—he suddenly found himself willing to embrace the changes wholeheartedly. Lying there in the dark, the warm body of his beloved Jenrosa by his side, the future had started to take shape, and he could see a path through the turmoil to a brighter and happier life.

Kumul propped himself on one elbow and gazed down on Jenrosa's sleeping face. She was like no other woman he had ever been with before. She actually loved him, and without reservation. Jenrosa did not seek power or influence or wealth; she wanted nothing but the chance to learn about herself and be with him.

Pride and loved swelled in Kumul and he leaned over to kiss Jenrosa's forehead. Without waking, she wrapped an arm around him and pulled him down so his head rested between her breasts. He closed his eyes and felt himself slowly drift off to sleep again, his fading thoughts measured by the beat of her heart.

The grass was too green and the sky was too pale, and the landscape was closed in by forests and wooded hills and streams and creeks. Lynan felt a stranger in his own land.

His army had left behind the Barda River two days after crossing the Algonka Pass and was now deep into Hume. The supply wagons had slowed their rate of progress, but his scouts were roving far and wide. That morning two of them had returned with three of their opposites from the army of Grenda Lear whom they had killed in a night action only hours before.

Lynan felt almost too tense to think, and he wondered if this was how his father had felt before a battle. Perhaps, he thought, but Elynd Chisal never had to worry about the consequences of attacking his own people.

He heard riders approach, and looked up to see Kumul, Ager, and Jenrosa.

"You wanted to see us, lad?" Kumul asked.

Lynan was not sure how to say what he had to say to them. They knew—they must have known—what would happen once they crossed into the east, but how ready were they for the reality?

"We have made contact with Areava's army," he said at

last. "They are only three or four hours' march to the east of our position. Korigan is preparing our forces to attack."

He let the words sink in. Ager and Jenrosa seemed frightened, and Kumul's face had paled almost to the color of his own skin.

"Well, we knew it would come," Kumul said huskily.

"It has to, my friend," Lynan said, wishing he had words that could make it easier for all of them. "I know no other way to end this, not now."

Kumul nodded stiffly, then said, "My lancers are ready. They'll be no match for the knights of the Twenty Houses, but against any other regiment they'll do fine."

"Jenrosa?"

Jenrosa breathed deeply. "As Kumul says, it had to come."

"And your magic? What does it say to you?"

Jenrosa had told no one except Kumul about her dream of Silona, not even Lasthear. "Sorrow, and . . ." She closed her mouth. She could not tell Lynan what she had seen. The dream might have meant nothing.

"And?" Lynan urged.

"If my magic is true, you will soon have the Key of the Sword around your neck."

Lynan's eyes widened in surprise. "You saw this?"

"I think so. I think this is what my vision showed me."

"And not the Key of the Scepter?" Ager said.

Jenrosa shook her head. "I did not see that."

"What can it mean?" Ager asked.

"I do not know."

"It is enough," Lynan said. "To win the Key of the Sword, we must win the battle."

"I cannot say," Jenrosa said, answering Lynan's unspoken question.

"Ager, do you ride with your clan?" Lynan asked.

"Of course."

"Then stay with me in the center with Gudon and the Red Hands. Kumul, I want your lancers in reserve. The enemy will be expecting horse archers, though not in the number we have. The lancers will be an extra shock to them, perhaps the deciding one. The gods go with us."

They silently regarded each other, each of them thinking something more should be said, but none knowing what it was. Kumul was the first to move, wheeling his horse around and galloping back to his lancers. Jenrosa followed him.

Ager gently tapped his horse's flanks, then suddenly reined in. "Lynan, are you prepared for what comes after the battle? Because I'm not."

Lynan did not know and wanted to answer truthfully, but said instead: "Yes."

"Good," Ager said, and then was gone as well.

Lynan felt nauseous and tired, and that somehow he was not only betraying the land of his birth but his friends as well.

"What's that?" Edaytor asked, pointing back the way he and Olio had just come.

At first Olio did not see anything out of the ordinary. The dawn sky was a pale, washed-out blue, and in the distance he could see tiny pennants fluttering from the masts of ships in the harbor. Then he noticed a ruddiness in the skyline above the old quarter. "I don't know."

For a moment they stood there watching, and then at the same time they saw the lick of yellow flame leap from one roof.

"Oh, no," Olio murmured.

Edaytor gripped his arm. "Go back to the palace and sound the alarm, your Highness. I will go with all speed to the Theurgias of Fire and Water. They can help." Edaytor ran off with all the speed his large body would allow him.

Olio started running toward the palace when he heard the alarm. One of the guards must already have seen the flames.

He stopped. There was nothing more he could do there. He was needed in the old quarter. He turned around and ran back the other way.

The spasm came so quickly that Areava could not help the groan that escaped from her lips.

"Damn!" she shouted, surprising Doctor Trion and the midwife who hovered nearby.

"Your Majesty, are you all right?"

"Another contraction," she said breathlessly. And then another wave of pain came. She pressed her lips together, but it was no good. She groaned again.

The midwife waited until the contractions had finished, then explored the queen again. Areava was so exhausted by the effort of controlling herself that she barely felt her.

"Two fingers' span. Good."

"What's best?" Areava asked her.

"A span of around eight fingers. Then your daughter will be ready to come out."

"Eight fingers! I have to wait for you to be able to shove—"

"Madam, please!" the midwife implored. "I do not shove—"

"I'm sorry. I'm sorry."

One of her maids stood beside her and placed a damp cloth against her brow. It helped.

"Is the pain really so bad?" she asked patronizingly.

"Are you a virgin or something?" Areava said shortly.

The maid blushed.

"God, you are," Areava breathed, and ridiculously felt like laughing. "And who's ringing those bloody bells?"

*   *   *

As soon as Galen received the message from Sendarus, he turned the regiments of knights around and returned to the main portion of the army. They got there just over an hour later, when dew still covered much of the ground. He saw that the army was being deployed, facing west across a wide, mainly flat plain. Archers lined the rise midway across the plain, and the infantry were arrayed into loose columns behind them and were in the process of marching left and right along the line to form the flanks. Some cavalry was already positioned on the far left flank. Galen found Sendarus in deep conversation with Charion, and was pleased to see they were not shouting at each other as they had been for most of the time since leaving Daavis.

"What has happened?" he asked as soon as he reached them.

"A few scouts on our left flank failed to report in," Sendarus said. "I sent a larger scouting party to find out what was happening."

"And they haven't come back either," Galen guessed.

Sendarus nodded and pointed to the west. Galen could see clouds of birds winging their way. "Whatever's stirred them up is very large. Salokan?"

Sendarus shrugged. "How could he have made such a wide detour without us detecting him? It must be him, but I don't understand how he's done it."

"It may not be Salokan at all," Charion said seriously.

"What do you mean?" Galen asked.

"Her Highness thinks it may be a second Haxus force, coming in from the Oceans of Grass."

"Mercenaries? This Rendle that Areava was so angry about?"

"Possibly."

"If it is, do you think he has been in touch with Salokan?"

"No way of knowing. If he has, we can probably expect him to be bearing down on us already, but whether to hit us on the flank or to join Rendle before making a combined assault, we don't know." Sendarus licked his lips. "There is another possibility."

"Which is?" Galen asked.

Sendarus and Charion spoke at the same time. "Lynan."

A whole street seemed to be on fire. Flames belched into the air as houses built from nothing but old wood and thatch ignited. Screaming people were jammed into the street, some of them on fire, some of them bleeding from burns and wounds caused by falling timber. Children slipped and if not caught up right away by their parents were trampled underneath by the panicking mob.

Olio tried to force his way though the mass to get to the stricken, but could make no headway. He grabbed one man by the arm and showed the Key of Power. "I am Prince Olio!" he shouted. "Help me get these people out of the way!" But the man shook his arm free and fled as fast as his legs could carry him. He tried with another man, and then a woman, but their reaction was the same as the first.

"God's death!" he shouted. "Will no one help me?"

The mob swept by him, forcing him against a wall. He heard a crack above him and looked up to see a roof smoldering, and then all at once catch fire. Flames seemed to leap over his head to the roof of the house on the opposite side of the street, and it, too, went up in flames. The heat was unbearable. He retreated to the end of the street, ducked in a doorway and waited for the mob to pass him by. When he emerged, he found that a handful of men and women had also stayed their ground, desperate to do something but not knowing what. He went to the nearest, a woman, and showed the emblem of his authority.

"Where is the nearest well?" he asked.

"A block away!" she said. "But we have no buckets to get water!"

"Make sure there is no one left inside these houses," he shouted, pointing to all those homes that were still free of the fire. "And collect as many buckets and pans as you can—anything that will carry water!"

The woman nodded, passed the word to another, and then another. In a short time there was a gang of about twenty people, all with a container of some kind.

"Form a chain to the well. We need to douse with water all the houses in the next street so the fires doesn't spread."

Other people came to see what was happening and, without being asked, joined in, but in a few minutes Olio could see their efforts were wasted. They could not get to the other end of the street where the fire was still spreading, and they could not carry enough water at this end to make any difference. The fire was leapfrogging houses now, sparks blowing from roof to roof, shining in the dark, smoky sky like miniature shooting stars.

"It's no good!" Olio told them. "Get to the harbor. Carry any who cannot get there themselves!"

At first some people ignored him, desperately trying to save their homes, but eventually the heat from the flames even drove them away.

Olio found an old man with only one leg who was struggling to keep up with the crowd; he was leaning against a corner post, bent over and gagging. Olio hooked an arm around the man's shoulders and helped him along.

"Thankin' ya, sir," the man said between bouts of coughing. "Thankin' ya."

A little way on they came across a small child, crying, standing by herself under the lintel of an open door. Olio shouted to a passing youth to take the man, then went to the child.

"What's your name?" he asked, picking her up.

"I can't find my mumma," she said.

"We'll find her, darling. What's your name?"

"Where's my mumma?"

The contractions were now less than two minutes apart. Areava was covered in a film of sweat. Her nightgown and the sheets on her bed were soaked, and the smell of them made her want to gag.

"A span of five fingers," the midwife said.

"Find Olio," she said desperately. "Find my brother. Find Prince Olio."

"There is nothing he can do for you, my lady," the midwife said, trying to sound stern.

"He has the Key of the Heart," she said. "The Healing Key. He can help the baby."

"Your Majesty—"

"Find him!" Areava screamed, and the midwife scurried off. A second midwife took her place and curtsied.

"I don't believe this," Areava moaned, then tensed as the contractions started again.

The first flight of arrows fell short, and even as the second flight was on its way Lynan was suddenly surrounded by twenty of the Red Hands. This time the arrows found targets. One of the Red Hands screamed and fell from her horse. Lynan heard other screams nearby.

"Spread out!" he ordered his bodyguard. They ignored him. "Listen to me, we're just making a bigger target for them! Now spread out!"

It was not until Gudon repeated the order that they reluctantly moved away from their charge. Another flight of arrows fell among them. Ager galloped over to him. "Where are they shooting from?"

Lynan pointed to a rise about three hundred paces away.

He could clearly see a line of archers dressed in Charion's colors. "They belong to a Hume regiment," he said.

Ager squinted through his one good eye. "God, they're hopeful. They're shooting at their maximum range. Let them waste their arrows, I say."

Lynan agreed. Gudon and the Red Hands were spread out in a line to his left, and on his right extended Ager's warriors. A hundred paces behind him, Kumul had drawn up his lancers into two wedges. Farther on his flanks the rest of the Chett army were still getting into their starting positions for the attack.

Someone on the other side must have realized the archers were wasting their time because the volleys ceased. The ground in between was sparsely coated in arrow shafts sticking out of the ground.

Over the next few minutes riders came to Lynan telling him that their respective banners were ready. Lastly came Korigan. She reined in beside Lynan and Ager.

"Everyone is in position," she said.

"Give the word, then."

"Do you want my people to take that ridge first?" Ager asked. "I could clear those archers away in five minutes."

"We don't know what's waiting for you behind the ridge. We go as planned. Flank movements first."

Korigan nodded and rode off, and for a while the only sound anyone could hear was the beating of her horse's hooves on the plain. When they stopped, there was a moment of complete silence. There was no wind, and all the birds had long fled.

A cry that sounded like the wailing of an angry grass wolf pierced the air. The cry was taken up by twenty thousand throats, and the ground seemed to rumble like thunder.

"I stopped the archers," Charion said, embarrassed at her own troops panicking like that.

"How many arrows have they left?"

"Half a dozen each, but I've ordered up more." She pointed to a supply wagon being quickly trundled up the ridge by hand.

"Let's hope the enemy don't charge in the center first before they're restocked," Galen said dourly.

Charion glared at him, but Sendarus held up a hand to each of them. "No time for this. Has anyone here fought with the Chetts?" Both commanders shook their head. "I don't suppose anyone here has fought *against* them?"

"If they had, you don't really think they'd admit it, do you?" Charion said. "The only people to fight against the Chetts in the last two generations have been slavers, mercenaries, and troops from Haxus."

"What tactics do the Chetts use?"

"Until now, small-scale tactics," Charion said. "The Chetts have never fielded an army. The largest clan can put up three or four thousand fighters, given time, but no one has ever seen this many warriors before."

"And never one under the command of a Rosetheme," Galen added, the contempt clear in his voice.

"You are sure that pennant represents the Key of Union?"

"What else?"

"But they are all horse archers," Sendarus said, changing the subject. He did not want to think about being in battle against his own wife's brother, no matter how much she hated him. "So if we keep our discipline, keep our lines intact, we can wear them down."

"And when the time is right, charge with our own cavalry," Galen agreed.

"That's the hard part," Charion said. "Knowing when to counterattack. The Chetts are good at fooling their enemies into foolish charges, then isolating and destroying them."

Suddenly the air was rent with the most terrifying cry they had ever heard.

"At least," Charion added, repressing a shiver, "that's how the Chetts behaved before they had an army. Who knows how they fight now?"

It was close to midday, but smoke hung so thickly over the city and its harbor that it could have been midnight. Dark figures moved like ghosts through the gloom, lost and aimless. Olio did his best to help organize refugees into groups that came from the same street or the same block so that families could be reunited, but the sheer number of people fleeing the fire made it impossible.

By now magickers from the all the theurgia were present to help, the most successful being those from the Theurgia of Fire—their most powerful spells were able to impede the progress of the fire by lowering its temperature. Mostly the magickers assisted by adding extra bodies to the long water chains that led from the harbor to the worst affected areas of the old quarter. Priests were everywhere, lending a hand and consoling where they could. Royal Guards arrived to help keep control of the crowds, and to distribute food and wine sent down from the palace's own stores.

The fire had not spread much farther north than the old quarter, where the buildings were uniformly old and badly maintained. Homes beyond the original city gates were spaced farther apart and there were servants and other workers to help landowners defend their property.

Still, it was a larger disaster than Kendra had experienced for many decades; some were saying the worst since the storms that had devastated the whole city one summer day a generation before the late Queen Usharna was born.

Tired and dirty and ragged as he was, Olio was recognized by some members of the Royal Guard and immediately assigned an escort to take him back to the palace. At first he refused to go, but when a brazen cleric pointed out he was more a distraction than a help, he reluctantly left.

The escort took him through that part of the old quarter the fire had already blazed through. Olio could smell charred wood and thatch, and the sickly sweet smell of the occasional burned corpse—sometimes a dog or cat, but usually human—that littered the streets and the burned out shells of what had once been homes. Near the edge of the quarter, where some of the homes seemed less damaged, they came across an inn. The inn's front wall had partly collapsed, but the roof was still in place and supported by intact beams, and dozens of people lay on the floor. Olio stopped and looked more closely. The people were all injured, and a few uninjured people worked among them to make them comfortable.

"Your Highness," one of the guards said, "we had best keep moving."

"Wait here," he ordered them, and went into the inn. The guards looked unsure but did as they were ordered.

Olio first came across a woman. She had no burns, but one of her legs was broken in several places and she was suffering intense pain. Olio knelt down next to her.

"How did this happen?" he asked her.

"It was the crowd, sir. They trampled all over me. Lucky to have only one leg broken."

Olio could feel the Key of the Heart warm suddenly. He needed no prompting. He took it out with his left hand and gripped it tightly, then put his right hand on the woman's knee. She winced in pain but did not cry out, almost as if she knew instinctively what was about to happen. The power surged through him so quickly he had no time to mentally prepare for it. He reeled back, blacked out for a moment. When his vision cleared, he saw that the woman's leg was completely healed and that she was falling into a deep sleep. Blue energy seemed to crackle around him.

He stood up and felt immediately dizzy, but still made his way to the next person on the floor, another woman,

younger, with blackened skin all along her exposed chest
and stomach. He did not even talk with her, but bent over
and ever so gently placed his fingertips against the curled
rind of skin that marked the edge of her burn.

"Soon now," Trion told Areava. "You are almost there."

She was crying, and was in too much pain and was too
tired to feel embarrassed or ashamed about it.

"My brother," she whispered hoarsely. "Where is he?"

Trion shook his head. "I am sorry, your Majesty, I don't
know. The midwife and some of your guards are searching
for him."

"He can't be far," she said. "Please find him for me. My
baby will die . . ."

Trion patted her hand. "We're doing everything we can."

Someone coughed discreetly near the door. Trion looked
up and saw Orkid standing there, his face furrowed in concern. Trion went to him

"How is she?" Orkid asked.

"She is doing fine, but the baby has turned. The contractions are causing her a great deal of pain. Has Prince Olio
been found?"

"No."

"Then I suggest you send out more guards to find him.
She calls for him all the time." He swallowed. "The baby
comes too early to live."

"Does she know?"

"Yes. I think so." He looked desperately at Orkid. "Only
Olio can help."

"The palace is stripped bare of guards," Orkid told him.
"There has been a terrible fire in city; most of the old quarter had been burned down."

"God's death!" Trion hissed. "So that's what the bells
were about."

"We have no idea how many have died, but the guards are helping to keep things going down there."

A horrible thought came to Trion. "You don't think his Highness is down there, do you?"

Orkid could only shrug. "We will find him and bring him to the queen as soon as we can." He looked across to Areava and saw her arch her back as another spasm of pain rippled through her. He gasped and looked away; he could not stand to see her suffer so.

"Believe me, Chancellor, Areava is young and strong. Nothing will happen to her."

"Is there anything I can do?"

"Wait patiently for nature to take its course. And find Prince Olio. I think more than anyone else, Areava needs her brother."

Lynan had no real idea how the battle was going. From his position in the center he could not see if his army's flanking attacks were succeeding or being driven back. As the Chett horse archers closed in on the enemy, loosed their arrows, then retreated out of range again, the grass was slowly trammeled to the ground and then destroyed. Clouds of dust were now spiraling into the air, obscuring the view. As well, the lay of the land was not completely flat—there were dips and rises—leading to strange consequences. Lynan could hear the clash of weapons and the cries of the wounded and dying in a skirmish on the far left flank between a troop of Chetts that had been surprised by a sudden charge by light infantry, but he could hear no sound at all from another skirmish much closer on the right flank between Chetts and a small band of Hume cavalry.

Ager, next to him and Gudon in the line, was able to make more sense of goings-on and could tell when the Chetts had the upper hand or when they were on the receiving end, but in one way this made it harder for Lynan. Having given the order for the attack to start he could do little to influence events until he decided to let the center or the reserve join in, and he was loath to do that until he had some clear idea of what the situation was like on the flanks. He needed to know what kind of troops his horse archers were encountering, and whether or not any had met the knights of the Twenty Houses. He had to know what quality of troops they were fighting, and whether or not they were determined or demoralized. He knew Korigan would arrange for riders to bring him information when she had the opportunity, but it seemed that the attack had already been going on for hours.

"Your center is getting itchy," Gudon said.

Lynan glanced along his line and saw that the Red Hands and Ocean clan warriors were looking frustrated. They were constantly shifting in their saddles, pulling on their bow strings and drawing and resheathing their swords.

Lynan kicked his mare into a canter. He first rode in front of the Ocean clan, making sure they noticed him, then back to the Red Hands. When he had the line's attention, he stopped before them.

"Our time is soon, but you must be patient. After this battle, no one in Theare will ever be able to stand against the Chetts without feeling fear!" The Chetts started to cheer. "You are *my* warriors, and I *will* lead you to battle today."

The cheering became louder, and he rejoined Ager and Gudon.

Gudon slapped him on the back. "Truth, little master, that was not bad."

"Not bad at all," Ager conceded. "No Elynd Chisal, but not bad."

"And what would my father have said?"

Ager grinned at him. "Charge."

Lynan was surprised. "Just charge?"

Ager shrugged. "More like 'Charge you fucking sons-of-whores,' but you get the idea."

Word had spread about the miracle worker. More and more of the injured were being brought to the inn.

Olio was no longer completely aware of what he was doing. The healing surge that coursed through his body was like a river of blue fire in his mind. His vision had narrowed to the point where he could barely see the victims being brought before him. His hand would go out, touch a hand or an eye, a burn or a puncture, and then another would be placed before him.

After a while he could hear a voice in the back of his head, and it sounded familiar but he could not put a name or a face to it.

He needed to stop, but did not know how. He tried to say "enough," but no sound at all came from his lips.

And all the time there was this voice trying to tell him something, something he was sure was important.

More victims. He felt himself fall, but hands picked him up and supported him. The river of fire grew wider and wider, his vision dimmed more and more, and there came a time when at last all he could see was the river. He wanted to step into it, to leave this place, and even as he wished it, it happened. He was adrift in the river, and slowly it covered him over until at last he was drowning in light. At that moment he heard the voice in the back of his head for the last time, saying a single word over and over, and he recognized the voice as his own.

And then it was gone.

"The infantry cannot take much more of this," Charion said, shouting to be heard over the din of battle. "Both our flanks are starting to cave in. Most of our infantry and light cavalry have been destroyed. We have to commit our heavy cavalry!"

"No!" Galen shouted back. "It's not time yet. The Chett center is still uncommitted. If we move the knights into action now, we will have nothing more to throw into the battle. The infantry have to hold or all is lost."

Both commanders fell silent and turned their gaze on Sendarus. He had visited each flank himself and seen the casualties they were suffering. A Chett troop would gallop in, let loose a volley of arrows, then retreat to be replaced by another troop. None of the volleys by themselves did much damage, but cumulatively they were starting to inflict significant casualties and damage morale. All their attempts so far at counterattacking had only resulted in the destruction of the pursuing units. But Galen was right. Until Sendarus knew what Lynan intended to do with his center, he had no choice but to hold back the knights. Still, there was one thing he could do to help the flanks.

"Move the archers from the rise," he ordered Charion. "Shift them all to the left flank. They have a greater range than the horse archers. When the enemy attack starts to flag, transfer them to the right flank."

It was not what Charion wanted to hear, but she was smart enough to know it was the most she would get from Sendarus at this point in the battle. She hurried forward to give the orders to the archers.

"That will leave our own center vulnerable," Galen pointed out.

"And offer a tempting target for Lynan," Sendarus countered. "Once he moves, we will know where to commit your knights. I hope he commits sooner rather than later."

Galen silently agreed.

It all seemed so unreal for Jenrosa. Beside her, sitting on one of the big stallions taken from the victory at the Ox

Tongue, Kumul stared straight ahead, occasionally turning his head slightly one way and then the other. His face was almost blank; the smallest of frowns creased his forehead. Before her, she could see the thin front line of the Red Hands and Ager's clan warriors. Beyond that there was a muffled, metal noise, like the sounds from a busy kitchen heard from the street. A cloud of white dust slowly drifted over the whole plain.

She tried to see inside her own mind, but there was nothing there except her own confusion. She wondered what Lasthear and the other magickers who had come with the army were thinking right now. The previous night she had asked Lasthear if there was some incantation they could use to help ensure victory, and Lasthear had laughed at her. "We might make it rain," Lasthear said, "but I can't see how that could help. Or we could start a fire and hope it spreads the right way on the grass, but I can't see how that would help either. No, best to strap on a sword and join someone you are prepared to die with."

Well, novice with a sword though she was, she was by Kumul, and there she would stay.

A rider galloped up to them. "His Majesty asks that you come to him."

Kumul nodded, and he and Jenrosa followed the rider back to Lynan. Ager, Gudon, and Korigan were already there.

"Any sign of heavy cavalry?" Kumul asked.

Korigan shook her head.

"What of Areava?"

Again Korigan shook her head.

"But they have brought up archers to their left flank. I am starting to lose riders. If I pull my forces back from that wing, the enemy commander will just switch the archers to the opposite. If something isn't done, our whole attack will stall, and I'm certain their infantry is close to collapsing."

Kumul and Lynan looked at each other.

"Your lancers have their target," Lynan said.

"The baby is starting to come," the midwife said. "I can feel her crown."

"Keep on pushing, your Majesty," Trion said, grimacing. Areava was gripping one of his hands so tightly if felt as if his fingers might break.

Areava kept on pushing.

"Olio?" she panted.

"I'm sorry. He isn't here yet."

Charion was starting to breathe a little easier. Her foot archers had forced back the Chetts, giving her infantry time to remove their dead and then reform their lines; the infantry crouched low and in straight lines, their shields covering their heads and sides, their spears held vertically to give some interference against flights of enemy arrows. The queen was about to send the archers across to the other flank when there was a new sound. It was not the rolling galloping of the horse archers darting in, but something heavier, slower. There was a glimmer of something as yet indistinct behind all the dust.

Sendarus joined her. "What is that sound?" he asked.

Charion shook her head. "I'm not . . . God, it can't be."

The dust cloud had parted for a moment, and she had seen what looked like massed cavalry, and they were carrying lances. She looked at Sendarus. "Tell me I didn't just see Chett cavalry starting a charge."

"Can you hold them?" he asked.

"I don't know." There was a note of desperation in her voice. "We'll try."

"It is time for Galen and his knights to play their part," Sendarus said. "Hold for ten minutes more, that's all I ask."

Charion ordered her infantry to stand and move to alter-

nate ranks, filling the gaps between the lines, then told the
front rank to go to one knee. The first two lines dug the buts
of the spears into the ground, holding the points out at forty-
five degrees, each succeeding line holding their spears a little more vertically than the one before. The maneuver was
just completed when the horse archers appeared again, the
sound of their coming hidden by the deeper thunder now
swelling over them. A hail of arrows fell among the more
closely packed infantry, and then another. The foot archers
hastily moved out of marching order into some kind of line
and started shooting back, but only sporadically.

Charion swore as her infantry, almost involuntarily,
started to edge back.

"Hold your ground!" she shouted at them. "Whatever
you do, hold your ground!"

But the infantry were starting to waver. One or two soldiers dropped their spears and ran, others looked over their
shoulder to see them flee and were on the verge of doing the
same. And then, as quickly and silently as they had come,
the horse archers disappeared.

Before any of them could breathe a sigh of relief, a wall
of solid horse appeared before them with glittering spear
points; leading them was a giant man on a giant stallion, and
each infantryman felt that the giant's sword was pointed directly at his head. The sound of the enemy's coming filled
their ears

The line crumbled like a sand bank before a flood. The
infantry threw away their spears and fled, running as fast as
their tired legs could carry them, but it was too late. The first
wedge of Chett lancers ignored them and carried on to the
now defenseless archers, ploughing into them with savage
ferocity, but the second wedge chased after them, their momentum carrying them through any resistance.

Charion galloped away from the onslaught, looking for
any troops she could use to form a second line or just to

throw in the way of the Chett attack so Galen's knights had time to get into action, but all around her were fleeing for their lives.

Kumul tried to recall his lancers, but they were carried away with bloodlust. *Lynan kept them on the leash for too long,* he cursed. *They've gone crazy.* The first banner was still together and under his command, but the other had broken into smaller groups intent on hunting down and killing every enemy soldier they could find. Around him were the remains of what had been a Hume regiment of archers. At least they would no longer be a threat. Now, if only he could get his own banners to reform, he might even be able to carry the battle to the enemy's center, or maybe even the opposite flank.

He gave command of the first wedge to Jenrosa and personally corralled a handful from the second, and from that small core started to reorganize it. When the battle was over he would make damn sure they knew how much they had failed him, failed Lynan, and failed as trained cavalry.

The wedge was almost completely reformed when he looked up and saw single riders galloping back. *About bloody time,* he thought, but as they drew closer, he saw the fear on the faces of the riders and realized they were fleeing from something. And there was only one thing he believed his lancers would be afraid of. He peered north, toward the enemy's center. A silvery line shimmered in the middle distance. He saw pennants and horsetail plumes. He knew what it meant.

Now what? he asked himself. His first wedge was still pretty fresh, but the second was sitting on a lot of blown horses. He rode to Jenrosa.

"Take back the second banner. They cannot move quickly, but get them out of the way. Tell Korigan we need horse archers up here, quickly."

"What are you going to do?"

"Give you the time you need to get away."

"No," Jenrosa said firmly. "You tried to do that once before, remember, for Lynan, and *he* came back. I'm not going to leave you now."

"This isn't for me," Kumul told her levelly. "It's for the four hundred Chetts who make up the second banner. Get them back to safety for me. You are one of Lynan's companions. They will obey you."

"I can't leave you to die."

"We will all die if someone doesn't tell Korigan to hurry up. Can you use your magic right now?"

Jenrosa shook her head. "I need time to prepare—"

"There is no more time. Get these troops away and come back with Korigan. That way there's a chance we'll both be alive after all this is over."

Kumul did not wait for her to reply, but turned to give orders to his first banner. It moved forward at a quick walk, flowing around Jenrosa and then leaving her behind.

Sendarus rode forward with Galen. Everything now depended on saving their left flank and repelling the Chett lancers. If they could do that, they could win the battle; if the lancers went unchecked, nothing would save them.

The knights rode forward in three straight lines, each line with around five hundred knights. They moved at a slow canter and so closely together that Sendarus could reach out and touch the shoulders of the riders to his left and right.

They first met their own infantry, fleeing unarmed from the field. Close behind them were scattered bands of Chett lancers, but Galen refused to break his lines to go after them. The lancers saw them and quickly retreated in panic. The knights, the best trained cavalry on the continent, smoothly increased their pace to a quicker canter on Galen's order. No words or oaths came from their lips, but everyone on the battlefield could hear the jingling of their mail and wheel stirrups, the tattoo of their stallions' hooves on the now bare and compressed ground. Ahead, they could now see at least two wedges of enemy troops, and the giant who led them; they all knew his name, and hated him. Galen shouted a command, and they couched their lances in one swift and uniform movement and automatically increased their pace to the gallop.

It was at this point that things started getting confusing for Sendarus, his head almost completely closed in his traditional Aman helmet. The horizon jiggled crazily through the narrow slits from which his eyes peered, and all he could hear was his own breathing. He concentrated on staying mounted during the rolling ride as the line charged the nearest enemy formation.

Then something loomed in his restricted vision. He straightened his sword and bent his elbow and shouted his own country's war cry, the roar of the great bear. Suddenly, there was a great crash. Horses screamed and went down, men cried in shock and pain. Sendarus could hear metal rending metal, and the softer whack of flesh and bone being butchered. He kept on going. Having obviously missed his target he reined in, wheeled, and charged in again, but in the confusing melee ahead he could not make out who was a knight and who was a Chett. He took off his helmet and hurled it away angrily. A Chett rode past, lance held overhand, and Sendarus went after him. The Chett must have heard his horse despite all the din because he turned just in time for Sendarus' sword to drive through his chest instead of his back. Sendarus twisted it free as the Chett fell off his horse, already dead. He kicked his mount further into the fray, pushing aside the riderless mare. In front of him, two Chetts were getting the better of one of the poorer knights—who could afford only a sleeveless mail hauberk—and both his arms were bleeding profusely. Sendarus hacked into one, dropping him almost immediately, but was too late to save the knight, who was struggling to pull out the lance that had been driven through his neck. The surviving Chett reached for his sword, but was not able to unsheath it before Sendarus cut off his head. The dying knight had disappeared by then, his horse panicking and taking him away from the battle.

Sendarus found himself in the clear, and it was obvious to him that the knights were winning this battle easily. They outnumbered the Chetts by at least three to one, had better body armor, and all wore helmets. The Chetts were fighting desperately, though, and most desperate and dangerous of all was their leader, Kumul Alarn. He swung his sword as easily as an average man could swing a twig, slicing off limbs and heads with terrifying ease. Galen and three other knights were already moving around behind him, but Kumul seemed to physically pull the stallion around with him. His sword rose and fell, cutting through the helmet and the skull of the luckless knight underneath. The knight fell back, his blood fountaining over his comrades, taking Kumul's sword with him. Kumul swore, punched another knight in the face and took his sword, but as he raised it high to strike down on another enemy, Galen saw his opportunity and struck, sending the point of his own sword deep into the armpit of the giant. Kumul let out a terrible bellow and for an instant seemed to freeze in place. Another knight sent a slashing blow into Kumul's back, the blade sinking deep. Galen and the knight drew out their swords at the same time and Kumul visibly slumped over the front of his stallion, then slipped sideways to the ground. A great wail went up from the Chetts and the sound of it chilled every knight who heard it.

Jenrosa had led the banner of exhausted lancers to the rear of the Chett line, the whole time looking around desperately for Korigan, but the queen was nowhere to be seen. She thought of Lynan and headed toward the center. She could see him there, surrounded by Ager and Gudon, looking out over the battle. She called out to him but he did not hear, and rode closer. She opened her mouth to try again, but another sound cut across her, a sound of such pain and sorrow and anger that she knew immediately, instinctively, what it heralded. She added her own voice to the cry, and heard other Chetts do the same.

Then she heard Lynan's scream, and it was as if a real grass wolf had taken human form. Before anyone could stop him he charged forward, straight for the enemy's center.

The Chett lancers had fought with more courage and tenacity than Sendarus had ever encountered before in an enemy, but they were all dead now, lying in bloody heaps on the ground with their leader. He sighed with relief, because now he knew the Chetts were going to lose the battle.

He ordered one of the knights to tie Kumul's corpse to his horse so he could parade him in front of the enemy, letting them know that nothing—and no one—could defeat the army of Queen Areava Rosetheme of Grenda Lear. When it was done, he rode off toward the center, an escort of knights on either side. When he saw the single Chett rider coming straight for him, he thought it must be some madman. Two of the knights spurred forward to kill the Chett before he reached their general, someone they had learned to respect and admire despite his Amanite blood.

Sendarus watched the madman closely, amazed and horrified by the fanaticism the Chetts had shown throughout the battle. He noticed that he seemed to have no face. Sendarus squinted and saw that indeed there was a face, but it was so pale it might almost have been nothing but a skull, the white bone shining in the sun.

He watched as the two knights lowered their lances and

charged. The Chett waited until the knights were only paces from him, then swerved to his right. The knight on his left had too much momentum to change course and rode past, but the other had only to change slightly his grip on his lance to redirect it. Sendarus saw the lance go through the Chett's body, and at the same time saw the Chett's sword cleanly take off the knight's head. The Chett slowed, the end of the lance wobbling in the air in front of him.

"He doesn't know he's dead yet," one of his remaining escort joked.

By now the other knight had wheeled and was charging back. The Chett looked over his shoulder and then down at the lance impaling him. As Sendarus watched, the Chett grasped the lance with his free hand and slowly pulled it out of his body, then twisted in his saddle and hurled it toward the charging knight. The lance struck the knight in the eye, propelling him off the back of his horse.

"Fuck," another of the escort said.

The Chett turned back to Sendarus and his escort, kicked his mare into a gallop and whirled his sword in the air above his head. And behind him, just coming over the rise, was the rest of the Chett army.

Sendarus' heart froze with fear.

"Her shoulders are coming through!" the midwife called excitedly.

Trion was wiping Areava's face and throat. "Your daughter is almost here, your Majesty . . ." He stopped because he could feel something warm near his arm. He turned and saw that the Key of the Scepter was pulsing with light.

"Your Majesty . . . ?"

Knights kept on getting in Lynan's way. He sliced through necks with his sword, punched faces with his free hand, even used his teeth when he could. He felt lances pierce him, but there was no pain. He felt swords fall on him, but they could not break his bones. One by one he got rid of the annoying, armored flies, and went straight for the man who still held his ground, the man whom Lynan in his fury did not recognize, the man with Kumul's body tied to his saddle by a length of rope, the man with the Key of the Sword hanging over his heart. He said nothing, casually brushed away the man's sword, and thrust his own weapon deep into the man's throat.

Areava screamed suddenly in terror and pain, her back arching off the bed.

Trion, taken by surprise, jumped back.

The midwife tried desperately to keep her hands on the baby still half in, half out of the queen. Before her eyes, a wound opened in the baby's throat and spouted blood all over her. The midwife fainted.

Lynan pulled the sword out and thrust again, this time into the man's heart. The man fell forward over Lynan's arm and keeled sideways, still hanging in the saddle. Lynan put his other hand on the pommel of his sword and drove it in farther; he saw the point emerge out the man's back, then threw him off his horse.

Trion cursed and rushed to save the baby, but before he could touch her, Areava, shouting and screaming, sat up and grabbed her by the shoulders. She pulled the baby out, lifting her up to her arms, the umbilical cord dangling between her legs. Even as she did so another wound appeared in the baby's back. Trion put his hand over the wound, but blood seeped over his hand and spilled down his arm. He was crying now, shouting in rage, but he was helpless. The baby's head lolled back. Her eyes opened once, seemed to stare at him, and then lost focus.

Trion stood back, in shock.

Areava held her daughter to her, the baby's blood mingling with her own. She wailed in grief and pain, and the whole palace filled with the sound.

Ager was the first to reach Lynan. The youth was huddled over Kumul, holding him in his arms, rocking back and forth on his knees. Ager stood there, not knowing what to do. Then Jenrosa was there, and she leaped from her horse and joined Lynan on the ground, held her beloved's head, and kissed his pale, blood-flecked face.

The Red Hands and Ager's own warriors, led by Gudon, had swept on, discarding their bows and using their swords to drive into the main body of knights. Their fury gave them each of them the strength of two men, and even the knights could not withstand them. When Korigan arrived with reinforcements and drove into the enemy's flank, some of the knights started to turn and gallop off.

But Ager could see the reorganized Grenda Lear infantry, most of them carrying long spears, approaching from the left. They were led by a small, dark-haired woman who marched with them on foot. Soon the Chetts would be sandwiched between the infantry and the knights, and fortune would turn against them once more.

They had lost this battle. Only barely, but they had lost it.

He knelt down next to Lynan and put his hand on the prince's shoulder. "Lynan, we have to withdraw."

Lynan looked up at him. His face was stained with tears, and at that moment Ager once again could see the youth he had first met in the Lost Sailor Tavern all those long months ago.

"What can I do now, Ager?" Lynan cried. "What can I do without Kumul?"

"Fight again another day," Ager said. "Fight again to revenge his death. But not here, not now." He put a hand under

Lynan's arm and helped him stand, then pointed to the battle still raging nearby. "We have the upper hand and can retreat without much chance of pursuit, but if we wait too long, the enemy infantry will arrive and most of our forces will be trapped."

Lynan wiped his face with the back of his hand. He looked down at Sendarus and recognized him. "She sent her lover," he said dully, then bent down and took the Key of the Sword from around Sendarus' bloody neck. Ager brought his horse and helped him climb into the saddle. "I will bring them back, Ager, but you must look after Kumul and Jenrosa for me."

"They will be safe, I promise."

Lynan nodded and rode off to save his army.

⬡ 30 ⬡

DEJANUS slept through the night in a drunken stupor. A sergeant found him lying in his cot, smelling of wine, and threw a jug of water over his face. Dejanus woke spluttering and angry. He grabbed the sergeant's jerkin and pushed him against a wall.

"I've gutted men for less than that!" he roared.

The sergeant did not seem to care, and this confused Dejanus.

"Maybe you're hard of hearing—"

"The queen lost her baby," the sergeant said.

"—but I said I've gutted . . ." His voice faded.

"Last night," the sergeant continued. "I heard say that it was a girl, but that she was spitting blood when she came out of the womb. It was a demon child. It almost killed the queen."

Dejanus let the sergeant go. He could not believe what he was hearing.

"And the old quarter in the city burned down. Hundreds are dead. They say the demon did that, too."

"The old quarter? All of it?"

"Almost. I've just come from there. Your guards have been helping where they can, but things are a mess. We need the constable to come down and take charge." The sergeant looked at Dejanus with sudden interest. "You *are* the constable, aren't you?"

Prelate Edaytor Fanhow and many magickers were working with priests and guards to help clothe and feed all the victims of the fire. He knew it could have been worse, that if the fire had taken hold earlier in the night an untold number would have been caught in their beds, but with so many homes destroyed the city still had the problem of finding shelter for thousands of people.

He overheard two of the victims talking about the miracle worker in the inn at the north end of the old quarter who was healing the dying and badly burned, and knew immediately who they were talking about. It took him an hour to find the inn. Two weary guards were still standing outside.

"Is the prince inside?" he demanded of one.

The guard looked frightened. "He went in this morning and still hasn't come out. He ordered us to stay here. There was a weird blue light . . ."

Edaytor let the guard babble on and entered. There were hundreds of people there, most injured in some way. He could not see Olio. A man was walking among the people with a large ewer tied to his back and a cup in his hand, offering water. Edaytor went to him and asked about the prince. The man nodded to a small bundle squatting in one corner, his face hidden from view.

Edaytor went to him and called out his name, but the prince did not answer. He put his hand under Olio's chin and lifted his head.

"God, your Highness, what have you done?"

Two blank eyes stared right through him. The prince's mouth was slack, and saliva dribbled from one corner.

"Stand up," Edaytor said, and struggled to help Olio to his feet. When he let go, Olio was able to stand alone, but he made no further effort to move. Edaytor wiped the prince's mouth and chin and then took his hand. "Come with me," he said, and Olio obediently followed.

When they went outside, the guards snapped to attention, then looked agog at Olio.

"What happened?" one of them asked.

Edaytor thought he knew but saw no need to speak of it. "Take him to Doctor Trion at the palace."

The guards each took one of the prince's arms. "What about you, Prelate?"

"I'm going to see if I can find anyone among the theurgia to help him. Tell Trion I'll join him as soon as I'm able. Now go."

The guards left with their charge. Edaytor closed his eyes and shuddered. He wanted to weep, but was too tired and had seen far, far too much destruction in the last few hours. He was sure there was no magic to cure the prince. After all, what could undo the work of one of the Keys of Power?

Primate Powl was crying over the corpse of the baby girl lying in rest on the altar of the Royal Chapel. He could hear the murmured prayers of several priests in the pews behind him, but no one else shared the altar with him.

Dear God, he prayed silently, *tell me why you have done this thing? Why did you pierce the flesh of this child? There is no demon in her. She is just a babe, slaughtered by some power, and aren't you the source of all power?*

He stroked the head of the baby. She had wisps of dark hair. The little body was black with blood, the skin bruised to the color of wine.

Is this your curse on Kendra for my sins? Is your vengeance that terrible? Will you murder other children in your name?

Powl stopped his crying and took deep breaths.

In your name, Lord, if we only knew what it was.

* * *

"I have posted sentries," Galen told the new commander of the army, "but I do not think they will be back."

Charion had never been so tired in her life before. "We must do something with Sendarus."

"We have no means of preserving him. He must be buried."

"Then take out his heart. Pack it in a casket with salt. Areava deserves to get something of him back." She looked at Galen carefully; she had been curious by his show of grief for the Amanite. Although Charion lived a long way from Kendra, she was well aware of the antipathy members of the Twenty Houses felt for the nobles of the kingdom's lesser provinces, including her own. "What did you think of him?"

"He was a brave soldier, and a clever captain. I think I liked him. I am sore for Areava. His death will devastate her."

"He died a hero, at least," Charion said, trying to make Galen feel better, a reaction which surprised her. "He drove off Salokan, saving Hume, then drove off a second and unexpected invasion by the outlaw Lynan."

At the mention of that name Galen shivered. "Lynan has been transformed into a demon."

"Did you see him?"

"Only from a distance. I saw what he did to eight knights and to Sendarus."

"Demon or not, he has gone."

"For now, your Highness, but do you think for a moment that he will not be back?"

The Chetts had recovered most of their dead. When night fell, they laid them out with their weapons in a shallow pit they had dug. Jenrosa had counted over fifteen hundred of them, nearly a third of them lancers. In the middle of the line lay Kumul. She stood before him, watching his face. He looked remarkably peaceful there, surrounded by his fellow warriors, his sword set lengthwise along his body.

"Kumul Alarn," she said. "Constable of Grenda Lear. Captain of the Red Shields. The General's Giant. Father to Lynan Rosetheme." Her throat constricted, and tears came when she thought she had no more tears go give. "And beloved of Jenrosa Alucar, apprentice magicker from the Theurgia of Stars."

He was the last and the greatest to be named. She stepped back into the arms of Ager and Lynan.

"It is done," she said, and a thousand Chetts moved forward to finish burying their dead.

Areava lay in her bed. Maids and servants silently stood to one side. Hansen Beresard stood at the foot of her bed, and Orkid Gravespear near the head. Doctor Trion finished examining the queen and stepped away. He signaled to Orkid.

"She is physically fine. I cannot speak for her mind. She has not spoken since . . . since the birth."

Orkid went back to the queen. He picked up her right hand. "Your Majesty, your people grieve with you for your loss."

Areava gave no sign she heard him.

"Is there anything, anything at all, that we can do to help—"

"Where is Olio?" she said suddenly. A few of the maids and servants jumped, but she had spoken quietly, even gently. She looked at Orkid. "My brother, Chancellor? Have you seen him?"

Orkid turned to Trion, who hurriedly came forward.

"He is . . . unwell . . . your Majesty," Trion said. "He is in my care."

"Bring him to me, please, Doctor."

"I do not know—"

"Bring him," Orkid said, and Trion knew by the chancellor's tone that it was an order he dared not refuse. Trion left.

"Is there anything you need, your Majesty?"

Areava sighed. "He is dead, you know."

Orkid assumed she was talking about the baby. "Your daughter. Yes, *she* is in the royal chapel . . ."

"Oh, I know she is dead. Her name was Usharna. Did I tell you that? Usharna is dead. That is how I know Sendarus is dead, too."

Orkid blinked. "I don't understand, your Majesty."

"He was stabbed in the throat and then he was stabbed in the heart. The second time the sword went clean through him. He died quickly at least. It was Lynan who killed him. I saw it in my mind. The Key of the Scepter let me see everything."

As soon as Areava had said the words, Orkid knew it was true. He did not know what to say. A thousand thoughts and feelings flooded his mind, including grief for his nephew. And what of the army he led? Was it destroyed? Had Salokan succeeded in taking Daavis?

But she had said Sendarus was killed by Lynan. How was that possible, unless the prince really had been serving Haxus?

Trion returned, holding Prince Olio's hand. Orkid gasped. He had not seen Olio for two days, and the person who stood before him now was not the same man.

"Your Majesty," Trion said. "Prince Olio is here. But I must warn you—"

"Bring him closer," Areava said.

Trion led Olio to his sister's bed. Areava reached out and took his hand from Trion. She studied her brother's face for a moment, and then with some effort sat up. She groaned with sudden pain.

"Your Majesty!" Trion cried and came forward.

"Stay, Doctor," she ordered, then leaned over and took

the Key of the Heart from around her brother's head and placed it around her own. It chinked when it rested against the Key of the Scepter.

"Dear Olio, you will not be needing this anymore," she told him, her voice still gentle. "You have failed me for the last time."

AREAVA started walking two days after the loss of Usharna. She had still been in bed when a carrier bird had brought a message from Daavis. Orkid had brought it to her immediately. She had said nothing since taking Olio's Key, and the chancellor hoped the news would elicit some response.

"This is from Queen Charion, your Majesty," he told her. She turned her head to look at him, which he took as a good sign.

" 'I regret to inform you,' " he read, " 'that your husband, Prince Sendarus, was yesterday slain in battle. He was murdered by your outlaw brother Prince Lynan who was in command of an army of Chetts invading Hume. Before his death, Prince Sendarus guaranteed victory for your army over the Chetts, and in the days before that battle had saved Daavis by forcing King Salokan of Haxus to flee back to his own territory.

" 'I know that this must be a grievous burden for you to bear, but take comfort in the knowledge that he sacrificed his life in your service, and in service of the kingdom of Grenda Lear, and in so doing protected those he loved most in this world.' "

"Is that all?" Areava asked.

"That is all, your Majesty."

She put out her hand and Orkid gave her the note. She read it quickly, and then again, more slowly.

"So it was not a nightmare," she said at last.

"No, your Majesty."

"I have lost a husband, a daughter, a third of my capital and, I think, a brother, all in one day. Do you think any ruler of Grenda Lear has ever managed so much?"

"It was for a cause, your Majesty. Your husband—my nephew—died to protect the kingdom. I have been told by Edaytor Fanhow that your brother sacrificed his sanity to save many of the victims of the fire."

"And what cause was served by the death of my daughter and the deaths of so many of my citizens in the old quarter?"

"I cannot read the mind of God, your Majesty."

"And I do not want to read his mind, Chancellor. I am sure I would hate him for it." She threw the bed covers back and tried to swing her legs over the side.

"Areava!" he cried. She glared at him. "Your Majesty, forgive me, I was startled, but please do not move! I will get the doctor—"

"You will do no such thing. I am queen, as you have so constantly reminded me, and have my duties to perform. It is time I went back to them."

"But so soon?"

"I cannot simply grieve, Orkid. I would go as mad as Olio. Give me your hand."

He helped her to her feet, and for a moment she stood still, getting her balance and getting used to the pain.

"My gown," she said curtly.

Orkid rushed to get the gown from the end of the bed and helped her into it.

"Now walk with me."

Step by step, her arm in Orkid's, she left her chambers. When word got around that she was abroad, maids and servants and courtiers scurried after her, but she shooed them all away until she was alone again with Orkid.

"I am sorry I have not yet offered you my condolences over the death of Sendarus. I know you loved him, too."

Orkid could not answer right away, but eventually managed to say, "Thank you."

"Please make sure that his father and Amemun are made aware of what has happened."

"I will do that today."

They came to the entrance of the south gallery. Areava saw Olio standing by himself, looking out over the city. He seemed very small to her.

"What is he doing here?" Areava asked.

"He has been here for the last two days. He is taken away for meals, and at night, but he always returns. Shall I have him taken to his chambers?"

Areava shook her head. "I think I have the mastery of this walking business. Would you stay here, please?"

Orkid reluctantly let her go, and she slowly made her way to her brother. Olio turned his head when she stopped beside him.

"Did you know this is the largest city in the whole wide world?" he asked.

"Yes. Yes, I think I knew that."

"Berayma told me that. He tells me lots of things." He smiled at Areava. "But not nearly as much as you tell me. You tell me even more things."

"Your stutter has gone."

"Silly sister," Olio said. "I don't stutter."

Areava breathed deeply, holding a hand over her heart. "I forgot," she said, her voice not much more than a whisper.

Olio breathed deeply, too, and then put a hand over his heart. "Do you think we will see Mother today?"

When Areava started crying, he put his arms around her.

When she came to him, he showed her his presents.

"I have two of them now. I killed my sister's favorite to get this one."

She smiled sweetly and touched his cheek.

"And when I have finished destroying this world, I will have four of them. I will give them all to you, then."

"You are the sweetest of lovers."

"And you are the most beautiful of women," he said, and reached out for her. She floated away from him.

"You don't like my presents?"

"Yes, I like your presents."

"Why do you move away from me?"

"I want to show you something."

She seemed to disappear into shadows. He tried to follow her, but she was lost to him.

"I cannot see you."

"I am here," she said behind him, laughing.

He laughed, too, and turned around, but what he saw made the laughter die in his throat.

"Am I not the most beautiful of women?" she asked, her fetid breath blowing on his face.

"No," he said pitifully, and stepped back.

She reached out for him, held him by his arms and brought him closer to her. She kissed him, and her long tongue pierced the back of his throat.

Lynan woke in a cold sweat, panting. He got out of his bed and tripped over something in the dark. He fell onto his knees. The tent flap opened and one of the Red Hands came in.

"Your Majesty, are you all right?" she asked.

Lynan looked up, still disoriented. "Yes. Yes, I think so."

Someone else came into the tent. "I will see to him," said the second person, and Lynan recognized Korigan's voice. He heard the strike of a flint, and a lamp blazoned in the darkness. The Red Hand bowed and left.

"Are you sure you are all right?" Korigan asked. She put the lamp down on the floor and helped him back to his cot.

"Yes." He grabbed a blanket and put it around him.

"You were dreaming of Silona again?"

He looked at her, startled. "This is the second time you've known."

"I told you she has a presence; I can feel when she is near."

"She never leaves her forest," Lynan said, his tone dismissive.

"She does not have to, not with her blood in you. And you are closer to her forest now than you have been since being given her blood."

Lynan groaned. "They are not dreams, really, are they?"

Korigan sat down beside him. "No. But it does not mean that she controls you, if that's what you're afraid of."

Lynan swallowed. "In the battle, when Kumul was killed, I changed."

"I know. We all saw it. It has happened to you before. When we fought the mercenaries, and when you killed the grass wolf."

"Does she not control me then?"

"You change to protect or avenge those you love, I think. You have some of her hate and some of her strength, and her invulnerability to normal weapons, but you do not turn on your own, you do not drink the blood of those you kill. You are no vampire, Lynan."

"Then what am I?"

"You know what you are, I think. Finally, you know what

you are. The battle against the Grenda Lear army showed you that. You have a destiny."

"A destiny for what?" he voiced ruefully. "Killing my own people?"

Korigan shrugged. "I don't know. But others feel it, too. That is why you are so loved by your companions—Gudon, Jenrosa, Ager . . ." She hesitated, not wanting to say the name.

"And Kumul," he said. His eyes brimmed with tears. He turned his face away in shame. "I'm sorry," he muttered.

Korigan put her arms around him and held him close to her. She could feel his head against her heart, and wondered if he heard it.

"It is all right to cry for those you love," she said, and after a while the tears came to her eyes as well.

Kristen Britain

GREEN RIDER

As Karigan G'ladheon, on the run from school, makes her way through the deep forest, a galloping horse plunges out of the brush, its rider impaled by two black arrows. With his dying breath, he tells her he is a Green Rider, one of the king's special messengers. Giving her his green coat with its symbolic brooch of office, he makes Karigan swear to deliver the message he was carrying. Pursued by unknown assassins, following a path only the horse seems to know, Karigan finds herself thrust into in a world of danger and complex magic.... 0-88677-858-1

FIRST RIDER'S CALL

With evil forces once again at large in the kingdom and with the messenger service depleted and weakened, can Karigan reach through the walls of time to get help from the First Rider, a woman dead for a millennium? 0-7564-0209-3

To Order Call: 1-800-788-6262

Tad Williams

THE WAR OF THE FLOWERS

"A masterpiece of fairytale worldbuilding."
—*Locus*

"Williams's imagination is boundless."
—*Publishers Weekly*
(Starred Review)

"A great introduction to an accomplished
and ambitious fantasist."
—*San Francisco Chronicle*

"An addictive world ... masterfully plays
with the tropes and traditions of
generations of fantasy writers."
—*Salon*

"A very elaborate and fully realized setting
for adventure, intrigue, and more
than an occasional chill."
—*Science Fiction Chronicle*

0-7564-0135-6

To Order Call: 1-800-788-6262

Tanya Huff

The Finest in Fantasy

To Order Call: 1-800-788-6262